Clock Face of Ills

Also by the Author

Beyond all Doubt
Whisper of Death

Non Fiction
How I Write and Publish Murder Mystery

Writing as Jacinta Sequentez:
The Foreigner

Writing as Shelby Summers:
Fortunes Along the Boulevard

Clock Face of Ills

Paige Elizabeth Turner

Matador
9 Priory Business Park,
Wistow Road, Kibworth Beauchamp,
Leicestershire. LE8 0RX
Tel: 0116 279 2299
Email: books@troubador.co.uk
Web: www.troubador.co.uk/matador
Twitter: @matadorbooks

ISBN 978 1788039 833

British Library Cataloguing in Publication Data.
A catalogue record for this book is available from the British Library.

Printed and bound by CPI Group (UK) Ltd, Croydon, CR0 4YY
Typeset in 11pt Adobe Garamond Pro by Troubador Publishing Ltd, Leicester, UK

Matador is an imprint of Troubador Publishing Ltd

MIX
Paper from responsible sources
FSC www.fsc.org FSC® C013604

For Sue Ablett. In recognition and appreciation of her devotion to the Evesham Festival of Words.

Acknowledgements

Many authors rely on others' expertise and cooperation to help us develop and enrich our fictitious settings.

I am indebted to Mr Peter Dickenson, Estate Agent and Chartered Surveyor, of High Street, Bidford-on-Avon, for advice concerning conveyance and contract detail.

(NOTE: This story contains references to a property acquisition and sales contract. The scenarios are a product of the author's imagination and are highly fictionalised. They do not represent, in any form whatsoever, a process by which property might be obtained, purchased or sold.)

I acknowledge Mariusz Skonieczny for his informative book: *Gold Production from Beginning to End* (ISBN 978-0-9848490-1-7) from which I mined many gems.

To my brother, Peter, I extend gratitude for initial research of the Clogau gold belt.

To Mel, for providing the analogy of sweet words and ants.

And to draft readers Frederick Dickson and Albert Atifi, thanks for your review and comments.

Prologue

PHILLIP MCMASTER SLAMS THE BILL on the table. Two tumblers of Scotch whisky jump in protest. Heads turn from adjacent tables. Silence drowns alcohol-fuelled banter.

'You fix this, and make sure you fix that Angelo prat,' wheezes McMaster.

'Pay your own friggin' bill,' recoils Jeff Main. 'I'm here to do you a favour. I never wanted in on this in the first place. I'm the paperwork man, not an action hero you pull out of a Mattel box to perform at your beck and call.'

McMaster extends his palms like a placating politician. 'Okay Jeff. Settle down. I've got the tab. Okay?'

Phillip, known to colleagues as Phil, a seasoned detective inspector who found his niche placement in a small regional office, has bedded down in career hibernation. He'd long ago settled into a comfort zone; happy to drift from one file to the next, to do only as required, and no more. Promotion and career progress – dissolved aspirations of the once eager officer – have melded into the nicotine-infused ceilings of Worcester CID.

Five years' earlier, his sonorous instructions boomed across offices with the mellifluous harmony of Placido Domingo. Today, McMaster huffs like a punctured blacksmith's bellow, legacy of his daily 60-cigarette habit. His physique also resembles the bellow: puffed up and full of hot air. At 42 years-of-age, and after 22 hard years in the constabulary, Phillip McMaster personifies the role of desk sergeant. His medical records should note 'obese', but the constabulary chooses to play down the condition as 'slightly overweight'. Spider veins criss-cross his sun-deprived complexion. Glowing cheeks and nose pay homage to Dewar's redeeming powers. Thin, peppered hair wavers like wheat stalks ravaged by a locust plague, and the skin beneath his eyes hangs like a pair of old saddle bags drooping from the bony back of a prairie horse.

For McMaster, life parallels the game of Snakes and Ladders. He slides beneath promotional opportunities; he falls into pits of depression propagated by marital disharmony; and his alcoholic dependence drops him into a fantasy criminal underworld.

He'll climb out of allegations of impropriety, and he'll step up the pace of an investigation until he nails his suspect. His mental capacity is top of the game. Locked away in his cerebral safe are the names, faces and crimes of every person he's arrested and prosecuted during his generally non-eventful career. He also remembers the few he's freed, his eyes closed to the activities of those he believes capable of furthering his agenda; and he zealously guards mental profiles of those recruited into his clandestine empire of chicanery and scams.

McMaster lives by his self-conceived doctrine: 'financial security is the ability to seize opportunity and shield it from authority's eyes'. He applies the creed to all manner of deceptive conduct, from swapping bar codes on B&Q's power tools to returning items of clothing for refunds after wearing them to one-off functions. *Why rent a dinner suit when I can buy one from a retailer with a lax return policy and claim a full refund the following day?* If the sales assistant objects, he coolly removes his wallet and lays it on the sales counter – making sure it falls face up to clearly display his police warrant card. The hapless assistant buckles to the innocent intimidation and cheerfully assistant buckles to the innocent intimidation and cheerfully completes the refund.

He has learnt through several misdealings that success and happiness are born of intelligent coercion and communication with the right people. Invariably, those 'right people' have no respect for law. For the past five years, he's held permanent ownership – under the auspice of 'reservation' – over a table inside the Knight's Arms. The 'Arms' – as abridged by the locals – is a renowned rendezvous for informants of dubious background who provide information for both his judicial and personal interests. It carries its history from the late sixteenth century, when, as a tavern, it hosted lords' and earls' messengers en-route to delivering sealed vellum pouches of taxes to King Edward VI. While England has matured into the twenty-first century, the Arms stand as a snapshot of 500 years past. Its tiny rooms remain intact; the telltale odour of hops and malt and stale tobacco hover about the low ceiling, and the pungent sweat of daily toil clings to walls like calcified mist on a Perspex shower screen.

The small room is still, as if a mute button has silenced the pair of widescreen televisions hanging above the bar. A six-square-metre ceiling of straw, mud and cowpat render, crudely brushed with the mandatory magnolia, and illuminated by six 25-watt power saving globes, reflects glistening perspiration from Main's brow.

McMaster glares: 'I know you're the paperwork man. But I'm the head man, aren't I? For the past year, I've papered your pocket with real bills – tens, twenties and fifties. Now, I'm thinking that if you want our little arrangement to continue, we have to come to an understanding. Right? There has to be some sort of hierarchal order. Right? You see where I'm coming from?'

Main knows exactly where. He'd once skimmed profit from McMaster's share portfolio after being instructed to sell 12,500 shares in a small trading company. Main had no way of knowing that Phillip McMaster was the major shareholder of that registered company, and that McMaster knew exactly what the sale should have returned.

McMaster had turned the tables to his advantage. Rather than report Main for criminal deception, he recognised the ingenuity as an exploitable trait. To date, his scams and schemes have lined Main's pockets with more than £40,000.

McMaster continues: 'You remember how you tried to, shall we say, rip me off?'

'I've apologised for that a thousand times. You never let me forget – it was a poor business decision.'

'And I make the good decisions, right?'

'Yes, Phil. Always.' Main shrinks into a small-time thug, afraid of his menacing Mafia-styled boss.

'Angelo's not pulling his weight. We've got to get that property deal sewn up. Quick.'

'Yes. Of course. I thought we'd sealed it.'

'Well, we haven't. You were too soft on that fuckin' wog bastard.'

Main turns to the cash register's beeping shrill. 'Better keep your voice down. There's not enough distractions.'

McMaster sets a ferocious scowl. 'Only fucking distraction here is you.'

I

The brass mail flap snaps shut. Letters topple to the floor. I grab the bundle and shuffle the envelopes like a deck of cards; throw aside a BT bill, Office Plus stationery account, a window envelope addressed to my business name – Watts Happening? Investigations – and a large, brown Readers' Digest envelope promising to excite me because I've made the final cut in their 'Last Chance Draw' £1,000,000 prize pool. I hadn't even entered the damn thing!

Since establishing Watts Happening? Investigations six months ago, I have undertaken enquiries ranging from missing persons to untimely deaths. I take credit for helping a lawyer solve a suspicious family death – an enquiry which resulted in my contribution solving two related mysterious casualties. With good fortune, I continue to swim in a stream of interesting enquiries.

I'd originally set up in Worcester, but over-reacted to the scale of the aforementioned family death enquiry by moving to Newquay in Cornwall as part of a career, slash, sea change. I later succumbed to the magnetism of my geographic roots after a chance Worcester file pulled me past my old flat and office. The 'To Let' sign dangling from the window hung as an omen – a divine invitation beckoning my return. But the task wasn't easy. On trying to re-lease the property, I struggled to convince the landlord of my reliability. My previous two years' unblemished tenancy apparently stood for nothing because I had to assure him that I would not go 'hopping around the country', at my earliest opportunity.

To enunciate my point, I slipped in the clincher: 'Looks like it's been vacant since I left. You're obviously overwhelmed with offers.' Flushed with funds, I flashed six months' advance rent before him and, well, he couldn't resist the sight. Then again, might it have been my loose, flouncy top, teasing him with an ample hint of mauve bra strap? Turns grown men to water. Too bad for them. Whilst there's not much in the bra, it's the hope of getting their hands on the merchandise that hypnotises them to my commands.

I am about to head out to deposit Alexander Beecham's £2,000 cheque when the phone stops me.

'Hello. Olivia? Superintendent Jack Thornton.'

Shit! I recognise the surname. I should have returned his call last night. I freeze. Even the innocent freeze when a police officer calls. But this is business. I hope. I learn that I am required for 'a spot of observing'. Excitement rises. *Nothing better than the chance to get my teeth into a big one.* I relish assignments of a covert nature; the darkness of tailing and watching; slithering around – chameleon like – tracing a target's every move. I explain my reluctance to enter another working relationship with police, especially after having been castigated over my association with DCI Stafford, whose assistance I'd sought during the latter stage of my employment as a detective sergeant with West Mercia Police. Ironically, it was Stafford who recommended me to Thornton.

Thornton describes a situation requiring external sources to penetrate an internal investigation. He confides that I'm chosen because of my belligerence, devotion to duty, and ability to utilise every available resource to achieve resolution.

Documented in my Personal History File is the cruel analogy: 'like a dog with a bone'. I accept the term as a compliment, but the world of officialdom would infer negative connotations. I would be Thornton's eyes in my petite, girl-next-door body. Such is the private investigator's role: uncover things that your instructor cannot; use the shield of anonymity to extract information, and then gawk in awe as he receives slaps on the back for a job well done. On the other side, should the investigation turn sour, *I* will be the scapegoat.

I profile him as a compatriot stickler for detail. Not that I object to that, but he stretches the trait too far, wanting complete separation of our roles – which actually suits me – and insisting that I not contact any other police member during the term of contract. I anticipate his use of the term 'observing' as a full-on, intense survey of a senior police officer whose identity would be code named throughout the investigation. His real name might never be revealed. What Thornton does not know, is that I am one who shifts the earth to uncover little snippets concealed from all but those immediately beneath command.

I am uneasy about spying on former colleagues. It is not a pride bolstering role, or one to gloat about at Christmas parties, but I do recognise the need for underhanded surveillance to keep the constabulary scrupulous.

I arrange to meet Thornton at the Worcester CID office, an inconvenience I will defray into future invoices – assuming I agree to the collaboration.

II

On completion of an enquiry into the ownership of recovered stolen goods, McMaster heads home along the A44, a BBC broadcast of the third Test between England and New Zealand blaring in the background, and smoke curling from a cigarette in the foreground – contrary to the constabulary's 'no smoking in police vehicles' policy.

A red Renault flashes by. Blonde hair trails from the driver's window. McMaster tries to overlook the infraction because he proudly avoids vehicular policing and revenue-raising. Had the driver not been a young female, he would continue his journey, counting six-ball overs and sweating to the escalating required run rate. Instead, he maintains a steady eighty-five miles per hour behind the Renault, flashes his headlights, and then, in a move more dangerous than the offending driver's actions, pulls alongside the car, thrusts his badge to the passenger window, and motions her to the verge.

Both cars retreat to a convenient lay-by where McMaster withdraws from his Vauxhall, lights another cigarette, and approaches the driver. A flustered young woman grimaces: 'Sorry. I've had a bad day.'

McMaster studies her: about twenty-years-old, bottle-blonde hair, deep brown eyes of Mediterranean or Middle Eastern background and skin glowing like Crème Caramel. Black eyeliner rolls down her left cheek. She wears a white blouse, a black lace tie pinched at the neck and a black linen skirt riding high on her thighs.

Conscious of McMaster's seedy glare, she drops her hands to her lap.

'So, what's the rush?'

'Just late. I'll be honest. I just wanted to get home. I know I was going too fast, but I was careful.'

'You work in a restaurant?'

'No. Heavenly Spirits. I'm a manager.'

'So what's that, a fortune telling shop?'

'No. We sell wines and spirits. Specialise in spirits – the wine's just a sideline.'

'Girl after my heart.'

She cringes.

McMaster had once faced a disciplinary hearing for taking personal details from a woman. The Internal Affairs panel heard the allegation and dismissed the complaint as a vengeful objection to a traffic fine.

'I'll have to make a note of this. What's your name and address?'

'No please. I can't afford to be fined. I'm going through a rough patch of personal problems.'

'I'm not saying you'll be fined, but I must record your details as a person I've spoken to whilst on duty.'

'Rose Maree Hernandez.'

McMaster scratches Rose's details into his notebook, together with her work location. He lectures the dangers of speeding, and finishes with an abrupt: 'You may hear something within the week.'

* * *

McMaster pulls into the driveway of Ashton Hill. He'd discovered the property eight years' earlier during an afternoon's cruising about the countryside in an unmarked police car. By the most intriguing circumstance, he was tasked to investigate a complaint of vandals smashing windows at an abandoned property. The offenders, in true fashion, had decamped before police arrived, but that didn't obviate the need for McMaster to complete crime reports, which might later be required by the property's owners or an insurance company. After searching Land Registry details, McMaster located records noting the Medicinal Trust as owner. Further checks disclosed that the Trust had long been liquidated, and its few assets dispersed to creditors. Then he found the diamond: the property was sitting in limbo pending transfer to the crown.

He jumped at the opportunity to acquire the property. Whilst claiming to be a proud Brit who would lie down for his country, he abhors the monarchy's accumulation of wealth while the average citizen struggles to pay rent or mortgage, council tax and television licences, and contents insurance for their few possessions. He therefore instructed solicitor, Steven Weston, to obtain the estate 'at all costs'. McMaster defined 'at all costs': 'to encourage those in authority to reach a favourable agreement either by legal threat or cash under the council chamber's table'.

Seven months' later, Steve Weston secured Ashton Hill's title.

Over the following two years, McMaster and his wife, Gloria, worked tirelessly to restore the property to its original condition. Expenditure soared beyond the purchase price, brought about by Phillip's insistence that one wing be totally remodelled. The faded title document decreed that no major departure from the building's original structure be allowed. McMaster chose to interpret 'major departure' so loose that its inclusion became superfluous. Because McMaster is not one to capitulate to authority, it is no surprise that he also flouted conditions of the listed buildings' register. With selfish pride, he boasted: *they can't tell me what to do with my property.*

He stared at the title's scaled-down cross-hatched area near the rear boundary. A bold stamp read: 'Do not Plough'. Colouration denoted a 165-metre strip, extending from the centre of McMaster's property and into the neighbouring Blackshaw's Mill. The McMasters had no intention of ploughing. Nor had they plans to develop the rear acreage. Renovating the new home was a priority that pushed the title document's discoloured markings into the background – but not too far from Phillip McMaster. To a detective, the addendum hid like a jewel in a pot plant: *Why would an owner of rural land affix such a clause?*

In trying to answer the conundrum, he considered the prospect of unstable earth, underground caves or tunnels, and the likelihood of buried relics or graves of long-passed clan. But no evidence supported the hypothesis. A painstaking sweep with a hired metal detector revealed nothing – discounting his worst-case scenario of the field being riddled with century-old sub-surface rabbit traps. The trauma continued: *What can I find out without ploughing? Who the hell would know if I do?*

It was curiosity, trumping the detective's penchant of leaving no question unanswered, that compelled McMaster to research Ashton Hill's history. The estate's original plans survive in Westlands Council archives. Records show the property had been constructed in 1822 to the order of Lord Stevenson, a then prominent member of the House of Lords. At the time of lodgement, only the owner or tax collector would have reason to inspect the huge sheet. Stevenson would have had no inkling that in 190 years' time all manner of council proprietorship over its residents' rights to privacy, and the willy-nilly granting of Freedom of Information applications to all and sundry would reward every nosy-parker with information to which they were not, and should not be, entitled.

On Stevenson's death in 1860, the estate passed to his only child, Penelope, who remained a hermit in the property until consumption claimed her in 1884. To comply with her father's wish that the estate pass to charity in the event of there being no lineal family descendant, the property was gifted to the Medicinal Trust, whose charter it was, ironically, to research prevention of communicable diseases.

On inheriting the property, trust custodians planned to convert the ground floors to research facilities, and the upper floor to office space. The south wing would house the Trust's physician. The custodians' foresight, however, was shattered after discovering Lord Stevenson's covenant demanding the property maintain its original facade and fit out. They could not successfully renovate the estate. Nor could they sell it – the slightest infraction would deliver the property to the crown. As a consequence, the trust forsook the bequest, leaving Ashton Hill vacant and neglected for 97 years.

The twenty-first century parallels the nineteenth, insomuch as males' acuity ranks high. Both eras judge personal standing and credibility by wealth. Stevenson flaunted his by erecting the palatial 17-room mansion on a prominent rise, but discrete enough to escape the cacophony of galloping hooves and crackling carriage wheels emanating from the nearby Worcester to Evesham road.

Today, McMaster flaunts the renovated mansion under duress of whining lorry tyres, screaming four-cylinder, ten thousand revs-per-minute motorcycles, and the morning and evening commuter procession that swells to hundreds of weekend tourists who alone have elevated the status of the once rutted track to the well-travelled A44. His foresight in planting a parallel stand of cedars and willows mutes the busy thoroughfare's traffic noise.

Bordering the McMaster property lays Blackshaw's Mill. Surrounded by 25 fertile Worcestershire acres fronting the River Avon, the former textile factory was long ago converted to a family home. Today, the only survivors of the eighteenth-century mill are two huge water wheels that once drove a score of antiquated bevelled cogs which creaked and groaned crude mechanical agitation to the wash and dye rooms.

For the past fourteen years Giuseppe and Maria Caruso have lovingly tended the property. Its heyday returned a regular income from sheep sales, baled hay, and grazing the local pony club's horses. Today, wild grass baled into cheap chaff withers in the fields.

Giuseppe is one of Britain's early invasions of European migrants, having arrived with his parents in 1962 and settling in Manchester – home to a strong Italian community. At sixteen-years-old he joined his father, Giuseppe senior, who was a master craftsman in laying terrazzo. With the advent of fibreglass and resin shower bases, and vinyl and ceramic tiled flooring, terrazzo lost favour with builders. Young Giuseppe could have followed fellow tradesman into kerbing and paving, but laying daily expanses of dull grey concrete failed to excite as did the sparkling, glittery medium he had enjoyed for twenty-odd years. He disappointed his father by joining Royal Mail as a sorter.

Employed behind the counter of Manchester City Post Office was Postal Clerk Grade Two, Maria Mazzini, a stunning beauty of classic Italian proportion, coached to shun male attention. Never could she wear down Giuseppe's proposals for an evening at the cinema; she had no chance, because Giuseppe walked into the Post Office every day at 4.45 p.m., moseyed up to her counter, and purchased six first class stamps. When they married in 1985, twenty-seven months after first setting eyes on each other, Giuseppe presented Maria his tin of 2,484 stamps – six hundred and twenty pounds worth.

Maria is now the archetypal rotund Italian grandmother – living only for her family of six children and four grandchildren. Three daughters drifted away on the wave of marriage, and two sons chose to settle in Italy after a backpacking holiday convinced them that more opportunities lay in their ancestral country than did in England. The sibling's exodus came about not by heartfelt wishes to embark on their own life, but of their own volition to escape violent arguments lifting the Caruso roof.

Giuseppe Caruso is the quintessential master of the home – and of his wife. Tall and silver-haired, his dominant bearing often resulted in elder siblings having to rescue their mother from his wayward fists. The soft-natured young man who'd swept Maria from the Post Office floor had hardened like clay in a kiln. From the oven stepped a strong-willed bully who wanted everything his own way – and would get it. He created arguments from the most trivial circumstances: late meals; clothes not ironed properly; overspending at the supermarket; and his wife's frequent molly-coddling of their youngest child.

Conceived late in the Caruso's marriage, Angelo was a heaven-sent gift. The special son's name credited His divinity. However, from the dawn of his teen years, Angelo disappointed many. Became a nightmare. Walked with the devil. Lashings of attention which had extended into mid-childhood, slowly diminished, leaving Angelo with little supervision. He compensated by doing as he pleased, growing independent and gaining self-assurance while ignoring the wishes of others – including his parents, who sat a distant second on his list of personal ties. The taste of self-sufficiency moulded Angelo's template for the future.

He grew up, encouraged by his brothers, to rush to his mother's defence. He is now, other than God, his mother's only saviour. The most recent intervention saw Angelo punch his father to the ground. His elderly namesake did not retaliate; he banished Angelo from the family home. In defiance, Angelo continues to maintain regular contact with his mother in a relationship motivated only by his desire to cement a place at the forefront of his parents' final bequests. Today, few words are spoken between Angelo and Giuseppe Caruso.

And few words flutter between Giuseppe Caruso and Phillip McMaster.

III

Phillip and Gloria McMaster befriended the Carusos after moving in to the restored Ashton Hill six years' earlier. Their rapport lolled around casual 'hellos', as opposed to the over-cordial friendships of longstanding rural residents. That suited the McMasters, for they barely exchanged a word between themselves. Phillip though, did extend the Caruso's Christmas cordiality by delivering wine and chocolates recycled from constabulary well-wishers. Gloria too, weighed in with Avon testers that failed to meet her pretentious expectations. The insincere gift-giving merely paves a path to favours. Building a credit bank. Such is McMaster's modus operandi – graft others into his debt.

A fortnight earlier – shortly after Christmas – he'd approached Giuseppe, hoping to resolve a boundary problem. The issue arose after McMaster found what he believed was a discrepancy on his council tax notice. After recovering a copy of the original title document from one of his safes, he compared the land area with that specified on the council notice. It didn't resolve the dilemma. Both figures tallied. But McMaster wasn't satisfied. He buzzed down to the rear boundary and paced out the measurement. One stride to the metre; proven reliable over years of pacing out crime scenes, marking-out evidence locations, pinpointing positions of deceased or injured, and taking measurements of vehicular skid marks. Scene of crime officers (SOCO) would later confirm his computations – to within a few inches – with their scientific apparatus or humble measuring tape.

The rear measurement accorded with both the tax notice and Land Registry title. He thrust a cigarette into his mouth, moved to the side boundaries and paced the parallel fence lines, pulling up six paces short of the official measurement. He double- and triple-checked to ensure he had not miscalculated by a whole six metres. He hadn't.

The legacy of McMaster's twenty-plus years of police service has taught him to check all facts before conducting an enquiry, whether official or domestic. He attended the council office to detail his problem and received the fob off: 'We rate by the title information. We have no reason to dispute official documents. Your argument's against the neighbour, not Westlands.'

'I'm not here to argue with anyone. All I want is to verify that council's measurements are correct.'

McMaster had expected the council to pass him off because council does not make mistakes. His temper-testing thirty-minute query was ultimately rewarded with a folder of archived material. The historic sheets detailed dates of acquisition and ownership changes, and confirmed the accuracy of official records. Only then did McMaster concede that a discrepancy did exist between those records and *his* measurements.

Before returning to Ashton Hill he bought a 100-metre 'Guaranteed to not Stretch' nylon/fibreglass tape. Subsequent measurements confirmed his suspicion: the adjacent landholder – in years or centuries prior to the Caruso's taking possession – had moved the rear boundary by 5.7 metres. Nearly six metres, or 20-odd feet over 544 feet, is a substantial chunk of land. As efforts to retrieve it could spark a full-blown dispute, McMaster appointed surveyors to repeg his estate.

The boundary discrepancy brewed ill will between the neighbours. Caruso called him 'infantile' for haggling over the small strip of land. 'I don't have a problem,' he said. 'You take the land if you're sure it's yours.' The proposal was sincere and generous. Caruso would not miss the sliver from his 25-acre holding.

'Thank you, Joe, but no.' McMaster responded. 'What's fair is fair, right? If I've made a mistake, I don't want to see you deprived because of it. Proper checks will give us both the detail and evidence we need, right.'

'You police. Always evidence, evidence, evidence. Why we no have the gentleman's agreement still? One handshake. Everything done.'

'It's a different world, Joe. Everything has to be right, right? And legal. I can't even order a black coffee without fear of being called a racist. Can't eat bloody white bread anymore; only order multigrain, right? – saves the drama. And don't even get me started on my black pudding!'

Giuseppe shot McMaster a quizzical look. 'How's a surveyor tell if the boundary's been moved?'

'They mark out the land to the exact measurements as noted on the original land title documents. I might even get in a mate to do a geological survey; run a scanner across the surface, bit like an X-ray of the earth. I'm sure we'll find a sign of fence or gate posts; maybe decayed roots of an old hedgerow or even a course of stone from an old dry wall.'

'Good luck to you. Like I'm say, I don't care. I save you the trouble and give the land.'

One week later, the West Midland Surveyors' report read: "We hereby certify the property described on Plan of Subdivision XD83642BS as Lot 29, now known as Ashton

Hill, is deficient in length of eighteen feet and five inches on the West and East boundaries, respectively. We have duly pegged intersecting boundaries with approved stakes."

McMaster dug holes for fence posts. Scooped out dregs by hand. The second handful sparkled. Darts of light pranced about like effervescent bubbles jumping from a carbonated drink. He ran his fingers through the fine silt. Sifted it from one hand to the other. Spat on his shirt sleeve and wiped a small stone. Swivelled his head as if he were about to shoplift a block of chocolate. And then he slipped a fingernail size gold pebble into his pocket.

He dropped posts into the holes and paced back to his house. On a table lay the laminated topographic estate plan. McMaster's interest focused on the lower section: 'Do not Plough. Preserved land.'

He mapped an imaginary vein, rich in gold deposits, worming its way beneath his and the Caruso property.

Across the border, Wales holds a place in the annals of British gold, when, in 70AD, scavenging Romans picked up the shiny ore. Over succeeding centuries, exploration and production gained momentum, right through to the late 1930s. In Gwynedd, North Wales, commercial operations began in the 1850s, where significant development enriched the small country until, in 1999, flattening gold prices and adverse economic conditions closed the mine. Other mining companies followed, citing strangling Occupational Health and Safety laws, environmental concerns – including the new emphasis on carbon emissions – and to top it all off, unrealistic union demands.

McMaster's relentless research uncovered details of a licence granted in 2010 to allow mining within a 120-square kilometre area known as the Dolgellau Gold Belt in Wales. He hoped a stratigraphic relationship would exist between Dolgellau and his find in the West Midlands. The Cambrian mountain range rose between the two locales, and it was that phenomenon that convinced McMaster that his finding might well be a satellite artery of Dolgellau.

He hoped that since Giuseppe had been so willing to forsake a small strip of land, he might be receptive to selling the whole farm. During subsequent over-the-fence banter, he made a veiled offer for the Caruso property. Giuseppe was not so restrained and forcefully rejected the proposal: 'We no want to move.'

You'll move. Such was McMaster's resolve. Never one to quit a challenge, he forecast reaping millions of pounds of instant wealth – with or without Caruso's land. The burning problem flared before him: *How do I extract riches from my property without arousing the Caruso's interest?*

Days later, while inspecting the new rear fence, McMaster noticed Maria Caruso tending her vegetable garden. It was no coincidence. McMaster complimented the lush rows of green foliage and freshly turned earth.

'I'll be doing a bit of that soon.'

'You like the gardening, Mr Mac?'

'Only for business. I'm going to set up a farm. Vegetables. Plenty of them. Maybe nuts and olives too.'

He steered the conversation to Blackshaw's Mill. Maria confided that she'd long dreamed of moving to a small village. 'My Giuseppe, he's just want to stay here. He's not want the trouble of packing and moving. He's just say this is our home – nowhere else there will be family. I'm say, "the family's gone". He's so stubborn is my Giuseppe.'

IV

Dennis Stonebridge slides the knife through the envelope. Peers inside. Smiles. Taps the wad of £20 notes and sinks the envelope into his jacket. He hands McMaster a certificate and shakes his hand with the vigorous pumping a car salesman injects into a prospective customer he hopes will generate substantial commissions for the lavish, dangling gold chains, the chronographic watch and the diamond encrusted dental work that radiates the salesman's permanent dazzling persona.

McMaster releases his prey. 'Thank you. I'm sure we can do business.'

On Stonebridge's recommendation, Westlands Council's planning department approved McMaster's permit application to erect a huge barn, or in twenty-first century parlance: maintenance shed. The application cited needs to house tractors, a small excavator and other earth moving plant to prepare his acreage for heavy agriculture. The council also approved construction of a one million litre dam to irrigate crops, although at the time of application, McMaster had not specified the variety of crops he would sow.

To justify the approval, and to shift attention from his forthcoming project, McMaster has planted an acre of cabbage and cauliflower, intending to consign the new crop to a local farmer to manage through to harvest. Whilst McMaster's ability to wheel and deal is limitless, his knowledge of agriculture and permaculture would be on par with the Chancellor of the

Exchequer's nous of the financial needs of the average British citizen.

The permit had not been rubber-stamped as McMaster had expected. The proposed siting of the 60 by 30 metre shed alongside the shared rear boundary of his and the Caruso property sees the completed building soar ten metres above ground level – the height of a two-storey building.

Giuseppe Caruso spat: 'What for you want the large shed? It's bigger than your house.'

McMaster explained his farm proposal and the necessity for an equipment and packing shed. He brushed off his indecision with the explanation that on-going climate research and soil evaluation would determine further crop selection.

Giuseppe Caruso vehemently opposes change. He formalised an objection, citing loss of amenity, destruction of natural fall of land with the consequent loss of water to his property, and then, contrary to his stance, complained that runoff from the 100-square-metre roof would flood his property – despite two proposed 50,000 litre storage tanks capable of collecting every raindrop.

Stonebridge weighed the objectors' concerns, and had been keen to deny the application after accepting the Carusos' submission citing loss of their 'precious views' of the Malvern Hills. His about-face followed McMaster's promise to resite the erection. McMaster also pledged to soften the galvanised monolith with jasmine, wandering Jew and climbing roses, creating a panorama of evergreen foliage.

Satisfied that the grounds of the Caruso's objection no longer existed, Stonebridge reconsidered the application – prompted by McMaster's incentive, discreetly left on Stonebridge's office table. That was inconsistent with McMaster's usual practice – his deals generally flourished *under* the table. The language of money is historic, as both trading currency and corruptive power. It is that element that conscripted Stonebridge to Phillip McMaster's payroll.

Ecstasy was short-lived. The project suffered further delays after Caruso sought a court injunction to overturn the Westlands Council decision. The action fuelled McMaster's rage toward Caruso, who by now had recruited fellow 'local farmers' – some of whom were more local to John o'Groats than the dales of Worcestershire – to support his objection. Caruso, however, soon learnt that when a government authority stamps a decision, nothing will reverse the ruling – even if the pronouncement is flawed, or an outright abuse of statutory power. Relations between the feuding neighbours turned so bitter that none of McMaster's sweeteners could reinstate the friendship.

Works commenced soon after council dismissed the objection. Concrete footings seeped into the earth, steel girders rose, and the frame peaked over a ten-hour shift before roof contractors fixed rafters and purlins. As dusk bleached the surroundings, the final sheet of olive-green corrugated iron roofing muted the topography.

Giuseppe Caruso stood within his boundary, yelling abuse and obscenities at the workers. The foreman countered with his own barrage, only for Caruso to complain to council that the works contravened planning permission. He had no foundation for the complaint other than his belief that McMaster would take shortcuts or request last-minute changes to the approved plan.

McMaster though, had exercised stringent control over the construction. And, although eight feet shy of his intended siting, he had sited it directly over the 'Do not Plough' section identified by the land title.

Angelo Caruso approaches McMaster as he attaches lattice panels to the shed's rear wall. Angelo has been 'on-side' since McMaster turned a blind eye to a small marijuana crop, sheltered by a stand of Willows, growing inside the Caruso's side boundary. Angelo knows his neighbour is a police officer; he's known it since the McMasters took on Ashton Hill. To lift the atmosphere, Angelo rolls two joints and offers one to his neighbour.

McMaster recalls photos of his late father drawing on the illicit tobacco back in the days of Vietnam War protests – a cause western youth had pursued with vigour. Fred McMaster, following his ilk, had experimented with the popular drug before walking into adulthood. Phil McMaster pulls hard on the sweet tobacco, clamps his mouth, and savours the rollie's full power. A few drags transport him to his father's snaps of 1967, where the twanging riff of the Jimi Hendrix Experience 'Purple Haze' reignites his first sexual encounter with a girl – whose name he didn't even know – under a blanket in Hyde Park. Later that night, he'd tried to swim across the Thames after missing the last bus.

Now, he contemplates a market for the popular weed. Four fellow detective's names come to mind; immediate candidates for a few wisps of enhanced weekend relaxation. He considers a partnership with Angelo, but decides to not risk his mantle as a threatening power. He draws again. 'Been a long time.'

'Wait no longer, then. You don't need an agricultural degree to grow this.'

'Too risky. Remember I'm in the job. One of those bloody detector dogs would sniff me out from ten miles away.'

But McMaster doesn't reject the idea. *Maybe I could grow a couple. Test the market.*

Under darkness, he returns to Angelo's crop and shakes seeds from a mature plant. A few hours nurturing inside his AGA-warmed kitchen will see them spring from pots within a fortnight. He'll then transfer them to crudely constructed troughs made of plastic roof guttering, in a section of his new shed. *If tomatoes and strawberries flourish in hydroponic trenches, why not marijuana?* It could prove to be a highly profitable low-maintenance hobby, *and* generate an immediate black-market income. The vision clashes with his prime aim.

A low-loader, struggling with excavator, buckets and augers, and a diesel generator, rumbles along McMaster's drive. As Phil rushes to direct the driver, he notices three Caruso faces gawking over the dividing fence. With a sarcastic wave, he yells: 'Nice afternoon, isn't it?'

Giuseppe returns unintelligible insults.

McMaster ignores him.

The driver off-loads the machinery.

McMaster, in a clearly defiant act, commandeers the small excavator, rattles over to a pre-pegged area close to the Caruso boundary, and scrapes off the top soil. Dumps it nearby.

Two cigarette breaks later, he returns to the shed, drops the roller door, and scrapes a ten-foot square of earth from the shed floor. He transfers scores of cubic metres of earth to the swelling pile beside a proposed dam. The growing mountain will surely provoke fresh complaints from the Carusos. And it will get bigger. McMaster recalls a geology manual stating that to extract just 15 to 30 grams of gold from the earth, he will have to sift through a ton – 2,240 pounds (1,000 kilograms) or, in physical terms, 500 shovelfuls of raw earth.

He continues the onerous task of pursuing criminals during the day, and of an evening, firing up the excavator to scoop earth for five hours. As the excavator's six-metre boom reaches its limit, the sizeable pit shows the beginnings of a fully fledged mine entrance.

The next phase is much harder. Physically taxing. Pick and shovel. Breaking through lime, rock and shale. Jarring wrists and shoulders. Shattering chunks of the renowned Cotswold stone. At ten metres, the three-section extension ladder begins to sway. He logs that as the maximum depth.

Encouraged by the familiar glitter-like sparkle in sections of the shaft wall, he strikes out a landing and carves a lateral tunnel. The metal detector buzzes and flashes strong readings of metallic substance, propelling McMaster to ferociously pick into the new section. Fear invokes reservations about channelling along a lateral trajectory. He has no experience of the occupation where cave-ins, wall collapses, and respiratory problems have taken lives. His knowledge comes only from skims through mining books and manuals, and reliance on carpentry instructions for shoring up the secondary tunnel. Safety demands the horizontal shaft be supported by five inch square beams, which in turn means further investment. He reflects that it might have been far more practical to disclose his findings to Caruso, and then embark on a joint venture. He just as quickly discards the thought. Never has McMaster been one to share.

He catches his breath. Organises his head. He rests the pick against the jagged wall and drops a large bucket at his feet. Waves the metal detector across the face of the new cut. Retreats from the high-pitched shrill. He drops the detector, grabs the pick, and slams it into the wall, sending chunks of clay and rock splintering to the floor. Shovels the lumps into the bucket and checks the pulley rope.

He scampers up the ladder like Spiderman scaling a wall, and then heaves the huge bucket to the surface where he upends the contents onto a large plastic tarpaulin. He then sifts the earth thorough a makeshift sieve fabricated from an old insect screen.

Two marble-sized pieces of dull gold roll like dice in a Roulette wheel. His temperament lifts as the rewards of success dissolve the pain of long laborious hours – finally justifying his huge investment. No one can learn of his find. Secrecy will guarantee his financial future, whereas bragging would surely see the Crown step in and take possession of all beneath the surface.

V

'Miss Watts?' A young constable approaches and escorts me to Thornton's temporary office. I suppress my knowledge of the building and its stalwarts, preferring to leave that history smudged on dusty architraves and faded blue curtains.

I have not previously met Superintendent Thornton, and nor have I had reason to, given his attachment to London's MET office. The introduction springs disbelief. Thornton stands in contrast to my perception of senior officers, typically typecast as five years' pre-retirement, anaemic complexion – save for the liquor-reddened nose, the uniform-issue fifty-inch belt buckled into the third extra hand-punched hole, and a wealth of RetireInvest prospectuses hidden beneath unsolved-crime files. He is a surprise: elf-like: short in stature, ectomorphic frame, and glows as if he'd minutes earlier completed the London Marathon – or just finished 'interviewing' a young female constable eager to suck her way to promotion.

'Hello, Miss Watts. Pleased to finally meet you.'

Why? Small talk, or has my reputation preceded me? 'Thank you sir.' I don't know why I call him 'sir'. Force of habit – the indoctrination of hierarchical respect instilled in me by my police officer step-father and reinforced through school and college.

Thornton sedates the atmosphere: 'Call me Jack please. You're not in uniform now, although I must say your resignation was a loss to the constabulary.'

He heard? Through Stafford or the rampant grapevine? 'One of those situations, sir. I hope you understand the discomfiture I faced. I felt extremely uneasy about overriding DI Marchant, but when we pledge to represent justice I believe that justice must receive the best opportunity of being served. Idealistic? Maybe. But as my presence here attests, I'm a person who stands by her word.'

'And that's precisely why you're here, Miss Watts, because of your ethics.'

'Better forget the "Miss Watts" then. It's Olivia.'

Needless to say, I wondered what was coming. Why recruit a recently resigned member who'd lagged on a superior officer? And why is this driven by the upper echelon – a superintendent for goodness' sake?

Thornton presses on: 'The target is a private investigator. Gillian Trotter. Know her?'

A queasy uneasiness chills me. I feel second-rate, a second string to his preferred outside help. *Reporting the activities of one of my own. That's* worse *than investigating a copper.* It revives the fallout of the Worcester CID incident, the very reason I'd left the constabulary. I'm still recovering to this day, not through emotional stress but through the regret of having sacrificed a magnificent career and all of its financial benefits. But there's a rider: I'm far happier for having started my own agency. Now, a potential conflict slaps me in the face.

'Never heard of her,' as if I keep a log of every registered and unregistered investigator in England. And that's good, because if I did know Trotter, I would instantly decline the job.

Thornton proffers a long-winded analytical speech in which he convinces me – not that I need convincing – of the need for accountability: 'it benefits taxpayers; it's their money,' and, 'not all police officers are squeaky clean; think of the bad apple syndrome.' He smiles and opens a manila folder. 'We have a situation, and I think – no, I know – that you're the one to look into it.'

I've seen the bad apples, including a couple rotten through to their core. I glare at the folder, trying to decipher the upside down print.

'The situation is, Olivia, we have an officer, an inspector at that, who I believe is treading a thin line. I want to nip this in the bud before the IPCC gets wind. That should not compromise your role because I have instigated mechanisms to ensure we are one step ahead.'

'We have strong reasons to suspect that the investigator tasked to inform us of matters pertaining to that detective inspector is not acting in our best interests. We suspect Trotter is short-delivering investigatory material, and, that she may be *too close* to the target. Your task is to shadow Trotter and update me. There's a leak somewhere – it's either her, or we have an internal problem. On that basis, I can't afford to have information flowing to anyone but me. I will be your only – and I stress *only* – contact, and you'll submit invoices only to me.' Thornton pens his mobile number on the back of a card and hands it over. 'For all intents and purposes you don't exist.'

I don't mind not existing; it's been on my wish-list for some time. But what haunts me is whether Thornton will outlay £45 per hour from his own pocket? If so, that suggests the enquiry is most definitely not *official*. On the other hand, hundreds of scenarios deserve varying levels of confidentiality. Mine is not to question, but to do the job and deliver results. And bank the money. Still, I am confused. Being head-hunted to inform on a fellow PI is not my idea of a rewarding contract. Employees are held to account by many devious means – it's quite normal to read about stings in papers or to see the results of a covert operation on television. But when you're in the epicentre, radiating shock waves through immediate surrounds, colleagues and friends, it is an entirely different Tupperware bowl of fish. I fear losing my last threads of credibility. It's not as if I have to subscribe to the 'beggars can't be choosers' philosophy; I have plenty of work and enquiries, although not on the financially rewarding scale of Thornton's proposal. I glance at the bloated folder. Eagerness displaces apprehension. 'I'll do it.'

I love the thrill of winning a new contract. Ignites the Hollywood lights around my dreams.

Thornton spills the folder's content across the table and points to three photos. Trotter. He briefs me about her 'installation' in the Knight's Arms as a part-time bar attendant to work hours that coincide with McMaster's lunch breaks and shift completion. Gillian Trotter looks every bit the expensive escort, overdressed and over made-up. And over ugly. The snaps fail to disclose whether she is in disguise, but her proximity and demeanour with McMaster oozes passion of a family reunion.

Other snaps of the officer complete the cast. DI Phillip McMaster. I don't flinch or speak. I remember him from my days at Worcester CID. We worked opposite shifts. Had I ever have been given the choice of working under either McMaster or Marchant, I honestly can't say what my decision would have been. Today, I'll approach this with an open mind.

On Thornton's winding up the meeting, I accept his recommendation to 'trial run' the Knight's Arms for a spot of lunch. On my own. *May as well eat and bill the MET for my time.* Since migrating to the ranks of the self-employed, I am obsessed with extracting as much income as possible from every working hour. Never crossed my mind in the constabulary. Paired up with one of the guys, we'd stop at Maccas for coffee, chat for maybe half-an-hour, and think nothing of it. We were in the public domain, providing 'police presence' and available to respond to any emergency. We'd each earn £8 for those thirty minutes. Multiply that by a few timeouts each week, factor in hours spent exchanging gossip with colleagues and local business owners – which we entered on our duty sheets as information collation – and we'd probably cleared about £70 per week for a few bouts of joviality. Of course, there was a balance. Many after-hours call-outs and unpaid overtime was deemed part of the job.

I walk into the pub with the confidence and deportment of a female CEO. Flop on a seat in a dusty alcove beneath a flickering fluorescent light. Difficult to see, difficult to *be* seen – but I do recognise the face behind the bar. No need to pull out the photos to double-check Gillian's profile.

With good fortune, a separate meals counter provides a haven for me to order a Chicken Schnitzel and cappuccino. I am conscious of standing out in a pub. Many times, I've cringed at guys' reactions: elbows in the ribs; the sly comment, 'get a load of her'; and then wallets appear and money changes hands after some poor sucker refuses to make a move on the woman who's 'asking for it'. Yeah, most guys believe that a single woman in a pub is on the make. I know different. Excuse my crassness, but they're thinking with their dicks. Why can't they accept that a girl has to eat, and might just want to drop in to a good value pub for a meal and a glass of cider? The greasy £2.99 café should not be the only venue where we can sit undisturbed.

I swipe away time on my mobile, checking emails,

blogs, and message boards. Three little characters, A44, prick my attention. The road is one of my most travelled out of Worcester. I skim through a rant about sleazy coppers who patrol the A44. I know most of the locals, but I object to the blogger's use of plural, in referring to 'coppers'. I type out my alter ego cyber chick response: Yeah. Agree wid ya. I had an old fogy try it on. Reckoned my car would fail an MOT check but sed hed let me off if we could cum to an agreement. I havent done nothing yet coz Im scared of what might happen. Cant afford to fix my car. I spose the best thing in these situations is to stay strong. They cant do nothing if we dont give them the chance.

By the time I arrive home there'll be twenty more replies.

I had not been fully briefed about Gillian's tenure in the pub. The terms of appointment are crucial, because the owner or proprietor could be a weak link if he knows that his de facto barmaid is informing on customers. I hope that Thornton hasn't instituted the arrangement under such perilous circumstances. Gillian, meanwhile, flits about like the perfect barmaid. Has the job down pat. Perhaps too well.

Bugger me. Talk about a trial run. I've barely put down the guy's photo when he walks in, strides up to the bar, orders a drink, and strokes Gillian's hand.

From beneath the table I aim my phone and snap off a couple of quick shots. Their intimacy might be totally innocent because I too, have performed the role of prospective lover, enamouring myself to men solely to win their confidence and trust. Perhaps Gillian is over-playing the role, but my interest is tuned not to dizzy gazes but to their conversation.

While Gillian ogles McMaster, I pounce on the opportunity to gain essential background knowledge. I flick through

Thornton's notes. Thumb to Gillian's address which I assume will be a budget rental somewhat like my own: lounge room converted to a home office, main bedroom demoted to a lounge room, and the second bedroom barely accommodating a king-size bed and small dressing table – a dual purpose establishment set up to claim tax deductions on home purchases that will be defrayed as office expenses. I've purchased a leather settee under that very scam. The settee became part of my clients' waiting area furnishings, which I later replaced with a budget sofa.

I take the scenic route home – a circuitous thirty-mile detour – to check out Gillian's address. I locate the average, two-bedroom terrace in one of Cheltenham's quieter back streets. It reeks of rental: weeds sprout across the frontage; cobwebs span windows' corners, and flakes of white paint fall from windowsills like coconut off a lamington. In the local paper, real estate professionals would declare it a 'renovator's delight awaiting tender-loving care'. I dump my car in a side street and trek back to the building. Knock on the door. No reply, as expected. I disadvantage myself by standing in view of the half-dozen neighbours who have little other to do than gawk from their windows. That rules out lock picking and window forcing. I reschedule the search and find mission.

Cheltenham is laid out in the grid pattern popular in the late 1700s. Running parallel with major streets are barely traversable lanes allowing access to the homes' rear yard. I often use those lanes for covert surveillance – a purpose far disconnected from their original function of providing discrete access to collect night tins. I canvass the narrow thoroughfare, checking for entry points along the squiggly line of battered corrugated iron fences. Frenzied ivy strangles trees, rickety fence panels and dilapidated gates. I leap over soiled nappies and plastic shopping bags bulging with household refuse, and sidestep smashed beer and spirit bottles glinting on the cobblestones. The odour of a departed pet assails my nostrils.

When faced with rows of cloned pre-war red brick, grey-slated roof, two up and two down terraces, a problem exists in trying to identify a specific property from the rear. The fail-safe method is to scan the roofline and count back chimneys from the end home.

I tally five clay pots holding up skewed television antennas, and arrive at Gillian's rear gate, one of few intact. It is padlocked from inside. I peer through the hand-hole. It is clearly Gillian Trotter's home. She uses my brand of security: curtains left open, old tops and underwear left on the clothes line, and one that truly impresses me, what appears to be a redundant store mannequin sitting behind an upstairs window. The alternative is unthinkable.

For now, I'll store the information for the later mission.

Three hours after downing a chicken schnitzel at the Knight's Arms, I fancy a cake-hunting stroll along Cheltenham's High Street mall and swanky arcades. I've walked only fifty metres when a flashing sign attracts me: Heavenly Spirits. It is heaven-sent because if not for a faulty electrical component known as a fluorescent starter, I would have continued blindly by the bottle shop. I take advantage of the find to top up my two-bottle alcohol cupboard. I enter the store, acknowledge a young woman stacking shelves, and browse the liqueur section. I snub the droned 'Can I help you?' with retail customers' stock response: 'Just looking thanks.' To negate any perception of ignorance, I look up, and after making eye contact, read the staff member's name badge: Rose Hernandez.

I scan the kaleidoscope of coloured liqueurs in peculiar bottles. I seize my standby Bailey's Irish Cream, approach Miss Hernandez, and ask if a new taste sensation has recently captured the market. She assesses me as if I am crazy and looks about ready blurt, 'How the fuck would I know?'

It's all about product knowledge, isn't it? If I go to a library or bookstore and ask for a book written similar to, say, John Grisham, a knowledgeable librarian might recommend Scott Turow or Lisa Scottoline. Equally, if Jackie Collins takes my fancy, I might pick up Danielle Steele or Nora Roberts.

'Sorry,' I stutter. 'I thought you might suggest something nice. I don't want to waste twenty quid on something I'll later tip down the sink.'

Hernandez switches from the couldn't-give-a-damn attitude to sales mode and suggests I try Orange Shock which sells in 375 and 750ml bottles. I grab the smaller sampling and grace the 'Customer Service' podium, which has become a sugary description of the cash desk.

I pass the bottle over the counter and hand her a debit card along with one of my business cards as egotistical self-promotion.

VI

DETERMINED TO AVOID HIS FATHER, Angelo visits his parents' home only during Giuseppe's habitual afternoon nap. On this particular Saturday, his mother raises *the* topic that continues to shake her marriage. Maria offloads her stress over the boundary dispute, claiming that the mammoth shed wreaked the final blow; Giuseppe so enraged by Westlands Council ignoring the rights of a seventeen-year responsible ratepayer in favour of an upstart hobby farmer.

'Angelo, you speak more sense than your father. He thinks of the past, not the future. You talk to papa. You tell him just don't look the shed too much, look other way and if you're still angry you don't need to talk to Mr Mac. You better with words. I no say things with the same sense like you.'

'You know papa and I don't talk. He'll think I'm trying to tell him what to do and how to run his life. I don't want to make trouble, and you know mama; it will make trouble for you also. I think I'll go now and see you later in the week.'

* * *

With a whole afternoon before Saturday's late shift start of 6.00 p.m., McMaster settles in his conservatory to enjoy a home-cooked lunch. His estrangement from Gloria means that the meal of eggs, sausages, bacon, beans and tomatoes, smothered with chilli sauce, is 'home-cooked' by himself.

Don McLean's 'American Pie' wails from a pair of Bose speakers. McMaster utters the interesting proposition: Why has no one composed a song about Spotted Dick? An opportunity awaits an aspiring artist prepared to deliver a unique rendition through one of many talent productions: *I get my kicks from Spotted Dicks.*

Beyond the rear garden's green expanse he notices a black Audi parked at the rear of the Caruso's property. *Angelo.* A Caruso get together could be discussing his purchase offer: McMaster's wishful thinking. He'd earlier considered convening a meeting to present the bid and embellish the benefits to his small audience. However, their fractious relationship dashed the prospect of his doing so, leaving hope of cordial negotiations as distant as the likelihood of resurrecting his marriage.

His intense observation of the Caruso property fuels paranoiac thoughts of the family plotting against him. Desperate to satisfy his curiosity, he abandons his meal and creeps to the rear boundary where he shields behind a stand of straggly poplars. He lights a cigarette but quickly crushes it into the ground lest the smoke disclose his presence. The conversation is barely perceptible, although a snatch of Giuseppe's gruff voice wavers across the boundary: 'I no want him here. He always do what he wants. He have no consideration for others.' And then, like a blaring commercial injected into a silent movie, a cacophony of yells and screams explode from the Caruso kitchen.

Angelo exits the back door, walks to his car and falls inside. Doesn't move.

McMaster recognises the trait. He adopts a similar ritual to calm his temper or collect thoughts. But he isn't calm now. He takes the slur to heart: *I no want him here… He have no consideration for others*. Marchant clenches his fists. Fails to consider that the comment might have been made against Giuseppe's own son.

When a police officer rushes to a domestic disturbance, an ethical dilemma presents itself: intervene to avert a potentially volatile confrontation, or turn a blind-eye and let the quarrelling participants resolve their own differences. It disturbs him that hostility could fracture the lifelong relationship of the devoted couple. McMaster has attended numerous domestic conflicts – triggered, in the main, by the male partner. Consequently, he harbours great resentment against instigators of domestic violence, and that compounds his predicament: act or retreat?

He returns to his conservatory. Slugs another double shot of Dewar's and heaves in unfiltered cigarette.

'Mr Mac. Mr Mac. Come quick. My husband. He's a fallen down. Not good. Not good.'

McMaster guzzles the remaining inch of whisky like a toilet cistern dropping its ten-litre flush. Races to the back door. 'Maria, what is it? Joe's hurt?'

'You musta come quick. Please.'

McMaster realises that Maria has hobbled 300 metres across uneven pasture to his door. He helps her to his car, and moments later halts at the rear of the Caruso property. He prises open the back door and tiptoes across the terrazzo floor. Enters the kitchen. The room reeks of a commercial galley whose aromas of garlic, tomato paste and boiling pasta cling to walls and ceilings. Giuseppe lays motionless on the floor, face down, arms outstretched above his head. McMaster checks for a pulse. Nothing. He commences CPR – preservation of human life taking priority over yet-to-attend paramedics and crime-scene investigators. He pumps his patient's chest – 100 to the minute. Nothing. Repeats the series: press and press and press and press. No twitch. No sudden jerks. No eye movement. No sign of recovery. He heaves air into the man he has for the past few weeks treated with disdain. Maria fills the doorway, hands clasped to her face.

'Phone 999,' McMaster yells, while silently berating her for having not already done so instead of wasting time running a cross-country marathon to his home. *Panic. Does strange things to people.*

His resuscitative efforts fail, as do those of paramedics who arrive twelve minutes later.

McMaster's investigative instincts beat 220. During recent protracted discussions with Giuseppe, he'd witnessed no sign of a heart condition or other physical ailment. That's not to say that Giuseppe isn't riddled with cancer, but to Phillip McMaster the death of a seemingly healthy person is *not* normal. He switches to police mode: 'Maria. Your husband on medication?'

'No Mr Mac. He's take nothing. He's healthy. He'll be all right?'

McMaster looks to the paramedics and exhales a desperate sigh. An officer shakes his head. His colleague, wise to the situation, avoids eye contact. McMaster accepts the grim task. Pulls himself from the floor and takes Maria's hand. 'I'm sorry, Maria. He's gone. Could be a heart attack. We'll know more once these gentlemen have finished. Is there someone I can call?'

Maria clasps her hand to her chest and lets out a piercing 'Noooo.'

McMaster tries again. 'Let me get someone to sit with you. Who can I call?'

'I have my Angelo, but I'm prefer be alone.'

He leads Maria to the lounge room and returns to the kitchen. Makes a pot of tea. Notes furniture placement and removes evidence of disarray. And then he wipes the back door frame and latch.

The Coroner notes a fracture at the base of Giuseppe's skull. He will not comment on whether the break was caused by the deceased falling to the floor or whether it was occasioned pre- or post-mortem. He confirms the cause of death is subject to autopsy, but does offer a preliminary determination of death occurring between 2.00 and 4.00 p.m.

Maria Caruso must now accept the possibility of someone having murdered her husband.

* * *

Over succeeding days McMaster works tirelessly, offers consolation to his neighbour, maintains the property, distributes feed to the few chickens, regulates watering systems, ensures gates are locked, and even collects weekly shopping. He tends Maria's tiny vegetable garden and is rewarded with take-home casseroles and home-baked bread. 'I can't cook for only me,' Maria cries. 'I'm always cook the big pasta for Giuseppe. Now I'm give some for you and Angelo.'

McMaster accepts the gifts, but seizes the mention of Angelo's name as a means to further his own agenda. He had thought that Angelo would step in and take over the bulk of his father's responsibilities. His conclusion is shattered when he learns that Angelo has no interest in working from dusk to dawn to grow what he could buy for less in Tesco. McMaster sees the once pristine farmlet blowing away with Midlands' gusts: 'Maria.

This is not the life for you anymore. It's not just the upkeep of the property. Taxes and maintenance will worry you more than you can imagine – especially while grieving for your dear husband.'

To a less sympathetic person, the patronising, romanticised language would be nauseating. He continues: 'You could be so happy in a small retirement unit. You'll have all your mementos and memories close by; your children will visit; and you'll make friendship with people in similar circumstances. I'll buy the property. Remember I told you I'm thinking about farming? I'm closer to my dream. If I buy your land, I can develop an especially productive operation.'

'I don't know, Mr Mac. It sounds good idea. I tell you I asked for Giuseppe to sell, but he's just say I want to complicate his retirement. Maybe it's not fair if I sell. Is like disrespect to my Giuseppe.'

'No Maria. Giuseppe would want what's best for you. He would want you to think of him and pray for him in peace. You can't do that when you're fighting council over taxes or trying to get plumbers to fix broken water pipes can you?'

'Mr Mac. You're like my Angelo. He's always know the right thing to do. I'm speaking to him later. I think is good idea. I'm not liking being here where my Giuseppe's passed away. That's what is, how you say, disrespectful?'

McMaster smiles. *I'm on a winner.* 'You're right. You speak with Angelo. I'll write up an offer so you've got something to discuss. And I'll tell you what I'll do. I'll insert a clause that lets you stay here, rent-free, while you plan your future.'

'Thank you, Mr Mac. You're a kind man. I'm tell that to Giuseppe when you offer to pay for the boundary mistake. I wish he's just taked the money and then he's maybe not have the stress that kills him.'

McMaster realises that his fortune lies not only beneath Ashton Hill and Blackshaw's Mill, but also with Angelo Caruso.

Angelo Caruso is a disappointment to his parents. He has pulled from life little other than perfecting (rated on his own scale) the art of deception. As a seven-year-old, he artfully deceived imprudent school students, graduating from sleight-of-hand swap card rorts to extorting Gameboys and mobile phones. His teen years saw him scam money, clothes and anything else he could lever from his younger and smaller victims. Angelo learned that verbal threats did more for his image than the anonymity of pickpocketing and general thieving. He was a true product of his environment, having grown up in a pressure-cooker of power and violence. How could he not believe that domination reaps rewards?

Still hoodwinking the public, he now spends most of his working week in a twenty-four-hour gymnasium. With no qualifications or school certificate, he lounges behind the membership desk in runner's shorts and tight muscle shirts. He's never 'trained' a client in his three years of employment, but deceptively wears the self-aggrandising title of personal trainer.

Angelo is a flesh covered rock. Victims of his extortion practices readily part with cash and valuables rather than risk an altercation with the ruffian. Built not from hours of sweat and toil in the hard-core gym, Angelo follows the fool's guide to gaining size: eat all you can and down a regime of illegal steroids and Human Growth Hormone. His diet of pasta and oil-saturated cuisine ensures he exceeds the calorific requirements, and working in an environmental magnet of shady characters ensures he has easy access to banned substances.

It was during his final school year that Angelo fell into the drug scene. Since then, he's immersed himself in the trade, starting out by purchasing small wads of marijuana and dividing them into smaller saleable quantities. He furthered his standing after creating a mini processing station in the loft of a disused barn on his parents' property. To dispel questions about the amount of time he spent in the barn, he set up two easels and decorated the walls with pieces of artistry that wouldn't sell from a cardboard box in the back corner of a charity shop. His drug equipment – bowls, racks, a small drying oven and two sets of scales – were passed off as necessities for making and mixing paint pigments.

The barn eventually gave way to the practicality of importing. Adopting modern multi-level marketing techniques, Angelo found it easier and safer to act as middle-man by purchasing the product from overseas. He now cuts and divides it, and wholesales the lot to a dealer to distribute through his own network. Angelo takes forty percent of the street value for doing next to nothing – and with little risk. But there's a catch. The imported product is inferior. Ever the thinker, he overcomes that problem by using his own quality crop as samples, and then fills the orders from the inferior product.

In responding to his mother's call to 'look some papers' Angelo ogles McMaster's offer. The glowing £360,000 sale price is like reading the dividend of Lotto's Division One prize pool. He visualises *not* what he can do for his mother, but what he *could* do for himself. He peers to the future. 'Mama, this is a good idea. You don't need the land. With Tony and Vince overseas, none of us can help. You've got no crops and no stock. All you do is pay for hay cutting and then lose money selling it.' He takes his mother's hand and offers rarely imparted sincerity:

'Mama, with this, you'll have it off your mind. You can have an easy life. You have the offer. You don't have to worry about advertising and agent's costs; you just sign and let a solicitor do the legals.'

He narrows his focus to the end-benefit. Grabs a local paper from the recycling pile. Checks listings of similar properties in the surrounding area. Sees that McMaster has offered a fair price. He phones McMaster and compliments a passion fruit screen, and then slips in that he is dealing with the property's sale process, save for the actual signing. He requests a meeting to discuss settlement.

McMaster knows that a person who deals drugs has the requisite mind-set to pluck a quid from helping an old lady cross the street. On hearing the words 'passion fruit', he suspected that Angelo was sizing him up. McMaster has used the deflection many times: 'How you going Shorty. Get those half a dozen bottles I sent you? By the way, got that name for me?'

Angelo cuts short the visit to his mother. 'Mama. I'll go and see Phil. We have to know if he's serious about this. After that, I'll go home, look over the documents, and come back later.'

Slouched in McMaster's conservatory, Angelo sips beer and drags on a thick joint. 'So what's the go with my oldies' farm?'

The abrupt question doesn't flummox McMaster. 'Mutual benefit,' he replies. 'You should know your mum will find it hard to cope. I'm looking to maximise my land potential by planting out crops. With an extra 25 acres, I'm sitting pretty. I'm not desperate though, so it's a take it or leave it offer. There's no pressure on your mother.'

'You're trying it on.' Angelo can't visualise McMaster

abandoning suits and handcuffs for baggy coveralls and pitchforks. Nor can he see the white-collar worker adapting to life on the land, especially in an era where farmers themselves stress over underproduction and falling financial returns. 'So what are you going to grow?'

'Not quite sure. Depends on soil evaluation and how much actual acreage will be available. That's where your parents' land comes in.'

'Okay. No big deal to me. I'm just the messenger; helping with the documents.'

'Fine. Probably the least you can do for her.' McMaster extends a handshake, knowing full well that Angelo's level of written comprehension would rise no higher than Muscle and Fitness magazine.

With Angelo Caruso dispatched, McMaster sets about formalising the deal. He advises Jeff Main of the proposed transaction and details preliminary instructions, stressing that no legal obstruction should compromise the conveyance. Main accepts the file with accompanying fear of McMaster's penchant for getting what he wants, be it by treading on toes, sacrificing relationships, or discarding ethics.

Back home, Angelo studies the contracts. Looks for a means to fill his wallet. He knows that any scam must allow the documents to pass through both the vendor's and purchaser's solicitors. Angelo's résumé of schoolyard extortions and immature pranks wouldn't succeed in an illicit gaming hall, let alone cut the mustard against the legal fraternity. His ambitions exceed his ability and his status as a small-time, bit player in drug and protection racquets. Those ambitions do, however, include the successful entrepreneur's prime attribute: confidence. Prosperous self-made men and women of the world uphold one ideal: Anything is Possible. Angelo poaches the Nike Corporation tag line: Just do it.

He switches on his computer, slides the original offer into the scanner, and with a Character Recognition program, copies the document into his computer. The Contract of Sale fills the screen – a replica of the offer proposed by Phillip McMaster. Gloria McMaster's signature joins her husband's, in name only, for Gloria is to Phillip as Gibraltar is to the United Kingdom – joined in sovereignty but separated by distance, culture and emotional attachment. Angelo drops the cursor onto the sale price, changes it from £360,000 to £270,000 – at the same time adjusting the ten percent deposit and balance figures – prints out three copies and slips them into a folder ready to receive his mother's signature. He then photocopies the original document and inserts both the original and its three copies into a separate folder.

He returns to Blackshaw's Mill with a tray of pastries. His mother welcomes the snack, preferring to talk about cakes and Cannolis rather than property matters. When Angelo insists on working through the documents Maria pushes them aside.

Just as I expected, he smiles, before opening the folders and displaying the contracts. The top copy notes the agreed price of £360,000, but the lower copies reflect £270,000.

Never a procrastinator, Maria pushes Angelo's finger-pointing aside. 'I'm a just sign here and here, and you're witness there and there.'

Angelo blushes at his mother's trusting naïvety. The execution is simpler than signing a credit card transaction at a supermarket. Maria flicks over each of the five pages to scrawl her signature alongside fluorescent green Post-it notes. Angelo divides the contracts into two folders and smiles to his mother: 'I'll return your copy later, after the solicitors have filed and stamped.'

Maria has no reason to suspect ill doing. What loving parent would ever dream that their devoted child would attempt to scam the proceeds of their life's work? She's attuned herself to moving, and is now preoccupied with financial projections and trust funds. Her mind spirals back to the day, fourteen years ago, when she and Giuseppe purchased the run-down property for only £66,000. Tears sting her eyes.

Mercilessly, Angelo excuses himself with the pre-arranged obligation of having to cover a shift at work. In his eagerness, he leaves a folder of signed contracts on his mother's kitchen table.

VII

Phillip McMaster pulls the contracts from the envelope.

The discrepancy stands out like a Rolls Royce on a council estate. He drops the wad of papers on his table, scurries to his study and retrieves a copy delivered by Maria Caruso. The head page discloses the sale price as £270,000. There's been no further negotiation, and there's been no correspondence notifying a lien or escape clause to reduce the sale price. He snatches the phone and calls Jeff Main: 'This contract's not as agreed. What's going on?'

'What are you talking about? All's above board; signed and witnessed by both parties. Two hundred and seventy grand, our fee calculated and displayed as an "on attendance" basis.'

'Two-seventy bullshit. I've got the original here – a legal document – that shows I offered £360,000 for Blackshaw's Mill. Are you trying to pull another one over me?'

'Just a moment.'

McMaster smoulders as the phone clicks through the switchboard.

'Phil. Hello. Steve Weston. Jeff tells me you have a problem.'

'Fucking problem all right,' McMaster counters before declaring the contract's conflicting details.

Heated discussion ensues until McMaster, having repeated the contract's irregular detail, bangs down the phone, furious that both Weston and Main refuse to accept responsibility for the contract's execution. He scoops up the documents and charges to the offices of Craggill, Weston and Rubenstein. After ditching his car in a No Standing zone (confident he'll smooth over any parking infringement with the council) he wheezes up two flights of musty concrete stairs to the solicitors' office, bypasses the receptionist, and barges straight into Weston's suite.

'What the hell's going on here?' roars McMaster, flinging the file onto Weston's desk. 'Someone's doing the dirty, right, and it ain't bloody me.'

Weston buzzes his secretary: 'Grab us a couple of coffees will you, Jade.' He turns to McMaster. 'Now listen, Phil. If we've got a problem, we'll sort it. Take a breather, then show me what you've got.'

McMaster points to the folder. Reaches for his cigarettes.

'Sorry Phil. O.H.&S. Can't let you smoke. You should give those things away.'

'That's fine for you to say when I'm frazzled by problems caused by your office.'

Weston ignores the comment and scans the head page. Draws his brow into an inverted 'V'. 'Something's grossly wrong.'

'That's what I've been telling you, and that halfwit, Main!'

And then the unconscionable thought strikes: *The old granny's ripped me. No one rips Phil McMaster.*

* * *

'No, Mr Mac. All I do is sign for you. Why I change something? You fair man and offer good price.'

'Mrs Caruso. I've just returned from my solicitor's office. Here's the original contract – see, £360,000.'

'I already sign that. I tell my Angelo you want to buy and

he read and say, "Good mama, go ahead" and he gives me the papers and I'm signing. I'm having the copy right here.' Maria hobbles to a kitchen drawer and removes a manila folder. Lays it in front of her guest. Opens it. 'Whatsa happen. I thought I'm having the papers. Maybe Angelo's take for something. Why you ask about this?'

McMaster removes a folded copy from his pocket. 'Because this is what I've got.' He points to the £270,000 and Maria's signature.'

'Yes. I'm sign that.'

'But look, two different figures.'

'Angelo's tell me the fees and the commissions and the taxes. I don't know more about the figures. Angelo's help with the paperworks; he's reading and taking to solicitors and I'm bring the papers to your home for my Angelo. He's such a good boy.'

'All right. Let me speak to Angelo. I can't wait to hear what he says.'

'He's no here. I give the number. And I give also the address. Angelo's fix for you. He's know the paperworks.'

McMaster leaves his neighbour's home wondering how such a straight-forward transaction has morphed into a giant crisis. The setback accompanies him to his office. Contracts flutter into and out of his head and pens march across his desk before assembling in perfect rows of a ceremonial army parade. Maria Caruso is the drill sergeant, a pleasant, upstanding grandmother who's never uttered a harsh word in his presence. She has no motive or malicious morals to take advantage of anyone. Likewise Weston. He showed a distinct lack of knowledge about the bungle. Could be a good act, but believable, nonetheless.

That leaves Jeff Main. He's tried it on before. Would he

dare repeat an act he'd already failed? Does time heal all wounds and leave an unblemished complexion? Not for many. But how could he think he'd get away with it? And then there is Angelo Caruso. He did say he was handling it all – for his mother. Could he have handled it for himself?

McMaster springs to a computer and runs a criminal check on Angelo Caruso. The screen throws up six years of petty-crime. *Perhaps he's come of age. Time to enter the big time. But not at my expense.* He doesn't raise an official enquiry, but confirms Angelo's address and scribbles names of his known associates into his notebook.

* * *

The Criminal History screen jolts McMaster's memory of unfinished business. He clicks in the name Hernandez. Rose. A red bar flashes across the screen: Rose has served six months of two years' probation. He creases a wry grin at the accompanying report: Convicted of theft.

That'll do fine.

Set to action both the Caruso and Hernandez files, McMaster scrawls his absence on the duty board. En route to Caruso's home he stops by Heavenly Spirits. Rose stands beside a counter, wearing the smile of a person who loves her work.

The smile shrinks as McMaster approaches. 'Coffee? I have something to discuss.'

'Sorry. I'm on my own. There's no one to cover me.'

'Excellent. No trouble. I'll grab the coffee.' He turns and leaves the store.

Rose stands with mouth agape. She can't stop him. Nervous tension prompts the thought: *Why would a police officer want to conduct a meeting in a shop over coffee?* A previous experience taught Rose that police are hospitable only when they want something.

McMaster returns and sets two coffees and a cardboard tray of croissants on the counter. 'Relax, Rose. I'm not here for work. I was passing by and thought I'd call in to make sure you're all right. I think I might have upset you yesterday – I want to put that right. How about a guided tour?'

Rose scrunches her face in sync with the question: 'Guided tour? It's a small shop. What do you mean?'

'Just an ice-breaker. Don't want you feeling nervous.'

She stalls. Looks to her feet. She returns an informal, but thoughtless, response: 'I'll give you anything if you'll keep me out of trouble.'

McMaster grins, not knowing whether to take her words as an over-exuberant reaction or a veiled invitation. He slurps the froth off his cappuccino. 'So, you have a secret locked away? You're afraid I'll out you, and that'll be the end of your career?'

'Something like that.' A tear rolls from her eye. Head drops. 'You know, don't you? You checked on me.'

'Yes. Part of the procedure, right? I'm sure we can come to an *agreement*.'

McMaster has built a career on agreements, siphoning information from informers, covering his fellow officers' indiscretions for reciprocated favours, and overlooking the criminal element's offending in exchange for a percentage of their loot.

'An agreement?' Rose is no stranger to the male's interpretation of 'agreement' in such a context. Remember, she works in an environment where alcohol-fuelled men unmask more bravado than in any other place – save for the bastion of maledom: bucks nights. She foresees her interrogator's motive. Fear wraps around her like a straitjacket compressing apprehension into her core.

McMaster relishes her distress. 'I think I could lose your details in exchange for a little cooperation, right? I've a project we can work on together, but for the moment I'm in need of a couple of bottles of Dewar's. I'm sure you could, er, consider a goodwill donation?'

Rose is amenable to anything that might absolve her from further trouble, but she knows there *is* a limit. 'I can't do that. You know I've already been done for theft; why would I do it again?'

'It's all right, Rose. You don't have to. I'm only suggesting a means to an end. Thought I might save myself a spot of paperwork, right? Gee, I meant to review the sentencing protocols for breach of probation.'

Rose spits out a threat: 'You can't do that. I could report you.'

McMaster warps his cheeks into an evil grin. 'Of course you could. You reckon you'd be up for a job in the prison canteen?'

'All right. All right. I'll get two bottles, and then we're done. Okay?'

'Sure. You have my word.' He lights a cigarette, directly in front of a 'No Smoking' sign, while Rose creeps to the spirits shelves. 'So what say I meet you at Cheltenham McDonald's? Let's make it Friday after work, eh? Six-thirty?'

With refusal spinning her head, Rose nods, unable to refuse. She does not know that many before her had relied on McMaster's assuring words, only to later find that the guarantee had dissolved like a mouthful of fairy floss.

A wisp of grey smoke follows McMaster from the store, knotting another victim to his team of innocent conspirators.

* * *

The glass-fronted apartments are trademark office block conversion, courtesy of the Thatcher Conservative Party's privatisation sell-offs of the 1980s. At first glance, the frontage is at odds with the heavily tattooed Angelo Caruso. McMaster revises his opinion as he appraises the Harley Davidson Softail tucked under a blue plastic tarpaulin. Sundry oil containers, chain lube, and a well-worn tyre litter the porch. He raps on the door. Creaking floorboards signify occupation.

'Hello Angelo. Nice to see you.'

Hesitation. 'Why? Is this official?'

'Not yet. But it could be. We're going to talk about a contract your mother signed.'

Angelo flushes the guilty face a child exhibits after being sprung sneaking biscuits from the pantry.

McMaster dismisses the stunned response and steps inside, forcing Angelo back into the hallway. McMaster has made a career of conducting business in hallways, corridors, on doorsteps, in pubs, on railway station platforms, in shadows of cobblestoned alleyways, and the lowest of all – a toilet cubicle. His claim that all of those dealings were official carries no substance.

Angelo closes the door: 'Yeah. Mum's happy to sell and very happy for you.'

McMaster fixes a glare. 'Yes, but my offer was 360 not 270. What do you know about that?'

Angelo's vacant gaze betrays him. He is trapped, so adopts the best defence: spit out the truth and talk his way out of trouble. 'I don't know how to put this. It might make me sound like a bastard, but I was snipping a bit from mum. She was happy to let me do the running around and negotiations, so that meant she wouldn't go scrutinising all the copies. And I was right. You've ended up with one of the dud contracts which you're not supposed to have. In fact you're not supposed to have any of them. I was going to sort them and drop the 360 copy at your place and post the others to mum's solicitor. She was only trying to help, but mum interfered by taking the documents from a folder I stupidly left at her place.'

McMaster stretches a gleeful smile. 'You reckon you were going to take her for "a bit"? We're talking ninety large. A few grand and maybe no one's the wiser. But fuck me – ninety grand? So where's the proper contract? You can't dupe anyone other than your mother by proceeding with the two hundred and seventy grand contract. How could you even think you'd get away with it? The way I see it, right, is that only I can guarantee your little scam remains between you and me. That'll cost you a little 'incentive'. It's what we call a win/win situation. The difference here is that I win big-time, or, I trot 'round to your mother's, drop the two contracts on her table and sympathise with her reaction on learning that her own son's shafting her.'

Angelo stands his full height. Sucks in his stomach. 'She won't believe you. Mama trusts you. She thinks you're a great neighbour the way you've helped her with the farm.'

'And she's right. I *am* a great neighbour – great enough to protect her from the likes of you.'

The roundhouse swing catches McMaster off guard. He falls against the wall, dazed and embarrassed about being jumped by the amateur embezzler. Angelo follows with a barrage of punches to McMaster's stomach, winding him and sending him to the floor.

McMaster wheezes: 'Twenty years ago you'd be down here. For the moment I'll forgive you. Let's just say that by the time I recover, and I won't need long, you'll have come to your senses and realise that you need me. Putting your mother aside for a moment, there's legal process that penalises financial deception. I'll mind the Harley for three years while you're in the big house.' He pulls himself from the floor, brushes past Angelo and exits the front door. Crumples into his car, clutches his ribs and rubs his kidneys. Lights a smoke. He will not be made a fool of. McMaster knows only two ways of dealing with Caruso's kind. Dominate them. Or recruit them.

* * *

Angelo kicks the door shut, wondering how he will explain the predicament to his mother. *What she don't know won't hurt her.* He plans to show McMaster that he won't be bullied by anyone, and that he, and only he, will oversee his mother's interests. He straightens a hall runner, realigns a group of family photo frames, and rights a hallstand knocked askew during the fracas. Angelo regrets voicing his devious plan, so plans to sew the conflict into an effortless settlement.

Thirty minutes later, he charges to McMaster's home, weaving and dodging, and ignoring the British motorists' honourable code of respect. His arrogance extends to tail-gating a slower driver and intimidating the young woman until she pulls to the kerb. He swings out of the congestion, floors the accelerator, and for a full five miles, relishes the rural landscape he has forsaken for his council flat in Worcester.

Dust flies from the loose-topped drive as his black Audi skids to a halt in Ashton Hill's corralled car park. Alerted by the crackling stones, McMaster bursts from the door, a Winchester XPR rifle snuggled under his arm. He recognises the visitor.

Rushes to the car. Easier to negotiate with the driver caged in his vehicle. He secures the rifle between arm and chest. Places his hands on the door frame and pokes his head through the window: 'Hello there. Sorry, I was cleaning this. Don't mean to appear threatening. What can I do for you?'

'Let's start again Phil. I think we can reach a deal.'

Angelo motions to exit the car. McMaster leans against the door and hoists his brow in surprise at the man attempting to steal his thunder. It is *he* who put deals to others – not vice versa. But the proposal arouses interest. 'What sort of deal?'

'Fifty-fifty. That's forty-five Gs to you for nothing, or, put another way, for copping a bit of roughage earlier on.'

'I cop roughage from the likes of you every day of the week. Why the fuck would I want to deal with you when I've got a perfectly legal contract sitting on my solicitor's desk? Your mother signed the contract, she delivered it, and I've verified its authenticity as a legal document. Too bad. Why would I accept half when I got a ninety gee discount on my offer? Thanks for nothing. Now piss off.'

Angelo's face reddens. No one makes him look like a dill. He raises his fists – an absurd action while facing a man clutching a rifle. 'You can't do that. I'll see our family lawyers and explain what you're doing.'

'No. I don't think you'll do any such thing. You'd have to incriminate yourself. Fraudulently altering legal documents for financial gain, conspiring to defraud, and not to mention having to defend my claims of assault, injuries which will be treated and photographed. Yep, reckon you could earn a stretch of at least seven years. Now, please respect my stones on your way out.'

* * *

From his wallet's coin pouch, McMaster removes a tiny gold pebble. At £990 per ounce on the official market he could pocket nearly £4,000 for his first sale. Here, inside the fashionable retail pawn shop that changes its trading name every year, he'll receive less than half. And that is after serious bartering.

Behind the counter is long-time acquaintance, 'Onions', the adopted street name of Daniel Owens. He does not know that the tag insults the memory of George Oliver Onions, British author and short story writer of 1873 – 1961.

After rejecting the common 'Danno' tag – popularised by Steve McGarrett's sidekick in Hawaii Five-O – Daniel inherited the unusual moniker from a drunken associate who slurred his surname as Onions. The name stuck. And rightfully so, because Daniel is a human simile of a mature onion: his large elliptical body balloons at its circumference, his mind precipitates tears in those who cut into his territory, and his cauliflower ears float beside sprigs of hair that appear as straggly, withered stems of a dried onion. Today, he is physically incapable of scampering from trouble. But his mind isn't.

Fifteen years earlier, Onions had fallen foul of the then Sergeant McMaster, when, as a sprightly, street-wise entrepreneur, he'd commanded most of the drug and stolen goods deals in Birmingham. Onions would arrange for his competitor's hauls of contraband – from highly saleable stolen goods through to methamphetamines discreetly wound into tampons – to be retrieved in a process Onions likened to 'criminal recycling'. Contrary to public perception, there is no honour amongst thieves.

McMaster respects that trait as a valuable asset in his stable of dealers and informers, for he frequently unloads wares unsuitable for regular retail channels.

'So what do you reckon?' probes McMaster as he removes the pebble from a knob of tissue paper.

Onions holds the piece between thumb and forefinger: 'Haven't seen anything like this for a while. Certainly not some granny's melted-down heirloom. Low grade though—'

'Low grade, bullshit. We go back a long way. You know I only cop good stuff – no matter what.'

Onions scratches his head. 'Man's got to make a quid, don't he? I can't easily shift a piece of rock. Jewellery? Not a problem. Counterfeit tenners? Done. But raw minerals? I got to wholesale it myself through the guild. Don't think I got any contacts.'

'Well get one. I know how you got tabs on everything illegal. You got more of a pulse on the street than in your arteries. See this little piece of "low grade" rock as you call it; there's plenty more. Unlimited. Reckon I can deliver kilos of the stuff, right? So you create a market and I'll supply the demand. Now, what are you going to give me for it?'

Onions stands his ground: 'Here's the deal. If I can move it, I'll give you a good price. Leave it with me for the day and I'll get back to you.'

McMaster accedes. Throws in the last word. 'Don't try shafting me on this, Onions, because I know it's just shy of four ounces. It is high-grade purity and even your questionable appraisals should reward me with forty to fifty percent. On that basis, you'd better arrange some cash.'

Onions waits five minutes and jumps to the phone. 'Albert please.'

'Lowenstein.'

'Alby. Onions. Need a price on some gold. I can tell you I know the client – straight as a die – and he tells me there's an unlimited supply. Piece of action for both of us.'

'How hot is it?'

Onions stalls. Surprised. He's known Lowenstein for many years and has referred a lot of business to him during a mutually beneficial relationship. But he's not comfortable being queried about the source of his product.

'All I can say is that it's reliable. I'll put my stamp on the stuff and guarantee the supplier. Oh, all right. Between you and me – and this didn't come from me or I'm done for – the guy's on the local Bill. Got his fingers in everything. Goes by the name of Mac. That's all I know, but I assure you he's reliable.'

'Good enough for me. I'll get back to you.'

Onions hesitates. 'Tell you what. I'll speak to my seller and call you back. You in all day?'

'What do you think? Can't make money sitting on my arse.'

VIII

Jeff Main stands in the office toilet block gelling his satin-black hair into ocean waves. At six-foot-two, his square shoulders and hips fill the mirror. His round head, and left hand set in a claw – the result of a failed Carpal Tunnel operation – has earned him the name: Lego Man.

He is of capricious character, one minute exhibiting the strength and determination of a Scottish Highland caber tosser; the next, assuming the soft, gentle disposition of a needleworker threading yarn through tapestry. He frequents nightclubs as a hip, trendy player, often seen with the most glamorous women, and sometimes with quaint-looking young guys. Jeff is defensive about the latter, claiming he helps them with legal advice about entering the modelling profession. Full points for initiative.

The mirror tells more. He struggles to suppress tears brought on by McMaster's admonishment; his misty green eyes reveal scarred personal pride after his client suggested that *he* had tried to manipulate the property contracts.

A thump on the bathroom door commands his return to the office. He splashes water over his face, swilling away spent emotion and embarrassment. As he saunters past reception – shielding his reddened eyes – the receptionist nods her over-made-up head towards a gentleman sitting in the waiting area.

Main gulps, glares at the receptionist with a look of *why didn't you warn me?* and strides with new-found confidence to the waiting client. 'Afternoon Phil. What a surprise. Come on through.'

McMaster extends his hand. 'Excellent. Sorry to land unannounced.'

Main shudders at McMaster's stance: powerful (above the calorie-thickened waist) intimidating, conceited. 'This way. We'll use the conference room.'

All prestigious legal offices have conference rooms – an eloquent description of its poorer synonym, the meeting room. The table spans six metres, its top planed from a one hundred-year-old slab of Californian Redwood, lacquered and polished to a bottomless lustre. Fourteen chairs surround this focal point. Winter's sun streams through a wall of windows, spearing framed certificates and mirrors on the opposite wall.

Main motions his client to the table's side. McMaster ignores him, side-steps to the head of the table, rolls out a plush leather high back and plonks himself into the body-hugging chair.

Round one to McMaster.

'Thanks for seeing me,' he says, smooth as strands of silk spilling through a weaving loom. 'You know I'm concerned about this contract, right? I've spoken with a person, no names mentioned, who admits manipulating the contract under the charade of "wanting to skim a few quid".'

'And you're talking ninety grand?'

'Yep. However, by my reckoning, that makes me the beneficiary of his intended scam. The property owner has legally executed the sale contract by signature, and, as you know, there's no cooling off period for a seller.'

Main warps into surprise. 'Legally executed? Aren't I the one to determine what's legal and what's not, Phil?'

'Cut the formalities, Jeff. One thing we should get straight right now is that *I'm* the client and the client's always right, right? Remember that from college, Jeff?'

'You're missing something. That might work in some tin-pot haberdashery where the customer is *said to be* always right, but here, if the client is always right, well, there's no need for me. May as well call it a day.' Main shrinks into his seat and contemplates whether to hold ground or scamper off to Steve Weston to suggest that *he* take over the file. Then he sees the downside: Weston would be furious to learn that a contractual error had escaped scrutiny.

McMaster leans across the table, slides Main a copy of the fabricated contract and steadies his glare: 'Now, you tell me who's right. You're representing me. This is a contract that falls £90,000 short of my instructions.' He plucks the original instrument from a folder. 'Let me tell you what's happened. I made an offer, as you know, to purchase Blackshaw's Mill for £360,000, right? A person known to the vendor intercepts the contract and thinks he can make a quick quid for himself. He keys in a fancy computer-generated duplication of the contract by changing the agreed selling price to £270,000. This person, for argument's sake we'll call him Angelo, has the vendor sign the dud document *and* duplicates of the original offer before collating them into sets for each party. You get the picture, right? We now have two sets of 'legal' contracts; one selling the vendor's property at three-sixty and the other at two-seventy.

'Consider you're getting this first-hand. His close association with the vendor means he had no difficulty convincing her that she is entitled to only £270,000 of the proceeds. Now, you might question how that could happen, right, but I have it on good authority that this Angelo is very influential.

He apparently convinced the vendor that deductions for commission, surveyor's fees, solicitor's fees, land tax and capital gains tax would account for the ninety gees. The vendor has my sympathy.

'So, this Angelo character plans that on settlement, he'll pull £90,000 from the proceeds and hand the vendor a banker's draft for two-seventy. The vendor's none the wiser, right? But how's this? The vendor, believing she is helping the process, has inadvertently delivered the false copies to me!

'To summarise, what's supposed to happen is that I pay the three-sixty and Angelo laughs all the way from the bank after duding the vendor. Bloody brilliant, if you ask me.'

McMaster continues: 'Now, the way I see it, since you've sanctioned this transaction, right, I'm standing my ground as contractually bound to two-seventy. I'll leave it to you to arrange how to fund the balance to the vendor.'

Main's mouth forms a huge 'O'. His left eye twitches like a motor-drive camera snapping off shots of a lingerie model. He shifts in his seat, turns and looks out of the window. A tattered career returns the glare.

'So, what do you want me to do, Phil? I could do my job and my Practicing Certificate over this.'

'That's not my concern, Jeff. There's a thirty-day settlement. That should give you ample time. But there's another catch. The vendor's just lost her husband, right? I don't want you dropping this shit on her. Finding out that someone's tried to swindle ninety gee from the deal would just about see her into her own grave. What say we get our heads together and strengthen our solicitor/client relationship with a pint over lunch? Keep your billing open. Remember, there's no such thing as a free lunch.'

Too right, Main hisses as he escorts McMaster from the room. He flashes reception a smile: 'We're out to grab a bite.'

McMaster rues the day government banned smoking in pubs and clubs. 'A man can't enjoy his pint anymore,' he complains to Main as they hijack a beer-sodden table in one of the lower-class venues cramped into the High Street. 'Now listen, Jeff. There might be a way of sweeping this whole situation under the table. I can keep quiet and reward you handsomely for your assistance. What I'm talking about is far more important to me than ninety grand. And, I'm sure you're more interested in keeping your certificate and progressing to the pinnacle of legal challenges.'

Main sips his lemon squash, tries to compose himself, but falters into prolonged babble: 'I don't know what's going on here. I received the contracts, couriered from the vendor's solicitor, with the instructions: "Both parties are agreed; simple conveyance," and so proceeded to complete what I expected to be a routine document execution. You now claim the document has been amended. How was I supposed to know? You say I'm wholly responsible, yet you offer to fix the mess?'

'Got it in one, Jeff. Yes. But I have to know you're with me on this. Peace of mind, you know.' Phillip pulls a tenner from his wallet and slides it under Main's glass. 'My shout. By the way, I'm not here in official capacity, so whatever we discuss stays here, right?'

'Goes without saying.'

Main returns with another pint of lemon squash, a pint of Guinness and two bags of cashews. A waitress follows with a crab-pot shaped Fisherman's Basket chock-full of crumbed Haddock, scallops, prawns, crab sticks and steaming chips.

'Go ahead,' Phillip gestures to his newly-indentured

partner. 'As I was saying, now that we're in this together, Jeff, if the document *is* legal we will proceed with the sale. There could be interference by this whacko, Angelo. Not to worry though – the guy's an idiot. With me so far?'

'I guess so, but he won't be happy losing ninety grand.'

'Got it in one! I've already dealt with him – in a fashion. As it stands, he hasn't got a clue what's going on. He'll be on edge because I left him an open-ended threat. He'll be swivelling his neck like one of those sideshow clowns that gulp table tennis balls, expecting me to crop up out of nowhere. But he's a pussy. He'll be more concerned about the vendor finding out what sort of a person he really is.'

Main picks his way through the basket, singling out the prawns and scallops, leaving McMaster to grind an over-battered piece of fish and a few crinkled chips.

'I'd better be getting back, Phil. Steve'll be wondering what's going on.'

'Not a problem.' McMaster whisks his mobile from his pocket and jabs a speed dial number. 'Steve. Hi there. Phil McMaster. Sorry about hijacking young Jeff. I've got another deal coming up. Wanted to discuss it with you, but since you'd delegated the current file to Jeff, I thought it more appropriate to brief him. We're over the road, be back in fifteen.' He flashes Main an agreeing smile and slides the phone back into his pocket. 'Now where was I? Yes, the subject property could have a fortune lying beneath it. There's evidence of untapped natural resources on my land with the prospect of it extending into the adjacent property. Where you come in is to brief me on mining rights and relevant applications. I want to keep this legal.'

Main returns a curious frown. 'How'd we get from a dubious contract to mining applications?'

'More on that later. First up, we've got to seal that contract. There's a lot more at stake than an argument over ninety grand.'

They part with the wariness of a developing romance: rejoicing in the euphoric high of their union and forming dreams of the future, while simultaneously insulating themselves from the emotional distress of incompatibility.

Main returns to his office. Only four years out of university, he's had the fortune to begin in a mid-level practice; the misfortune of inheriting a file of dubious merit; and now, the shock of being drafted into his client's confidence to undertake research totally unrelated to his area of expertise. Fear of deceiving his employer perches in the forefront of his mind like the cuckoo waiting to pounce on the hour's strike. On the positive side, he warms to a heightened level of excitement and enthusiasm.

He retreats to the practice's library.

* * *

Rose Hernandez sits at a fibreglass table watching children whiz, slide and swing in Hamburglar's activity area. She has no children of her own and no inclination to change that. Thoughts of sleepless nights, nappy changing, expanded hips and sagging breasts convinced her that other people's kids satisfy both her maternal instincts and personal vanity.

She hasn't dated for ten months, after an ill-fated blind date turned to disaster. Shuddering at the thought of meeting the twenty years' older McMaster, she clamps her blouse's top press studs and zips her jacket to the collar.

McMaster bounds into the restaurant like a child attending his first Ronald McDonald birthday bash. He scans the dining area and fixes upon Rose's blonde hair shining like the miraculous star guiding the Three Wise Men to Bethlehem.

'Hello,' McMaster gleams as he glides into the bench seat. Drops his eyes to her jacket.

Rose folds her arms across her chest. 'I've got what you asked for.' She kicks a canvas bag toward McMaster's feet.

His gawk lingers on Rose's chest. 'Perhaps you've got something I haven't yet asked for?'

She blushes. 'Are we going to eat?'

McMaster peers inside the bag. 'You've excelled yourself. I hope you didn't find it too difficult.'

'I've only done this to help myself.'

'Don't be so harsh. You've got everything to gain.'

Rose draws on her tiny reserve of courage. 'I'm sorry I was speeding. I've done all you asked. Can't you leave me alone now? I promise I'll never speed again.'

McMaster smirks. By his charter, everyone has a purpose in life. McMaster proclaims that *his* purpose is to help those tangled in trouble. He *has* helped Rose evade a breach of probation penalty, so justifies that with the rationale that he is entitled to a little recompense.

Although Rose had braved theft charges through to court proceedings, she has no real grasp of police protocol. She is not convinced McMaster will overlook the minor offence and cannot risk the prospect of a prison term, or the humility of working under a Community Order. Either way, having already squirmed to McMaster's requests, she would lose her job together with further career opportunities.

McMaster continues: 'I don't care if you speed. It's none of my business, right? I'm more interested in seeing our little arrangement continue. I'm not here to take advantage of you or make your life a misery. Quite the opposite in fact. I think I can help you more than you realise. But I won't discuss it now. I've got to be off.'

Relieved of further demands, Rose bolts to the counter. Eases her tension with a cup of tea. Her father's words ring in her head: Never trust a copper.

She sips McMaster's menacing threat: *I'd just like to see our little arrangement continue.*

IX

GILLIAN TROTTER'S FIRST SHIFT AT the Knight's Arms had introduced her to Phillip McMaster's smooth-talk: 'Hi sweetie. Dewar's Malt. Double, no ice.'

Gillian, keen to allay the accommodating persona of over-friendly bar staff, quickly wrong-footed McMaster: 'It's not sweetie, it's Gill with a hard 'G', as in 'gherkin' – because I'm a hard woman.' With a forceful glare, she pushed the tumbler across the bar. 'Drink's on the house.'

'Thanks Gill. My profuse apologies. But I can't accept your kind generosity.' He folded £20 into her hand: 'Buy yourself something nice. You don't look too hard to me.'

Gillian Trotter commenced a private investigator's course after dropping out of the Cambridge School of Visual and Performing Arts. She had no particular credentials for undercover work other than inheriting her mother's lifelong trait of sticking her nose into other people's business, and her own desire to assume the role of other characters as a vehicle for demonstrating her acting ability. Her goal had been to join the cast of a local soap, believing she could springboard to EastEnders or Coronation Street. After weeks of cold calling studios and agencies, Gillian realised that fluttered black eyelashes and exposed valleys of cleavage did not lead to stardom.

She celebrated her Diploma of Private Investigation on her twenty-first birthday. Devotees of the industry would belittle the achievement as a 'Mickey Mouse' diploma, claiming that no one could learn private investigation from college and online tutorials. Only after many miles of 'hard yards' could a candidate come close to adapting to the demanding and often dangerous industry.

Proving the old adage of being in the right place at the right time, Gillian's social media and networking skills rewarded her with an assignment just three days after qualifying. She accepted a position with a local agency contracted by the Education Department, to identify leaders of a drug ring infiltrating West Birmingham Comprehensive School. Gillian's innocence enhanced her suitability, and her youthful appearance afforded entry to select grunge groups. She carried a smooth, pre-pubescent unblemished complexion, contrasted by rabid unmanageable tawny-brown hair which fell in clumps over deep brown eyes. A hint of Pacific Islands' olive-skinned ancestry, which, combined with her heavy stature, posed the threat of a British Bulldog.

Her charter was to mingle with students, collate information and pass it to a fellow agent planted in the student services office. Three weeks was all it took. The first to identify sources; the second, to form relationships and flirtatious dependencies on traders; and the third to secure video and audio recordings of transactions where tiny packages and money exchanged hands either direct or from pickup points beneath trees, in the school canteen, and in one instance under the wheel arch of a teacher's car.

In the years following that assignment, Gillian infiltrated criminal operations. High profile successes included apprehending a family operation specialising in retail goods theft, through to cracking a cartel of British-Euro car thieves who 'remanufactured' vehicles with new serial and identification numbers. She had twice assisted MET Police to penetrate operations where the constabulary sought to not risk the identity of their own members.

Her contact is Superintendent Jack Thornton, a seasoned officer of forty years' experience and a thorn-in-the-side to both the criminal element and police members. He earned the obvious tag of 'Thorns' from school, where he was regarded as a pain-in-the-ass. After treading on toes along the police promotional route, the nickname gradually morphed to 'Prickle' and ultimately to 'Prick'. Minor etymological contraction; major perceptional difference.

Thornton derives no satisfaction from investigating fellow officers. He is prepared to overlook minor complaints; often founded on vexatious retribution over traffic fines or domestic dispute warnings; he's overlooked or quelled complaints from female officers of sexual innuendo or unwelcome advances; and he's put down theft of property from secure evidence rooms to ineffective chain of possession documentation. The brotherhood.

One subject he won't overlook is the repetitive blather of DI Phillip McMaster operating beyond the fair boundary of policing. He authorised Gillian's installation in the Knight's Arms after learning of McMaster's not so secret meetings with city lesser-lifes. His decision to inject Gillian into the seedy pub was made after McMaster's unaccounted for absence from the officers' favoured after shift rendezvous. McMaster is believed to avoid the regular venue because of his aversion to being captured by new CCTV coverage. A flow of resignations and prosecutions evidence the merit of bugs now grazing in police watering holes. McMaster had either inside information about their existence, or God-given blessings in the form of a timely change of venue.

As McMaster motioned Jeff Main to *his* table, Gillian compiled a bullet-point description of Main: Height, a smidgen under two metres; Weight, 80 kilograms; Hair, black; Eyes, green; distinguishing features; an unusually square head. She trained a miniature security camera in their direction and tracked the conversation – a routine conveyancing matter. She recalled her briefing: nothing about McMaster is 'routine'. *So why convene a legal meeting in a pub, and why would McMaster insist on Main paying the bill and 'fixing' Angelo.* The latter is open to conjecture, but when a police inspector is under investigation, a conversation embracing an expression to fix someone must be treated with vigilance. The penny dropped after McMaster named a person up to the task. Gillian seized the words like an invitation to a premiere fashion launch.

Who is Angelo? Fix him for what? The gravity of the assignment took on greater weight as the enigma swelled into a larger picture: *Should I report this straight away or would my over-reaction convey an impression that I'm incapable of the assignment?* She resolved to pluck further information before painting a detailed mural of McMaster's activities.

From another snatch of McMaster's conversation, part of which she *knew* could not be official, she heard of a drug crop he was trying to establish. Those snippets satisfied her that Thornton's assumptions were correct: McMaster is a crook.

Ordinarily, Gillian would maintain considerable distance between herself and nominated targets, for both safety and discretion. No matter how high her confidence, she could never fulfil the Bond-girl role with bedroom rendezvous guaranteed to extract sacred information. However, during her third shift behind the bar, she accepted McMaster's syrupy invitation to dinner: 'Purely professional, I need a woman's perspective on some matters.' Many times she'd been propositioned – an occupational hazard founded upon her being thrust into testosterone-driven criminal activity. She'd filed away ambitious suitors' feeble excuses for trying to get a bit extra on the side. Women worldwide retch over the same drivel: 'our marriage isn't working'; 'we don't get on'; 'the marriage has been dead for years'; and untold other forms of denouncing the happy marriage to which the eager guy would return after an evening's illicit entertainment.

Gillian feigned surprise at the invitation: 'I'd be glad to help. I have no ties, so I'm free anytime.' She paused. 'I won't go to a pub because landlords talk and they'll think of me as easy meat, and I can't have a late night because I'm on earlies this week.' She blushed away her enthusiasm; no girl should sound too eager to help a stranger, more so to date one.

First score to Gillian. She seized the advantage by gaining a seat in the dress circle where the play to elicit prized information would soon begin.

* * *

Gillian Trotter had learnt during her briefing that McMaster is married, and had so been for 'twelve unhappy years.' The word 'unhappy' sprang from the dossier in fluorescent orange, presumably to warn Gillian that her target might be 'emotionally pliable'.

She accompanied McMaster to an Indian Curry House where the stinging aroma of hot curry and spices competed with heat radiating from beneath the table. McMaster, in true form, had extended the invitation by false pretences: his request for the female perspective queried a woman's commitment to career when she would forego the job on the first pangs of maternal yearning. He shifted the discussion to their life stories; he gloating about his 'exceptional' arrest rate; she enthusing over the anticipated advent of a bit-part acting role, at which time McMaster proffered the sly innuendo: 'If you're looking for a leading man—'

He stopped mid-sentence, as if expecting Gillian to jump at the opportunity. Instead, she deflected the try-on and cast out the line: 'My type would be more adventurous. I'm sure you're swamped with routines that compromise your private life.'

McMaster grinned. 'Nothing could be further from the truth. My private life is an escape from the drudgery of arrests, paperwork and court appearances, even though after accomplishing good in the name of the community, we have to justify our actions to some jumped-up civil libertarian do-gooder. Bah. Don't tell me you wouldn't want to escape from that shit.'

He studied Gillian, his years of experience effecting a snap assessment. 'Speaking of escapes, want a smoke?' He flipped open a pack of Dunhill to reveal the familiar gold-ringed cigarettes. He pushed a few aside, and from a lower layer removed a roll-your-own.

'Don't smoke,' Gillian replied.

'You don't need to for these.' An out-of-control flame shot from his ebony lighter.

Gillian panicked from the first whiff. 'Not here. You'll be sprung.'

'Come on Gill. No one'll smell this over that curry shit,

right? And if they do,' he patted his wallet, 'I've got the ultimate immunity idol. But I see your point. What say we continue this wonderful evening at my place?'

'I'd really love to,' she lied, 'but as I said, I'm on early tomorrow. A girl's got to get her beauty sleep.' She batted her eyelashes, further arousing her suitor.

'I love the way you do that,' sleazed McMaster.

'I'll remember it for next time.' She yanked her jacket from the back of a chair. 'Thanks for a nice evening.'

The following morning Gillian updated Thornton, first chuckling over her reintroduction to the drug scene before moving on to the serious business of McMaster arranging to 'fix' a person. She assured the superintendent that it wouldn't take her long to uncover Angelo's identity and connection.

She concluded the briefing by detailing McMaster's antics in Heavenly Spirits, and agreed to email time-stamped photos of his receiving bottles of spirit together with his placing the items in evidence bags and into his car.

Thornton's follow-up revealed that the bottles had not been logged in Worcester CID's property book.

X

I'd met Lowenstein by chance just prior to my leaving Worcester CID. I was working under Detective Inspector Michael Marchant, who'd struck more deals with the criminal element than he had with the Crown Prosecution Service. I am not saying he was 'bent'; he just had a manner that dovetailed him into the criminal element. Crooks stick with crooks and some crooks forever strike deals with a faithful detective who has taken them into his confidence. That's how Albert Lowenstein became part of McMaster's stable of informers. He loved to double-deal; loved to pad one pocket with profits of unlawful transactions, and the other with McMaster's payoffs.

I'd seen backpacks of jewellery and negotiable bonds pass through Lowenstein's 'wholesale' operation. On the surface, he ran an esteemed retail business – 'Jewellers to the Jewish community'. Beneath, backroom deals boosted his wealth and deprived HM Revenue and Customs six-figure annual returns.

I am intrigued as to how Lowenstein found me. I take his call: 'Yes. I know Mac. Used to work with him at Worcester, although not in the same—'

He cuts me short. 'Got a news flash for you. What's it worth?'

That's another thing with crooks. Everything has a value. A name? Fifty quid. An introduction to a fencing circle? A share of the proceeds. I once saw a crook swap a Cornish pasty for one chocolate biscuit. Crooks and chocoholics share a remarkable addiction – they'll trade anything for their next hit. 'You wouldn't have anything of value to me. I'm not in the job now.'

'I know. That's why I'm calling. Word is, McMaster's under investigation and you're a big part of it.'

I'm constantly perplexed how word travels faster through the underworld grapevine than a village women's network cultivates gossip and innuendo over husbands' infidelities. 'I can't and won't do deals. I'll never be tarred with the brush that's blackened some of your previous associates.'

'I'm on the level, Liv. Always have been. All I'm interested in is doing my bit for the law.'

His 'good citizen' parody nearly makes me puke. *And* he called me "Liv". But I run with it. 'All right. Go.'

'Got a guy wanting a price on gold. Claims he has an unlimited supply. Mean anything to you?'

'Could. Why call me?'

'Because I'm thinking there's something sneaky going on behind the scenes. When you have a shifty trying to push merchandise for a third party, I've found from experience that things usually turn dirty. If I can nip it in the bud without implicating myself, I'll do it. All I want is a good word put in of how I helped the coppers.'

'I told you. I'm no longer a copper.'

'But you can see it gets to one.'

I try to figure his angle. 'So, you want to do the deal, but if it falls over, you'll use me as a safety net?' Such was Marchant's MO – I just want to hear it straight from Lowenstein's mouth.

'Miss. I already know you've severed all ties. You run a tight ship, if you get my drift. I can give you an opportunity to make up for lost income.'

Severed all ties, nothin'. I'll run with it. Could be worth credos from Thornton.

'Okay. I'm up for it. When's the deal?'

'Soon. I'll call you.'

I tell him I'm 'on the road', so offer my mobile and landline numbers, and an email address.

XI

Detective Sergeant Roy Street snatches the file from his desk. An 'Urgent Action' Post-it note curls on the blue cover sheet. He pulls a gold-nibbed fountain pen from his Harris Tweed jacket and scrawls 'Rec'd April 20th / 2pm' on both the cover sheet and Post-it note.

Most members of Worcester CID have never seen a fountain pen, let alone watched someone actually use one – especially a young copper of only twenty-five years of age. It is not a pretentious front; Street stands by his conviction that the fountain pen is an avatar of sincerity. It paints his character: refined, precise and ostentatious, sewn together with a thread of mystique. He rises above the average detective's 99p bulk pack of blue or black throw-aways in favour of strength and longevity of the historic, cigar-shaped instrument.

In the field, it is the most impractical implement of modern times. It smudges in the damp and wet, won't write when upside down, and deposits deep blue splodges inside his shirt pocket. Worse still, he has to blow-dry the ink before closing his notebook. On the positive side, he can leave it on his desk and no one, save an opportunist seeking a few pounds from a pawn shop, would think of stealing it. Street idolises the famed Sherlock Holmes – some colleagues claim he is just as fictional – the fountain pen symbolising Holmes' quill. He'd even sought a Baker Street rental property – in Worcester – as his dream address, but instead, settled on Barker Street. He is a career go-getter; striving for promotion at every opportunity, studying hard and passing exams, diligently applying himself to enquiries and investigations, and working endless hours to demonstrate his worth to force command.

He flicks through the file of phone transcripts, witness statements and a coroner's preliminary report which notes Giuseppe Caruso's passing was 'in circumstances not consistent with natural cessation of life'. *Gobbledegook*. He turns the page: extradural haematoma occasioned by a blunt instrument to the base of the skull. The coroner parenthesised a piece of timber, pipe or similar object as a possible weapon.

Scene of Crime Officers had photographed the Caruso's kitchen area as a possible crime scene. The absence of blood, Caruso's age, and the credibility of McMaster's observations and knowledge of the deceased, together with Maria Caruso's account of the situation, drove detectives to circumvent usual procedures and record the death as natural causes.

Heads rolled after the coroner's decision hit the desk of the Worcester CID superintendent. Crime officers swamped the Caruso property to re-examine the kitchen – then two weeks after the tragedy – and seized a rolling pin and a wooden cylinder used for storing spaghetti.

Armed with that information – albeit without forensic results – DS Street grabs the nearest idle detective and rushes to the Caruso property. Maria, when asked if she wants to call a solicitor, replies that she has no need.

The interview quickly strays from pleasantries to tormenting discomfiture. 'Mrs Caruso. You told police on April the fourteenth that you found your husband lying on the floor. What did you first do?'

'I'm call his name, he's no answer so I'm shake him, see if he's answer. He's say nothing so I'm run to Mr Mac's house for help.'

'You're referring to Phillip McMaster, the policeman?'

'Yes. I'm call him always Mr Mac. He no mind.'

'Good. Then tell me. Was your husband a healthy man?'

'Yes. He's go for the walks and he's not smoking the cigarettes. It's strange when I'm finding him because it's smell cigarette in the room. I don't understand, because Giuseppe, he's never smoke, and Angelo, he has the tobacco, but I'm not letting him smoke in the house.'

Street motions to his colleague to make a note to check the forensic report for evidence of cigarette butts or ash.

'And you've told us earlier that Angelo is your son. Is that correct?'

'Yes. I'm have other sons, but they're living now in Italy.'

'So what happened next?'

'Mr Mac drive to my house, he's saying it quicker than run, and he's check Giuseppe's wrist for the pulse, he's saying nothing there, then he's pushing the chest like lifesaver on the beach and he's saying "come on Joe, come on Joe," and he's look at me and saying call 999 but maybe he's saying that first. I'm in panic and not remembering when he's saying exact, but he's telling me ring 999 and I do that and then they're coming in the house ten minutes after.'

Street unravels his brow. He struggles to grasp Maria's convoluted English and is relieved to not be typing the narrative into a Record of Interview. He continues: 'What did Mr McMaster do then?'

'He's make the cup of tea and he's talk to the police and then he's going home.'

'Mrs Caruso. I need to ask you this: What were you doing before you found your husband?'

'I've been talking to Angelo. He's going home and I'm going to the bathroom because I'm having too much the cups of tea. When I'm in the bathroom I'm hear shouting, but not words. It was noise like the pain. I know one's Giuseppe but the other voice, I'm not understand. Then I'm coming back to the kitchen and my Giuseppe's on the floor. I'm saying Giuseppe, Giuseppe, and he's say nothing. Then I'm running to Mr Mac's—

'Yes. Right. Tell me about Angelo. How often does he visit?'

'He's coming only sometimes in the week. Not often. He's not having much, what you say, friends with his father.'

'You mean he doesn't get on with his father? They don't talk?'

Maria grimaces. She finds it difficult to find the right words for English conversations, but has no problem understanding that Street has boxed her into a corner. 'They're both having strong persons. Angelo's coming to the house only when his papa sleeps or goes the pub with friend.'

'But you've said Angelo left before you found your husband on the floor?'

'Yes. That's what happen because Angelo's already go through the door and then I'm going to the bathroom and Giuseppe's must be come from the bedroom and he's shouting "not welcome in the house" and when I'm coming back to the kitchen that's when Angelo's already gone and my Giuseppe's on the floor.'

Street's mouth creases into a warped smile. The sleeping name on his lips awakes and crystallises as a person of interest. He concludes the interview and circles Angelo Caruso's name.

* * *

DS Street circles the apartment block before rapping on his suspect's front door.

Angelo squeezes his head into the half-open entry: 'Yeah?'

Street introduces himself and WDC Plumpton. 'We have a few questions. May we come in?'

'Sure. What about?' Angelo's facade of innocence and readiness to assist the constabulary fools no one. He leads the pair to his reception room, where he pushes from a couch a few *Men's Health* and bodybuilding magazines, *Guns & Ammo*, and folded local papers.

Street remains standing. 'It's your late father. When did you last see him?'

'You're sick. At the fuckin' funeral of course.'

Street blushes. A grammatical slip throws him onto the back foot. 'I'm sorry. I thought you'd accept that I meant before your tragic loss.' DS Street knows full-well that a guilty person, or one with something to hide, will try to deflect questions from the focal issue – exactly as Caruso has just done.

Angelo continues: 'Don't know what makes you think it was a tragic loss. I rarely saw him. He pissed me off long ago. About a fortnight before he croaked it – I mean that's when I last saw him.'

Street doesn't chide the disrespectful term, but stows it as a relationship blueprint.

'And when did you last see your mother?'

'About a week ago.'

Street pauses, allowing Plumpton to take notes. 'You sure? You haven't visited more recently?'

'No. It's a fair trip. I took her shopping in Cheltenham, so the last time was April nine. Got a Tesco docket to prove it. I put mum's shopping on my credit card and she gives me cash.'

'So, you're sure of that? April nine?'

'Yep. Got no reason to lie.'

Street's experience has instilled in him that every suspect has a reason to lie about something. It falls to the smart interrogator to outwit the suspect into admitting the deception. He removes a folder from his leather attaché. 'I'm going to read a passage from an interview with your mother: "Mrs Caruso. I need to ask you this: What were you doing immediately before finding your husband?" Her answer: "I've been speaking to Angelo. He's going home and I'm going to the bathroom because I'm having too much the cups of tea. When I'm coming back to the kitchen my Giuseppe's on the floor. I'm saying Giuseppe, Giuseppe, and he's say nothing. Then I'm running to Mr Mac's—". '

Angelo throws his hand to his head, faking a flash recollection. 'Oh yeah, I was there then, but I didn't see my father.'

'That was April fourteen.' Street feigns confusion as he sets up Angelo for the big one: 'But I asked you specifically when you last saw your mother.'

Angelo throws a stern look: 'Just a minute. You came in here and said you wanted to speak about my father. You asked when I last saw him and I told you something like "I hardly see him, a fortnight maybe". Then you ask when I last see my mother. To me, that means when did I last see my mother in context with seeing my father. Don't try to twist the subject and make it look as if I've done something wrong. I know your form, but it won't wash with me. Yes, I did see my mother on the day my father died – but I didn't see him.'

Street carries on: 'So when you say you last saw your mother on April nine, you weren't being totally honest with us?'

'Yes,' Angelo smiles. 'I was perfectly honest. I did see her on that day.'

Street casts an exasperated look to Plumpton. Like most detectives on a path to nowhere, he changes tack – a ploy to unsettle the interviewee. 'Okay, Angelo. Have you seen your mother recently?'

'Yes. I'm helping her with some paperwork,' he replies. 'She's decided that the farm's too much for her and is selling.' Angelo slows. Thinks. 'Perhaps you're better off speaking to her about that.'

'We will. So tell us how you heard about your father's injury?' Street slips in the teaser, designed to elicit information privy only to one or two persons.

'Huh? I didn't know he *was injured.* Mama told me on the phone it was a heart attack. I was nearly home when she called my mobile.'

'And what time was that?'

'Easy.' Angelo pulls his phone from his pocket, flips through a menu. 'Three fourteen,' he says, and turns the screen to Street.

Street flashes a glance to Plumpton. Without reaction, she grasps her colleague's message: *There's more to this guy than he lets on.*

Street continues: 'Do you remember what time you left your parents' home?'

'I had no reason to look. We'd finished our discussion about the lack of family interest in the farm – it was a conclusion of sorts, it was time to leave. If it's any help, the trip to my place is around forty minutes.'

'Mm. That'd make it 2.35 p.m. That's all for now. Thanks for your help.'

Plumpton, remembering her colleague's prompt during the previous interview, injects: 'Sorry, one more thing Mr Caruso. What brand of cigarettes do you smoke?'

Angelo flushes. 'Rollies. Shit, you're not going to do me for a bit of weed, are you?'

'We didn't even know about that, did we sergeant?'

Angelo farewells the couple, locks the door, and wonders what the hell they are up to.

The chivalrous DS Street opens the car door for Plumpton. He slots into the driver's seat. 'Well, Lor, what did you make of that little sideshow?'

'Cocksure prat. All over the shop. And what about that "seeing my mother in context with seeing my father" crap? Reckon he's trying to weasel out of something.'

'Yep. Think we'll have a chat with the illustrious Inspector Mac. Could be an education.'

'He would have made a statement for the coroner, wouldn't he?'

'Yep. But the rules have changed since the coroner's report. You know they recently took stuff from the Caruso place for examination?'

'How could I? You've buried me in crap shoplifting files.'

Street starts the car. 'Call the office. Find out if Mac's on. If not, try him at home – his number's on the after-hours list.'

'He's in the office now. On lates,' bellows the radio.

Street yells into the mic: 'Ask him if he'll be there for a while. We need to chat.' And then to Laurel: 'Ever interviewed an inspector?'

'Only in the college – if that counts.'

'I'm not talking about role play shit. This is for real. We'll do this by the book. Can't have the guv in the shit if he missed something. Let's just hope his observations tally with the Caruso woman's version. We could also win a further glimpse into Angelo's movements.'

Little interaction has passed between Street and McMaster since Street's recent appointment to Worcester. Such is typical of small offices where 'sounding out' periods extend from one week to eternity. Responsibility falls to the new incumbent to ingratiate himself with the troops. Street though, cares nothing for acceptance or rejection.

Accompanied by his equally withdrawn partner, he approaches McMaster's office.

McMaster snaps to attention with a Tom Cruise smile, hand extended ready to welcome a prospective member to the Church of Scientology. 'Come in Roy. We don't see much of you. And DC Plumpton. Laurel, isn't it? What can I do for you? Take a seat, take a seat.'

Street is fresh, but he isn't naïve. He's entertained the door-to-door sellers' persona too often. False, and easy to penetrate. 'Thank you, inspector. I've copped the Caruso file. Don't know why. I think you should run it, with respect sir, because you were on the spot, first up.'

'Roy, call me "Phil", behind closed doors. Not a problem. I think they passed it down the line because the deceased was my neighbour. Thought it'd be too traumatic for me – or a conflict of interest. You'd reckon the hierarchy would know by now that we're dealing with death every day, right?'

Street lounges into a chair. Plumpton becomes a lady-in-waiting.

Street continues: 'They don't think like that. It's all numbers to them. Farm them out, wrap them up, and then table a report highlighting the great solution rate, and at the same time demanding extra funding to "keep up the momentum".'

McMaster forces another laugh. 'Got it in one Roy. So what are you doing? Showing young Laurel the ropes with an easy one?'

Street turns to the blushing Plumpton and lifts his brows as an advance apology. 'Yeah, she's been tied up with shoplifters. Thought I'd show her the real stuff. Just want your thoughts of the Caruso situation. You knew the old man, Giuseppe?'

'Knew him? We were just about related – we'd been neighbours for that long. Six years I think. Pretty much kept to himself. Slowed down in recent times, that's what age does, not that you two will experience that for a while. Good family man I gather. Couple of kids overseas, another couple married off, and another one who comes and goes. I will say his passing was a surprise. We'd haggled over a boundary discrepancy – which was resolved – and I'd made an offer on his farm. I'd ask you to keep this under your hat: I'm looking at early retirement and going into full-time farming. Could be crops, could be bleedin' Alpacas – I'm just whizzing things through my head. So, to cut a long story short, I'd seen Giuseppe on a few occasions of late and all seemed hunky-dory. Couldn't have picked that he'd croak it.'

'He was on the kitchen floor when you found him?'

'Yeah. Pummelled him with CPR, and got his wife, Maria, to call the ambos. They arrived within minutes, did their thing, and pronounced him dead.'

'You know they're now calling it suspicious?'

McMaster stretches another smile. 'Yeah. Can't see what for. The guy clearly died of a heart attack, right? Seen enough of 'em in my time.'

'Any thoughts of the wife offing him?'

'Not a chance. They're just a lovely old couple who'd probably planned to share the same grave. Have their arguments, like anyone else I suppose. Catch the right breeze and I cop it all. Usually about their delinquent son.'

Street pounces on the opportunity. 'Angelo? I've had the pleasure. Didn't remember whether he'd been there or not.'

'He knew he'd been there,' Plumpton pipes in, 'just wouldn't come clean with it.'

Street swings her a glare, but elects to not admonish his partner in front of McMaster. 'I take it you got through to him. Had Angelo been there on the day?'

'Too right,' says McMaster. 'Got a black Audi. Parks out the back in a spot visible from my place. He left, er, must have been only minutes before his mother came and got me, right? In fact, there was a yelling session around that time. I didn't have the breeze so I can't tell you who or what it involved.'

XII

Gillian must discover why Angelo is implicated in McMaster's property transaction. She obtains his vehicle registration number and will rely on Thornton to provide name and address details. She will have no problem drawing McMaster into her web. He's already made a move – on their second meeting – inviting her home for nightcaps. She'd declined, but only because she hadn't then mapped out her objectives. Later, she realised that it is irregular for a married man to invite a woman back to *his own* home.

Her opportunity arises when, in a dull corner of the Knight's Arms, McMaster and Main erupt. Gillian records the shouts, ears tuned to McMaster's words: 'We'll have to kill the prick. Either you arrange it or I will, the only difference being if I arrange it you'll be going too.' McMaster passes Main a slip of paper. 'Here's a number. Call after 8.00 p.m. You'll find the person *very* accommodating. I'll be expecting confirmation at 8.30. As a legal professional, I'm sure you'll see this in your best interest.'

Main crunches his brows. 'Who's 'The Jill'?'

McMaster leans forward. 'I'll tell you who she is. She's an enforcer who'll solve our little problem. Russian bird, though she doesn't sing too sweet. Jilonova or some tennis player name pulled from half the alphabet; took the initials of her given names – friggin' mouthful if you ask me – to make 'The', and then anglicised Jilonova. Da-da—The Jill emerged. Must have thought she was sharing fame with the mono-labelled Madonna or our old pet, Jordan, aka Katie Price. We could use the courts to resolve this, which would, as you know, take months or years; or we can use this business incentivator. Don't go looking for that in your legal dictionary; let's just say it's an informal word for "encourager".'

'I'm a bloody lawyer. These things take time. I'll work this Angelo in my own way. We'll get the contract sorted, but I won't get involved in bloody underworld shenanigans.'

'Listen Jeff. The only thing you're involved in is taking instructions from your client – me. Remember the objective? I want that parcel of land. For some reason, that Angelo weasel is stalling this. He's not going to shaft me out of my rightful purchase. Anyway, I'm sure you'd prefer that over the Law Society investigating your processing a transaction at 90 thou' under.' McMaster pushes his point, making it clear to Main that his career, and possibly his life, is in jeopardy.

Main folds the note. 'I'll set up a meeting.' He flings back his seat and storms from the pub.

McMaster jabs his phone: 'And how are you, wonder woman? You're going to get a call from a solicitor, a prat called Jeff Main – that's 'M' for main, not 'P' for pain. The guy's a loser, right; supposed to be representing me in a property transaction. He's stuffed up by not noticing his client's tried to stick me big time. I need to show him I mean business. Discretely. Needs to see the error of his ways.'

'I can handle that. What about a two-for-one offer?'

'Not at this stage. I think our Mr Main will come to the party.'

The situation alarms Gillian; she is shocked to hear, right in front of her, that a senior police officer is plotting revenge on an adversary. She considers the 8.30 p.m. call. Surely, he won't take a call like that at work? Nor would he accept it on a mobile, unless he has an unregistered Pay as You Go. There is only one place to receive such a call.

McMaster broods behind two empty glasses. Gillian treats him a pot of coffee. 'I hope you're all right. I saw your friend's tantrum. Thought you might need a sedative. Wish I could join you, but the boss is watching. Enjoy.'

McMaster smiles, sculls one cup, drops a tenner on the table, and rushes from the lounge.

Gillian shadows him through the door.

She pulls to the edge of a grass verge. Two hundred metres farther along the A44, McMaster slows, turns left into his tree-lined avenue and parks in front of his home.

Gillian studies the property and calculates that a police inspector's salary, even bolstered by abundant overtime, would not cover council taxes and upkeep. She cannot imagine McMaster as a descendant of the gentry or privileged family line with inheritance rights to estates and worldly chattels. Some people *are* born lucky.

At four in the afternoon, the spring sun dips behind a huge turret, igniting the ground floor windows to a soft yellow hue. Gillian proceeds to a potholed lane skirting the property. Parks and waits. Four hours' later, with phone and penlight, she creeps through the darkness, back to the main road.

A carved timber panel: 'Ashton Hill', headlines the driveway. Keen to avoid crackling stones, Gillian negotiates the drive's centre where wild grasses squelch beneath her runners. A sliver of moon trickles over the track while a delicate breeze swishes away her footsteps. After creeping through the double row of cedars, she negotiates a huge expanse of lawn and passes a trickling fountain heralding the memory of Lord Stevenson. Eight-twenty-five. Window by window she takes in the property's sprawling facade. Homes of such grandiose proportion are the mainstay of society's wish-lists.

The double-glazed windows dull the electronic shrill of McMaster's landline telephone. Gillian duck-walks the final four metres to the front of the house, thankful that McMaster has paved over the courtyard of crunchy white stones. A silhouette shuffles behind a curtain. Gillian creeps up to the sash window and peers through a leadlight pane. Inside, McMaster smiles as if he's just won a hard-fought divorce. He opens an antique cabinet, removes a crystal decanter, and pours a half glass of golden spirit. *Guess he's in for the night.*

Inching down the terrace steps, she clips a cast-iron plant stand, knocking it to the ground. Cusses herself. Light spreads from an upper window: a female silhouette on canvas. The front door clicks open. McMaster.

Gillian darts across the lawn, hurdles over dwarf rose bushes and a box hedge. She twists, turns and zigzags, sees no one chasing, and then slows, confident she's shaken her pursuer. Wrong. A shot rings out. Four follow, in two-shot bursts. She identifies the crack as a small pistol, gleaned from firearms training taken as an adjunct to her Investigator's course.

She dives to the ground. *Minimise the target.* Far across the lawn, a figure stands beneath the portico, bathed in light, arm extended, sweeping to fix on his prey. The upstairs curtains swish back into place. *Must be the wife. Too bad. What she can't see won't hurt her.*

Gillian slithers along the ground in a commando crawl, scraping elbows and knees until she reaches the stand of trees.

Hunched over, she waddles along the rutted lane, slowing only after fathoming McMaster too inebriated to walk beyond his front steps. Perhaps that was his reason for using the firearm. Or was it an exhibition of supremacy? She slumps into her car, pulls in a lungful of breath, and calls Thornton. Arranges a meeting at the nearby McDonald's, under cover of high-calorie snack seekers and methadone-dependant youth desperate for a Caramel Super Sundae sugar hit.

Slouched behind a table alongside the drive-through, she spills the evening's events: 'You won't believe what I've just been through. There's serious shit going on. McMaster's hooked up with a lawyer, but I haven't determined what they're up to, other than to say someone is hampering a land settlement. I have identified a stumbling block as a person known as Angelo. Anticipating important info, I followed McMaster home. Shit, you should see the place. No straight copper could afford that.'

Thornton is aware of McMaster's property holding. That is why he had authorised enquiries to establish its current value, but stopped short of researching history of acquisition.

'I thought we'd agreed that his home is out of bounds.'

Gillian squirms. 'Yes, but I heard him arrange a call for 8.30 p.m. When he didn't return to his office, I knew he'd take it elsewhere. I had to follow him. I only realised we were at his home after I saw the 'Ashton Hill' sign. It would have been counterproductive to have just driven off.' Gillian praises herself for the impromptu explanation. She continues: 'I sneaked into his property and approached the front door. I hoped for an invite for a drink. That's his form, as you know – he's already put it on me. I lost my nerve and turned around to leave. It was dark. No outside lights. I knocked over a plant stand and then high-tailed it across the front lawn. Next thing, I'm dodging fucking bullets.'

Thornton grins, not at her predicament, but at her graphic account. He considers Gillian's fictional embellishment. He will not accept McMaster firing live rounds at a person – even if that person were trespassing.

The courts had, in January 2000, in the case against Anthony ('Tony') Edward Martin, discarded the long-standing legal maxim – 'A man's home is his castle' – of an owner having the right to protect his home. The full weight of the law once crushed those who sought to breach the code. But no longer. Martin was sentenced to life imprisonment (later reduced by appeal) for the shooting death of a youth who was burgling Martin's home. Many now see offender's 'rights' surpass those of respectable, law-abiding citizens.

'You're saying McMaster shot at you?'

'Yes, I am. I know when I'm being shot at, although it's not something I experience on a daily basis, and not something I thought I'd encounter when I took this on.'

'You were running across the lawn. How can you positively identify McMaster as the shooter?'

Gillian ponders. 'When you put it that way, I can't be a hundred percent. But I saw him bolt out of the front door. I turned, and then came the shots. I couldn't justify hanging around to get the serial number of his fucking weapon just so I could satisfy a later enquiry.'

'Leave it with me.'

That'll mean the boys' club cover-up, Gillian reasons, too afraid to vocalise her barb. She then details the Knight's Arms conversation, particularising excerpts of McMaster's and Main's heated discussion, and confirming that the ebullient young solicitor is the go-between for a contract killing on 'Angelo'.

The underworld is full of Angelos.

Satisfied he'd both reassured Gillian and exhausted her material, Thornton calls his office and orders a search of the Solicitors' Practice Register for the name 'Main'. The righteous Jeffrey John Main has a clean sheet; no traffic violations, no radical university activisms, no drug use, and no flags for suspicious activities. The absence of adverse data leaves Thornton with nothing to link Main to criminal connections. He suggests Gillian probe further if she intends to darken a solicitor's character.

Thornton's only sure bet is that McMaster can *never* be excluded from *any* form of illicit dealings.

XIII

It had been practical to change her name to Jill.

Treena Harriet Engelada Krusenjilova tired of the questions: 'Please spell that for me'; 'How do you pronounce that?' It happened every time she introduced herself; and it happened every time she had to complete a form, government documentation, or restaurant booking.

Jill grew up under the hard hand of military-devoted Bulgarian parents. She was the youngest of five siblings and the only girl. Instead of Barbies and crocheted teddies, she played with plastic rifles and hand guns. Upon unwrapping Christmas and birthday gifts of traditional female companion toys, she'd retreat to her bedroom and later emerge with transformed jungle warriors – their faces coloured with crayon, fatigues hand stitched from khaki handkerchiefs, and weaponry fabricated from ice cream sticks in paint-by-numbers watercolour.

By the time she entered Botevgrad Senior School, Jill was fully indoctrinated into military protocol, authority and self-preservation. She regularly exploited her repertoire of combat and defensive strategies to quell snide sniggers and name calling. Jill was not a cover girl – and never would be. A pubescent estradiol imbalance flattened her forming curves, morphing her school-champion callisthenic figure into a granite block of weightlifting behemoth. Capitalising on nature's flaw, she won three consecutive Bulgarian National Powerlifting Championships and two European shot-put gymkhanas.

In school's final year, her world collapsed with her parents' decision to join the former Soviet Bloc avalanche into Great Britain. Adapting to the new country and language was not easy. She evaded school and fell from the pinnacle of her parents' expectations. Successive failed job applications confirmed her inability to secure employment.

Jill presents an intimidating aspect, her vast bulk overshadowing her taller than average five-foot-nine. Never has she rewarded a male with heart palpitations, although a few non-conformist men express desire for sexual debaucheries that Jill would never consider. For the past five years, she has experienced more comfort and understanding from her own genus than any male could provide. At twenty-five-years-old, the only male relationships Jill enters are professional. And her profession is contract killer.

To describe how Jill joined the exclusive band of contract killers – as one of the inaugural female professionals – would be a project of comprehensive commentary. For this exposé, her association with DI McMaster rewinds seven years to her first month in England when she attended an employment interview for a Worcestershire police district interpreter. The interview was held in McMaster's precinct, where the comings and goings of police and criminals flowed with the same regularity as traffic on the M25.

As she detailed Bulgarian life, McMaster found affinity with Jill's weapon proficiency and ability to identify black market firearms – a market that McMaster held, for various reasons, close to his heart. It was during that account when a suspect being led through the precinct broke free from his escort and rushed McMaster, grabbing him from behind in a stranglehold. 'You bastard,' he uttered before Jill rushed the attacker, dropped to her hands, and in a whirlwind sweep derived from karate or Thai boxing, swept the assailant's feet from the floor. McMaster swayed on the toppling seat while the drug dealer he'd arrested months earlier, lay sprawled on the floor with Jill sitting above him with *her* arm across *his* throat.

McMaster's appreciation founded a close relationship from the incident. So when he decided to 'encourage' Angelo Caruso, Treena Harriet Engelada Krusenjilova materialised as the obvious candidate.

She lumbers into the offices of Craggill, Weston and Rubenstein. Fronts reception. Whispers: 'Jeff's expecting me.'

Directed to Main's office, she props in the doorway.

Main bolts upright. 'Er, hello. Jill? Shall I call you Jill?'

'Call me what you want.'

Main flushes and reclines in his chair. 'You're here to assist with a complex file?'

Jill scans a wall of certificates and diplomas. Shoots her gaze back to Main. 'I don't know how I can help. I thought I am here about an inheritance.' She responds with caution, offering no scope for a third-party to identify the source of her contacts and instructions. Always vigilant, she fears bugs, scanning devices and concealed audio-visual equipment planted to capture incriminating material that might later glow in vibrant colour on a high definition screen in the Royal Courts of Justice. And then there's the Arrest Warrants. With that in mind, she suggests relocating to safe territory: 'I don't know about you, but I'm overdue for breakfast. How about we hop over the road for a snack and drink?'

Main agrees, pleased to remove his personal dealings from the office. 'There's a spot down the road – makes a good meal and the cider's okay.'

They saunter into the Knight's Arms, the pairing of such physical compatibility it appeared a successful union of an offbeat dating service or hillbilly matchmaker. Main defers to Jill's table selection which overlooks the entry foyer and offers line of sight to the bar and rest rooms. Her bulky jacket balloons her to Michelin Man proportions. It is oversize for a reason: to accommodate tools of trade.

Main returns from the bar with two pints of non-alcoholic cider. 'Sorry. Don't drink while I'm working. Can't have the boss sniffing around for whoever's trashing his office with alcohol breath.'

'Let's cut the jokes.' Jill drops her elbows to the table and drills a glare straight into Main's eyes. 'What's the deal? I'm not one of your dumbos trying to settle debts or matrimony. We both know why we're here, so let's have it.'

Main lowers his eyes. Scans the bar and its surrounds. 'I want you to persuade a client to complete a business transaction. Your customer service and negotiation skills have been recommended.'

Jill continues the sounding board. 'I have a full client list. I don't know that I could accept new contracts.'

'This would be worth your while, you know, for a mutual friend.'

'No names. I don't have friends, and name-dropping will serve no purpose. *If* I could find time, what sort of service do you want?'

'It's all in here.' Main folds back his jacket lapel to display an envelope. 'Simply put, a motivational session. The guy's a little laxed in his administration skills and is delaying a contract my client wants finalised.'

'And how do I contact this guy?'

Main removes the envelope and slides it across the table. Jill squeezes open the top. Peers at a sheet of typed instructions, a map, a business card and block of £20 notes. Jams it into her own jacket pocket. 'I'll have a look when I've got time. I'll get back to you.'

Main hands her a business card.

Jill brushes it aside. 'Don't need two. I know how to contact you. If I didn't I'd hardly be any good at my job, would I?'

They exit the Knight's Arms, Jill with the envelope comforted inside her jacket, Main trailing like a lost lamb. He shuns pandering to the likes of McMaster, but simultaneously applauds him for recommending Jill. He momentarily considers offering a larger incentive to recruit her to his own advantage, and thereby eliminating *two* problems. Main knows the form: Jill wouldn't give a damn about the hit's identity – provided the money is right. A job's a job.

* * *

Gillian hunkers behind the bar, browsing the dozen shots she's snapped with her mobile phone. She attaches the snaps of Main and his Trojan warrior to an email, jabs in a pre-dial number and presses 'send'.

Thornton replies: *Message received.*

McMaster makes the call.

'Yeah, Angelo here.'

'Phil.'

A short silence. 'Hello.'

'What's the go with my contracts?'

'I haven't a clue what you're talking about.'

'Your mother tells me she's left it to you.'

'Ah, that. Yeah. Word is that it's held up with your solicitors. Something to do with extending the settlement to fix an anomaly. Far as I know we don't have anomalies. You made your offer. Live with it.'

'Listen good, right. I got no problem living with my offer. Truth is, you're keeping your mother in the dark so she doesn't find out you're ripping her off. She's got confidence in you handling it – not that you're not doing much of a job. Might be time for me to pay her a visit, right, and put her in the picture.'

Angelo forces his words: 'It's none of your business, man. That's what solicitors are for. If you don't like it, too bad. Mum doesn't need you lobbing on her doorstep dropping accusations she'll never believe. I'm sure she's not busting to sell, but since she's gone this far, I suggest you regard me as a friendly neighbour and let this matter take its course, otherwise mum might just decide that we're not interested in your offer.'

'Listen you little fucker! There is no "we". You've not heard the end of this.' McMaster jabs the 'end call' button. Clenches his fists. Thrusts them against his thighs. Ashton Hill shakes. The parquetry floor splinters.

He is finished with Angelo Caruso.

And he is finished with Jeff Main.

* * *

Never trust a copper. Rose replays the words as McMaster

swaggers into the bottle shop. Evidence of alcoholic overdose. 'Hello Rose. You all right? I've been thinking how lucky I am to have met someone like you. Reckon you could spare another couple of those Dewies?'

No, not again. Rose flushes. Blurts: 'Just take them and go,' preferring to be rid of him and resolve the matter under 'breakages' on her daily stock count rather than endure further conflict.

McMaster grabs three bottles, hands them to Rose, helps her bag them, and with a coarse sneer slurs, 'I'll be in touch.'

Rose spends the rest of the day flooded with distress. She has no one from whom to seek help. On leaving home in her seventeenth year, she severed family contact after being told: 'You'll not make it on your own. Once you walk out that door there'll be no coming back' – the words of her father. There was no reason behind his attitude other than to respect the Spanish culture of conserving the family unit. José Hernandez took his daughter's intention to leave home as an insult.

To Rose, it was part of growing up. Leaving the nest. Spreading her wings. There was no suitable employment in Jesmond, her home town near Newcastle. Her successful application to Heavenly Spirits promised a regular income with incremental increases, enabling her to take on a nice bed-sit in leafy Cheltenham.

There is no going back. Despite Rose's deep affection for her family, she cannot, and will not, ever forgive her father for exorcising her from the home. Too proud to forgive, and too fearful of further rejection, Rose elects to wade in her own shallow pool of resources.

She shares her fear of McMaster with the fear of losing

her job. No one knows about the theft she'd omitted from her job application. Who would volunteer *that?* But now, over the space of a fortnight, she's stolen seven bottles of expensive liquor from her employer.

And it isn't over.

XIV

FROM THE REAR OF HIS mother's property, Angelo scans Ashton Hill's panorama. Rolls a joint to contemplate McMaster's insistence on purchasing his parents' farm.

Why 'intensive agriculture' when he's farmed nothing over the past six years? And what of the newfound desire to 'maximise' the land's potential? Why this sudden interest in working the land? And why a whopping £360,000 gesture to 'help' his mother? McMaster had insisted their respective solicitors execute the contract with haste. They'd exchanged blows over the issue, albeit of Angelo's own doing. And most recently, McMaster had countered with the abusive and threatening phone call.

Angelo wonders if McMaster might have inside information about spiralling prices of small property holdings, or advance notice of revised planning guidelines. If so, his neighbour could then slice Blackshaw's Mill into small farmlets and reap instant riches. Should that be tabled, Angelo vows it will be *he*, not his neighbour, who will benefit.

The euphoric influence of marijuana has blunted his senses. Too late he reacts to the crackle of dried lucerne. The black glove flashes through the air and pummels into his stomach. He buckles and drops to the ground. Turns to identify the attacker. Adrenalin fuels natural defence mechanisms as he rises to the crunch of a sharp kick into his stomach.

An oversized black lace-up boot compresses his chest. He

grimaces submission. The assailant towers like Gulliver over the Lilliputians. Black balaclava. Black jacket. Thick shoulders. Heavy-set. Wispy voice: 'I see I've got your attention farm-boy. Listen up.'

Angelo glares. He cannot determine whether his pain emanates from his chest, his abdomen, or the embarrassment of being floored by the surprise mugger. 'And who the fuck are you? Black Samurai? You got a problem with me, sort it out face to face, no mask. Bet you haven't got the bollocks to show yourself instead of attacking from behind like a back-stabbing moron.'

'Nice analogy, farm-boy. You're good with insults. I have a message. Complete the paperwork. Comprendo? You'd better, because if not, I may be called upon to return, and who would I be to refuse?'

'Yeah, right. And who pulls your strings?'

Angelo wheezes as the boot exerts 100 kilograms of Bulgarian muscle onto his ribs. 'Need to know basis. And you don't need to know.' The boot sinks into Angelo's chest. Ribs snap like popped bubble wrap. 'Think you'll need a few strings yourself.'

Angelo protests, wincing with each breath: 'Hang on. Hang on, what the fuck are you doing? Who put you up to this? I've got nothing to do with paperwork; it's with the lawyers. I've got more to worry about than acting as a middleman for a contract that's got zip to do with me. It's between the neighbour and my mother!'

Jill swipes an envelope of documents across Angelo's face. 'See this? It's a reminder of the contract you dudded. Don't tell me you've got nothing to do with this because I know better. Understand? I have sources. I have up-to-date information.

Now get this. You're going to go to your mother's solicitor's office and you'll instruct them, on your mother's behalf, to effect settlement forthwith. Your reward is that I will ensure this dud contract doesn't go to the police, and for your troubles, you'll get to keep ten grand of the ninety. The other eighty will go to your neighbour as compensation for the hiding you gave him. By my reckoning, that'll make everything even. You've got twenty-four hours. Should I learn that you've failed to do so, I would truly look forward to receiving further instructions. One more thing: you'd better get those ribs checked.'

Angelo twists down to the envelope and moves just in time to dodge a swinging kick to his head. He fumes at being beaten by a professional – his snapped ribs merely a warning. He opens the envelope. Tips it on end. Glances at the contracts. Instant recognition. Handwriting. All capitals: 'REMEMBER ME. REMEMBER YOUR INSTRUCTIONS. I KNOW ENOUGH ABOUT YOUR LITTLE OPERATION TO PUT YOU INSIDE FOR A LONG TIME.' He rips it to pieces and hurls it into the air.

He salvages his elephant-hide mentality. *I do what I want when I want. I won't be intimidated by anyone. Next time you won't catch me with my guard down.* Typical. How many display the tough, impenetrable bravado, only *after* the threat has passed?

He limps back to his mother's home. Crashes through the kitchen door. Heaves for breath.

'Angelo. What's happen to you?'

'Tripped over the bloody long weeds. We should do something about this farm.'

'We can't. I tell you I'm sell it to Mister Mac. It's too much for me and you no come to help. I don't want the worry. With your papa gone there's nothing here for me.'

'Tell you what, mama. I'll buy it and develop it. I will surprise you.'

'Angelo. Ever since you little boy you have the dreams. Nothing but dreams. Never do we see any good from them. You no have achieved nothing; just hang around with the friends. You no visit much your mama. And papa? You visit his grave? No, Angelo. You won't have this and destroy it too. You destroy too much of us already.'

Maria wipes a tear. She's erased the hurt of police bringing him home as a ten-year-old for stealing from shops, and she concealed from his father the Chief Constable's warning. She's cried over his petty thieving, gambling and stand-over tactics which began in his early teens – at least – earning him his first stint in Ashfield young offenders' institution just three days shy of his sixteenth birthday. The Children's Court magistrate expressed regret at having to incarcerate the young Angelo 'for his own good'. He would be disappointed to learn that no 'good' came of his pronouncement, for the name Angelo Caruso made regular appearances on court lists.

Refusing to accept his mother's berating, Angelo storms out of the house and returns to his flat. Too proud to seek medical help, he cuts the shoulder straps from an old gym singlet and pulls the remainder over his head until it compresses his chest like his sisters' 'boob tubes' of old. A half roll of silver duct tape secures the binding, leaving him like a statuesque knight in armour.

That done, he swirls a glass of beer into a frothy eddy of the week's events. The television blares an afternoon chat show: Jeremy Kyle satirising a couple – after outing them in front of 20 million viewers – who need help with marital problems.

Banter between the recently wed pair fuels Angelo's rage. Why do partners opt for public airing instead of engaging professional resources to help restore matrimonial harmony? He pulls his mind from the screen and plans revenge against McMaster. Or eradication.

Angelo knows that to achieve his objective, he must leave no clues. Hours of planning and preparation do not guarantee the perfect murder – only the fortunes of fate reward the lucky few.

He considers various means, many of which are better performed under night's silence. Creeping through an open door and emptying a cyanide-filled syringe into McMaster's arm is one option. However, opportunity would be scarce, and forensic examination would discover the needle puncture. Sure, he could mask poison by mixing it with food or alcohol, but again, forensic analysis would identify toxins. He turns his mind to conceiving something new, using his own resources, as had the fictional 'MacGyver', renowned for fabricating weaponry from on-hand scraps.

As a rite of passage into maturity, thirteen-year-old Angelo had learnt to fire a rifle. Blackshaw's Mill had little need for armoury, other than to abate the threat of foxes against livestock. Giuseppe Caruso endorsed the long-standing custom of raising his son to early manhood by evading twentieth century pampering, political correctness, gay bars and soft sports. 'This will make you a man,' said Giuseppe as he handed young Angelo the gleaming Remington 700.

That frightening day of eleven years' past spawned in Angelo a lifetime hobby of collecting firearms with the enthusiasm of a Teenage Mutant Ninja Turtle fan seizing every

Turtle, sword, shield, dagger, and nunchaku he could afford. His 1960 Browning .32 is a favourite for concealing in an ankle holster, while a Smith & Wesson Model 29 Magnum, made famous by Harry Callaghan in the iconic 'Dirty Harry' movies is his preferred frightener. Angelo knows the menace of death reaps more productive results than mere execution, although execution is the favoured means of *convincing others* that a threat is real. The administration of threat renders *anything* negotiable. On the down side, vengeance and retribution posed by others means that Angelo must heed his own self-preservation – a matter he neglected in the field attack. He had settled in a comfort zone, but should have known better, because renegades circle Angelo like crows above a carcass.

Redirecting his thoughts to McMaster, he has confidence in picking him off with one shot. Perhaps, as he arrives home from work. Darkness would befriend him as he shrinks alongside Ashton Hill's tree-lined driveway. He also considers a ploy such as a workplace accident or auto mishap, but concedes the element of risk as too great. While Angelo's DNA is cloned from creative crooks, he reverts to the tried and true: a gunshot to the head. Quick. Clean. And no trace evidence (he believes) awaiting investigators' evidence bags. A formidable plan – in principle. Angelo oils his Magnum, sights his image in the bedroom mirror, and then jams the hardware behind his back.

* * *

He downs two cans of Beck's Lager as he hides in the same spot as was Gillian the previous evening; far enough to be out of the way, but close enough to monitor all peripheral goings-on. His disadvantage is not knowing when McMaster will arrive.

A practiced killer would know his (or her) target's movements to the half-minute: when and where they eat; the time and method of commuting to and from work; time spent visiting acquaintances; locations and duration of shopping trips; right down to monitoring light switchings within the home.

He's prepared. The closed driveway gate will catch McMaster off guard and allow Angelo to empty the six-round chamber into his rival's head. *One shot will do. An extra two or three to be sure. Damn it, why don't I maximise the satisfaction?*

That scenario compels Angelo to abort the mission. For now. He has no silencer. The shots would attract attention. A local resident, possibly his mother, would call police. Sirens and flashing lights would rush the scene like fire engines to an epic blaze. Angelo is known to police. Easy pickings.

When planning a murder, many variables must be considered. One must forecast a range of outcomes to safeguard both the operation's success and the killer's anonymity. Preparation is akin to a screenwriter stitching together plots and scenes, establishing time-lines, and illuminating the manner by which the killer will escape prosecution. Later, the movie buff will tense before the huge screen – double-bass thumping through his ears – engrossed in an experience so convincing and far beyond the realms of fiction.

I can do that, murmurs Angelo.

XV

TOO FEARFUL TO ANSWER THE phone, Rose flicks it to answering machine. McMaster's words: 'I'll be in touch' shake through her fingertips.

She's had an extra deadlock fitted to her front door, and a security door fixed to the rear. Every mile travelled, whether by car, train or foot, is now inched with trepidation, neck swivelling 180 degrees, peering along lanes, behind trees, and at shop window reflections. The strain follows her to bed, for Rose has not enjoyed one night of unbroken sleep since McMaster's impromptu visit to her shop.

She shuns television news bulletins warning women about stalkers targeting anyone from royalty to screen star. A profile of a deranged male posing as a normal member of the public would jump from the screen. Horrific Crimewatch re-enactments and college warnings urge students (taken to mean girls but not openly stated for fear of abusing political correctness) to use floodlit walkways from evening tutorials, and to avoid walking unaccompanied within, and beyond, the campus grounds. Like most women, Rose had once defied warnings with the clichéd: 'It'll never happen to me' – a reasonable notion for those living in safe, rural, Gloucestershire. Now, she is a target.

Her mood lifts on McMaster not leaving a message. It drops just as quick when her mobile shrieks to life. She glares at the screen, 'caller ID blocked,' and answers the call.

'Hello sweetie. How are you? I thought since you'd helped

me out so well I'd return the favour.' McMaster's sleazy salutation.

'Sorry. Can I call you back? I was just going out.'

'You're not going anywhere, right? We have an arrangement to consider. I'll be there in half an hour. If you're not there, you can expect to find a summons dropped through your letter box on your return.'

Rose recognises she will gain no advantage by leaving. McMaster would find her at work the next day or the next week. He wouldn't give up. All she can do is play along and hope that the 'arrangement' will not elevate to a woman's worst fear. Never has Rose needed to rely on self-defence measures, but now, with panic intensifying, she tapes a large bread knife under the kitchen table. She can't imagine using it, but its presence will be akin to a protective talisman.

'Smoke?'

'No thanks.' Rose trembles.

'Come on. It'll do you good. You've never smoked anything like this.' McMaster drops an envelope onto the kitchen table. 'Business opportunity. Everyone who drinks enjoys a good smoke. And this is the best. You could make a heap – and it'll encourage me to tear up this traffic report.' He pulls the report, complete with summons, from his pocket.

Rose's face falls into disarray. Agreeing to any kind of arrangement will cement her obligation to McMaster. She struggles against the principles of right and wrong, as she had in her early teens when facing young love's elations and traumas. Her mind floods with memories of the school library where an older male approached her. She'd secretly adored the out of bounds school teacher – twenty-six-years-old and married, and one who ignored the old Berlin Wall standing between teachers and students. In the aisle indexed Geography, he'd leant over her shoulder and whispered, 'Meet me here after class. 4.00 p.m.'

Rose spent the rest of the afternoon confused – as she is now. *If I get involved with dope, I'm sunk forever. If I let him file the report, what happens? A speeding fine? Big deal. He wouldn't dare say anything about the theft; how would he explain that? That could be my ace.*

Along with her enforced parental detachment, distance has also diluted the few close friendships founded in Jesmond. Rose has no one to whom she can share her problem, and she daren't discuss the dilemma with work colleagues because admitting theft would end her career. She has only one choice: an independent third party. Anonymous. Her approach akin to a couple taking their fractured marriage to a church counsellor.

She plucks Olivia Watts' card from her handbag. Jabs the number into her mobile. Presses 'send'. Pokes 'end'. Drives her thumbs into her forehead. Nerves. Two minutes' later she redials: 'Hello. You met me at the bottle shop and left your card. It's Rose Hernandez. Could we have a chat – not on the phone – it's important. Something I hope you can help me with.'

They meet outside Cheltenham's HSBC and exchange a limp handshake before scrambling through the lunchtime rush to Wetherspoon's pub. Olivia takes the lead and flops into a booth. Her experience in dealing with women – striking up discussions, taking part in debates, and conducting fully-fledged interrogations – doesn't find a starting point with

Hernandez. She goes with the obvious: 'You even *look* worried. What is it?'

Rose stalls. 'Remember how you replied to my blog; the one where I wrote about not trusting coppers?'

Olivia's brow crunches into a corrugated road. 'No. I don't mind admitting my posts, but how do you know it was me?'

'I'm not stupid. Sorry, didn't mean it in that way. I'm not angry. When you gave me a business card I was surprised to see that you were an investigator. Truth is, I thought you were a girls' girl trying to make a move on me.'

Olivia smiles, hoping to not telegraph that the thought had crossed her mind. For all she knows, Rose might reciprocate, but professionalism must rise above lascivious desire.

Rose continues: 'Anyway, I thought it was quite ingenious the way you'd placed the question mark in the middle of your business name. The only time I've seen something similar is the exclamation mark attached to Yahoo! So, I was curious, because it registered that I'd recently seen a question mark in another identity. I scrolled through my blog pages and there you were – couldn't have been anyone else: 'WH?I' At the time, I thought it was a person who couldn't spell, or that they just wanted attract attention to the disjointed word. On deciphering the letters, I came up with you.'

Olivia welcomes the break. 'Well done. I'd never thought of the correlation between the two, but the way you put it – well, it's obvious. I might change my blog identity because it could create problems if the wrong person uses your uncanny powers of deduction.

'Okay, I'm a PI. Before this, I'd served seven years in the police, finishing as a DS. I responded to your blog because I agree with you. I have my own experiences of shonky police members. Fortunately, there's only a few, but the shame is, it tarnishes the whole constabulary – the bad apple in the barrel syndrome.'

Rose holds her drink to her lips. Doesn't sip. Doesn't breathe. Cocooned in hibernation, she collects her thoughts. And then spills them: 'I've met one of the bad apples. It's a long story – I'll give you the condensed version. I got pulled over on the A44. My fault; I was over the limit, but not by much. The officer, in plain clothes, took my details and said he'll have to consider whether my offence is serious enough to report. I didn't hear anything for a week until he walked into my work. Told me to give him a couple of bottles – Dewar's – and he'll forget about the report.

'I'm sorry I have to mention this, but I have to be up front. I've been done for theft, just a minor shoplift. Sorry, I suppose to you that no theft is minor, but this was just a top. I'm on probation now, so I was terrified of being breached. I gave him two bottles of Scotch. I thought that would be the end of it, but he fronted a week later and put it on me again, this time saying he'll report the matter of the two stolen bottles – even though he pressured me.

'And now, just earlier, he gave me this package, pre-bagged tobacco – grass, I suppose – and told me to sell it to my customers. How the hell do I do that and get away with it? I don't want to, but I'm scared of what will happen if I don't.'

'Shit!' Olivia lets fly the tame expletive. Sits deep in thought. 'Okay. Who is he?'

'I don't know. He's never said. He showed ID when he first pulled me over, but I was too panicked to look properly. I think he intentionally held his thumb over the name, although I did see 'Detective Inspector'. It only came to me much later to question why an officer of that rank would target someone for a minor traffic infringement.'

'That's a shame. Can't do much without a name, and we can't be sure that the ID was legit. When's he going to see you about this package? You have to sell it all within a certain time? Is there an arrangement to contact him?' Olivia is so concerned by an officer using a woman's licence as a dating agency recommendation, that she forgets the interrogator's rule: one question at a time.

'He didn't say anything about a next step. I suppose that protects him, doesn't it? – so no one can confront him.'

Olivia checks her watch. 'Um, I can't hang around on the off-chance he'll front tomorrow, the next day or whenever. What I can do, and it won't be expensive, is have a tech install a camera behind the register. It'll have a ten-hour recording capacity. You only need change or reset the SD card each morning. As for the package, what's the cost of each bag?'

'Twenty quid. Means I'll owe him two hundred for the lot.'

'Okay. Here's what we'll do. Give me two; I'll give you £40. I'll seal it in this bag and type up a declaration that we've made the exchange for investigatory purposes. Later on, I'll lodge it with a trusted police member. For the moment, lay the bags on the table so I can photograph them. That'll cover us both.

'Don't even try to sell any. You don't know if it could be a set-up. When the guy returns, you hand him the cash. He'll be glad to get anything, all dealers are the same. Try to set up a meeting. But don't get into long discussions or make things difficult for yourself. Tell him you've been too nervous to approach too many customers. If you can, try to take control and tell him that once you've done this there'll be no more.'

‘I already said that about the Scotch. He doesn’t listen. He’s too demanding.’

‘Trust me,’ says Olivia, with little conviction. ‘The position he’s in, he won’t take the speeding or the theft any further. I’ll have my guy, Hamilton, drop in tomorrow and set up the cam. In the meantime, if the creep does drop in, call or message me.’

XVI

A LAY-BY CUT INTO THE roadside verge provides an uninterrupted view of Ashton Hill. Angry shadows of giant elms and straggly willows fall over the rental van as morning traffic zooms along the adjacent road. The driver twiddles the radio to calming music as McMaster swings from his drive onto the A44.

Confident of a free reign, he turns the van out of the lay-by and into McMaster's drive where he pulls on white overalls, high-vis yellow safety vest, and yellow helmet. He stands fluorescent-orange safety cones behind the van and removes a chainsaw, bar lube, trunk wedges and a four-litre tin of two-stroke fuel.

From the twenty-two tree guard of honour, he selects the third from the front gate. Estimates its height using a formula spouted by a television gardening guru: 'Take your best guess and then double it.' The precaution means nothing, for this operator has no regard for consequential damage. Quite the opposite.

The trunk's circumference measures four feet – a tough challenge for the stolen Husqvarna eighteen-inch bar with tungsten tipped chain. Camouflaged by the morning shade, the chainsaw's piercing shriek will soon radiate its presence to all within a two-kilometre radius.

He tugs the start rope in rapid motions as he would yank unruly weeds from the earth. A cloud of oily smoke billows from the tiny exhaust outlet, followed by the 120cc motor's throaty gurgle. The engine splutters excess fuel and spent carbon as it revs to the high-pitched squawk of a model airplane enthusiast's balsa wood baby circling overhead.

Into the trunk he slices a huge 'V' – facing straight into the driveway. From the opposite side, he cuts downwards, holding tight as the saw bucks through the chunky bark. He panics as the tree creaks like a rusty barn door. It sways in protest. He buzzes a quick slash into the widening crevice, causing the tree to groan and crash to the ground, straight across McMaster's driveway. Part one accomplished.

After completing a task, he prefers to recuperate with a smoke or coffee. He craves approval and accomplishment that he never received at school. Here though, he cannot risk leaving a sign of his presence. Eighteen months' earlier a patch of phlegm and spittle convicted an associate for his part in a service station robbery. DNA. Follows you everywhere. Drop a hair? Sprung. Spot of blood? Might as well plead guilty. Cotton bud? A globule of sickly, cholesterol-laden earwax could earn you a stretch in Her Majesty's big house.

He moves to the next tree, cuts another 'V' notch and continues to slice through its trunk. Again, the saw protests, spitting chips and sawdust at his feet. This time he stops short, leaving the tree standing with a huge yawning yellow mouth. He rushes the equipment back to the van and steps out of the overalls. Throws them in the back. Ties a black windcheater around his waist to complement the black polo shirt and black track pants.

He retrieves the orange safety cones and returns the van to the lay-by where he scoffs two jam rolls and drowns them with a bottle of Coke. He crunches two bags of Salt and Vinegar potato crisps into his jacket and returns to the property. It could be a long wait.

The afternoon is comfortable. Calm. Many times he has loitered, waiting for the right moment to exact vengeance on those who'd deceived him. He would usually mix with pub patrons, down a few pints, grab a meal if necessary, and exchange banter with locals. The target toe-rag would swagger into the pub, scull a couple of pints and within half an hour, dart to the toilet. He would dawdle behind, and safeguarded by a crony covering the door, would pummel his adversary to within seconds of unconsciousness. It is the proven means of obtaining information and debt recovery. A few extra punches to the lower stomach sees his foe pleading for mercy. Result? Another faithful devotee. Today, McMaster will have no opportunity to beg for mercy.

After lying in wait for nine hours he considers giving up. His temper has rocketed into the red zone with thoughts of McMaster held back on overtime or having got lucky at the pub and now enjoying a round of nocturnal entertainment. He is thirsty; he's scoffed all the crisps – his only sustenance since the morning rolls, and is now busting for a major toilet break. He could construct a 'bushman's dunny' of the type seen in Australian camping magazines; but he is a step ahead because he knows that a white jacketed forensic scientist would later examine his huge Pringle-infused turd. DNA. Follows you everywhere.

As he strains against nature's urge, a pair of white halogen headlights turns off the road and bounce into the driveway like courting fireflies. And then they stop… suspended in time… shining over the fallen tree. His target pulls up in the perfect position.

McMaster sits in his car. Awestruck. *What the fuck? We had a storm or something? How the hell would one of these fall?* A blue hue seeps from the car; the familiar backlight of a phone keypad.

The anxious vengeance-seeker swings into action and pumps a hand saw through the pre-cut trunk, heaving to and fro with the speed of an illegal logger. The trunk creaks; he belts the saw faster and faster, to and fro, to and fro, faster and faster, while the trunk heaves and groans until it collapses like a spent jigolo. He smiles. Birds flutter. McMaster's terrified glare shoots out of the open car door. The huge tree crashes onto the roof, crushing it and snapping the door from its hinges. Glass shatters. Pine needles and splinters fly in rhythm to crunching metal and snapping branches – a concerto piercing the evening's silence. And McMaster's ears.

The antagonist has only moments to flee. With saw in hand, he approaches the car where McMaster lays sandwiched between the crumpled roof and flattened seats. One leg splays in a physiologically unnatural angle. Spatters of blood decorate the passenger window.

Part two. Check.

How's that for a deal, copper bastard. Only the night's silence prevents him vocalising his venom. *No one tries it on with me, least of all a fat bastard trying to take advantage of an old widow.* He smiles and takes a diagonal path across the property to his van.

And then the adjacent property's porch light flicks on.

As the crash shakes the ground, Gillian jerks to attention in her small Fiat sedan. She scans the road for mangled cars or trucks. The east and west horizons are bare. From the darkened roadside, a black outline glides across the road, into the lay-by, and then throws some items into the back of a van. Logic connects him with the thunderous noise she heard moments earlier. Too late now, she curses, as the van drives off. *Why didn't I jot down its number?*

Intuition. A private detective's life is built upon suspicion: suspect everything and be prepared. It follows that a van without occupants in a darkened lay-by must be suspicious, unless a secret humping is bouncing about the mattressed cargo area.

Gillian tries to gain a better vantage point from which to view McMaster's home. There is no clear sighting from where she stands; the house is in darkness. It remains so after she crosses the road and observes the property from the front fence. She edges toward the driveway, sharing the darkness for fear of being spotted by McMaster. From bar girl to stalker.

Gillian has done her utmost to get close to McMaster. The Knight's Arms though, was a no through road. She could not risk dedicated socialising at work – she has to be everybody's dream. Sell more drinks that way, her boss tutored. Although not an employee, she is still expected to perform as do other staff, and that means returning a profit.

She harbours the pain of having broken the unwritten creed: Don't mix work with pleasure. Gillian has a job to do, but she's allowed her heart to rule her head. She sees in McMaster qualities that very few others, including his estranged wife, ever see. He embodies a single-focused determination contrasted by soft sincerity. Only days earlier, McMaster took her hand as a gesture of thanks for the bonus shot of Dewar's. His warmth flowed through her like a blood transfusion. Yes, she should have withdrawn her hand. She couldn't. Desire conquered rational judgement. Her eyes said what her lips couldn't: *I want you.*

McMaster responded with an offer to dinner. The rain cheque is uncashed.

Gillian recognises that *she* now has a problem. *Am I watching his house to get info for Thornton, or am I watching out of jealousy?*

Two steps into the driveway, Gillian reels at the root of the pandemonium. She runs along the stones, almost tripping in shock on seeing the mammoth tree compressing McMaster's car into the driveway. Snapped branches and dense, spindly foliage scratch her arms and legs, hampering access to the vehicle. She strips small branches from the trunk. Cuts her fingers. A faint gurgle reverberates from inside the car. She crawls under one branch and over another in a prickly version of a funfair mud run. Through the shattered rear window, she makes out the crude outline of McMaster, who, by a spontaneous act of self-preservation, had shrunk into the driver's side footwell, straddled the console and forced his head and shoulders down to the passenger floor. The roof sandwiches him.

Gillian is pleased that McMaster will not be able to identify her, although that is the least of her concerns during the vital moments where her actions, or lack of, could determine his fate. She calls through the window: 'Stay still. I'm getting help.' She yanks out her phone and swipes 999.

'What happened?' McMaster groans.

'Don't know. I'm just passing by. I've called an ambulance.'

'What happened?'

'Just keep still and quiet until help arrives.'

A shrieking voice in the background: 'Oh my God. Oh my God.'

Gillian turns to see an elderly woman tottering along the

driveway. 'Mister Mac, mister Mac,' she bellows. 'Whatsa happen? Whatsa happen?'

'You know him?' Gillian asks.

'Yes, mister Mac. He my neighbour. Whatsa happen?'

'I don't know. I've called an ambulance. I'll wait for it on the road.'

Gillian rushes back to the road in time to see the horizon alive with flashing red and blue lights. She waves frantically, directing the approaching ambulance to the driveway entrance. As it rustles into the drive she lunges across the road, races to the lay-by, and climbs into her car. Still clutching the phone, she notes the time: 9.40 p.m. She calls Thornton.

'When did this happen?' he asks, in between mouthfuls of expletives.

Gillian imagines him watching television, beer in one hand, phone in the other. 'Just now,' she replies. 'Very suspicious, but I can't remain at the scene. I called the ambos; I think Mac's in a bad way. He's been well and truly set up. Someone dropped a tree across his drive. He had to stop. Another tree crashed on to his car, flattening the roof. Perfectly executed. Sorry, bad choice of words.'

'He's dead?'

'No. Pretty bad though. No way of getting him out of the car without the jaws. I missed a clue by not getting the number of a van parked nearby, but at the time it meant nothing. Some guy dressed in all black rushed over from the location and decamped with haste.'

'Okay. I'll take over from here.'

XVII

I TOSS ABOUT MY THOUGHTS. Question my rationale for taking on Thornton's operation. PI versus PI. 'Give me everything you can,' he instructed. Every moment spent in Gillian's shadow rewards me with pages of valuable information.

Gillian makes a sly exit from the Knight's Arms and scoots to a nearby Pay and Display. I cringe at the sight of her vehicle, a tacky baby blue end-of-season clearance or back line sale. Easy to follow though; no losing it amongst all the whites and silvers cramming our congested roads.

My second sense tells me she'll be heading for the A44. I smile with recognition as she criss-crosses Worcester's back streets. As usual, I am right. I've witnessed three cosy connections between Gillian and McMaster at the Knight's Arms so it is not unreasonable for me to expect that she will pry further into his lifestyle.

I follow her into a lay-by off the A44, a neatly cut arc beneath narrow blotches of shade. The refuge is clear of wayside stoppers, save for a white rental van propped ten metres from an overflowing rubbish bin. I grab a shopping bag from the floor, fill it with discarded biscuit and chocolate wrappers and head for the bin. Gillian drops her head as I approach. She doesn't fool me – her fixation on McMaster's property is obvious. I press the bag into a small gap. I'm not the first, and I won't be the last, to spring clean my car in a lay-by. I lock away the registration number and return to my car.

Gillian must have seen my car in her rear-view mirrors. Too bad her professionalism is so far below par that she didn't realise she'd been followed from the Knight's Arms. But that doesn't concern me as much as my current predicament. Why has she chosen to watch the property from here when there are more advantageous positions?

When a deafening thud pierces the night's silence, Gillian scurries to the roadside. She returns just as quick when an unknown person rushes across the road. I assume it is the van's driver, because distance drivers habitually stop en route – in the most inappropriate places – for a toilet break. They don't however, park in a lay-by and *cross* to the *other* side of the road to take a leak.

I face a threefold challenge: watch the anonymous figure; ogle Gillian; or check the source of the crash. I tail Gillian to the driveway. The spectacle floors me. I've seen similar devastation on news reports of typhoon-flattened communities. Here, compacted in a small area is similar destruction. Gillian takes control of the scene and renders help. I call emergency services – just in case Gillian does not share my presence of mind.

On seeing her speak to an elderly woman, I race back to my car. And that's when it hits me that I am embroiled in hell of a lot more than a spot of 'observing'. I call Thornton. Engaged. I wait. As one able to spot a penny coin from twenty paces, I see a white clump shining like a lone star where the white van had been parked. A glove. A workman's glove; right hand, soft leather palm with hardened fingertips, a smear of grease across the palm and a moist patch on the rear of the wrist – a sign of someone having wiped their brow during hard work. Specks of sawdust cling to its moist canvas webbing. Not having the official resources I once had, I place the glove in a Glad sandwich bag; my version of the police evidence bag. Watts Happening? Investigations might not be 'high-tech' but it is highly adaptable.

Again I swipe Thornton's number.

'What now?'

'Excuse me?' I say with rising inflection. 'It's Olivia. I wouldn't call unless it was important.'

'Sorry Liv. Had bad news. Think I can guess what you're calling about. You're on Trotter's arse, I take it?'

'Yes. And I have a situation for you.'

'She's already phoned. You know where you are?'

'Not exactly. Close to Pershore?'

'That's McMaster's property you're on to. Mac's stranded in his car. Why the fuck would someone do that to one of our own?'

'No idea. Yet. Seems strange that your super investigator just happens to be watching McMaster's home at the exact time he's taken out.' I could think of a thousand other reasons, but I'm certainly not going to get off-side with Thornton. 'Emergency services have arrived. I'll hang around. Trotter's gone, but there's a woman here who seems to know Mac. Not his wife, from what I can gather. I'll head back and see what I can find out.'

'It'll be a crime scene now. Trees don't just fall across driveways onto cars.'

'Okay. I'll make myself scarce.'

But I don't. I race back and approach the distressed woman who is standing alongside the driveway. She's been swept aside by paramedics and emergency service workers who flap around the wrecked vehicle. I hand her my card and ask, in my most sensitive voice: 'You recognise the man in the car?'

'Mister Mac. He my neighbour. I live over there.' The woman indicates the farmhouse with the illuminated front porch.

'Mr McMaster? The policeman?'

'Yes. That's him. Mister Phil.'

'You know what happened here?

'No. I hear the crash and then nothing. Then I remember I hear the same noise this afternoon so I wonder what it is. I think maybe something's fall on mister Mac's house; the roof or something, so I'm come outside and have a look but I see nothing. I think what if something happens and he's in trouble so I walk here. I hope he be all right.'

'The noise you heard earlier. Do you remember what time?'

'Yes. I'm always make the cup of tea after Coronation Street, so I know it's minutes after two o'clock. I hear the chainsaw; I know chainsaws because my Giuseppe always makes the firewood. It's not mean nothing to me because people always make the firewood – soon there be no trees left.'

'Could you identify the worker's truck, anything like that?'

'No. I'm not looking for anything.'

I feel sorry for her, jittering and shaking as her neighbour is extricated from the flattened vehicle. 'Let me walk you home. I'll make you a nice cup of tea.'

A mobile crane, splattered with signwriting of a nearby commercial hire company, lowers its boom and unwinds cables which jockeys sling around the tree atop McMaster's car. A nurse feeds an intravenous drip through the shattered passenger window.

'I musta see if mister Mac good.'

'I'll let you know. I'll find out what hospital he's going to.' I take the woman's arm and guide her across the paddock. In retrospect, we should have walked around the fence line where it is brighter. That would have spared me the effort of propping her up each time she fell into a rut or tripped over clod of dirt.

A black Audi squats in her driveway – I can't imagine this frail woman behind its wheel. She breaks from my grip. 'Angelo, it's mister Mac, he's a been hurt.'

The male stands like a sentry in the doorway. 'Mama, I've told you not to worry about the neighbours. We take care of ourselves.' His eyes bore into me as he asks his mother: 'And who's your friend?'

I answer for her. 'Hi. I'm Olivia. I helped your mother home from next door. You been here all the time?'

'What's it to you? You've done your good deed, you can leave now.'

'Fine with me. I just thought it would have been nice of you to help your mother through the dark.' I guess that he has been there only a short while, my assumption supported by the Audi's cooling motor pinging contraction ticks into the night.

'Thanks for your concern. You can see she's okay now so there's no need to take up any more of your time. Bye.'

Arrogant bastard.

I return to the hive of activity in McMaster's driveway. The entrance is taped off. Doesn't deter me. I squeeze between the fence's wire strands straight into an astute constable in charge of fluttering yellow tape. From my bag I display an emergency card: "Watts Insurance Services", and ask: 'Which hospital is Mr McMaster being transferred to?'

She consults a paramedic: 'Worcester General.'

XVIII

I NAVIGATE THE WAITING ROOMS and corridors of Worcester General, expecting to see a throng of family and police appended to McMaster's bedside. While four colleagues crowd the small ward, Gillian fusses around the nurses' station, pleading for a private minute with McMaster. My curiosity piques. *What is her interest?* Here is a supposedly professional person engaged in a professional capacity, seeking to grace the bedside of the very person she is paid to shadow. Talk about conflict of interest. The thought bubbles through me like a concoction frothing in a mad scientist's test tube: *Could* she *be trying to dispose of McMaster?* With further thought, I wonder if she might be double-dealing. But for what purpose? *She's failed the first hit, but now fronts up to finish him off?* I could so easily be right, but then again, I am prone to spearing off on outlandish tangents. I switch back to reality – report the conduct of Gillian Trotter.

On seeing two suited gentlemen swish through a curtain, I am drawn to the private suite of the critically injured McMaster. The harsh reality of police service hits me. I've seen my share of road accident victims: the worst where a crumpled car wrapped itself around the victim like joint of pork re-packed in burnished tin foil; I've seen motorcyclists' limbs splayed in more configurations than I once twisted with my stepfather's pipe cleaners; and I've seen the zombiefied walks of the wounded who clamber from a vehicle, displaced of presence, of location, and of their own identity.

McMaster's legs hang from ceiling-suspended stirrups – perhaps scavenged from the maternity ward, and a shoulder is swathed in heavy gauze bandage. An adjacent machine pulses and beeps. Wires snake into a bank of monitors flashing and buzzing like a Las Vegas gambling den. That does not surpass the shock of seeing Gillian's hand clasped around the patient. I am sure she has moulded a relationship far beyond her charter.

I now have the strongest possible motive to ransack her home to obtain *proof* that the relationship is more than undercover subterfuge. For balance, I will also view the McMaster mansion.

Ashton Hill sits in silence. A slice of silver moon pierces the misty darkness and soaks into the slate roof. The driveway is bordered by the two felled trees, pushed aside to free the thoroughfare and facilitate further evidential examination. I note both trees had been sabotaged, thereby excluding any possibility that McMaster had succumbed to horrific storm damage. The neat slices and woodchip particles dotted around the stumps are prime evidence of chainsaw use.

Ribbons of police tape lay twisted and curled, and glass fragments sparkle like diamonds in a clique of gossip-mongering footballers' wives. I assume McMaster's car is now imprisoned within a police compound awaiting forensic analysis. It will yield no clues. A person so meticulous in their efforts to eliminate another takes great care to leave not one smidgen of evidence. Investigators will return at first light to scan the surrounds. They *will* locate the most seemingly inconsequential piece of incriminating evidence that *will* propel the investigation into full momentum.

Hoping to skip ahead of the police, I scratch around and walk the driveway's length, gravel crunching and crackling like breakfast cereal beneath my feet. I take in the property's awe-inspiring silhouetted presence. Sepia photos of the 1900s spring to mind: gardeners tending roses and clipping hedges into formal, geometric patterns bordered by strips of box hedge alongside weedless white-stoned paths; maids in ill-fitting shoes struggling with cane baskets of crisp laundry while others glow with perspiration in the huge scullery; and a footman preparing a hansom carriage for his lord. I imagine the imposing structure once being the main topic of the parish church's women's auxiliary. In a past life I might have been a historian, delving through archives, tracing property ownership of Lords and Earls, and of the Industrial Revolutionists who made their fortunes off the back of sheep, iron and steel fabrication, while exploiting the super-human efforts of lowly-paid child workers sweating out product from dark, noisy factories.

Back to the present, and reasoning from my own selfish perspective, the good thing with older properties is that no matter how well they're maintained and restored, they are comparatively easy to breach. I don't include those that boast huge steel cross-bars barricading doors like a fortress, and plunge bolts that sink deep into the earth or upwards into stone lintels. I refer to owners of the less structurally sound who believe that fitting two or three locks will double, or triple, their security. Wrong. Such over-security is effective only when activated from inside – it's when the doors are locked from the exterior that the property becomes most vulnerable. Their owners think because they're surrounded by acreage, no one will risk exposure trying to access the home. Wrong again.

Owners sympathetic to the period do not interfere with original fittings – to avoid compromising authenticity. So, they don't fit deadlocks or window locks. McMaster's back door proves my theory – secured only by a flimsy latch. I pull my knife from its ankle strap and probe between the door and the architrave. Seven seconds' later I'm inside, fighting the stench of stale tobacco.

I believe most mansion owners pretentious. The homes feature upwards of ten to twenty rooms, with only four or five seeing regular occupation. The remainder honour the owner's crowing lifestyle, buttressed by tax-deductible mortgages.

I dart into the first doorway. A study. Small enough to preserve the aroma of leather and furniture polish, but large enough to display a whisky collection, framed photos of police graduations and functions, and copies of media releases headlining McMaster for a succession of high-profile arrests. The yellowing pages are ten years' old. I train my torch's narrow beam to a neat Cherrywood desk. I rifle its drawers, three of each descending beneath one another at each end of the desk, and find departmental notebooks, personal stationery, stamps, and a small tablet computer. There is no laptop in the room so I assume there's one stashed elsewhere. Or might it now be a kaleidoscope of blacks and greys decorating the back seat of his car?

I take the tablet. It looks well-travelled; buffed edges scream trauma of slipping into and out of McMaster's multi-purpose briefcase. I switch it on. Password protected. Predictable. I don't have a lot of info on McMaster (although I do have means of obtaining it) so my attempts to login are futile. I suspect it might be his MET service number, which I will find on nearby documents. A flick through manila folders shatters my presumption.

I shamefully admit that some of my investigative skills parallel television criminology. That's why I look for a safe behind wall hangings, paintings and the framed certificates. It might also explain why I find nothing – McMaster doesn't watch the same programs.

But as the torch light waltzes from wall to wall, it settles on a window sill. I probe further, thinking that I've chanced upon a piece of shoddy restoration, but soon find that the whole sill, a huge block of granite or bluestone, is not fixed to the surrounding masonry. Why wouldn't a tradesman squeeze out a few beads of that silicone stuff we women are supposed to know nothing about? I tap the slab. A wooden thud replies. It is a brilliant piece of restoration – moulded fibreglass with a stone texture. Perhaps it's not *really* part of the restoration. I remove the sill, which I could not have done had it been genuine granite, and set it on the floor. After reeling to the musty pong of an old drainpipe, I throw in the torch beam. It spots a small strong-box. I reach into the cavity with the same tenacity I once employed when leaning over my neighbour's fence – as a six-year-old – to wrest tomatoes from their tall plants. The box is not locked. No need, I guess, when it is so well hidden. I remove two Berretta 92 series revolvers. Leave three boxes of ammunition. A smaller box, also unlocked, contains bundles of £20 and £50 notes. More than £20,000. I assume the hoard is not the constabulary's Christmas bonus.

Hugging the edge of the void, stand three tall Post Pack tubes of the type used for mailing poster prints, house plans and artists' canvasses. I open the first. Find a huge sheet of paper of similar size as that once used by butchers to wrap meat. As it unfurls, the plans of the manor flatten before me, each end kicking up like a baby's first kiss-curls. The second tube holds Land Registry documents, and an enlargement of the estate.

A series of cross-hatches forms a pattern near the rear boundary and extends into the adjacent land. On first sight, I consider it the work of an idle public servant doodling away an hour between morning tea and lunch breaks. Then I see a detailed 'legend' box at the foot of the page. I decipher the scale computations and symbols for gates, fences, trees to be retained, but stall at the cross hatch. It commands my attention, but disappoints me with the one word reference: 'reserve'. Reserve what? It certainly can't be a reserve as in public land – there is no designated right-of-way. More puzzling, the marking extends into the neighbour's land. Such notations would usually pertain only to the land described by the title.

I open the remaining tube. A translucent sheet provides a full topographic layover of the Ashton Hill property while another details measurements and cross-hatching of Blackshaw's Mill. This plan displays red dashes, inked across a line six metres parallel to the boundary, suggesting that McMaster might be, or has been, involved in one of Britain's most common disputes: property boundaries and fence lines.

Neighbourly friendships have been lost and destroyed over this phenomenon. As a police officer, I'd attended my share of quarrels of neighbours ranting about incorrectly sited fences. One complainant demanded a fence's removal and realignment; another claimed entitlement to a four-inch strip because the fence palings had been attached to the 'wrong' side of the frame; and another complained that a neighbour's hedge had spread so wide, it reduced her rear garden by 'two-feet-nine-inches'. Before I'd learnt to pass off these complaints as civil matters, I advised that particular neighbour to trim back the offending hedge. 'But then I could be charged with wilful damage,' replied the complainant.

Two weeks' later, my partner and I attended a dispute at a familiar address. This time it was the house next to the former complainant. It transpired that the neighbour had trimmed the hedge. The hedge died. I tried hard to conceal my embarrassment because it had been my naïve advice that caused the predicament. All I could do was take a hard-line stance by insisting the complaint remained a civil matter as no crime had been committed. 'Surely it's wilful or criminal damage?' the complainant contested. I would not debate the delicate legal distinction, so deflected the question: 'I'm sure your neighbour's intention was only to reduce its size, not kill it. It's a shared responsibility; perhaps you could have assisted with the trimming.'

'But that's her side!'

'My point exactly. You can't then complain that she's done something wrong.' At that juncture, we excused ourselves before becoming further embroiled in the trivial exercise of a neighbour's quest for one-upmanship.

I refocus, and wonder if a similar dispute had festered between these two property owners. Sure, I was drawing a long bow if I were to conclude that the felling of a tree directly onto a vehicle was part of a property dispute, but nothing can be discounted in the battle of cross-boundary war. I make a mental note to further examine the trees on my way out. Tomorrow will be too late – forensics will burrow through them like termites.

Before returning the items to McMaster's sill-safe, I probe inside the crevice in the event some remaining gems have evaded me. This might sound very 'Treasure Island' – but it is likely that a secret map or document has been expressly secured. It's a common trait of the paranoid. They see everyone as a threat: the postman; the census statistician; and the relations who believe they're entitled to a share of their bloodlines' wealth – yet those same people are reticent about sharing anything of their own. I've discovered secret bank accounts, wills, share scrips, Birth Certificates and pornography stashes taped beneath drawers, behind bookcases and in freezers. In one memorable instance a shelf had been hollowed out with a router and a £200,000 share certificate concealed before the shelf was restored with a veneer edge. The only reason I discovered this was because the shelf housed only a few books in an otherwise crammed bookcase.

Perseverance rewards me when I pull two books from the depths of the void: *Gold Production from Beginning to End* and *The Crown Lands Act 1702*. Why the frig, I wonder, would these be hidden instead of standing in the adjacent bookcase? My knowledge of statutes informs me that the *Crown Lands Act* governs the ownership and use of the Queen's land holdings, which, as most Britons know, comprise vast acreages set aside for fox hunting and exercising Corgis.

I flick through the gold production book and note the recent publication date. Hadn't British mining been wiped out in the 1980s – courtesy of Arthur Scargill some would say – whose 1984-5 miners' strike sealed the workers' fate? I learn about lode deposits (original gold formations) and placer deposits – fragmented remains of the original lode which have been separated by erosion, land movement or previous prospecting activities. I skim through tunnelling, gold separation, and refining. This is serious reading.

McMaster's obsession with mining stuns me. Nothing here suggests he has a financial interest in either North Sea oil exploration or overseas mineral deposits. And I don't see him as a weekend warrior lugging around a B&Q metal detector pinging the earth for Roman coins and gypsy treasures. I suddenly wonder whether his attack might have something to do with this interest. I replace the items and restore the false sill to its correct position.

Padding through other rooms reconfirms my impression of McMaster: slovenly and careless. The washing is stockpiled – both dishes and laundry – and telltale cobwebs crave a tickling from John Dyson's latest invention.

Rich beeswax draws me to the main reception room. It appears rarely used, reminding me of a 'best' room my parents cherished. 'Don't go in there Olivia, we might have visitors.' In my twelve years of living in that house, I saw guests on only three occasions, and that means, quite unequivocally, that the room was inhabited only three times.

This room is devoted to a cause. It enshrines McMaster's history like a buried time capsule; from schoolboy and sportsman to husband and father and police officer. A dozen photos of Phillip and his wife hang from the walls, and two gold-leaf framed portraits of a young daughter stand erect on each end of the mantelpiece. There is no evidence within the home of a wife and child – nor is there in many police officers' homes. The stress and hours become too much for the young couples, causing love and wedding vows to dissolve into the deepening well of crime and degenerating society. I'm one of few who proudly endorse the practice of remaining unmarried – but not necessarily unattached.

En route to a quiet exit, I pass another reception room,

or what might once have been a gallery or library. It oozes the gentlemen's clubs' décor I once experienced during an afternoon's spoiling by a senior police officer. A huge fireplace with a three-metre mantle of polished marble sits like a pulpit in a Gothic cathedral, and rich leather Chesterfields watch over period tables lazing on Brintons carpet. In the elliptic yellow of my torchlight's waning beam, a clock's luminous Roman numerals reflect fuzzy digits. The hourly divisions read not as II, III, IV, V, VI, VII; they diffuse a superimposed subliminal message. Although I shun any form of the occult and supernatural (I used to laugh at friends' tales of séances) as I study this timepiece, words leap from the numerals: bill, hill, mill, Jill, Gill, sill, quill and even more eerie, the clock's owner, Phil. I step back from this clock face of ills.

I retreat to an adjacent den which reconfirms McMaster's domestic habits of chaotic disarray. The bed is chaotic, sheets and duvet appear as abstract human entanglement, and a lipstick and eyeliner lay on the bedside table. Someone had fled the room, perhaps fearful of Mrs McMaster doing her utmost to spring surprise on her defiant husband.

Bedside tables provide many clues and bonuses to police and private investigators. I pick through the drawers. One side is empty, save for the characteristic stinging aroma of fresh pine. I taste varnish used to transform the £40 knocked-up setting into a £299 Edwardian reproduction befitting a Lord, rewarding retail copywriters with their industry association's 'Best use of Poetic Licence' award.

Its counterpart shocks. This guest room doubles as a love parlour. I guess McMaster's own bedroom is too personal and private to use for casual flings and nocturnal transgressions. On opening the drawer, I feel the same rush of nerves that felled me when I entered an adult DVD store – for official police business, of course. I ogle the variety of flavoured gels (and take a sniff for interest's sake), magazines, freaky condoms, a battery-powered cucumber, and a camera. I don't need a PI licence to query why one would have a camera in a guest room drawer. I power it on, and click through the digital frames. The first face to grace the screen is Gillian's – in a pose I choose to not describe.

Now I understand why Thornton commissioned me. Closer to my heart is the fact that Gillian has tainted my new profession. I consider taking the camera, but remove the SD memory card instead. Either way, McMaster will, hopefully during an amorous moment, realise that something is wrong.

I creep from the back door into darkness. *Bloody cigarettes.* A faint whiff of tobacco fouls the fresh rural air. I put it down to residual stench from the McMaster home.

XIX

ANGELO SLOUCHES AGAINST A TREE in his mother's garden, drawing on a cigarette. He winces with pain as fractured ribs protest against the pressure of deep inhalations. He fixes upon a flickering light in an upstairs window of Ashton Hill. Experience tells him it is a person wandering by torchlight from room to room. And he knows it isn't McMaster.

Despite Angelo's issues with his neighbour, he has to act – his mother's home could be next. He races across the paddock, pumping and flexing ready to meet any challenge. A creaking rear door forecasts an imminent exit, so he crouches against a wall. Darkness is also his enemy, for he is unable to identify the retreating figure. He shuffles a few paces. Prepares to rush the intruder to the ground. A shard of moonlight strikes the prowler's face. Angelo recognises the profile and wonders why the woman who'd assisted his mother is now slithering away from his neighbour's house.

He ditches plans to attack, clings to the wall, and allows her to continue through the night. Reporting the intrusion to McMaster could restore his favour. Just as the phrase 'knowledge is power' is professed by academia, so too is the cliché a bastion of the criminal element, and Angelo is its number one advocate. The reality of his proposal unnerves him: *Refer it to McMaster? The guy's supposed to be dead.* The alternative is unthinkable: *What if he's still alive?*

He darts back to his mother's house. 'I'm going now mama.

Have a good sleep.' As if asking for a cup of tea he follows with: 'By the way, mama, any word on how the neighbour is?'

'No. I know nothing. The ambulance takes him and that young lady who brings me home says she will let me know, but she's no come back.'

Angelo doesn't reply. Something else to play by ear at the appropriate time.

Maria ponders her son's attitude to the young lady and is disturbed to see her recently departed husband reappear through Angelo.

When faced with confusion over their offspring's direction in life, mothers across the world view a flickering newsreel of their child's journey to maturity. Maria has many happy memories of Angelo's childhood and his relationship with his brothers. Yes, he has been in trouble – just part of growing up, she defends. Today, he is as troubled as he had been in his teens. The short temper is indisputably inherited, but the fresh facade of fear and concern draws his face into a grim caricature of his former self – and of his father.

Perhaps the sorrow of his father's passing has finally hit. With the fire of denunciation ablaze, he might now regret having not resolved their differences when opportunities arose. Maria also wonders if the burden of handling the sale contract might have ignited his spirit.

XX

Minutes after midnight, I race home to check McMaster's family snaps. From my investigator's kit I pull out the superseded Fuji el-cheapo camera which I've permanently ejected from my weighty handbag. The introduction of efficient mobile phone cameras has converted me to a Samsung Galaxy. My downfall is failing to list the old Fuji on eBay.

I press the power button. A faded menu appears. I slot in McMaster's SD card. A bedroom scene springs to life – one I might enjoy as a participant, but not as a home viewer. I flick through the photos. Frame four bares Gillian accepting McMaster's animalistic advances. Talk about mixing business with pleasure! I ogle more frames of the motel room romp, clearly identified by a 'Premier' logo on a background 'Rules of House'. *Now* I have something.

Photo eleven is a steamy image – in more ways than one – of a contortionist's act in the shower, and frames twelve to fifteen depict a huge shed. The abrupt change of venue confounds me – I haven't a clue where it is or what it means. The next shots perplex me even further.

Abysmal lighting. No flash. I squint and scrunch as I decipher grainy images taken in a cave-like tunnel with chiselled walls. One shot aims down a shaft, capturing the depths of what appears to be a disused wishing well. A timber structure resembling tangled house framing supports the walls. I try to link this to the preceding intimate moments. Vivid imagination conjures a discipline dungeon where McMaster role plays with a tribe of fur-clad hunters and gatherers. I discount its relevance to a police investigation because of its inclusion within a series of *very* personal shots.

I flash back to the 1997 movie, *Dante's Peak.* I wasn't supposed to be watching TV; it was way past my bedtime. I snuggled up to mum, and, well, you know mums are a sucker for a bit of a cuddle. So I got to stay up late that night. Much of the movie was shot in a mine, and it is that setting I see in McMaster's photos. Nothing is suspiciously illegal, other than signs of a peculiar interest. I click to the next series of photos.

Two long-range shots portray photographic skills of an amateur trying to claim professional status with sub-standard equipment. I've done it myself when snapping a clear shot some 200 metres distant with a measly 4x zoom. Dead loss. But in this shot, I recognise him: Angelo on a bike. Appears to be a Harley, but I can't discount the possibility of it being one of those thumping V Twin Japanese impersonations. Another snap shows him applauding a mature marijuana crop. The next is an unposed pic of Maria Caruso beside her back door.

I've seen shots like these. They're not family snaps. If they were, they would not have been taken from a distance. Nor would they be for evidential purposes. For a start, no electronic time-stamp appears on the frames, and, as I've identified, they are within a collection of personal snaps. Conscious of McMaster's reputation, I think these are fuel for bribery. He could command immense power wielding the threat of exposing Angelo's marijuana crop. The photos are meant to threaten: *we know where your bike is and will steal it if you don't cooperate,* and the big one: *we know your mother – she wants a long life, doesn't she?* I hate to think that McMaster would sink so low, but resign myself to the possibility.

The next few show the interior and exterior of The Knight's Arms. These have been taken covertly. The shots are out of focus, but there is no mistaking Gillian at the bar. A pic of an executive-looking gentleman entering the pub arouses my interest. I've no idea how anyone could capture such a good close-up of the guy slipping an envelope into his jacket pocket. I have to assume the photos were taken by McMaster, possibly with a remote action. Given the location, and Gillian's inclusion, I make a second assumption that this string of shots was taken for 'insurance' – the envelope exchange being the focal point. It also becomes my focal point: what was in the envelope and to whom was it given?

I've spent enough time with the camera, so copy the card onto my computer. I write a quick statement detailing what I've seen and how I've come by the various items. It has no legal standing, but will supplement Thornton's enquiry.

As I list shots fifteen to eighteen – depicting the structural formwork – all comes clear. There must be a tie-in between the photos and the goodies I'd found concealed in the window sill.

The change of pace revitalises me. I check the remaining shots and pause over the last few. A young girl. Miss Average on a shopping expedition along the High Street. Could be his daughter or relation. But it's not, because the next snap of the girl strolling into Heavenly Spirits stitches it together. *Shit! Rose Hernandez.*

XXI

McMaster lies rigid, neck craned toward a television mounted high on a robotic arm. He flicks the remote through a sequence of channels: *bloody housewife television. Is there no sports channel?* Presses the power button and crunches the remote onto a bedside trolley. Finding nothing on TV is more traumatic than the broken leg and arm, dislocated shoulder, and two ruptured discs.

On being told he will be hospitalised for up to five days, McMaster objects with the predictable male psych: *what do you think I am? A pansy? I can walk out of here and return to work tomorrow.* Pain does not blunt McMaster's temperament; nor does the high dose of Valium jade his mind.

The 'accident'. He chastises himself for stopping at the felled tree: *I should have questioned the closed gate; should have seen the sawn trunk; should have realised that pines do not fall of their own accord; and I should have known that Main and Angelo would seek retribution.*

A nurse discusses family visits. Gloria McMaster is faintly inked on his suspect list. Whilst content to live on 'her side' of the home, the lure of life insurance and a healthy payout from the police pension fund would provide her an incentive to shed the matrimonial burden. For some, a simple, no-fault divorce carries no excitement. The aggrieved enjoy bouncing tales around the gossip table, clutching each sympathetic consolation: 'Oh you poor dear, you shouldn't have to put up with that'; 'Come and stay with me for a while – we'll put all this behind you'.

McMaster hands the nurse a slip of paper: Jeff Main. 0755 245 1314. The name shadows his wife's on his suspect list. Main, threatened with career-ending exposure to the Law Institute, has the number one motive at his fingertips: self-preservation.

McMaster wakes mid-morning on the following day with enemies duelling in his head. Fulfilling one of Nostradamus's unwritten predictions, one of those enemies enters the ward. En-route to an early court appearance, Main mutters the patronising: 'Hi. How are you Phil?'

McMaster casts a contemptuous glare. 'You know who's behind this?'

'Behind what? I see you're in a bad way. What happened?'

McMaster details the incident, voicing greater concern over the destruction of his prized trees than his injuries. He recounts a fuzzy memory of a young woman consoling him; his strained words to a paramedic who caused more pain through inserting the intravenous drip needle than he had suffered from the impact; and he replays the painful extrication of his shattered body from the crumpled wreck.

'And why would anyone want to see you hurt?' Main asks.

'I could give you a thousand reasons, right, but let's start with the topic of our previous discussions. That'd help, wouldn't it?'

Blood drains from Main's face. 'I followed your instructions to the letter. Mechanisms had been put in place to accelerate the transaction. I'm sure that'd have nothing to do with the painful spot you now find yourself in.'

'Bullshit. You speak to Jill?'

'Yes. And she confirmed acceptance.'

'She's reported back? Is there a result?'

Main looks at his watch as if to say: *What do you expect?* 'It's not yet twenty-four hours. I'm sure these things take some planning. Look Phil, I've had a complex case fall in my lap that requires undivided attention for the next three months. I have to release a few clients; I know this isn't the best time, but you could consider it an opportunity to source another practice.'

McMaster sees Main's backpedalling as more than cold feet – he sincerely believes that his compulsion to withdraw is clear admission of his involvement. 'What the fuck are you on about? If I wasn't incapacitated, I'd throttle you on the spot. You don't dictate terms. Weston know about this? I bet not. You can't just go picking and choosing your clients like you do with your swanky aftershaves: "Ooh, I've had enough of Gucci. I think I'll go a splash of Armani". Plus, as I'm sure you're aware, the Law Society would show great interest in a practitioner who plays one client against another.' He wheezes a lungful of sanitised air: 'Now what say we set a time for me to receive the fully executed documents so that when I'm out of here, and I expect to be within a few days, I can start planning my new property. And I'm over this for now so I thank you for your compassion and interest. I'll touch base with you soon.' He rolls over and feigns sleep.

Main withdraws and swears *he* will no longer yield to McMaster. He didn't get the chance to relay the mining information he'd unearthed. Twenty-four pages of obligations under the *Land Registration Act 2002, Land Registration Rules 2003*, and a host of information about 'Mines Royal' – administered by The Crown Estate. With McMaster now placing more emphasis on the property transaction than his rehabilitation, Main believes the vital information must be linked to the land purchase.

He steps into his Range Rover. Glares at the windscreen. McMaster's words bounce off: '*... the subject property may have a fortune lying beneath it. There's evidence of untapped natural resources on my land with the prospect of it extending into the adjacent property.* The prophecy rattles around his head like coins in a tumble dryer. He wonders if Blackshaw's Mill might be worth more to McMaster for its subterranean potential than its improvements above ground. And, his knowledge of McMaster's investment portfolios confirms two points: McMaster would not embark on a half-hearted mission; nor would he invest half a million pounds in a dream.

Main vows to learn more, but how? Professionally adept with archives and files, he is totally inept with field investigations.

Elasticised minutes and hours in a hospital bed affords patients time to reflect, and chart future hopes. Few people prepare for death. By the time they're in hospital, it's too late. McMaster is nonchalant about committing to a Last Will and Testament. He'd once applied to see a specialist, but cancelled after his wife and daughter vacated the new home within months of moving in. His wife's subsequent return failed to reignite his enthusiasm to restore the will-signing appointment *and* the marriage.

A doctor performing morning rounds shatters his reflections. Doctor Ramesh checks McMaster's pulse, enters 142 on the chart and murmurs: 'Nurse will advise you of discharge details. For the moment, you're fine.'

'For the moment?' McMaster's question chases Ramesh from the ward. *Bloody doctors. Won't commit – pass the buck to the poor nurses.* "For the moment" contaminates his mind.

McMaster had parroted the same spiel to the seriously injured: 'You'll be fine, it's only a small cut' (to an elderly road casualty whose leg was severed to the bone); and, 'It's missed the major arteries,' (speaking to a gunshot victim whose stomach seeped from two ·22 calibre bullet holes.) He is, therefore, cautious of Ramesh's dispensable consultation and chooses to 'get his house in order' as is the office euphemism.

He presses the nurses' station buzzer: 'I'm sorry. It might not be an emergency, but I need to call the police association to arrange my will.'

'I'm sure you're not going anywhere soon, Mr McMaster,' the nurse consoles. 'I'll arrange a phone, so long as you confine business to visiting hours.'

That same evening, Walton Bryant attends with a briefcase of documents. Salesmen forgo seats at the FA Cup final or a Royal Command performance just to clinch a sales opportunity. Such is the power of commissions. McMaster signs over his estate not to his estranged wife, Gloria, but to Gillian Trotter.

Walton advises against the decision, given that the McMasters are not divorced. He predicts lengthy legal battles if the legal wife is excluded in favour of a part-time lover.

Phillip McMaster is prepared. 'Gloria won't fight,' he replies. Whilst easily led on by the 'take-him-for-all-he's-worth' brigade, her over-abundant pride would yell: *Stuff Phillip. Let his floozy have her share. I hope she's happy with it.*

He does not know his wife as well as he should.

Walton leaves the ward, treasuring McMaster's signature

like a philatelist holding a Penny Black. He has the signature. And the commission.

Gloria McMaster shares women's sixth-sense about infidelity. She'd long ago joined the throng of sisters who coined the term 'PWS' (policeman's wife syndrome). Its symptoms are universal. Hours of agony sweated in the pressure cooker of wonder: what time will my husband arrive home? *Will* he come home? And then there's the second- and third-hand tales of locker room frolics with new WPCs; the need to stomach the 'something's just come up' excuse; and forgiving their husband's (often welcome) wilting passion.

When Phillip *is* at home, Gloria wears the strain of initiating or continuing a conversation unrelated to police matters. Her husband has become so one track that shop talk is his sole contribution to domestic communication. 'We'll enjoy a good break soon,' he says. Days later he cancels or reschedules, all in the name of the job. No attempt is ever made to rebook.

Not content to pander to his needs and demands after being discarded to meal-making and laundry duties, Gloria took over the remodelled wing of the home, preferring to carve her own life as an artist, rather than rely on friends' or council's emergency accommodation. With no interest in immediate divorce or financial settlement, she fully supports her husband's negotiations to buy Blackshaw's Mill, knowing full-well that one day she will take him to the cleaners.

During an afternoon's sporadic pleasantries, Gloria pours her husband a tumbler of whisky and purrs 'we need to talk.' Most divorcees will attest that when a marriage enters its final chapter, there is little left to discuss. Gloria allows the marriage to float across the seas like a message in a bottle that will never wash onto a distant shore. A bottle full of unrequited love, unspoken apologies, and silent wishes for a prosperous future, all left to fade away on a piece of rose bordered parchment. But she fights to delay the inevitable: 'We need time, Phil,' she says, 'to discover ourselves and contemplate the future.'

Phillip replies with trademark sarcasm: 'If we haven't discovered ourselves in twelve years of marriage, we're not likely to. And don't think sweet words will make us stronger. They might just encourage ants to eat us both.'

They continue to share the home, by address only, in their respective wings. Gloria is not blind to the goings-on in her husband's life; the flow of female visitors; his implausible offer to acquire the adjacent property, and his inexplicable interest in farming. She's queried the growing mountain of soil, the huge shed, and the hired excavator.

Phillip fobs her off. 'You don't want to go down there. Boy's toys,' he smiles. 'Going to make the place pay for itself at last.'

Since the day Eve trained her eyes over Adam, curiosity embedded itself in the genetic makeup of the female gender. Gloria McMaster has inherited an overabundance. During a tranquil afternoon while Phillip is at work, she ventures to the shed to satisfy that curiosity. As expected, the snooping mission leads to a locked door. Through a pinhole in the covered window, she sees rows of lights, channels of white troughs sprouting plant life, and an outdoor setting for six. *I've never even seen two people here, let alone six.* Gloria cannot fathom the purpose of the huge shed, but knowing Phillip as she does, she is sure there is more to his new-found interest in primary production. She resolves to find the side door key or bound into his botanic paradise with a tray of coffee and biscuits.

If the farm is going to pay for itself, she will ensure that she, too, will share its benefits.

XXII

Jill sits in her rental car, envelope open, the musty bouquet of aged banknotes transporting her to an exotic place. One thousand pounds. Little value in England. Riches in Bulgaria. 'Half now, the other half when you're done,' Jeff Main had whispered.

She's honed her trademark assertive manner in dealings with middlemen and their associates: talk hard and act fast. Strong character is the vertebrae of her industry – and it must reign at all costs. Lying in wait is a kingpin-elect anxious to snap in two any underling who threatens, or has the potential to threaten, her journey to the pinnacle of Gangland Management. If Jill were to display a trace of indecision or physical frailty, she could fall to second best – a ranking she will not accept. She respects the need to maintain those ideals, for Main is a man of two faces – and she trusts neither of them.

For three days, she's tailed Angelo from morning until night, logging lunchtime café visits, profiling habits, and recording weekend activities – all of which form a databank of intelligence from which she will later create a calamity.

Jill aspires to fulfil engagements with efficiency and neatness – and without complaint. She insists a textbook 'hit' should confuse investigators and remain for many years – perhaps forever – a crumpled page or incomplete document in the 'unsolved' file. Complex hits have, in the past, seen the deceased falling from a cliff face – no witnesses of course; a self-inflicted gunshot wound to the head – with the victim's own handgun; and conceivably her best handiwork, a job that earned her accolades throughout the underworld – death by electrocution.

That particular job sits in Jill's repertoire as her most callous, and one envied by colleagues around the world. She had been contracted by a disgruntled husband – the name's not important – whose young wife, Stacey, was involved in an affair with a male work colleague. Mimicking similarly adventurous women, Stacey created sound alibis of nights out with the girls: surprise lingerie parties and unforeseen overtime.

Her husband discerned that Stacey spent far too much time pampering herself in the bathroom if she were attending a 'boring party' of overpriced lingerie or perfume.

Jill agreed.

'Ideal setting for her downfall,' suggested the husband.

Jill didn't argue. Nothing safer, from her perspective, given that suspicions surrounding a spouse's death will first fall to the partner.

A self-anointed entrepreneur of human termination, Jill advocates originality and abhors copying others. She is not content to battle with drownings, for the ironic reason that the victim would suffer an agonising death. She is also not prepared to regurgitate common film and television crime scenes – tossing a toaster into the bath, for example – that have been done to the death. Jill always fulfils client's wishes with an extravagant plan. And this job was no exception. From a 10-metre electrical cord, she stripped back two metres of the external insulation, snipped the earth wire, and stripped back the two remaining wires to bare, shiny copper.

The next stage required talent recovery from her youth.

Basket weaving. Jill wove the two wires over and under a bath mat's platted fabric until they resembled the sidings of Paddington Railway Station. The material's density concealed the wires, but did not hinder their function. Content with her handiwork, she rolled up the mat, coiled the remaining six metres of flex, and stared at the clock. At that precise moment, Stacey's husband would be disabling the master circuit breaker on his electrical fuseboard. Jill hoped he'd not have the common sense to use gloves.

At the prearranged time, she attended Stacey's home where the excited, and soon to be widowed husband, snuck her into a spare-room wardrobe – conveniently adjacent to the bathroom – where she would hide until alerted by the hissing shower. The husband darted off to the local pub to drink down a watertight alibi.

After forty-five minutes of modelling a wardrobe of outfits, Stacey made final preparations for her evening dalliance. Footsteps pattered from bedroom to bathroom, transferring clothes, robe, makeup bag and other items the pretentious, over-adorned, philandering woman would wear to impress her beau. Silence took over until the shower spluttered and gushed – as did Jill's heartbeat.

She pulled the mat from her bag, crawled along the hallway, slithered beside the bathroom door and removed a damp shower mat. Stacey didn't have a clue what was going on as she lathered up and gurgled a Celine Dion hit from twenty years' earlier: *my heart will go on forever…*

Jill smiled: *I don't think so.*

Jill could have re-enacted the shower scene from Alfred Hitchcock's Psycho – but she had something better. She took her bespoke mat, slid it in front of the shower cubicle door, and then ran the extension lead to a hallway power point. Flicked on the switch. Instant 220-volt shower mat – no towel required.

After an agonising wait, the singing stopped, the water ceased, the shower screen slid open and Stacey stepped out. Buzz. Shriek. Buzz. Thump.

Jill crept to the bathroom door. Stacey lay lifeless, her white feet criss-crossed like a serve of toasted waffles. Jill reached back, and with gloved hand flicked off the power switch. Ripped out the plug. Rolled up the mat and replaced the original. And then slid out unnoticed.

A rehydrating lemon squash at the local, a subtle nod to a gentleman at the bar, and she was on her way.

Jill snaps back to the present. One thousand up front. Balance on completion. Angelo's exodus presents an interesting challenge because he is more alert than previous targets – save for his lapse at Blackshaw's Mill. He knows there is always someone bigger, and tougher, in the world of drugs, scams and illegal gambling. Occupational hazard. If you're crooked, there's always someone wanting your piece of the action, just waiting to undermine you. Jill has learned of McMaster's accumulated enemies, not only a consequence of ripping off colleagues but also because his aggressive temperament has alienated so many people. Jill figures *that* will provide a background for Angelo's demise. And since he hasn't taken heed of the first warning, the second will be an ultimatum.

The plan is simple. She'd once likened the task to writing a memoir-based novel: conceive an idea; write the draft; refine and adjust, and then sit back and critically analyse the plot. She applies the formula to Angelo's blueprint, starting with three ideas: a night-time bashing outside a club – that particular environment being one where everyone is blind and patrons daren't whisper a word about anything or anyone. Jill knows the drill: 'I don't take notice of who's who and who's not. Sorry.'

The second option carries a higher degree of risk, but is quick and easy: knock him from his beloved Harley on the motorway. A seventy-plus miles-per-hour motorcycle accident on a motorway would be horrific, more so should an eighteen-wheeler be gobbling his slipstream. If he didn't die, he'd surely get the message.

The third alternative has been successfully practised since Horace Smith and Daniel B.Wesson joined forces in 1852: shoot the bastard.

XXIII

Recent intelligence hastens my urgency to discover how deep Gillian Trotter is enmeshed with McMaster. It is an honour to be engaged by police to pursue a file. For that reason alone, I am incensed that Gillian seemingly sat by, watching the scene unfold in which her target was nearly crushed to death. In contrast, her compassion at the hospital leaves me at odds with her motives.

I now regret having not parked closer to her vehicle. I was narrow-minded: focusing on Trotter instead of the surrounds. Why didn't I question her presence? There was no silver Vauxhall sparkling in the distant parking bay, meaning that McMaster was not then at home.

If someone had targeted McMaster – and nothing convinces me otherwise – Gillian was close enough to identify the perpetrator. Her presence in the Knight's Arms empowered her with knowledge of exactly when McMaster wasn't home AND his most likely arrival time after leaving the pub. Accepting that, I added Gillian to my list of people from whom to squeeze information about McMaster's injuries. I don't see her as wholly responsible, but I sincerely believe she can push me toward whoever is. My gut feeling shouts either Main or Angelo. I haven't excluded Gloria McMaster, although she's buried at the bottom of the list – for one reason only. Heaven knows how many marriages have been annulled by the murder of, or by, a spouse, an aggrieved boyfriend, or a lover possessed of perfectly sane mind who flips at emotional rejection and turns to stalking. But I don't see Gloria McMaster as one who'll fell a forest to kill a termite. Least of all by her own hand.

When I trace back to the starting point, I arrive at two common denominators: the Knight's Arms and Phillip McMaster, with the meeting between McMaster and Main as the spark that detonated their tempers.

My advantage of police methodology sets me on a trail towards Angelo. There is no way I'll gain from McMaster or Main information that will implicate them in illegal activity. For that, I will need evidence more watertight than the National Marine Aquarium.

Angelo, although having exhibited an aggressive disposition towards me, might inadvertently let slip why someone would want rid of him. I must also consider that he might not even be aware of the arrangement. Perhaps I can tip him off. I fancy myself as a Good Samaritan – the angel of saving grace. Abandon that. Angelo would reject me on sight.

I see Blackshaw's Mill as a repository of family history; a place where I can flesh out detail from the trusting Maria Caruso. She'll remember my assisting her home, so I'm sure she'll not hold back when I offer to help her son.

I first attend the Knight's Arms to verify Gillian is on shift. She preens herself behind the bar, oblivious to my presence. I raise my hand in one of those sorry-I-can't-see-who-I'm-looking-for motions, retreat through the front door and rush to the rear car park. I locate Gillian's rusty, pale blue Fiat. Ideal undercover transport.

A trail of local youth mill about the parking lot, so I crane my head as if looking for my car, a legacy of shopping centre and hospital car mazes. I return to Gillian's vehicle, unscrew the front tyre valve cap, and soften the escaping hiss as my nail depresses the valve. The front tyre choice is not random. A driver can easily limp to a repair garage with a flat rear tyre. Try it with a front and you'll snap your forearms trying to steer the wretched thing.

Vandalism accomplished, I set off for Grosvenor Street in Cheltenham where I cruise a nearby street for a parking bay. I look to God, drop my head and fluke a spot adjacent to the access lane that services Gillian's and nearby properties. I grab my blue clipboard to imitate wanderers tasked to survey home owners or sell an electricity company's latest budget plan. I check the rear of the property; give the gate a passing nudge. Locked. I continue along the lane and wind back to Grosvenor Street. Stride up to the front door of number seventeen. No answer. Bonus.

I do not know Gillian's living arrangements. Flatmate or partner? Nup. I peg her as a one-night-stander – six nights a week. She'd thank the Lord for the Sabbath. I don't hang around the front door. Mr and Mrs Nosey Parker could be logging my movements; one snapping a redundant disposable camera, the other reading the Neighbourhood Watch Procedure Sheet.

I'd determined my entry point from the earlier visit, so I saunter along the lane, avoiding piles of refuse along the way. I leap over the gate in a clumsy Fosbury Flop, and fall into the chaotic back yard. Now I'm sure Gillian doesn't own the property. The state of disorganisation screams 'rental': clumps of weeds and thistles erupt from once pristine lawns. A furrowed path is defined by a marathon-running dog; unpruned geraniums swell into frenzied shrubs; a clothes line imitates the Leaning Tower of Pisa; rear fence panels crave paint and alignment; and a former outhouse bulges with garbage bags, flattened cardboard boxes and empty bottles.

The rear door is double-latched. A security conscious landlord wants no one breaking into *his* property. The kitchen window is of the modern variety that winds open and shut. It is tightly closed, its frame offering no means of exploitation. Give me the old sash window any day. The next window along the back wall is small. Exceedingly small. A toilet window. Thank goodness, because I'm used to finding toilet windows upstairs. The good thing with toilet windows is that most people leave them open a smidge – for obvious reasons. They consider the tiny window non-negotiable. Wrong. I will squeeze into an attaché case if need be. Erm, make that a suitcase.

This window is a modern wind in, wind out type. It offers no challenge to a skilled illegal entry practitioner like me. I pull on a pair of latex gloves, grab a wicker laundry basket from beneath the clothes line, place it under the window and step on. I distribute my weight at its outer edge – but not carefully enough. My 52 kilograms crumples the basket, and me, to the concrete footpath. Okay, not so skilled.

From the junk-filled outhouse I grab an old milk crate stamped 'Property of Eastern Dairies' and invert it under the window. Remove a pair of pliers from my back pocket. Yes, I am prepared. I've learnt that a good break and enter can be achieved with one of three implements: a knife; a credit card, which I use for releasing latches and unsnibbed deadlocks; and the pliers, which are multi-functional, but today will twist and snap the window's winding mechanism from its housing. And that's exactly what I do.

With the window free on its hinges, I pull myself up from the ledge and manoeuvre my way inside. The word 'manoeuvre' might infer elegance. To the contrary. I cannot rotate within the window frame so I drop, head first with arms outstretched, to the floor. It isn't a soft, dancer's tumble but a thumping crunch. I reassemble myself and peep into a small hallway. Clear. My heavy landing has not alerted anyone – nor is a dog with open jaws sizing me up.

The kitchen is not dissimilar to the rear yard. Total disarray, and reason for eviction. It reminds me of kitchens showcased on reality shows that portray landlords' losses from careless and disrespectful tenants. The sink overflows with unwashed plates and dishes; the servery is stacked with open food packets, jars and tins – some of which host partying flies and insects; McDonald's wrappers litter the benchtop and abseil to the waste tidy; the microwave boasts an allergy to Spray n' Wipe; and the floor looks like a fly-tipped section of country back road. All this from a woman who spends more time in front of a mirror than she does in charge of a bottle of Cillit Bang.

I perform the mandatory rummage through kitchen drawers and cupboards, not really expecting to find anything, but mindful that I'd once had a memory stick stolen from my own utility drawer. At that time, wise to the merit of multiple backups, I wasn't overly concerned about the missing files. What did irk me was the fact that *I'd* been outwitted by a crook. Anyway, the kitchen cupboards are comparatively clean – and under stocked. The woman obviously lives on takeaway. I continue to a small lounge room. It also displays convenience living: scattered magazines and empty Diet Coke cans, a throw rug that validates its description by having been sloppily 'thrown' over a couch, a small television with inbuilt DVD, and a table on which stands a computer keyboard, matt black speakers, wireless mouse and other hi-tech paraphernalia. But there is no computer. The set-up mirrors a method I'd once used when, to hasten my typing speed, I'd plugged in a *proper* keyboard to my laptop.

I now face a real predicament. Several USB memory sticks of various colours, together with a portable hard drive, sit on the table for my taking. I grab the sticks and drop them into my bag.

Stupid bitch, I chastise. Ridiculous move. I plunge into the bag, retrieve the tiny plastic stubs and restore them to the table. If I take them now, Gillian will realise that whoever had broken in had entered with a specific purpose. She would then beef up security, making it difficult, although not impossible, to regain entry.

On the other hand, I could abort today's mission, consider it research, and return better equipped with my small tablet into which I could transfer all the goodies lying around the desk. I elect to continue my exploration. A concertina folder contains wads of services' bills, credit card statements, extended warranties for a toaster and kettle – which I consider superfluous because the toaster is unused – and a few pages of notes, doodles and hieroglyphics. I pay little heed to the papers until the word 'Knight's Arms' jumps from a page.

I check the document and read a summary of Jack Thornton's instructions. I am not surprised – I already know Trotter's role is to report on McMaster's activities. But what does surprise me is the detail she's acquired: his address (which *I'd* been told was out-of-bounds) and phone numbers and associates names, most of which mean nothing to me. Nonetheless, I copy them onto a scrap of paper: Angelo. Main. Hernandez. *That's some serious tailing.* The name 'Hernandez' grabs me. Surely it can't be. Not Rose. The distinct possibility of her being under

Trotter's nose means I have another loose end to seal. I then flick over a file tab headed 'Worcester General Hospital'. Inside are McMaster's phone and ward numbers.

I proceed to the bedroom and bathroom and find nothing of interest. I slump on to Gillian's toilet and do my business. Crane my neck to the window. *Shit.* By twisting off the winding mechanism I'd shattered a small section of window frame. I climb onto the toilet bowl, clamp my pliers onto the winder and try to return the winder to its former shape. Fat chance. I push the mounting back into the frame. It looks original. Save for the splintered timber.

I've previously exalted my ability to think on my feet: when the going gets tough… I race back to the kitchen. Scan the cupboards, again. Remove a bottle of soy sauce and a jar of peanut butter. The peanut butter resembles a rocky chasm of the Grand Canyon. But I'm not here to eat. I take a dirty teaspoon from the sink, scoop out a half spoon of peanut butter, add a few drops of soy and stir it into a smooth brown paste. Thankfully, the peanut butter is of the smooth variety. Smells like crap, and looks like it too. I race back to the toilet, take a dollop of the goo and press it into the splintered wood. The best wood putty ever seen. As added security, I rip off a couple of sheets of toilet paper, fold them into a small square and wedge the wad between the window and frame to secure the window in its original position.

I find the rear door and study the night latch. I unsnib the old Yale, open the door and slide out. I clamber over the rear gate and dance back to my car knowing that next time will be heck of a lot easier.

The real work starts on return to my office. I launch Google and type in Main. Bloody hell. Pages and pages of businesses, main men, *Main Course* by the Bee Gees, Main Street Auto Wreckers, and thousands upon thousands of people named 'Main'. With no first name it is a futile exercise. The same for 'Angelo', which could be either a given name or surname.

Hernandez is a different story. There are no fewer than fifty names listed under the cross-section of businesses and the Hispanic community. I play my gut instinct and scroll direct to blogger Rose Hernandez, whose activities comprise condensed drivel over pages of worthless comment and information. I wonder why she invests in seemingly useless trivialities. And then I am glad she does.

Everything happens at once when I'm on a computer. My objective is to unmask the names Gillian had collected. With Main and Angelo, I've struck out, so I hang my hopes on the Hernandez girl having posted another clue. Whilst her unfortunate harassment by a police member distresses me, I'm still perplexed as to the reason her photo was on McMaster's camera. Nothing fits. I can't fathom how, or why, Gillian has Rose's name – unless she is the subject of another theft enquiry, or, heaven forbid, an accessory to McMaster's rorts. Hernandez's cries of helplessness are shaping up to be a case of the boy crying wolf. With that filling my mind it is only by chance I notice the flashing email icon. I open the 'Urgent' message: 'Please phone me. Thorns.' I smile at the irony of an important matter being softened by the Superintendent's nickname.

'At your service,' I smile into the phone.

'Olivia. We have a situation. You up to speed on what's been happening?'

My smile shrinks. 'Yeah. So much that I haven't been able

to get back to you.' I press his silence against my ear: Thornton wondering whether I'm on the level.

'We've got to get together. Today. How about lunch at an out-of-the-way café, say Pierre's Pastries in Cheltenham?'

'Yeah. I know it. One o'clock?'

'Twelve.'

'*Shit.* A girl's got to get ready. Make herself look appealing.'

'You're already appealing, Olivia. This isn't a date. It's a crisis. Twelve.'

I suspend my research and jump in the shower.

XXIV

Main sits at his desk, cold coffee at his side. Studies the contracts. Diverts his attention from the conflicting offers to the cross-hatched scale plan at the base of the document. *It must be coal.* Coal had been mined in Britain's most remote, and most unlikely, regions. Main's experience in land transfers constrained by covenants is limited, but he does recognise a familiar theme. Where a property sits atop or alongside mines or pits, the land is considered unstable and subject to cave-in. For that reason, title documents annotate the encumbrance in a variety of ways: 'no building envelope'; 'do not improve'; and 'do not plough' being three means of alerting prospective purchasers to the fact that the property might be subject to subsidence or similar catastrophic upheaval.

Main considers his position. Having been advised that McMaster's land comprises 'riches', he strives to find out exactly what his client is withholding. With McMaster in hospital, he can further the enquiry. The earlier boundary discrepancy legitimises an on-site query. Gloria McMaster should offer no resistance. Some enquiries return more fruitful information from spouses and partners than they do from the actual client.

'Jeff Main, Mrs McMaster. I'm sorry to hear about your husband. I saw him earlier today, and it's on his instructions that I must verify measurements for your purchase.'

'It's Gloria. And it's not my purchase. I don't know what

he's up to. Look at the monstrosity he's got there; noise all hours of the night. The only time I've had a moment's peace is since he's been in hospital. Never tells me what's going on and I really don't care. What measurements do you need?'

'These "do not plough" areas marked on the plan. I'll recommend insuring against any damage or injury that might occur within that defined area.'

Gloria looks unfazed. 'Doesn't worry me. I won't be out there. He's built that bloody shed over most of it. Can't you tell?'

'I was hoping you'd allow me to check inside – at the ground conditions.'

'Can't be too much ground in there. Carted it all out with the tractor. Bloody unsightly mess he's left down the back. Got our own bleedin' pyramid. Anyway, nothing in there apart from a few plants. I'll let you in. For goodness sake don't tell him you've been in there. I'm not supposed to have this key. Bastard tried to pull the wool over my eyes and tell me nothing's in there, but I've got his measure. Have done for years. Snaffled it out of his study and got one cut, didn't I. Need to keep tabs on his little ventures. You don't know my Mac, and you probably wouldn't want to.'

Don't be so sure, lady.

Gloria presses the side door key into Main's hand. 'Take your time. You don't need me. Just tap on the door when you've finished.'

Main grins at the ease with which he's obtained the passport to McMaster's emergent riches. He'd expected an abrupt: 'You'll have to wait until my husband's home.' He bounds down to the shed. Enters like a cinematographer capturing a 360-degree panoramic mural. After starting his career in small offices, and living the past four years in a two-bedroom flat, the enormity of the shed strikes him – as does the small tractor, a roof-truss mounted jib with block and tackle, and sundry piles of earth scattered about the ground. In a rear corner, rows of white troughs sprout plant life. Above them, wide-rimmed light shades hang like Asian farmers' straw hats. He recognises the marijuana – he's defended clients for cultivating that very product. He samples a strawberry. Walks to the centre where a plastic outdoor setting looks out of place, retailer's stickers still glued to the back of the chairs. He sits, and takes in the surroundings. The unmistakable hollow echo, like the thump from his bathroom floorboards, rumble in his ear. He lifts the corner of the plywood sheet. Darkness. Looks at the soil piles. No hint of coal. He laughs. *Old Mac's flogging a dead horse.*

He ambles to a small mound of sparkling flecks. *If McMaster's stumbled on gold deposits, is it no wonder he wants the adjacent property. 'At all costs,' he'd instructed. He's been holding out while I'm doing all the dirty work and behind-the-scenes research for a scale fee and an envelope of cash under the table. We'll see about that.*

He takes a few grains of the sparkling ore and folds it into a page ripped from his notebook. Takes another look under the plywood and studies the formwork bracing. It all makes sense. Looks to the jib and dangling chain and a bucket lying alongside one of the piles. Reflects on Gloria's words… *nothing in there apart from a few plants.*

So he's holding out on his wife, too. Can't say I blame him. He runs figures through his mind: the cost of a new apartment in Canary Wharf; his own practice on a lower floor; a Mercedes AMG…

He replaces the plywood cover, leaves the shed, locks the

door, climbs into his car, and sails out of the driveway toward a new life.

Main acts on impatience with characteristic sensibility. He pulls to the side of the road, delves into his pocket for his mobile, swipes 'internet', and Googles Gold Guild, the obvious starting point for preliminary enquiries about the commodity's quality and price. Saves the number into his directory. Makes an appointment. Considers it research for a client. He'll bill McMaster for the pleasure. *At all costs.*

He drives straight to Frederick Street in Birmingham, a nest of silversmiths, gem traders and diamond merchants. 'The Gold Guild' shines in gold leaf on double doors protected by a bulky black bullion-looking guard. 'Mr Lowenstein's expecting me.'

The doorman points him inside.

'Jeffrey Main.' (He formalises his given name only in situations requiring elevated status.) 'I'm representing a client with a potential high-yield mine. I'd be obliged if you would assess and value this sample.' Main removes the folded notepaper and tips its contents into a stainless steel tray.

'Your client will hardly get rich on that.'

'This is a sample. I'm hardly going to cart 'round 32 ounce nuggets, am I?' replies Main, compromising his professionalism with sarcasm.

'Leave it with me. And your card. One of my staff will contact you.'

XXV

The venue is an ostentatious Parisienne sidewalk café boasting a red and white chequered frontage with bold blue French windows. The two 'P's of the business name, artistically Photoshopped from two Eiffel Towers, soar above the front windows. Inside, the theme continues: red and white chequered tablecloths, blue placemats, an enormous chalkboard menu boasting croissants and baguettes, French toast, French onion soup and French vanilla slices. I spot a young couple French kissing. Assorted letters cover their table. Not French. I am Frenched out before I even sit. The theme ends when I hear the proprietor – presumably Pierre – speak English without a hint of French accent.

Thornton walks directly to the police table, so named because of its location in the back corner. Like a true gentleman, he withdraws me a seat.

I fold into a nervous posture and glance at the menu. Thornton studies me instead of the fare. I select Chicken Parmigiana, with a cappuccino up front. Thornton nods a Superglued smile to a waitress and doubles the order.

'Well, Olivia. How's that report? I thought you'd have got back to me by now.'

I stall, still not able to call him Jack. Most people who contract my services do so on a casual-cum-business relationship. This is different. I preserve formalities: 'Sir, I've been flat out from location to location. After I phoned you yesterday, I headed straight to Worcester General to find out Mac's condition. Er, I'll give you a quick rundown and later formalise it in writing.

'I was working on Trotter, tailing her. We'd pulled up in a lay-by 100 metres south of McMaster's home, Ashton Hill—'

'Yes, yes. I know where he lives.'

I hate being cut short, so hasten the pace: 'Sorry. Obviously, I didn't know what she was up to. While trying to fathom her reason for being there, I heard a crack, which I thought was thunder until I recognised it as splitting timber. A loud thud followed. Some of the next events are blurred but I'll correct the chronology on paper. Gillian withdrew from her car and looked along the lay-by toward a white van – which meant nothing to me at the time – before racing across the road and glaring at McMaster's home.

'Only after she was clear, did I too dash across the road to monitor her movements. I saw a tree lying over Mac's car. Gillian spoke to Mac, but I don't know if he replied or was even coherent; she made a call from her mobile, and shortly after conversed with a woman I later identified as McMaster's neighbour, Mrs Maria Caruso.

'At that stage I raced back to my car to phone you. Your phone was engaged. Anyway, while I was waiting, I spotted a white glove on the ground nearby where the white van had been parked.' I remove the Glad Bag from my handbag and pass it across the table. 'It's bloody whiffy, but you'll get good DNA. The van's registered keeper is Ray's Rentals. Plate number KH07 WMX. We should get a positive ID from the glove or the van. Doesn't mean the van's got anything to do with it, but the driver should be regarded as a person of interest, if only for his presence.'

Thornton glares: 'Yes, Olivia. I think I know the way it works.'

My cheeks flush. 'Sorry. Got carried away. After I phoned you I headed back to the scene and accompanied Mrs Caruso to her home. That's where I had the unfortunate displeasure of meeting her delightful son, Angelo – more on him later.

'There's multiple issues here. McMaster has tentacles wrapped around the whole country.'

I pull out the second Glad Bag. 'You'll find this to be medium to high grade marijuana. I've taken it from a girl who claims Mac's asked her to sell it.' I push over a brief report of the Hernandez events. 'I'll elaborate later. He's definitely collecting enemies. Do you want me to keep on this while he's in hospital?'

'Yes. You might learn more while he's laid up. You might also probe further into his association with Trotter. If there's more to that than professionalism, heads are going to fly.'

I am relieved to have his confidence. 'I'm actually pursuing that right now. Would be premature to discuss too much, but I'll soon have goodies that I'll share in person. Initially at least.'

'You've got concerns?'

'As I say, early days. Best to not speculate on this one.'

'Fair enough. Appreciate your honesty. Another coffee?'

'Yes thanks. They make a good vanilla slice here.'

Thornton takes the hint and orders two cappuccinos and two vanilla slices. We ease into informal banter: life after the constabulary; my old mentor DI Stafford, and then his surprise revelation that the local council is pursuing an employee by the name of Stonebridge for unauthorised dealings with Phillip McMaster.

Confused over the week's events, I leave the patisserie and

ruminate over having sat in my car while a former colleague drove into a death trap.

I rewind to Thornton's original request: *'The situation is, Olivia, we have an officer, an inspector at that, who might be compromising the ethics of the constabulary... There is a loose cannon somewhere in the office.'*

Taking into account the limited information I've acquired, I conclude that something of greater magnitude is unravelling. It would take much more than a copper's underhanded shenanigans to incite someone to kill him. I prioritise doing over Gillian's home. This time I'll be properly equipped.

* * *

'Olivia. Albert Lowenstein. You're going to love this. I've just had another guy come in to request a gold sample appraisal. Wants quality *and* price, which is interesting, because most amateurs are after quick cash. How's this? He's a Worcester-based solicitor. Jeffrey Main. I shouldn't put two and two together, but as you know, I've already got a sample from one of my Worcester cohorts and now here's another. That'd be like Halley's Comet reappearing during its 76-year cycle. But here's the crunch: both samples are of the same composition.'

'So why call me?'

'Because when a solicitor peddles the same merchandise as a street con and that merchandise ties in McMaster, warning flags flap. I don't care what you do; I'm being a good, upstanding citizen reporting an activity I believe is contrary to public interest.'

Bloody hell. Old Alby's after a spot in the Queen's birthday honours list. 'Okay, leave it with me. I'll give you a call. This could be too big for me – but you have my word you'll share in the final glory.'

This puts McMaster on a new stage. I have no reason to doubt Lowenstein; I've seen McMaster's stash of mining books and related paraphernalia. What disturbs me is that my charter is to report on Gillian. And then I wonder. Is she part of this? I wallow in indecision: a loose end dangling from a cable of severed nerves twitching about after a workplace amputation. No purpose, and no hope of recovery without professional help.

Forcing conclusions has countless drawbacks. Losing focus on the main objective is one. Maybe I should redefine *my* objectives. Perhaps I still think like a copper instead of a private investigator. I can no longer introduce myself as Detective Sergeant Olivia Watts, and expect an instant confession or privileged information. No. The rules have changed. Now, when I introduce myself as Olivia Watts, private investigator, I'm snubbed like a satellite TV salesperson. Is it no wonder I conduct business under the radar?

I must complete my current priority, and that is to extract as much info as possible from Gillian's flat. With McMaster in hospital, I expect Gillian to be glued to his bedside instead of pulling Guinness at the Knight's Arms. Minutes before the 2.00 p.m. visitors' exodus, I drift along the corridor past McMaster's ward. Sure enough, there she is, sipping orange juice, affably chatting to the patient. The question of the year resurfaces: *Why has she conjoined herself to McMaster?*

I contemplate the conundrum on my way to Grosvenor Street. I dump my car and stride to Gillian's front door like a meter reader hustling to complete his shift. Knock twice. No answer. A bright mid-winter sun warms me as I trek along the rear lane to the familiar gate. I climb into Gillian's backyard. Having prepared my mode of entry, I grab the milk crate from the outhouse, place it beneath the toilet window, step up and pull open the window. The wad of toilet paper falls from the frame, followed by a glob of peanut butter and soy.

I haul myself through the portal and replicate my previous landing: painful and noisy. After brushing off dust and pubic hairs, I head to the lounge room where the items on the table appear undisturbed. Not so. The keyboard has been moved. I presume information has been updated and saved on portable storage devices.

I remove my iPad from my jacket, pick up the closest USB memory stick, push it into my Lightning connector and click through sources until two folders flash onto the screen: family history and personal correspondence. I flick through both to make sure no documents are hidden within snaps of granny celebrating her ninetieth birthday.

The second USB is more promising. The first folder, 'Current', lists Word documents logging times and attendances at both the Knight's Arms and McMaster's property, cross-referenced to time sheets and invoices. I download the lot into my iPad. Another folder marked 'Legal' holds files relating to Craggill, Weston and Rubenstein, which means nothing – until I see mention of a meeting between McMaster and J. Main. *Aah, that's the 'Main' I found in her handwritten notes.* Download that also.

Another folder, 'H' details observations of McMaster at the Heavenly Spirits bottle shop. *Holy shit! Trotter's known about this all along and she just stood by?*

McMaster is not *my* concern, but I begin to find – as I do in most investigations – that rarely is a crime solved by one or two pieces of evidence linking the perpetrator. An overlap invariably blurs other findings. I copy the 'H' folder.

I click open the remaining folder: 'Mac'. At first glance it appears a duplicate because 'Mac' was prominent in the 'Legal' folder. But this collection of documents is a mixed bag; some clearly from police command – in particular, his service history and arrest record – which I'll later find interesting, and others of a personal nature: records of bank and financial transactions and half-a-dozen Excel spreadsheets displaying assets and liabilities. There is too much sensitive detail to have been obtained by a single investigator – the material is an authentic reproduction from financial institutions and police administration archives. I am sure big money has passed under one or two tables to get the data, otherwise 'information sharing' has taken a mammoth illegal step forward.

I download the 'Mac' file and am about to plug in the portable hard drive when I hear the front door unlatch. *Shit.* I am two rooms from disaster. I plunge the data cable down the front of my top, grab hold of my iPad and look to the window. Pointless. There is no time to open it and escape. That leaves two choices: I can prop behind the lounge room door, or seek refuge behind a settee backed up against the wall. Either way, my options aren't good. I choose the settee, knowing that I'll at least be comfortable.

I've only just stretched out when I actually *feel* footsteps pound along the hallway to the rear of the house. There is no way I'll chance my retreat on the presumption that she won't return to the lounge room. That is a welcome instance of intuition – women's of course – because moments later the footsteps creak into the lounge room. From under the couch I see steel-capped work boots, small enough to confirm their being worn by a woman. I can't risk twisting my head beyond the sofa's armrest, for obvious reasons. I confirm Gillian's presence after inhaling a whiff of cheap perfume. Women of class will support me on this: budget perfumes have a decidedly 'sickly' scent. We know perfume is a concoction of chemicals complementing a base essential oil. Budget scents however, comprise only two to six percent perfume concentrate, with the remainder, I reckon, made up of water and saccharin and similar elements to hoodwink the purchaser into believing their fragrance replicates those of Chanel, Dior, and others. In reality, they don't cut it.

And then I gasp a whiff of something else. Dog. *Fuck me.* Sorry. I'm not usually so crass. This mangy spaniel-looking cross-breed pokes its wet snout around the back of the settee and right into my face. It just stays there like one of those stupid Irish or English Setters that identify their prey and stand frozen on the spot like a young child catching his first glimpse of a person suffering elephantiasis.

I extend my hand, hoping my own unthreatening scent might pacify Woofy or whatever its name is. It sniffs. And growls. But doesn't bark.

Again, I offer my hand. And now it barks.

'Calm down, Benjamin. I know you're hungry.' Gillian's melodious voice.

I force myself to not snigger. 'Benjamin'? *Whatever.* I wish for dear Benjamin to pad off to the kitchen.

But Benjamin doesn't move. He growls. And barks some more.

'Come on boy. What is it?' Gillian's sing-song voice irritates me. She must think of Benjamin as a two-year-old child.

Bloody hell. I am about to be sprung. Gillian's footsteps

approach. I have is the element of surprise, but Benjamin has compromised even that.

Here goes. I safeguard the iPad inside my top and zip up my jacket for added insurance. With both hands I grab the frame beneath the couch and spring up like a Jack-in-the-box, hoisting the couch with me. It rises and rotates through the air like an Olympic gymnast tumbling across the competition mat.

She screams – in surprise rather than fright – and Benjamin goes berserk. To avoid the flying settee Gillian steps back, but not quick enough. The couch crashes into her midriff, the impact propelling her rearward into the table upon which the computer equipment sits. She buckles to the floor.

I rush to the doorway, Benjamin snapping at my ankle. He clamps onto my jeans' hem, causing me to shoot out a vigorous kick. The dog is wise, and retreats before I connect. That affords me time to bound out of the lounge and into the hallway. Bright light filters through the front door's leadlight panes. Heaven beckons me. What I don't see, or remember, is a hall runner – a ridiculous piece of carpet barely three feet wide; a sort of red carpet for poor VIPs (Very Insignificant People) or a budget means of dressing up a home for those who can't afford *real* wall-to-wall carpet.

I step onto the runner and flounder like a person without skates walking across an ice rink. I crash to the ground, and right on cue, bloody Benjamin barks, pounces and jumps all over me.

'Bitch.' The word resonates from the other room.

I don't need a PIs licence to know Gillian refers to me and not the dog. I jump up, gently kick Benjamin ('gently' meaning that no animals were injured during my escape) and start toward the doorway. The next moment I'm felled by a rugby tackle that sends me crashing to the floor – this time with my assailant landing on top of me. And it isn't Benjamin. Gillian's tackle would earn her a report in a World Cup match. She holds me around the waist while I heave for breath. I don't care too much for myself, but I do fear for my iPad. If I lose the information I've so carefully extracted, the whole exercise will be wasted, and I'll be bruised and battered for nothing.

Gillian is of substantial size. Without conveying discourtesy, I comprehend why she's been coined 'The Pig' by Thornton – and it has nothing to do with trotters. But, as any boxer or martial arts exponent will attest, 'big' does not a winner make.

I have marginal martial arts experience – snubbed because I can't apply myself to anything for longer than six months. I know I have to rely on the favoured 'attack is the best form of defence' strategy. With Gillian's arms wrapped around my waist (the first time I've been held in months) I sense she'll have difficulty removing them because our combined weight of 150 kilograms pins them to the floor. That places me in the fortunate, and advantageous, position of having my arms free.

In my predicament, there are few things a slight woman can achieve with free hands. I could elbow her in the stomach. She might wince, but her body mass would insulate her from *real* pain. I could punch her in the head, but my aim would have to be so well placed to cause *real* damage. I'd probably break my knuckles. Or, I could execute a precision poke to the larynx where I'd be assured of inflicting immediate discomfort. I twist my neck to the left. And then I do it. I fold my thumb under four fingers to form a prong of muscle and bone. I rotate my wrist.

Gillian diverts her attention to silence the dog.

Benjamin is the least of her problems. She doesn't see my arm spring from the floor. Doesn't see my pointed fingers plunge into her neck. And I mean *into*. I feel flesh up to my second knuckle. My finger nails, not long but daintily manicured, pierce her bacon. Blood spurts. Instant tracheotomy. Her torso rises as if pushed up by the San Andreas Fault. She clutches her neck. I push up and heave sideways, tipping her to the floor. Benjamin is frenetic. *Stuff the dog.* Gillian partially recovers and rises from the floor. I kick her in the stomach with enough force to wind her and send her crumpling back to the floor. (I'm ashamed of that because it's far from flattering to kick another woman – especially in the stomach. This was my only means of 'disabling the threat' as we'd learnt in the constabulary.)

I race to the front door and pause on the step – for the benefit of the neighbours – as if I'm waving goodbye to a most cordial afternoon. I hasten along to the next street and sprint to my car. I don my huge 'bug eye' sunglasses and drive off, cruising slowly past Grosvenor Street to see Gillian standing on the pavement, head swivelling.

I remove the iPad. The screen is shattered. A job for Hamilton.

XXVI

Gillian bristles with anger. Looks right and left along Grosvenor Street. Returns to the bathroom. Props in front of the mirror. Dabs blood from her throat.

She rights the upturned couch and restores the lounge room. In the bedroom, a drawer of jewellery and family mementos are untouched. *The intruder had nothing in her hands when she sprung from behind the couch.* And *that* presents a problem. Gillian dwells on the question of what *had* attracted the intruder to her home: *I've nothing worth stealing.* With no prospect of valuables being the target, she considers an alternative motive: *I've got something somebody wants?*

She hobbles to the kitchen. Benjamin curls in a corner, content, as if *he's* had an enjoyable afternoon. Gillian returns to the lounge room with a cup of double-strength black coffee. Five sugars mask the sharp aroma. She pushes aside the assorted USBs and computer peripherals, plugs in her laptop, opens the 'Current' file, and types a report of the break-in. A strict believer in regular back-ups, she grabs the red memory stick – which duplicates 'Current' – and presses it into the slot. A menu flashes onto the screen. Several files flag access within the past hour.

She scrolls through menus of the accompanying memory sticks and time stamps of recent activity. *So who's checking on me?* Two names hover: Thornton. McMaster. *Thornton making sure I'm on the level. That'd be his form – check on the outsider, make sure she's legit. Surely Mac wouldn't have arranged this? He's in bloody hospital.* Then it hits her. *That's what's driving this. He thinks I've got something to do with the accident.*

A phone screeches. She snatches it from the bench: 'Hello.'

'Hi. I'm home. Change of plans. Got discharged. What you up to?'

'I only left you two hours ago! You said you'd be out next week. What happened?'

'Bed shortage. They say I'll be okay. Gonna treat me as an outpatient. Just bandage redressing, well, except for this piece of plastic shit around my waist, and, um, the plaster around my leg. So, how are you, my sweet? Think you'll be up to having a visitor?'

'Strange you mention that. Already had one. Someone in my flat when I got home, hiding behind the couch. Friggin' bitch – yeah, it was a fuckin' woman. Think I beat her to the punch. Didn't take anything, though.'

'Don't worry. Local scum looking for cash. You wanna know about break-ins? Barely one in twenty are solved – and then only after someone's recognised their prized DVD player or circular saw in a pawn shop. You'd best beef up your security. You home this evening?'

'Yes. What about your wife?'

'Can't bring her. Sorry.'

'Smart arse. Phone me after six. I'm going to tidy up here. And be prepared. I'll have important news for you.'

'I hope that's not all you got.' McMaster's grin trickles through the phone.

Gillian dawdles to the toilet. *Fuckin' bitch.* Dangling from the wall glares a piece of window frame and the damaged winder.

She phones Thornton. 'I think we're onto something. Mac's out of hospital and he's asked me over. No idea what for – have to phone back after six.' She stifles a small chuckle. 'Not a problem for me. Must've played the flirt to perfection.'

'I'm paying you for information. How you get it is your own business.' Thornton bangs down the phone.

He picks it up just as quick. Jabs a pre-dial: 'Olivia. Glad you're there. The Pig's had a call from Mac. Apparently, he's been released and wants to see her. Something in her voice that smacks of arse covering. She suspects something's going on, but I trust her like—'

'Okay. I'm prepared. Can head over now. You know I might be restricted. It's a difficult location to eavesdrop without being seen, especially during daylight.'

'Might be premature for a full-on obbo. Nothing's happening until after six, so don't drop everything. Just tread carefully, Liv. You have my total support. Call me when you've got something.'

Liv. Why do they keep calling me that?

XXVII

At 2:30 a.m. creaking timber stirs Angelo from his sleep. He fluffs his pillow and dismisses the interruption as yawns of the aging four-level timber-framed stairway. He rolls over to snare another four hours' sleep.

An arm drops across his neck. Wrestler's sleeper hold. A momentary struggle defers unconsciousness. He submits. Plays dead. Works miracles. In theory. Save yourself for a surprise counter. He cannot identify the person pumping a syringe into his thigh. Doesn't wince as a second 100 ml shot of Deca Durabolin mixed with sodium thiopental seeps into the muscle.

'Deca' is Angelo's favoured bodybuilding steroid. He's made no secret around gym cronies of his obsession with the internet-sourced drug to help him gain muscular weight and size. It is intended to mask the sodium thiopental – commonly dispensed as Pentothal – a mild anaesthetic formulated for intravenous administration.

Angelo succumbs to the concoction.

Arms grasp him and hoist him over a shoulder. Strong. Heavy-set. Body odour.

Moving.

Out of the doorway.

Head crashes against the architrave. Bounce, bounce, bounce. Synchronised with descending steps.

The front door opens. Night's chill rushes his nostrils. Freshness stings. But fails to revive.

A car door unlocks. Remote controlled.

Powerless to brace himself.

Bashes his head. Metal.

Crashes onto a seat. Face down. Not bucket seats. A bench seat. The rear.

Recognises the scent. *Leather?*

Familiar smell.

Touches his tongue to the seat. Neat's-foot oil. Best leather preservative ever. Few know about it. Fewer use it.

Fuck. This is my fucking car!

The car starts.

Don't rev the shit out of my *car.*

Drives off.

Take it easy for fuck sake.

Sways from side to side. Can't discern the direction. Lost.

How long? Twenty minutes? Thirty?

Crunching. A gravel driveway.

What the fuck?

The car stops. Rear door opens.

Don't pull me by the fucking legs.

Crashes onto the ground. Chest first. Then face.

Fuck! Not heard.

Up and over the shoulder.

Not again.

Bounce, bounce, bounce. A door opens. Metallic. Ankles whack the doorway.

More bouncing. Halts.

Scraping.

Chairs in an empty hall?

Whop. A whoosh of air and a soft thump.

Fuuucckk!

Falling. Head and limbs crash and tumble. Feels like a lift

shaft. No cables. Solid walls. Slam from side to side. Somersault. Descending.

Where the fuck am I?

Thud, bang, wallop, thwack. Crash. Earth. Can't move. Can't speak.

Feel nothing. Blood trickles down my neck.

Scraping. Darkness.

A faint creak. Closing door.

The car drives off.

Silence.

* * *

Twelve hours' later, weighing McMaster's and Caruso's threats, Jeff Main pores over the Blackshaw's Mill contracts. Under threat of the approaching deadline, he ponders which of the two contracts to execute. Either way, horrific consequences loom. He favours McMaster because his contract is legal, *and*, he would retain his dress circle seat overlooking his client's forecast riches. Angelo's deal – returning the vendor ninety thousand pounds short of McMaster's offer – will render him liable to a malpractice suit.

He snatches the phone. 'Main.'

'Been waiting to hear from you.'

'Yeah Phil. Had a bit going on. You're on my list though.'

McMaster has dealt with every form of excuse and delay tactic. From the near-extinct 'cheque's in the mail' through to 'the bank's got a problem with my account.' It is always someone else's fault.

'You must have a long list,' he replies. 'My conveyancing file through yet? Settlement's due.'

'Coupla hiccups Phil. Not a problem, though. Should be on the way now.'

'So what are these hiccups? You should've told me. I can't afford to lose this property.'

'I know, Phil, and I'm sorry. As if I haven't had enough problems trying to fix this. I've had to sign affidavits about one of those erroneous copies. Declared the offer was amended because chattels had been recalculated. On top of that, the vendor changed heart – spoke of passing the property to the son – but just as dramatically reverted back to normal. Seems I've forgotten what normal is. I've gotta go.' Main slams down the phone.

The receptionist's voice crackles through the intercom: 'Telephone call. Mr Main. Line two.'

He grabs the phone again. 'What now?'

Silence.

'Yes. Main here.'

'Hello. Job's done.' The line clunks dead. Main struggles to identify the voice, the electronic disguise muffling the dialogue into an androgynous robotic mix. *What job?* He connects: Blackshaw's Mill. *What job's done? Has dear Jill encouraged Angelo to withdraw from the sale?*

He's expected the call since handing over the envelope of cash and instructions. Satisfied with the news, he switches to a routine matrimonial settlement but cannot concentrate. He flings the file from his desk, seizes his brief case, and rushes from office. 'Migraine. Back in the morning,' he grunts to reception.

In the sanctity of his car, he ruminates over Lowenstein's arrangement. He is not comfortable with unresolved matters fracturing his established routine. He also has little patience with those who make arrangements and fail to stand by them. Albert Lowenstein is one of those.

Frustrated, he makes the call. Lowenstein apologises: 'Sorry, Mr Main. I always try to respond with urgency to clients who show genuine interest in my business. I'm not sure if you understand my industry, but raw materials are sometimes harder to, shall we say, offload? No problem to discuss details. What about tomorrow at two o'clock? I'd say it would be in your interest.'

'I'll be there.' Main smiles, rubs his hands and visualises serious debt clearance.

Lowenstein flicks through his phone's menu.

'Onions. Listen up. Had delays. I'm set now. Got Mac's solicitor coming in at two tomorrow. Shouldn't need you both. It's up to you.'

'Comprendo. I was beginning to wonder what's the go. Why's a bloody lawyer on the case?'

'You'd have to ask Mac. I've had no contact with him – only you and the lawyer. Goes by the name of Main. Know him?'

'No. You trying to shop me or something?'

'I'm an honourable trader. Honouring my agreement. Said I'd call you, which is what I am doing. I don't know what Mac's up to – I told you I haven't spoken with him. All I know is that he deals through you. Doesn't affect me. If he's got someone else on a string, that's between him and you.'

'Yeah, my mother was honourable. Kicked me out at fourteen. Too right it's between Mac and me. I'll phone him.'

Onions is determined to not lose out. Either way, he'll get commission for striking a deal for McMaster's sample, or he'll be rewarded for tipping off Mac that his legal friend is about to scam him. He smiles, rubs his hands and visualises a new car – this time purchased off the showroom floor instead of stolen from a railway station park and ride.

Lowenstein swipes his phone.

'Hello Miss Watts. How lovely to speak with you again.'

Olivia recognises the distinct voice. Returns similar falsity: 'Mr Lowenstein. I'm equally delighted. How may I help?'

'Serious business, Olivia. I'm only doing this as a favour for my old friend Marchant. Don't know what good it will do, but I've tied up a deal for you.'

Olivia knows the deals Marchant had orchestrated – she'd witnessed his shortcuts to convictions. 'Told you I don't do deals, Mr Lowenstein. You want to capitalise on that community spirit you were talking of?'

'This is big. I know about McMaster, but ask no questions. Thing is, he's got a well-known fence *and* a solicitor brokering gold. I haven't a clue where it's from, other than there's supposed to be an unlimited supply – quote, unquote. Point is, I need to re-establish credibility with the MET. Let's say I had a licensing problem a while back and doing the Bill a favour will restore my good standing. You see where I'm coming from?'

'Yes, but I don't see where you're going. Unless you're sure this gold is stolen, there's nothing wrong with someone trying to sell it.'

'Then pray tell me why McMaster himself hasn't graced my doorstep?'

Olivia ponders the conundrum. If McMaster has found gold on his property, he will be obligated to the Crown. No owner of private property would make such an admission. To investigate him for that would be akin to charging a burglar with jay walking on departing a burglary. With the knowledge gleaned from McMaster's sill safe, she now wonders whether McMaster might be complicit in Giuseppe's passing.

'All right, Alby. What's the go?'

'I can deliver McMaster and Main in one hit. You do what you like with them.'

'I can't do anything with them. I told you – I'm no longer a copper.'

'Think about it, woman. The lawyer's given me an envelope of dirt and grit. I was lucky to find a pinhead of gold. That suggests he's acquired remnants, maybe from a slush pile. The fence guy – you don't need his name – had a couple of tiny rocks. I reckon he's doing Mac's dirty work – has done for years. You want info on McMaster? Come and get it. Main'll sell him out.'

'Don't be so sure,' says Olivia. 'Mac's the biggest seller outerer ever.'

'Main'll spill his guts if he thinks the police are involved. The guy'll back-pedal faster than a dyslexic speed-reader. I've let on to Mac's fence that Main's coming in; in fact, he should be onto Mac right now. Knowing Mac as I do, he'll be pacing my floor at ten to two tomorrow. It's up to you. Do a trade – their story for your glory.'

'Can't do that,' says Olivia. 'Nothing I can do will insulate them from what I believe they've done. I can't offer immunity from prosecution – but I know someone who can.' Cautious of Lowenstein's motives, she offers no further.

'If you bring the right artillery, no one'll be threatening no one.'

'Fair enough. I've got a contact who'll be there with bells

on. This is not cut and dried, you know. Main'll recognise me. Plus, he'll make a meal of anything that so much as whiffs of entrapment.'

'Hey, there's no entrapment. Main's coming here for a price *he* requested, and I'll bet my life that McMaster'll be here under his own steam to sort out Main.'

'Nup. Gotta do this straight down the line. I'll try to beat Main to the punch. I've got until tomorrow to save his butt from McMaster and score a major win for myself.' Olivia smiles and ends the call. Rubs her hands and pictures closing her enquiry with a substantial cheque and an offer of continued work.

XXVIII

Hamilton Holt is an easy person to forget – until a computer problem or electronics malfunction sparks the need for his expertise. That is my reason for messaging him.

Hamilton is the archetypal nerd who presents as a modern-day Ginger Meggs. He's cursed with wild ginger hair and blocky glasses so old they've encored as current designer fashion. A strip of blue, black and red pens adorns his jacket pocket. I would bet a crisp fifty he transfers them to his striped flannelette pyjamas each evening. For those not familiar with my earlier investigations, Hamilton is a former Police IT consultant who turned to his own consultancy. He is one of few in Britain able to acquire the tiniest scrap of information about anyone and anything.

He's also au fait with computer repairs, upgrades and tweaks one might not access from the regular High Street technician. I trust him with my soul and that's why I'd called him with a request to extract information from my shattered iPad. I haven't been game to turn it on since leaving Gillian's, just in case I fuse it, fizz it out, or whatever happens after a £400 rectangle of electronic wizardry is compressed under the combined weight of a 100-kilo *Biggest Loser* candidate and a wispy excuse of a female.

An orange-haired Orangutan flashes onto my phone screen. 'Hi Hamo. What you been doing.'

'Nothing as exciting as being with you, Liv.'

Here we go again. Hamilton's harmless, yet no matter how long the break between contact, he always lets go with sickly come-ons, similar to the pickup lines I reject in pubs and clubs. I once made the fateful mistake of following through and acceding to one of his invitations. Yuk. Never again. We *had* agreed to keep everything professional.

'Yeah, right. First up, how'd you go with that little installation in Cheltenham?'

'Not a problem. Did it the next morning. Your girl should be happy now. Tell me, what's the occasion?'

'I'm stuck. I've got an iPad that's thinner than the factory specs; cracked screen but the body's intact – bit like myself.'

'Come on, Liv. Nothing a bit of rejuvenation won't fix.'

'Let's focus on my iPad, and *don't* call me Liv.'

'Right. Don't mess with it. Don't turn it on. We might be okay. Has it been wet?'

'Nup. Just squashed. I was doing a job, turned rough and, well, I'll tell you when I see you. Can I meet you somewhere? Half way?'

Hamilton changes address every three months. He once explained that he gets bored in the same premises, but I suspect it has more to do with evading detection or keeping MI5 officers at bay. Last I knew, he was settled in a swanky Birmingham city apartment.

'Lunch, Liv. My place. And I'll fix it on the spot.'

'Swanky' understates the premises. An area marked 'Visitors Only' requires a Key Card, thereby preventing my access. I surmise that 'visitors' need approval for privileged parking. I venture to a nearby street to misappropriate a resident's spot. With none available, I roll into a ginormous Tesco. To legitimise my right to its car park, I grab a bag of groceries before returning to the apartment block.

The front is more secure than 10 Downing Street – without the police protection. There is no tenants'/owners' listing, and no intercom. *My kind of place. No hassles from door-to-door salespeople.*

I circumvent further stress by phoning him. 'I'm here.'

'Sorry Liv. I should'a told you about the rear entry. It's a ploy designed to deter intruders. Guess it worked. Just walk around the back and I'll meet you.'

I hedge around the corner and see Hamilton standing next to the rear electronic doors, glowing like a just-extinguished matchstick. A panel of apartment numbers and buzzers shine beside him. I disguise my ineptitude: 'I would have found this but I didn't want to keep you waiting.'

Hamilton smirks. 'Yeah sure.'

A stainless steel and mirrored lift propels us to the fifth floor. 'Probably the only lift in Birmingham that isn't graffitied.'

We walk into his apartment. I freeze, open-mouthed. 'You got a maid or something?' I've seen Hamilton's previous apartments; the stereotyped unkempt, chaotic and unlivable bachelor's space.

'No. I've turned the corner. There comes a day when everyone finds their true self. I was hiding behind a facade of immaturity; I cared nothing for neatness and order – except within my work. Now, it's my lifestyle.'

I can't believe him. Won't. It would be like Russell Brand cutting his hair and shaving. Some things *don't* change. I don't give up: 'You haven't turned the corner and joined the gay brigade have you?'

'You gotta to be having a laugh. I can't even score a plain

Jane, let alone a guy who's flamboyant, outgoing and particular. I'm still hanging for you, Liv.'

'You'll be hanging a long time. And please stop calling me Liv!'

'All right already. Let's get this show on the road. Hand over the goods, *Olivia*. What you got in there?'

I pass the iPad from my bag and detail the circumstances leading to its demise. I stress the importance of the stored information, and confide my inability to regain it with similar ease.

Hamilton lays the unit on a rubber mat and fixes a strap to his wrist.

'What the— What's that? You a gay fashion icon now?'

Hamilton grimaces. 'What's the sudden fascination with gayness? It's an electrostatic strap. Prevents static destroying capacitors and insulators and stuff. Bit technical; it's just a precaution. I bet you'd be into precautions?'

I ignore the oblique question.

I watch over his shoulder; an apprentice studying her master's craft. He separates the iPad into two parts, leaving the inner circuitry upturned on the mat. I see that two silver caps – and I don't know whether they are diodes or capacitors or chipsets or even a CPU – are bent. That alarms me. Hamilton pulls a data cable from the back of his laptop and clips the other end to a peg inside the iPad. I smile. The menu pops up on Hamilton's laptop. He selects 'All Files' from a program I've never heard of, clicks 'copy/transfer', and within moments my files, including my treasured photos and music, swim like sperm into Hamilton's computer.

He delves into a box beneath his bench and pulls out an iPad casing. I hope he isn't going to do what I think he's going to do, because I don't want a *white* iPad.

'What are you doing?' I query.

'Restoring your iPad. Updating.'

He does do what I didn't want him to do. I peck his cheek. My work is reinstated and I'm about to own a remodeled iPad. 'Where'd you get the case?'

'eBay. Probably hot. No identifiers though.'

I do the eye roll. 'Great.'

Hamilton smiles. Fires up the unit. Icons flood the screen. 'Okay Liv. Job done. Now, we'll have coffee and make love… ly use of these files, shall we?'

He doesn't give up. I hadn't banked on sharing the information with Hamilton, but it won't cause any harm. He might even be able to help.

There's something endearing about a man in control. Perhaps it's power, or maybe over-confidence. I'm not sure. But Hamilton bypasses the coffee making and goes straight to the 'Current' file. A list of twenty-odd Word documents paginate. Gillian is certainly methodical. Every filename is preceded by the day's date, which makes it easier to locate an item referenced to time than by name. I vow to adopt her system.

The most recent entries are time sheets, probably for Thornton's invoices. I click on a video icon I'd missed while rummaging through the menu at Gillian's home. Turns out to be excellent footage of McMaster and Main in the Knight's Arms. Sound is next to non-existent, but Gillian has excelled by including accompanying notes: *18/4 Screws on JM. 20/4 Knight's Arms. 2pm meeting with suit. Later identified as solicitor. Details in confidence relate to land transaction. 23/4 Tree down.*

Hamilton twists his neck from the screen. 'You know what all this is about?'

'Not all, but I'll figure it pretty quick. I know the Knight's

Arms. That's where Trotter, Gillian, whose info this is, works part-time. She's an undercover op' for Thornton. Remember the Super?'

'Thorns? 'course I remember him. But how the hell do you know that?'

'Because I'm also working for him.'

Hamilton stares. 'You're having a laugh. You're both on the same job?'

'No Hamo. This is big. I wouldn't tell *anyone* but you. Thorns thinks Trotter's bent. I'm tailing her while she's tailing Phillip McMaster, an inspector from way back. He's supposed to be pocketing goodies on the side. Thorns believes Trotter's tipping off Mac. I tend to agree. Some strange shit going down. I've got a side lead on McMaster which might be supported by whatever's in the 'H' file.'

'Be buggered. *Now* I'm making coffee. Come and check out the bedroom, woops sorry, the kitchen.'

'You wish.' I follow him into the kitchen where a huge black and chrome coffee machine holds a bench top to ransom. 'You working for MI5 or something? How'd you afford this?'

'Talent, Olivia. I'm a man rewarded for my talents. I help people who figure I should be adequately recompensed.'

'Yeah, right. If I see any bulletins about stolen cappuccino machines, well, mum's the word.' I stand beside the wheezing, hissing, emphysemic machine while Hamilton withdraws two mugs from an overhead cupboard. I study the gold leaf double 'H' adorning the cups. 'Shit Hamo. You must have won Lotto.'

'Come on Liv. Credit where credit's due. Self-gratuitous identification. What if they get stolen? At least they'll be traced to me.'

'Only if they're found.'

We carry our royal mugs back to the sweeping lounge which is so much more than a room. Hamilton reinstalls himself in front of the computer. I prop jealously beside. He closes the 'Current' file and clicks onto 'H'. Again, a menu of Word documents bursts onto the screen, but this time numbered, not dated. I ask Hamilton to open number one. *Spanish Angel with spirit. Eager to please. Couple of Dewies.*

'Crap code,' I laugh. I've met the girl, Rose. Spanish, I think. The angel with spirit relates to where she works – Heavenly Spirits bottle shop; not too sure about 'eager to please' because I'm on the fence over what she has to do with Mac. The 'Dewies' is Dewar's Scotch. He's bribing her over a minor traffic incident, or so Rose says. Open three.'

Hamilton complies. *Meeting at brother's. Ordered more Dewies.*

'Can we search 'McMaster'?' If he's got a brother, he's definitely not in the job. The only other 'Mac' I know is McDonald's – my second home. I wonder, give us a look: *'meeting at brother's'.* Mac's? He held a meeting at Maccas?'

'That's workable.'

'All right. What we got in the 'Mac' file?'

Fifty files fill the screen. A sub-folder marked 'Blackshaws' lies at the bottom of the reverse-alphabet listing. I ask him to open it.

The menu throws up three documents, each of ten pages. With the benefit of the 'Current' file detail, we confirm that McMaster is trying to buy Blackshaw's Mill. Nothing untoward there, except that the guy's on a DI's salary. And then the name Jeff Main jumps out – the same Jeff Main Gillian had spied with McMaster at the Knight's Arms. 'Something fishy here,' I say. 'Too coincidental. Solicitor/

client meeting in a pub where money and envelopes change hands.

'Hamo,' I drool in my I-want-something-from-you-smile. 'Do you reckon you could get me the goods on Main? I'll do the Land Registry and suss the property and check local agents for valuations.'

'Leave it with me. Think I'll get my plates gold-leafed for this.'

'Not bloody likely. But I will owe you.'

'That's what I'm talkin' about. A negotiable debt. Okay, *Olivia*, I'll get on to it.'

I click through folders while Hamo goofs off. It gets to the stage where I neglect his rambling because I am so immersed in a peculiar printout. The format is the same as court transcripts, but amateurishly laid out in the old-fashioned 'I said/he said' police format. It changes my whole perception of McMaster, for I now believe he's masterminding much more than minor scams.

I read through the preliminaries, the hellos, the how's things, and the hope your family's all right waffle before I begin my own mining:

PM	'We had a little win yesterday.'
JM	'What do you mean "we"?'
PM	'Our old man had a heart attack. The sale should now be a breeze.'
JM	'Don't bet your bollocks on that. It could delay the whole process because of probate.'
PM	'I've got my man, Angelo, onto it. She'll be smooth sailing.'
JM	'You sure it was a heart attack? You didn't put

too much pressure on the old codger, did you? Like you tried with me?'

PM 'Come now. You think I'm the kind of guy who'd do something like that?'

From what I've seen and learned, he most certainly is. As I'd earlier suspected, there *is* far more than coincidence surrounding the untimely demise of Giuseppe Caruso. That leaves me with an interesting proposition. Hand this over to Thornton, or first check its authenticity. I adopt for the latter. I also want to know if Trotter has passed on this information. Whilst I care nothing for her, I don't particularly want to jeopardise her investigation.

I thank Hamilton for his afternoon's work and for my new *white* iPad before heading home to read every word of my restored files. On the way, I break another law by using my mobile to arrange another meeting with Thornton.

* * *

When I hand over the photos of Gillian and McMaster, Thornton nearly falls off his chair. He flings back his hands, thumps himself in the forehead and lets out a huge, 'Fuck me. How the fuck could she get roped in by that bastard?'

'Works both ways,' I venture.

'She's invoicing me an exorbitant rate for professional services. I had no idea they extended to satisfying the whims of bloody McMaster. Now I can't rely on anything she's given me. Could be covering up a whole lot of mess here. I'll have her arse.'

Probably worn out by Mac.

He makes no reference to gold or mining. My inclinations are that Gillian must know, especially since McMaster has let on the fact to Main. Gillian holds meticulous records of the McMaster/Main conversations in the Knight's Arms and she has been close enough to McMaster to share out-of-hours activities. I consider the proposition that it is she who had contacted Lowenstein on McMaster's behalf. Lowenstein would never tell me that – and I wouldn't ask – but he might tell me if it were a man or a woman. Process of elimination.

Thornton yanks a phone from his pocket. Switches demeanours. The guy's a genius. Melts like toffee in the sunshine, eager to not telegraph the slightest hint of concern: 'Hello Gill, how are you? Can I catch a few minutes with you for an update? Tomorrow? Say, one o'clock, my office? And bring all you got on PM.'

I snigger, applying the reference to Theresa May rather than Phillip McMaster. I strain to hear the crap Gillian is dishing up, but fail.

Thornton ends the call and turns to me: 'She tried calling McMaster as arranged, but he hasn't answered. Could have gone cold on her. I don't know.'

'Think it'd be the other way 'round if you ask me.'

Thornton tramples my joviality. 'I'll get to the bottom of this. She'll fry if she's double-dealing. Now update me with the latest.'

I chronologise my observations from the Knight's Arms and the information I'd 'acquired' from her home; I detail her appearance at the fallen tree catastrophe, her closeness in the hospital, and McMaster's incriminating photos.

'For all the hours she's spent around him, I haven't got much in return,' says Thornton.

I won't comment on her professionalism, or lack thereof, but I do seize on the opening to further my own prospects: 'Now I'm familiar with all the players, I can take over.'

I expect the 'don't jump the gun' response and am pleasantly surprised when he says, without hesitation, 'Goes without saying, Olivia. Carte-blanche. The whole shebang. I want this sewn up as soon as possible and I want that McMaster's arse.'

My confidence soars: 'Gee sir, you're wanting a lot of arse out of this.'

'Remember who I am or I'll be having yours.'

You wish.

XXIX

I SHIFT MY ATTENTION TO McMaster. When I accepted this job, I thought I might drown in another contentious contest of criticising constabulary members. I'm happy to have upped my charter from the Gillian Trotter Activity Profile to a full shakedown of DI Phillip McMaster, who seems more a part of Trotter than she is of herself.

Part of my armoury springs from the teachings of American psychology guru, Dale Carnegie (*How to Win Friends and Influence People* (1936): to solve a dilemma, evaluate each positive and negative point on its merit. There will be advantages and disadvantages, just as each will have features and benefits. I heed his advice as I try to gauge the McMaster/Trotter relationship.

I understand Gillian's charter is to log activities that compromise McMaster's professional role, notwithstanding she has actually become one of those 'activities'. I can't pardon her behaviour at the hospital, all mushy-mushy and lovey-dovey in a billowing top, openly inviting McMaster's eyes to roll out of their sockets.

My concern is that she 'just happened' to be outside McMaster's home when the tree fell. Given what I *now* know, I believe she was waiting for his secret signal – *the coast is clear* – to allay any fear of Gloria McMaster bisecting their dalliance. It therefore makes complete sense that Gillian would wait nearby, rather than drive straight into the property and risk confronting the opposition.

I've encountered weird relationships in my time. In the mixed bag of human emotions, love and deception, I consider the possibility of Gloria either not knowing, or not caring, about her husband's extramarital activities. I'm ashamed to imagine the alternative: participation in a writhing threesome.

I must see Maria Caruso. Who better than a neighbour to diss Phillip McMaster?

In head scarf and black mourning dress, Maria opens the door.

'Hello Mrs Caruso. Remember me? Olivia. We spoke next door after the accident.'

'Yes. I'm always help Mr Mac.'

'He's doing very well. I've just come from the hospital.'

Maria offers a grateful smile.

'I'm working with the police, trying to identify who attacked Mr McMaster. Can you help? Did you see anything?' My contractual obligation to Superintendent Thornton qualifies "working with the police".

'No. Mr Mac's nice man. I think he's not have enemies.'

He certainly had one. I push harder.

'No. I see nothing. I'm not looking anywhere. My Giuseppe, he's die only three weeks ago.'

I look down, say nothing. Sometimes it's more respectful that way. One often says 'Sorry' and then we're left to wonder whether they're sorry for the loss or sorry for mentioning a departed loved one. I use the soft, female approach: 'You were married a long time?'

'Yes. Fifty-four years. Is long time. And he's not be sick. I'm knowing nothing wrong with him and he's just die there on the kitchen floor.'

And then I say it: 'I'm sorry.'

I throw in my new-found knowledge: 'Mr Mac is buying your property. Is that right?'

'Yes. I am going smaller place. Maybe village. Mr Mac's offer the good price. My boy Angelo, he's look the figures and say is good.'

'That must have been a surprise. Had you previously discussed selling to your neighbour?'

'No, nothing like that. My Giuseppe's never want to leave. He's think the family take over and pass to the generations. Mr Mac's just ask one day if he can buy because he's help me and wants to make the big farm.'

I feel the conversation circling. 'So what made you sell?'

'I'm talk with Angelo, and he's say is good idea for a fresh start.'

'Had Mr McMaster ever talked about farming or buying your property *before* he made the offer?'

'He's once ask my Giuseppe and he's say "No". Mr Mac's not talk much to me and Giuseppe, except the Christmas and sometimes hello in the garden. After he's offer the good price and Giuseppe's already gone, my Angelo's help and we decide sell because I'm not being able to manage the farm.'

That seems fair enough, but the haste by which Angelo took on negotiations with McMaster surprises me. From my cynical perspective, I see Angelo as more focused on selling the family property than he is in mourning his father.

I capitalise on the conversation's good fortune of spotlighting Angelo: 'So was it Angelo who was instrumental, sorry, who helped you with the sale process?'

'He's a good boy, my Angelo. He's do it nearly all. The papers, the going to solicitors, and he's see Mr Mac for the final figures. I'm just sign the papers and it's all done. But later he's come to me and says he wants to buy the farm. I'm laugh, because he's know nothing about the farming. He's not even feed the chickens.'

'Aah, yes. I met your son when I helped you home that night.' I remember Angelo standing like a sentry before a fortress. Granted, he didn't know me, but I see that as a reason to extend, not withhold, just a little cordiality. From my impression of Angelo, I agree that he might show determination to grow crops, but come animals and humans, he is grossly deficient in communication skills. I don't convey this to his mother. 'So you decided to sell?'

'Yes. Half decided. Angelo's coming later to me. He's say, "You're right, mama. You should sell. Clear the slate," is what he say, but I'm no understand the slate. Then he's start to cry and say nothing more and goes straight away home.' Fuelled by sympathy, Maria also cries.

'Don't upset yourself. I'll go now. I'm sure everything will work out.'

'All right miss. Can you tell the police when I get my things back?'

'What things?'

'When the police coming the second time, the take the things. They're saying we check for any sick and I'm know no one's been sick here, only die, so I'm not understand why they take the things.'

I almost piss myself – sorry, let go of my bladder. I'm no match for a linguistics graduate, but I easily piece together that "for any sick" translates to "forensic". 'What did they take?'

'I'm not see everything because they tell me sit in other room. But I know they take the rolling pin for the pasta and the wood jar for the spaghetti and the paddle for thrashing the dust from the mats. If there's more, I'm not missing yet.'

I used to supply an inventory of seized items to the property's owner or tenant. I can't see that procedure as having been revoked so I put the omission down to a detective's oversight, or Maria's difficulty with English language. 'I'll speak to the detective. You should get them back soon.'

My visit has extracted all information. The problem remains: Why would someone try to derail a property purchase? Mrs Caruso's physical frailty prevents her. She is happy to move. Angelo doesn't live there, but I can't discount him because of that. The only other commonality I see is McMaster's association with Jeff Main.

I hop the fence to visit Gloria McMaster. As I stretch through the parallel wires, a sprinkling of paper fragments, not unlike confetti, attracts my attention. I can't imagine the McMasters, or the Carusos for that matter, as the class of people to litter their own property. Putting that aside, my craving for nose-poking into other people's business obligates me to pick up a few pieces. They bear handwriting on one side and black typeface on the other. I don't need a diploma to discern the shredded matter is a business card. A flashback to my jigsaw solving days compels me to gather the pieces. From the small handful, I assemble the tiny fragments to form what appears to be part of a message: I KNOW BOUT YOU... REMEMB... OPERATIO... INSIDE FOR... NG IME.

I can't make much of the soiled writing other than to realise that it isn't a birthday party invitation. In context of where I've found it and the relationship between the opposing neighbours, I consider it to be something more sinister. When

I turn the pieces over to assemble the typeface, the words 'Jeffrey Main' and 'solicitor' spring from my palm. It follows that the card hasn't flown out of a rubbish bin. The only time *I've* ripped up business cards has been through frustration, a tantrum, or when I wanted to destroy what was actually on the card. Those scenarios dovetail with my find. I scour the immediate area, collect every visible piece, and drop them into a small Glad Bag.

Nearby, the remnants of a cigarette have been crunched into the ground. Roll your own. Stands out like a cat turd on a snooker table. I detest irresponsible smokers who throw butts from car windows; tread them into footpaths and marble steps of iconic buildings; stomp them into sporting grounds because the 'caretaker will clean them up later'; leave them scattered in front of shops and offices to flow into drains and rivers with the next downpour; and my worst pet-hate – as if there *is* worse than the foregoing – the desperados at railway stations who wilfully flick their lit cigarette to the platform as the train rolls in, and once within the carriage, exhale their filthy tobacco breath over every commuter in the vestibule and adjacent seats.

This particular butt – it is more than a butt; nearly a full cigarette – would not have aroused my attention but for the fact it accompanies the confetti-like scraps. I pick it up, using a Glad Bag as a glove like a responsible pet lover collecting her dog's doings from a local park. I hope it might prove useful.

One disadvantage of self-employment is that I no longer enjoy quality resources once at my disposal within the constabulary. Previously, I would log the card fragments and butt as exhibits in the Property Office, making them available for forensic examination should the need arise. Watts Happening? Investigations practises low-tech evidence handling – and most other things. I store items in my safe, accompanied by a sworn affidavit attesting to the time and date of their finding.

Satisfied with my treasure, I continue towards Ashton Hill.

From the rear, the property looks far more imposing than it does from the front. It rises from the ground like that huge monolith in the Australian outback. It was universally known as Ayers Rock, until the 1985 political correctness bandwagon handed the local indigenous tribes ownership and the right to convey upon it the aboriginal name of Uluru.

Up close, the confrontational mansion's two wings extend far behind the facade, each comprising, at my best guess, a minimum of six *substantial* rooms. Again, the thought strikes me: *How does a copper afford this?* And then I am double-struck. I glare at the huge window occupying the full gable end of the right-hand side wing. I imagine McMaster spying on neighbours, but as I edge closer to the wall, I make out what appears to be an artists' easel in the centre of the glazing. Never could I see the DI as an artist (although he does splatter good bullshit) so I deduce the apparatus must belong to his wife.

I continue to the front door. Lean on the bell. Jive to a melodic chime. Wait for a maid or butler. Nothing wrong with fantasy; so wild is my imagination of what I might find beyond the huge carved door. I drift into the nineteenth century… Rhett Butler, the staircase…

Whatever is there will complement the enormity and grandiloquence I'd witnessed during my night-time rummage. The door cracks open. A diminutive woman with an anaemic, pasty albino complexion, greets me: 'Yes?'

Great start. Like anyone attending a domain of the rich, I had expectations. High expectations. Designer dress – hand-stitched by a personal courtier – jewellery hanging off fingers and earlobes, hair piled high into a beehive bouffant, and a voice cultured through regard for personal elocution. I am disappointed.

'Yes?' she repeats in an Essex-tainted voice. She is the best representation of office gossip in the flesh I've ever seen. Think dowdy. Frumpy.

I introduce myself, slipping in that I am a former police member now charged with identifying Phillip McMaster's attacker. Poetic licence is a great asset.

'I don't share your concern. He hasn't been my husband for some time. Been carting 'round floozies behind my back. Most of 'em coppers, I'll bet.'

"Floozies". I haven't heard the word since mum labelled a neighbour with it when I was still wearing pinafores and knitted tights. Despite her vague admission, I continue: 'So you're Gloria McMaster?'

'Unfortunately. Don't I look like a rejected housewife?'

Don't get me started. She invites the sympathetic, consoling babble she's probably heard a thousand times from her society set: *You can work through it; think of how your life would be without him; you couldn't go back to a semi-detached in a council estate;* and all the other pompous ill-advised encouragement they hand out over cups of tea – pinkies extended as if they're broken at the knuckle – sweet shortbreads clenched in the other hand, all the while battling to elevate themselves up the ranking ladder of their husband's personal worth.

Not me. No way. I'd just tell him to fuck off.

The woman has problems. Proverbial chip on the shoulder. Perhaps I shouldn't blame her if she's been treated half as bad as some police wives. 'Did you hear anything on the evening of Monday, April twenty-third?'

She throws her head back like an actress rejected after an audition: 'Not a sound. Not a murmur. Might have been sozzled. When was the twenty-third?'

Shaping up to be a lost cause. 'Is there a possibility his attacker could have been a revenge-seeking part-time lover?'

'I don't know and I don't care.' She becomes even shorter: 'If there's nothing else, I'm preparing dinner.'

Play to their strengths when you're buying time: 'Detective Interviewing Techniques', Module Two. 'Sorry, I don't mean to impose. I just came from the Caruso's across your rear yard. That amazing rear window frames your easel like a painting in a gallery. You're an artist?'

'Try to be. Nothing else here to keep me occupied.'

'I wonder if you could cast your mind back to the kerfuffle on the twentieth, when Giuseppe collapsed. I believe Mrs Caruso ran over here to get your husband?'

As she couldn't remember the twenty-third, I don't know what makes me think she might recall the twentieth. But she does. Clear as one of her Swarovski vases.

'Waddled. She didn't run. Got the gait thing happening. Yes, she got Phil, didn't run back though – they went in his car. Total misfortune if you ask me. Phil was over there only minutes before Maria came waddling over. I thought he must have forgotten something and she was returning it. Until I heard all the yelling that is.'

'What? You're saying that your husband was at the Caruso's immediately prior to Maria attending here?'

'That's exactly what I'm saying. I was sitting right at the window waiting for the sun to cast the right light on the Malvern Hills. Phil wandered down back and had a smoke under the trees. You walked through them on your way here.

Goodness knows what he was up to. He climbed through the fence, into the Caruso's but re-emerged only seconds later. Sprang back to the house happy as Larry. Strange. He had a cricket bat or similar under his arm. No idea why. Who knows what goes on in his head? Next minute, he's sitting outside with his precious Scotch, if you want the full blow-by-blow description.'

I thank The Lord – if he still looks over me – for bagging the butt from that exact area. 'So you're sure it was the fourteenth?'

'Miss, I have a drink now and then, but sure as I'm standing here, it was the fourteenth. I'll tell you why. After Phil came back the second time, I asked what the ambulance was for and he said Giuseppe had collapsed. Moments later he was getting ready for work as if nothing had happened. He was on a 6.00 p.m. start. Saturday, my TV night. Just ask Maria and her son, the one with the black car. They'll confirm everything I've told you. Now, if there's nothing more, I should like to go inside.'

I thank her as she turns and closes the door. I am elated to have converted her from an uptight, deserted housewife, to a semi-communicable citizen – assuming she has told me the truth. If, heaven forbid, it is the truth – and I'm not going to vent this until I am absolutely sure – then DI Phillip McMaster could be in for one hell of a lengthy interrogation.

Gloria's perception, or belief, of her husband's pleasure practices, augment my expanding profile of Phillip McMaster, and push him closer to Gillian.

Whilst she is my prime concern, I cannot ignore peripheral matters. I look at it this way: I would rather be an old 32 volume Encyclopaedia Britannica than a toddler's brand new ABC reader. The more information in my arsenal, the better equipped I am to conquer the crims.

Back to Gillian, I wonder if she had been spurned by McMaster, or worse still, learned that he'd uncovered the true purpose of her friendship. It's not uncommon for a scorned woman to seek vengeance, and, she was undoubtedly in the right place at the right time when the tree dropped. But she didn't *physically* do it. Of that I am sure.

That doesn't mean she couldn't have arranged it. The script changed though, after the plan failed. To allay suspicion, she *had* to attend the hospital, and in pandering to his emotions, offer her one hundred percent devotion.

From what I'd witnessed, her display of affection is much, much, more than an undercover act. *So what* would *be her motive?*

Too hard basket. I'll sit on that one.

XXX

But not for too long.

I head to Angelo Caruso's home. I have no particular lead other than my screaming intuition: *there's something about him. His father dies and now he's dealing the farm.*

A Harley leans on the front veranda. My raps go unanswered, so I circumnavigate the premises. He could be anywhere; at work, on a run, or strolling to the local shops. I wait.

My patience wanes with the daylight. Two hours' later, I scribble 'Contact me please' on a business card and wedge it into the door jamb. I twist the knob. The door opens. *Why the hell didn't I do that two hours ago?*

'Hello, anyone home?'

No reply.

'Hello. Angelo?'

Again, no reply. I step inside. A pong assails me. Stale tobacco, beer and body odour. Not the best combination to greet a girl. I tip-toe along the hallway, poke my head into a sitting room and then enter a large kitchen. No sign of Angelo or anyone else.

I creep upstairs where a bathroom and bedroom squeeze into the vaulted roof space. At first glance, Angelo appears to be a remarkably neat person (for a male) which seems out of character, and conflicts with his aversion to opening windows. The contrast shakes me when I step into the bedroom. A pair of jeans lies over the bed end, a flannelette cowboy shirt hangs from the back of a chair, and black boots sit beneath. The bed covers are tumbled aside as if Angelo answered a call of diarrhoea. The prophecy gains credibility when I see his underpants on the floor beside the bed. I recognise the habit from a past boyfriend – Angelo is a 'Commando' sleeper.

I study the sheets, hoping to locate evidence. He sleeps on his own. The two pillows are different sizes, which isn't necessarily unusual for an uncoordinated male, but the pillow opposite *his* side of the double bed has no indentations. Whilst the sheets evidence the hills and valleys of restless sleep, one pillow is as smooth and white as a snow-laid vale.

My first reaction is to pick up his pillow, peek underneath and try to discern his musty, male scent. Alcohol or tobacco residue often provides valuable evidence. My training kicks in and warns me to not touch anything. It's not as if it is a crime scene, but given the events of the previous few days, it does have the potential to be one.

I lean over the bed (this may repulse some, but I've had to do far worse in my career) and draw in the pillow's scent. Stale male. Unmistakeable. The guy must sleep with the pillow under his armpits.

I poke around the bedroom, but nothing, other than a cluster of aftershave and deodorants sitting symmetrically on the dressing table, convinces me that Angelo is anything but a slovenly, arrogant pig.

Nervous about the time, I bound down the stairs. Curiosity propels me to a small alcove where a study desk cowers beneath the stairs. A high-tech laser copier dwarfs an old computer, whose CRT monitor hangs over the desktop edge. Newspapers, a Visa statement, and invoices for council tax and local services lie nearby. A manila folder peeps from the pile – a blight on its surroundings as is the London Eye to Westminster.

Also like the London Eye, the file attracts my curiosity. Inside, I find contracts of sale bearing the names Giuseppe and Maria Caruso and Phillip and Gloria McMaster. Tiny black dots and a grey streak along the left margin expose the documents as photocopies. It matters not whether they are copies or originals, for I have just learnt more about the relationship between the neighbouring owners. Only hours earlier, Hamilton's repair work helped me access the files I'd misappropriated from Gillian's home, and they clearly detailed the Carusos and McMasters as parties to negotiations. Main represents McMaster, and Angelo's role, as I'd learnt from his mother, was, or is, no more than a delivery boy.

I study each page in the folder and wonder why there are so many copies – until I detect two different sets showing a disparity of ninety thousand pounds. If Angelo has played an amateurish hand of forgery, it is no wonder others want to 'fix the prat' – to steal their words. And then I succumb to speculation: if they want to fix Angelo, had they already fixed his father?

McMaster is clearly implicated in an unsavoury transaction – formidable fodder for Thornton.

On leaving, I'm curious about the unlocked front door. I've been inside for half an hour. Add to that the two hours I'd spent waiting, my first inclination of Angelo running laps or tripping to the shops is baseless.

I had reason to dislike Angelo from the moment we met, although that's not the best attitude to guide an investigator through an open-minded investigation. His arrogance towards me at his mother's home was disconcerting. The logical extension could be that he harboured similar contempt towards his mother and father. Perhaps humanity in general. Might he have had a disagreement with his father? One of sufficient intensity to cause a heart attack?

To discover Angelo's movements on the day his father died, I decide to question police who had attended the original callout. On phoning Worcester CID, an officer pays me little regard. 'Drop in, someone might be able to help you.' The off-hand invitation usually yields little. Different story when they want information from me.

At the CID office, a WPC shows me to the senior investigator's room. Along the way, I pass uniform and CID members who once knew me as DS Watts. Their revulsion burns into me. To offset the discomfort – for both officers and myself – I fix my eyes on the auburn pony tail swishing in front of me.

DS Roy Street sits in a partitioned cubicle. Looks as if he's stepped off H.G. Wells' Time Machine. Could almost pass for a live promotional poster of the 1960 film. He stands with a slight stoop. I think he's checking his shoe laces, but then realise he is afflicted with a natural – hereditary maybe – gene carried by many tall people. Scoliosis: curvature of the spine. I feel embarrassed for him and ashamed of my mute chuckle.

Perhaps it is his peculiarity; his uniqueness that draws me to him. Not with the quick rush of blood that attracts lovers at first sight, but a calmer sort of blending of characteristics. He eyes me with a hint of recognition. I don't know why, because I've never met him. I would remember had I have done so. He wasn't around during my tenure at Worcester. I assume him to be one of the replacements for DI Marchant and two of his cronies who departed in protest.

I introduce myself, and then fall silent as if a giant full stop has been banged after me. How can I justify seeing him? I am carrying out an investigation on behalf of the MET and can't possibly let on anything that might align me with McMaster.

He races to the point by quizzing my interest in Giuseppe Caruso's death. I burble that I am assisting Maria Caruso with matters related to her husband's life insurance policy.

Street reveals little. 'We're too early in the investigation,' he says. I know he is holding back because SOCO would have examined the Caruso home with the scrutiny of a homeless drunk scanning the footpath outside Harrods.

I conjure my seductive tone: 'My only interest is who was at the home at the time of Mr Caruso's death.'

'We're yet to fully determine that, but there's no harm in saying that both his wife and son, Angelo, were present during the course of the morning.'

I remember the safe speak. "Present during the course…" Means they were there at *some* time, but not necessarily at *the* time of Caruso's supposed heart attack. That implies he possesses material he is unable, or unwilling, to divulge. I use the 'we can work on this together' strategy, a generally successful tack, but it backfires.

'What can you bring to the table?'

'Nothing yet,' I say, with the emphasis on 'yet'. I slip in: 'Doesn't it strike you as odd that Giuseppe Caruso's death and the attack on his neighbour occurred within only days of each other?'

Street gawks. He's missed the point of my question. 'Are you suggesting that Caruso rose from the dead, docked a tree on to McMaster's car and then high-tailed it back to the morgue?'

What peeves me is that he doesn't even smile. He is dead serious and not willing to accept that the two incidents might be related. 'No. I'm suggesting no such thing. What I am suggesting is that there might have been a motive behind the *sudden* casualties of the two neighbours.'

Street lifts his eyes as if my proposition is meritless. 'I assure you we will consider a range of factors within the investigation. I can't help you any further.'

'All right. Just one final question: Mrs Caruso is anxious to have the seized items returned. Will they be released or are they potential exhibits?'

'That's the rolling pin and wooden jar or whatever you want to call it? Yeah, she can have them. She'll have to sign a release.'

'What about the paddle?'

'What fuckin' paddle. We took two items. Fat lot of good they were; can't blame the boys of course. Just doing their job.'

I have no reason to doubt Maria's account of the missing paddle. 'Sergeant. Mrs Caruso is emphatic that a paddle was taken from a utility room.'

'News to me. I'm telling you, the old lady's senile. The boys took two kitchen items. End of story. If you think otherwise, you're paddling up the wrong creek.'

I take the sarcasm as my cue to leave.

* * *

The law of coincidence sets off my mobile. How I'd love to shut it down and divert all calls to voice mail. I switch to speaker mode.

'Olivia? It's Rose. He's just been in.'

Whoa. Settle down. Hold up a minute. Surprise, surprise…

It has been nearly two weeks since Hamilton installed the hidden camera. I expected to hear from Rose much sooner, but quickly grasp that with McMaster in hospital, he could not have attended Heavenly Spirits or anywhere else. 'Are you all right?'

'Yes. I hope it's all recorded. He really went overboard. I'm going to report him no matter what.' Agitation rattles the phone.

'It's okay, Rose. Calm down. When did he leave?'

'Just now, couple of minutes ago. Took your money and said it's not good enough. Wants me to sell more stuff. Says he has an unlimited supply and that I can make more than I ever could working here.'

'I'm sure you could, but for how long?' Could you deal with the prospect of a jail sentence hanging over your head?'

'I wouldn't do it anyway.'

'Good. Sit tight. I'll race over and grab the SD card, see what's on there and then we'll decide what to do.'

Rose restores tear-streaked make-up as I enter the shop. I lay my arm across her shoulder. Compassion and professionalism make bad partners. Despite the cosmetic restoration, she wears a distressed face. I wonder if McMaster had beaten her.

'Rose. What is it?'

'He's threatened to tell my family.'

'I thought you were on your own. He wouldn't even know them.'

She pulls a tissue from beneath the counter. 'Says he has "resources". You'd know what he means, wouldn't you?'

I do. Criminal Record checks, licence checks, registration

checks, information sharing through HM Revenue and Customs, access to electoral rolls, and the good old Google Search and Facebook can find just about anyone, anywhere. I play it down: 'Strict guidelines control access to information. Police have to justify their request with evidence of a legitimate enquiry. Anyone trenching for info without authorisation would face disciplinary action. He's just trying to scare you.'

'I… I… I have to tell you something. He touched me. Said I'm a cute girl and that he could make me really happy.'

Shit! How do I handle this? 'Are you all right?' *Idiot!* Stupid question in the circumstances. In all my years of policing, I've never dealt with such an accusation right out of the blue. I haven't served in sexual offence units, so I am ill-equipped to assist Rose. I'm not a good consoler. Give me the tomboy jobs any day: the truck drivers, labourers, builders and the brash entrepreneurs.

I'll do my best, woman to woman. 'Rose. I'm here if you want to talk. We should speak to a female police officer. I can arrange that if you like.'

Rose wipes away a tear. 'Thank you, but I've dealt with much worse in my life. I only mentioned it so you know what we're dealing with.'

'I think I know exactly what we're dealing with. Just a moment.' I scan the shelves for Hamilton's camera, looking in all the obvious places: behind display stands and advertising posters and along a refrigerator's top moulding. The geek's good. I can't find a lens or even a telltale wire. I resort to the embarrassing step of phoning him. After his laughing subsides he suggests I look in the ceiling for a non-functioning LED light. The supposed burnt out globe is the camera lens; the camera itself hiding above the ceiling.

'I could have shown you that,' says Rose.

Shit. Made a complete fool of myself. Got carried away and clean forgot that Hamilton would have shown Rose the camera's location so she could change the SD cards. I pull a ladder from the wall, climb up to the ceiling, shift a panel, and remove the camera. The compact digital is familiar, so replaying the images is not a problem. But it is a problem when I see DI McMaster leaning over the counter clutching Rose's shoulder.

XXXI

Phillip McMaster could not have risen through the constabulary's ranks to detective inspector – while simultaneously running scams – without owning a shrewd awareness of the criminal element, their motives and peculiarities.

During his flat-out respite in hospital, he'd struggled to pinpoint the perpetrator of the attack upon him. Colleagues reviewed recent convictions after confirming the falling tree was no accident. McMaster knew as much.

When quizzed about potential enemies, he countered: 'Why would I have enemies?' The list unfurling in his mind totalled ten. For starters.

The uniformed officer replied: 'Put it down to the job, sir. Probably arrested a few and aggrieved a few in your time. Mull over a few recent cases. Anyone come to mind?'

McMaster knew exactly who came to mind, and it wasn't a name he was about to present to colleagues. Since he'd had no high-profile cases during the previous three years, he knew his problems emanated from his own backyard – and his neighbour's. The run-in with Angelo pitched him as top pick.

Elevated to equal top was Jeff Main. On first impressions, Main presents as a fresh-faced schoolboy who would not even clench a fist. Beware of the quiet ones – a lesson from the past, origins unknown.

Numbers three to nine were out of the frame. They have

neither the ability nor the nous to drop a firecracker through his letter flap. Likewise, number ten – the beloved Gloria.

McMaster dismissed the young constable: 'I'll think about it and get back to you.' He had often dealt the same fob-off. His immediate reaction was to visit the Caruso property to sound out Maria. Whilst she would not deliberately implicate her son in any wrongdoings (and nor would she believe Angelo was involved) McMaster would need little effort to discover Angelo Caruso's whereabouts on the tragic evening.

* * *

Free of nurses and matrons, blood pressure and heart-rate checks, pressing and prodding, and regimented showering and eating, McMaster craves a stroll through his gardens to his shed. Brick and stone paths brew exhilaration far above the wheelchair excusions along shiny vinyl corridors.

Rural residents relish the joy of mid-morning walks in mist-laden valleys. McMaster's limping stroll reignites the passion for his precious Ashton Hill. Sadly, the manicured gardens bear symptoms of neglect; the lawns mimic a 1970s punk rocker's patchy haircut; the fountain base glows with green algae; and the small orchard – trees united by matted spider webs – awaits pruning. In contrast, deer on a distant hill prance and frolic on acres of glistening dew.

As he nears the shed, he concedes its monstrous proportions should have been rejected by council. Little wonder the Carusos objected. *Thank you Dennis Stonebridge for your pliable greed.* He opens the door. The huge interior swallows him. As does the engulfing reek of the maturing marijuana crop. He flops into one of the plastic chairs and absorbs the bare, galvanised walls. He's missed the evening operations and is anxious to return to the pit, despite the prognosis of a collapsed lung incapacitating him in the enclosed, stale environment ten metres below ground. The anxiety of prospecting just a little more, to pick out a few kilos of rock from the jagged wall, and to taste the dank odour of subterranean mustiness draws him to his underground vault.

He pulls aside the chairs and table, removes the plywood cover, and staggers back. The stench of death. Unmistakeable. Occupational hazard. He has often responded to calls of odours emanating from properties. After the first couple of turnouts he knew what to expect. If he was lucky he'd find in a derelict house someone's pet stoned to death by estate hoodlums. If he was unlucky, he'd break through a front door – with mask pressed to mouth and nostrils – and dry retch. He'd enter the next room to greet the maggot-ridden, fly-infested remains of someone's grandmother or grandfather.

And that is what he now smells. He hopes a cat or a fox has met its demise, but reality tells him the hypothesis has little merit. He picks up a torch and steps down the ladder into the mine. On the lower rung, he sees the crisis. A body. He drops to the ground, hooks one foot under the corpse's shoulder, and heaves, rolling the cadaver over as if it were a huge log. Its face is a platoon of predators, ceremonially marching into the mouth and wheeling from nostrils and eye sockets. Angelo's.

McMaster gasps. Shock. Regrets his earlier harsh words. He didn't want or expect this as an outcome, but he'd given the instructions and that puts him squarely in the frame. As soon as questions zip from one suspect to another, someone will surely nominate him as a contender for wanting Angelo out of the way.

That someone immediately springs to mind: Jeff Main.

First notions though, are rarely logic's sibling. He ponders: *Main is not beyond doing this. I'd told him to encourage Angelo. It's not inconceivable that he went too far. He knows where I live. Then again, he was supposed to liaise with Jill. Would she have done this? A payback for some reason? What the hell's she got to gain?*

Nothing makes sense. In his world of crime and deceit, little does. First instinct is to report the find. *Got sweet FA to do with me – I was in hospital. Beat that for an alibi.* He rifles through Angelo's pockets. Pulls out a business card: Jeffrey Main/Attorney at Law/Craggill, Weston and Rubenstein. On the flipside, he reads a scrawl: Ashton Hill, LHS A44, 1.6 miles from Pinvin turnoff. It makes no sense. Angelo Caruso has no need for his neighbour's address. It is a given – he'd known it for six years.

McMaster slips it into his pocket and scratches his head, a habit gained to buy time while interviewing suspects. Now, he doesn't need time; he needs to determine why Angelo Caruso would have Main's card. He considers the possibilities: his last conversation with Main commanded him to exert pressure on Angelo to ensure the Blackshaw's Mill property contract was promptly executed. *Hmm, it was the contract that was supposed to be executed, not the bloody client!* A forced grin foreshadows a ridiculous thought: Main is hardly going to introduce himself to Angelo and hand him a business card before killing him. And then his honed investigative skills trump. Main, perhaps with an ulterior motive, *had* initiated contact with Angelo and used him as a pawn in the estate transaction as a means of influencing his mother to hasten the process. Under those or similar circumstances, the existence of the business card is easily explained. McMaster has ample evidence of Main's propensity for double-dealing: once a crook, always a crook. If Main had convinced Angelo that a huge benefit glowed on the horizon – such as McMaster meeting a tragic accident – he has no doubt that Angelo would rise to the cause and become the proverbial putty in Main's hands.

The card could also be superficial, a decoy; its presence deflecting the real identity of whoever had disposed of Angelo's body on his property. *Why should it matter? How could anybody link Angelo to me other than by our acquaintance as neighbours?* He looks to his secondary career. What would a crim do? He'd do his utmost to conceal the crime. Period. He'd hoist the corpse up the ladder, wrap it in a blanket, drop it into the boot of his car – pre-laid with garbage bags or a blue plastic drop-sheet – drive to a quiet back street in the middle of the night, hurl the body over a railway bridge, and hope that by the time a dog walker or school boy discovered Angelo's mashed body, only DNA would identify him.

McMaster clambers up the ladder, replaces the cover and table and chairs and rushes outside for fresh air. It makes no difference. He can't undo what he's seen; he can't brush off death's scent. But he can undo the potential problem that will rope him into a murder enquiry. It will take little effort to conceal Angelo in a small dog-leg in the catacombs of his mine. Concrete and clay – the eternal preservative. That is a matter for consideration. For now, *someone* has dumped Angelo on his property and he urgently needs to find out *who*.

He paces back to the house, suspends events of the past half-hour, and defers to his drawing room. A tumbler of Dewar's provides divine intervention. The Saviour. With clear head, he concludes that twenty-four hours will buy time enough to learn who has set him up. That's exactly what it is. A set-up. A turncoat tipping him in for Angelo Caruso's murder. The trap is set, but the lid is yet to be sealed.

His throwaway mobile phone – the phone used for illicit dealings and anything he doesn't want traced, which in McMaster's case is *all* outgoing calls – is in the study. He creaks from the Chesterfield and hobbles along the hallway. Grabs the phone. Presses a pre-dial number. Waits. Voicemail.

'Hi. Sorry about last night. Change of plans. Come 'round as soon as you can. Urgent business.'

He jabs 'end call' and thumbs in another pre-dial.

XXXII

GILLIAN TURNS INTO THE DRIVEWAY, rear wheels sliding, stones tumbling across the grassy verge. She abandons the vehicle and rushes straight into McMaster's enfolding arms.

'Your wife home?'

'Don't worry about her. This is business, and it's none of hers.'

'What's got into you? Been demoted or something?'

'Will be if I don't resolve a problem. Now tell me; what's the deal? You've been coming on to me as if you want something. What's the go?'

'I beg your pardon? Yes, I find you appealing. And yes, I find you interesting. I've been hoping we can get together, especially after you told me your wife's out of the picture. That's not the first time I've been fed that line, but if you're going to chastise me like a little kid, you can stick our friendship and forget you ever met me.'

McMaster retreats. 'Calm down. I'm sorry. It's the job. Sometimes I feel as if you're scrutinising me.'

'Bloody hell, Mac. You summon me here and you claim *you're* under scrutiny? Fuck me. What about the trips to your boudoir – were they initiated by me? No way. How can you say that? You think I'm some spying bitch from MI5? Think your wife's paying me to tell her what you really get up to?'

Whack.

The slap whips across her cheek. Sends her to the ground.

Gillian's mixed it with the best in fights, but never has she copped a startling blow like McMaster's open-hander. The element of surprise. Always more powerful than the actual strike.

She rises. Heads for the door.

'No you don't. You're here for a reason. Come with me.'

'Fuck you. I'm going. Period.'

'Gill, I'm sorry. I lost it. This is very important.'

'Don't think you can treat me like one of your criminal pieces of shit. Five minutes. That's all you get.'

McMaster leads her to the shed.

Gillian dallies. Apprehensive. 'What you going to do, lock me up and have another go? You fancy some disciplinary action today?'

'Shut up and follow.' He opens the side door. The pair enter. McMaster closes the door. Locks it. Drags the table from the pit-cover. Throws the chairs aside.

Gillian's fascinated. 'So what's this? Another tantrum?'

'I'll show you tantrum in a moment, right?' He draws in a lungful of air before kicking back the pit-cover.

The whiff hits her with the same ferocity as had McMaster's slap. 'What the hell's that?'

McMaster grabs the torch and shines it down the shaft. 'It's *who the hell's* that? You know anything about this?'

'How would I? I've never been in here. It's always straight to the bedroom, as if you don't remember. So who is it?'

'My fuckin' neighbour, that's who. And I reckon you know something.'

Gillian blushes. Out of character. Ordinarily, nothing fazes her. 'So, Mr Detective. How would I know anything?'

'Because you have a habit of popping up in the right places

at the wrong times – or right times, depending on your point of view.'

'I work in a pub. I pull beers. And you. That's it.'

'All right. Yes, I am Mr Detective. You tell me just how you were on the scene within minutes of that tree crushing my car. Go on. You weren't pulling beers then.'

'I— I was coming to visit you.' She looks to the pit. 'Cover this up. He fucking stinks.'

McMaster replaces the plywood sheet. Grabs a bag of Blood and Bone fertilizer and sprinkles it around the floor. Absorbs one odour; introduces another. He glares at Gillian: 'You were saying?'

'I told you. I fancy you. I came to visit.'

'Yeah, right. Point One, Miss Suspect. You hadn't been here before, so there's no way you knew where I lived. Point Two. If you had come to visit, you would have followed me into the drive. I never saw lights behind me until the ambos. Shame for you, because I was conscious all the time. Even saw my neighbour. Point Three. I wasn't followed. Occupational obsession – always watch your back. Point Four, and this is the big one; the only reason you were here is because someone gave you my address. Now what I reckon is that you'd better come clean or you might find yourself joining your buddy down there.'

'Don't you threaten me. I don't recognise the guy and I haven't a clue how he got there. You're the copper. You ever thought about how many might want you taken out? Reckon someone might be setting you up? The way you're acting, I'd say they'd have very good reason.'

'If I was being set up, I'd have been snaffled by now. He's been there a while.'

'All right. So get back to basics. Have you had a run-in with him?'

'In more ways than one. He tried to shaft me.'

'But *you* wouldn't kill him, would you,' Gillian enunciates as a statement.

'Christ woman. If I'm going to waste someone, I'm not going to toss the stiff in my own fucking backyard. Look what I got over there. About five grand of choof, right? Perhaps I was wrong. You are too stupid to have anything to do with it. Let's get out of here.'

'But I'm not too stupid to hang around. I don't want your wife seeing me. That might be one of *her* lovers she's wasted just to get back at you. You thought about that, eh?'

What the hell else can go wrong, McMaster mumbles as he pours a scotch. Makes another call: 'Onions, it's me. What's the go with my deal?'

'Erm, had to shop around to get the best price. Sure you understand. I seen a trader, a good one. Coincidence, he just rang back.'

Onions started scamming as a twelve-year-old. One of his first enterprises was to sell his school's fundraising chocolate at a huge profit. Any kid can sell the product and keep the money. That's for simpletons. You'll be sprung. Inevitable. The parents pay the shortfall to the school and the thieving child suffers disciplinary action from both the school *and* the parent. Not so for Onions. He purchased small chocolates and Freddos from Tesco, swapped them with the larger fundraising confectionary and then palmed them off for the same price. Result? He handed the correct money to the school, and then scoffed and on-sold the couple of dozen larger chocolates for a handsome profit. His certificate of success was not the end profit, but receiving the headmaster's praises in school assembly for his devotion to fundraising. Refining his 'trade' over ensuing years sees *no one* capable of outwitting Onions.

Now, after receiving Lowenstein's advice about Main also tendering a gold sample for a price, Onions is cautious: 'My host's set up a meeting for Tuesday. Two o'clock. You want me there, or will you leave it with your solicitor?'

'What do you mean my fuckin' solicitor? I got no fuckin' solicitor on this, right? You're doing the deal; that's why I gave you a few hundred quid's worth of rock to shop around. We're not selling a crotchety old granny's nine karat wedding ring. So what the fuck are you on about?'

'Shit Mac. You don't have to crank off at me. Just passing on what the dealer, Lowenstein's his name, told me. I don't know what you got going with this, do I?'

'So you got a name of this fuckin' lawyer?'

'Main, he said. Someone Main.'

'Fuck me. I been scammed before by that prick. If he's going me again I'll fuckin' do him. Give me the address. I'll be there. You hang low. I don't want you getting caught up in this, although there's nothing wrong with getting a price from a reputable jeweller.'

'Fair enough. Sure you don't want back up? I got contacts.'

'You well might have, but they'll be not a patch on mine. I'll get back to you.'

XXXIII

Ever since my twelfth birthday I've insisted people not call me *'Liv'*. It's not that I dislike the contraction; I just want to preserve – in the nicest way – the nickname my step-father gave me. It's to his honour that I reject its use by other people, and that includes colleagues – close or otherwise.

When I pick up Thornton's call – *'Liv, the pig's off to Mac's right now'* – I've only just joined the A435 after leaving Rose to lock her shop and head home. I hurry to Ashton Hill.

Wary of Gillian's impending arrival, I hope to have at least a five-minute advantage. There is no way I'll prop in the lay-by again, just in case Gillian decides to dump her car and race cross-country to her beau. With McMaster's wife sitting at home, possibly spying on comings and goings from her upstairs window, I assume that Gillian won't brazenly waltz up to the front door.

I call on my knowledge of the narrow dirt lane – a service track that hasn't seen a grader for years – that runs alongside Ashton Hill. Partly concealed, it is used only by locals, because its bone-rattling surface discourages through traffic. I shudder at the wicked thought of riding my bicycle over its rhythmic ruts for an out-of-body experience.

I inch beyond McMaster's end boundary and park beneath a shady clump of oaks. I absorb the magnificent stand of trees, now separated by a void like a five-millimetre gap between a pair of bucky front teeth. The vista turns industrial when I set eyes on the huge shed.

It is mammoth; a galvanised shed that could double as an aircraft hangar. The query flashes before me: *What does he want with that?* Inquisitiveness compels me to find out, but I can't do that with McMaster at home. Or can I? A superficial scan reveals insufficient cover for me to creep around the side or rear of the construction. *But no one will see me tonight.* I reverse into a narrow space between two trees and wind back my seat. The driveway's entry point is out of view, but rattling stones will signal her arrival.

And they do.

The couple must have enjoyed a welcome reunion because it is ten minutes before they trek across the garden to the shed. I can't snoop on activities unfolding inside the giant steel structure. Perhaps I don't want to. It isn't the sort of retreat I'd fancy for a quickie, but each to their own. When they do emerge, it is not with a fatigued and dishevelled demeanour; it is with reserve and concern. I capture the moment with a few Samsung snaps. More evidence. I dispatch them straight to Thornton, partly to validate my efficiency; and partly to pump his ego for his spot-on assessment of Gillian.

As they return to the house, I claw the opportunity to dart to the shed. I huddle against the steel wall and press up to a blacked-out window. Plastic bin liner. The DIY method of concealing illicit activities from the public. A wrinkled edge permits me a pinhead view of a rear corner where rows of suspended lights hang over a flourishing crop of rich, green foliage. I don't need a botanist to tell me the plants' genus.

Thornton will be interested in that, *and* that Gillian must have seen it. My position is that if Gillian fails to tell Thornton about the crop, a cloud of suspicion must strangle her perceived integrity. What else then, is she concealing? For that reason,

I must procure specific evidence to confirm my findings and photos. I skirt the wall to a small door. Locked. That'd be right. I sneak a moment to decide whether to break in or continue pursuing Gillian. As the marijuana isn't going anywhere, I opt for the latter. I hustle back to my car. Await her next move. *Will she stay the night?*

At 2.00 a.m. I reverse count sheep to stay awake. So too, I suppose, does Gillian. As she proceeds along the driveway I start my car, hoping the crunchy gravel will drown the whir of my Focus's starter motor. I am disadvantaged by having to crawl along the rutted lane without headlights. By the time I reach the road, her taillights are two distant fireflies. I make ground fast, gratified that we are heading toward Cheltenham. If she is going home – and where else would she be going at 2.00 a.m? – I do not need to travel so close. I plan my tack: *what will I do if I approach her? Ask about Mac?* She'll tell me he's a boyfriend or colleague and I'd have to cop it sweet. Technically, I have nothing on her. I decide to wait and find out what she off-loads to Thornton.

I've achieved nothing concrete over the eight-hour drag. The few photos, sighting a small drug crop, and witnessing two people together who should not have been, is subject to further enquiry. Negative vibes gush through me as if I've let down Thornton. I continue to my flat, carrying with me the tensions of my vast and unpredictable workplace.

As a police officer, I'd often commiserated with employees of powerful organisations returning home to their loved ones where they suppress traumas of their daily grind. Even the self-employed take home similar dramas. We keep them to ourselves until they boil out of our pores, whether by the stillness of a lavender-scented bath, or the ferocity of smashing a stack of plates, Greek style, upon the floor, or kicking the cat – colloquially speaking of course. I've always envied the self-employed and the entrepreneurs, who, in charge of their own destiny, return home to their daily fold, excited, imbued with fresh ideas for the morrow, with not an ounce of troubles in their attaché case or smart phone, and not one smidgen of stress coursing through their body.

What a fool. I now carry home more stress than I ever did. I worry about the following day – how can I piece together loose ends?; how can I insulate myself from the loose cannons who had set out to neutralise McMaster?; and, will I ever see an eight-hour shift as a self-employed person? I pull myself from the doldrums, veer into a twenty-four-hour servo, and buy a one litre tub of Ben & Jerry's Cookies 'n' Cream and two 200 gram blocks of Cadbury's Fruit and Nut.

It is 3.00 a.m. when I slide between my sheets. I sure will have sweet dreams.

XXXIV

THEY LAST ONLY TWO HOURS before I wake with the need to revisit McMaster's shed. His interest in the monstrosity, coupled with the fact he's now toured Gillian through the enormous space, propels my belief – and mounting evidence – that they are in cahoots over something, and that something has to be illegal.

I approach the locked door. This time I am prepared with my set of masters, a gift from a grateful former client. Some may recall my working for Newquay lawyer, Alexander Beecham, for whom I investigated his mother's suspicious death. Through the most unfortunate circumstances, his sister, Roslyn, who was a local real estate agent, was murdered in her office. Alexander, on receiving his sister's possessions, regarded me – if you don't mind my bragging – as a worthy recipient of her master keys which she'd accumulated for emergency access to rental properties.

After a clean entry, the first thing to hit me is the magnitude of the Olympic size equine centre. Smells worse though; a musty, botanic pong fighting the odour of death. I offer that not only as professional recognition – but also from history. As a six-year-old I bawled my eyes out after finding my poor 'Tiggy' in a matted entanglement of stripped fur and fly-blown intestines. Subsequent scents of death assault my nostrils in much the same manner as mum's oven-baked chocolate cake – if you'll excuse the disparate comparison.

I check the marijuana plants, strip a few leaves and crowns and stuff them into a small Glad Bag. Evidence for Thornton. All right, I know, I know: paper bags for produce – but I'm not in the fruit and veg market now.

Curiosity leads me across the earthen floor, past small piles of sifted earth which rise from the ground like castings of a mole invasion. I cross a wobbly board supporting an outdoor setting. My footsteps drum a hollow thud. I prod and tap around the board as Gene Kelly, minus the rain and umbrella. Curiosity wins. I scamper to the window. Clear. I race back, slide the table and chairs aside and flip over the plywood sheet just like I'd done with Gillian's settee. *Shit!* Could well be, because the stench is unbearable. I can't see into the depths, so chance my luck on finding matches or a torch nearby. A small LED flashlight strapped to a safety helmet grabs my attention. I unclip the light and train it into the pit. A body shines back. Enough. The waft of decomposition tells me the person is beyond resuscitation. Instead, and it might seem a tad ghoulish, I haul a few shots into my Samsung. More evidence.

The situation requires urgent police attendance. In my former role, I'd call control and secure the scene. Here, as a trespasser, the scene is not so straightforward. I can't waste time, but I do have to get moving – my own well-being depends on it. I drag the board back over the pit and redecorate, before snapping off a few more shots of the locale. I clip the light back onto the helmet, which I've worked out is a crudely fabricated miner's cap, and return it to the tool bench. Further along the bench, a piece of polished timber lies among tools and cleaning rags. It's clearly out of place – unmasked by its dust-free sheen. Well, almost. A small blotch attracts me. And I recognise the blackened smudge of congealed blood.

Best guess is Maria Caruso's missing paddle. I won't leap to conclusions. The stakes are far too high. I snap a photo *in situ,* wrap a Glad Bag around one end, and jam it under my arm.

I exit with shaking hands. Hunched over like a trooper carrying a rifle, I run back to my car. Momentarily break down. Me, not the car. It's one thing attending a scene when we know what to expect. We prepare ourselves for shock, distress, and almost any eventuality. But in taking a midnight snoop (albeit six hours' late) for the purpose of snaffling marijuana stems, and to then find a corpse that McMaster and Trotter must surely know about, does test one's resilience. I delay waking Thornton while I race home to download the shed images into my laptop. Sleep must wait. I am pleased to have learnt the source of the mineshaft photos found in McMaster's camera, but disappointed to have not identified the body. Blame inadequate light or my reluctance to get down amongst it. I'm an investigator, not a hero.

Time: 6.30 a.m. I *have* to make the call. Whether to phone Thornton or Street is subject to a coin toss. Either way, I could alienate myself from a vital working relationship. Contacting Street in the first instance is the correct procedure, because the deceased lies in his jurisdiction. However, doing so will raise Thornton's ire for my not first reporting to him. Phoning DS Street is also fraught with danger. He will question my relationship with Thornton, and by deduction consider me the enemy. Result? Lost information source.

Loyalty wins over gut instinct. I detail my observations of the past few hours to Thornton and email photos of McMaster's shed and contents. I'm sure I hear his heart rate soaring – to the verge of shutdown, the self-preservation mode of the confronted: *I knew something was going on. Why didn't I act sooner? First, Mac's under a tree and now there's a body under his property.*

He is either mulling over the gravity of my report or examining the digital photos. I query his last contact with Gillian and hear about her call from McMaster. I continue with an account of the hours Gillian has shared with him, and imagine Thornton's eyes when I mention her 2.00 a.m. departure.

His voice competes with a police radio crackling in the background: *'Any unit available to attend Gatcomb Industrial Estate for a suspected vehicle on fire?'*

'Papa lima 408 receiving. Three minutes off. Mark us down…'

And then I send him beyond boiling point with news of the marijuana crop.

'Papa lima 408 to control.'

'Go ahead 408.'

'Vehicle's burning. Interior only. We've got the extinguisher on it. It's a black sedan, Audi. No plates, but got a VIN for you: WAUZZZ8K6AA103083.'

I jump at the words 'Audi' and 'black' as I continue with an overview of the McMaster/Caruso property transaction together with my take on Angelo's underhanded dealings. I don't reveal my source – and he wouldn't want to know – but I do reinforce that Gillian definitely knows every bit of information I've just relayed. I continue that if Gillian were on the level she should have already relayed the vital information about the body in McMaster's shed. There is no excuse for her not having done so. I move on to the timber paddle. He arranges for a car to collect it from my home.

'Papa lima 408. Your VIN comes up not recorded as stolen. Belongs to an Angelo Caruso, 63 Canning Road, Worcester.'

'Bloody hell. You hear to that? Caruso's car. I tried to see him at his flat. Wasn't there. I don't like the sound of this.'

'I'll get forensics onto it. Probably the local scum with nothing better to do.'

'It's more than that. This isn't a bunch of scroats joy riding and then torching the bloody thing. You'll find this is more, and since it's Caruso's car, I'm talking paybacks. And the ringleader'll be McMaster.'

Thornton placates me with one of his clichéd lines: 'Let's just wait and see what happens. In the meantime, I'll see what Trotter has to say for herself. Call me after five.'

His response is understandable: listen to both sides. Then he baffles me: 'What do we do now?'

I feel uneasy about offering my thoughts to a super, but I have to remember my charter – I am paid to provide information. My addendum is that I'm not paid to suggest direction. Never one for shirking the opportunity of promoting my viewpoint, I prepare both barrels. 'With respect sir—'

Any announcement or viewpoint prefaced with those three words grants the speaker immunity. I could call the Chief Constable a fat bastard, so long as I preface it with, 'With respect, sir.'

'With respect sir, I suggest you allow me to call DS Street, who is the officer in charge of the tree incident. I've already struck up a low-profile relationship. If I give the impression I have confided this discovery to him, it could cement my place as a confidant and reward me with ongoing information.'

Thornton's mind churns. 'How would you explain my involvement?'

'Easy. You might have read a report or been referred to the

Mac incident; you'd conveyed your best wishes to the hospital and as a follow-up you phone Worcester CI to discover what is being done to protect its officers. By that time, DS Street would have my information. He might seek accolades by offering you 'breaking news' of the body found in Mac's premises.' I hold my breath in time with the pause on the phone.

'Very good. Shows why Stafford recommended you. We'll go with that. Keep me informed.'

'One more thing, sir. I have a complainant who claims McMaster has been extorting merchandise from her shop. Your Gillian should have mentioned it; she's known about it for a while. Got her own photos of an incident.'

I admit that slandering Gillian is sleazy – even by my own standards. But if I'm doing the job, and she's not, well, I'll do my utmost to set up future engagements.

'News to me.'

'I also have a photo of him threatening her. Haven't got complainant's permission to make this official, but can do so fairly quickly.'

'Get it. We need it. Good work Watts.'

I end the call. I am *in*.

I restore my serious disposition and phone DS Street. He sounds edgy: 'Can't talk. Got a job on. A big one.'

Many detectives will claim a minor bout of shoplifting as a big one. Bragging rights around the office: the small Gucci purse becomes a whole set of Louis Vuitton travel gear.

'This is bigger,' I pronounce. 'I've got a body for you.'

'You know something I don't? We've just had a call from DI McMaster panicking over a stiff he's found in his shed.'

'I think I know plenty you don't. About this I mean. That's exactly why I'm calling. Don't get me wrong on this, but I can assure you there's something suss about anything involving McMaster.'

'You'd better be careful. You're talking about a respected, long-serving inspector. I'll approach this as I do everything else: with an open mind. Thanks for your concern. Gotta go.'

The phone clunks dead. Sounded like one of those old black Bakelite handsets crashing down onto the two silver pins. I didn't even get the chance to ask if I could tag along. Not a problem. I hold the trump card because I can positively ID McMaster entering the shed with Gillian. What I can't swear to is whether they had actually seen the deceased. With what Street has just told me, McMaster had. That, however, isn't my present concern. Getting to McMaster's property is.

I sit my Samsung on the table. I've done my civic duty. If all hell breaks loose, I'll feel consoled that I've acted professionally and am protected under Superintendent Thornton's wing.

I'll not add to my two hours' sleep, so I duck under the shower. My short GI hair allows me to sacrifice shampoo and conditioner. I pull on a black skirt, white chiffon blouse and tailored black jacket. The jacket is pure business; buttoned when speaking to women, floating free when eliciting information from males. The seductive appeal of a black bra beneath white chiffon reduces males to trance-like obedience, thereby enhancing the information-gathering process. A splash of an old Christmas cologne, and I am on my way.

XXXV

At five minutes after one o'clock, Thornton reads a list of McMaster's visitors during his confinement at Worcester General. Paces his office. Feels betrayed. Trotter's activities have not only insulted him, but are a blatant betrayal of trust.

The straightforward request elevated his temper after a nurse caustically replied: 'we don't log every visitor into the wards.' Worse followed: 'What do you think we are, a booking agency?'

Thornton wouldn't accept the young upstart's fob offs, nor consider that she might have worked a full night shift followed by four hours' overtime. He persisted: 'Can I speak to someone who might help with descriptions of his visitors?'

'I suppose you can,' sighed the disinterested respondent, complete with exclamatory huff of breath.

The phone clicked through: 'J Ward. Jeremy speaking.' In contrast, Jeremy was more proficient than an Identikit profiler. He painted perfect descriptions of Olivia Watts, Jeff Main, Gillian Trotter, other police colleagues, and an insurance salesman. Thornton smiled at the similarity between Main and Trotter as if they were both conceived from stem cells in a laboratory culture dish.

'I'll show you through,' the desk sergeant smiles to Gillian.

'Drop them on the table.' Thornton points to Gillian's laptop and carry bag. No hello. No greeting.

He glances at his guest. She is good. Red blush on one

cheek, but no sign of nerves as her eyes dart across certificates and children's paintings Blu-Tacked to the walls. 'Gillian. I've called you here today so we can catch up on the McMaster file.'

'Sure. I've got it all here. I don't mind if you call me Gill. I actually prefer it.'

A habitual stickler for formality, Thornton relents, knowing that acceding to her wish will allow the meeting to go ahead informally, which, in turn, will guarantee her candour. 'So Gill. How was your session with McMaster?'

'Sorry I didn't get to call you back. End of the line, I think. He's a different beast since getting out of hospital. Might be the tranquillizers. Seems more interested in pursuing a career in farming. He's spent buckets on doing up his property; put in a huge shed and the last I heard, started excavating. Whatever for, I haven't a clue.'

Thornton wheels out from behind his desk. Buckles his brow. '"From what I heard", you say? From whom?'

'Sorry, just a figure of speech. As you know, I've monitored his house and property from across the road. That's where I was when the tree came down.'

'And you saw him in hospital after that.' Thornton forces the sentence into a statement rather than a question.

Gillian stalls. Clicks through her memory, trying to recall whether she's mentioned that. Can't figure why she would have. 'Yes, I was there. If ever I was going to learn anything about him, catching him at his most vulnerable was essential. He'd be out for vengeance and I felt I could learn who he'd be after and that would probably lead me to the core of his inner circle – or so I hoped. It transpired the only recent contact he'd made, that I saw, was with his solicitor – and that was all business.'

'You think.'

'If you put it like that. Yes. But I'm confident it wasn't Main who did the tree. Different physique. Main's quite, er unique.'

'All right. Tell me about this shed.'

'It's massive. Mac, I mean McMaster, says he's considering farming. That's all I know. He doesn't talk much about it.'

'But you've been in there?'

'I never got that close. As I mentioned, I went to his home and he told me all this lovey-dovey stuff about how he's missed me and asked if he could see more of me. With our mutual interest of learning all we can about the inspector, I agreed. If we're going to nail him, I'll grab every break I can.'

Thornton drags a file from a plastic In Tray. Removes a laminated A4 photo. 'I can make this official.' He slides over the photo. 'Do you want to change your story?'

Gillian's face drops. Falls into silence as if caught cheating in a university exam. No way out. Considers a bribe. And then she turns to water: 'He threatened me. I had to go. If he knew what I was doing he'd kill me. I'm sorry sir; I just didn't know what to do. I still don't. You've got to cover me.'

Thornton receives the words as a poor attempt to deflect her lies. 'And you didn't think to inform me of the threat? We have a person under the microscope, and the very piece of information and evidence that would crucify him, you don't think to phone or text? When did this happen? You didn't seem too fussed when you walked in here, so it can't have been too much of a threat.'

'Maybe it wasn't. Maybe I over-reacted. I don't know. There's been so much going on, and my home's been broken into—'

She stops dead as if her vocal chords snap. 'Hang on. How'd you get that photo? It was only Mac and me. He's in the photo so he couldn't've taken it. It's his wife, isn't it? The elusive Mrs McMaster spying on her supposedly estranged husband to get enough goods to support a divorce action, or, to sink him once and for all. You'd better tell me what's going on here.'

'Doesn't work that way, Miss Trotter. You're telling *me* what's going on.'

'Nothing. I've worked through days and nights on this. I've got stuff on him right here.' Gillian produces photos of McMaster in Heavenly Spirits receiving a canvas bag.

'They're old news. You've already emailed them. Tell me what you were doing in McMaster's shed. There's a reason behind this, and I suspect you're trying to evade it. We're about two questions away from me ordering a Record of Interview.'

'Mac called me. Sounded real urgent. I had to go because I thought I might capture something important.'

'So why would he confide in you if you are discretely tailing him?'

'I was doing it my way, okay? I made him feel as if he'd landed me as a date, when all the while I'm doing my job of plucking every ounce of information from him. It's worked so far.'

'I wouldn't say a photo of a few bottles of *possibly* stolen plonk from a bottle shop constitutes working out okay. Let me spell it out. That shed which you've only just remembered being inside, is a crime scene from where a body is about to be retrieved. I'm pegging you're up to your neck.'

'All I know is, and I told you this a week ago, is that McMaster said something about having to fix someone. I later considered it just a figure of speech because he's shown no aggression since he's been under my observation.'

'Your red cheek evidence of his "no aggression"?'

'We were messing around.'

'Sounds too close for comfort.'

With Thornton's eyes blazing into hers, Gillian tries to reconcile the best way to handle the matter. She has become too emotionally involved with her target and is now so immersed in McMaster's activities that she truly fears the repercussions of telling all. And she knows whatever Thornton dishes out will be a breadcrumb compared to the loaf McMaster will serve.

Thornton fidgets through a further forty minutes of Gillian's diluted recitation. After sifting falsities from fact very little of the conversation will hook McMaster. Too little to justify the thousands of pounds shelled out on an undercover investigation that reveals only that DI Phillip McMaster is trying to buy a farm and *might be* receiving alcohol under false pretences.

'We're going to clean this up right now,' Thornton instructs. 'You've got fifteen minutes to load your files onto this.' He hands her a USB memory stick. 'Transfer everything and delete the material from your laptop. Make sure everything's wiped because I'll check it. Then, you can head home and type me a report of everything that's transpired with DI McMaster since I hired you. It'd better be complete, because by God I'll know if it's not.'

XXXVI

McMaster knocks on the door to his wife's quarters. 'Hi honey,' he offers with transparent deceit. 'Had a couple of strange events occur while I've been in hospital. You notice anything suspicious?'

'No. I was too busy enjoying your absence. You all right now?'

'As if you care. You weren't even interested enough to phone, let alone visit.'

Gloria smiles with tilted head and pouted lips. 'Come on Philly, you know I can't drive after a few drinks. One of your boys might arrest me. How embarrassing for you.'

'Shit, Gloria. Give it a rest. There'll be more than my boys here soon, right? There's a fuckin' body in my shed and I didn't damn well put it there. So who did you have hopping 'round here while I was wrapped in bandages and Christ knows what else?'

'If you told me what you were up to out there I could be more helpful. That lawyer of yours came here wanting to check measurements inside that monstrosity of yours. Goodness knows what for. I'm in the dark, aren't I?'

'Well he can't check measurements if the fuckin' joint's locked, can he?'

'Sure he can. I gave, er, I gave him permission. He had, er, a master key. Said he uses it in cases of clients not being available. No harm done. He only wanted to measure.'

'Fuck woman. You know what he's done, don't you?'

'No. Who needs to watch over a lawyer?'

McMaster huffs off and slams the door.

He removes all traces of the hydroponic set up and uproots forty harvest-ready plants. Bags the lot for quick removal. He'll later recover seeds from the mature plants. Waste not, want not. He also removes a strip of lights to allay any perception of professional drug cultivation. The remaining rows of strawberries look impressive – surprising the grower who barely fits the image of commercial fruit producer.

The excavation presents a problem. A string of questions will ask why a detective inspector has a huge pit in his oversize shed. It has been difficult enough explaining ownership of the prestigious property, let alone now having to justify what he wants to do with it.

With the incriminating botany removed, McMaster phones Jeff Main.

Main responds: 'Done as you asked, Phil. A little encouragement has accelerated the deal.'

'Tell me something I don't know, right. Whatever motivational speech you or she laid on him won't be doing him any good now. Caruso's sprawled out in my shed and he ain't going nowhere. Don't know who dumped him, or why, but you can bet your bollocks he won't be the last if word of our arrangement gets out.

'I've called the locals. Very soon there'll be cops crawling all over this place. So here's the solution, right: We've had a working relationship since Weston passed you my file. You'd noticed discrepancies and brought them to my attention and to the Caruso's solicitor, right. You never heard of Jill, and you never met Angelo Caruso. Just cite conflict of interest if need be. You've nothin' to worry about, so long as you keep that professional face of yours cool and detached. In the meantime, what's the delay with my settlement? Should be done and dusted by now.'

* * *

DS Roy Street pricks his ears at the mention of Caruso. He loiters around the office door like a vagrant picking up discarded betting slips from Ladbroke's floor. Street knocks and enters the inspector's office. 'Sorry I've got such big ears sir, was on my way out. Couldn't help overhearing the Caruso name. I've got the file on the old man; you got something new?'

'Plenty. We got another Caruso down. Angelo. Any connection?'

'Angelo's the son. We've crossed swords. Piece of work too. Has form for burgs, drugs and assaults.'

The inspector hoists an eyebrow. 'Well he won't have any more. Mac's just found him in his shed. Suggest you get over there right away. I'll arrange SOCO and support.'

'Something not adding up here. I'm just off the phone from that ex-copper, Watts, you know, the bitch who tipped in Marchant. She's somehow got her nose in everything and only just told me about a body in Mac's shed.'

'Have nothing to do with her. You've got an investigation to conduct. On your way. Hold up. What's her place in this? On second thoughts, you might make something of her getting bloody info before we do. Grill her. If she's as much as overstayed a parking meter, do her.'

Street shrugs his shoulders. 'All right. Are we to assume Mac's got something to do with it?'

'Come on Roy. You know the drill. We don't assume anything. We start with a blank sheet and do our job. Just make sure you follow the book.'

'The only way I work.' Street returns to the incident room and taps WDC Plumpton on the shoulder: 'We're off. Got a good one.'

They share a vehicle to McMaster's property, Street promoting general chat under the umbrella of learning more about McMaster.

'Never had much to do with him,' replies Plumpton. 'Sort of does his own thing. Inspector's prerogative I suppose. Got a reputation as a womaniser. Not my scene to go out with work colleagues, least of all a near-retired gov'nor.'

'He tried it on you then?'

'Nah. I don't even go to the pub. Anyway, I'm not his type. Lose a few kilos, I might come up okay. Happy enough with my pets.'

'Word has it he's on the take.' Street slips in.

'No go zone. I'm not getting into that. You're right, it's all around the office, but I've got no first-hand knowledge. I wouldn't be shoving my nose in there.'

'Wise. Very wise.'

They pull into Ashton Hill's drive and pass two stumps standing like lost children in a carnival – totally out of place, dwarfed by their surrounds.

'Look at the size of those mothers,' pipes Street. 'Must have been one hell of an impact.'

Plumpton scrunches her face. 'This is where it happened? Where the DI copped it?'

'Yeah. There's talk of rivalry between the neighbours, which explains why I have a drawer full of Caruso-related files: old man Caruso's suspicious death; the wife as a suspect; Mac's hit; and now Angelo. He didn't live with the oldies, but was there often enough. Won't be any more though – except in spirit.'

They edge along the drive, Plumpton in awe of the imposing mansion growing before her. 'Do we have to bow or curtsy? What is this place? Downton Abbey? Bit of the old silver spoon in the family?'

'I think that's enough, Laurel. He's still your inspector. But to answer, no one'll say. Holds his cards against his chest. Look, there he is.'

McMaster stands at the end of the drive motioning Street to continue to the rear of the property.

Street parks. Approaches McMaster. 'Hello. Very impressive.'

'Thanks. What you're about to see isn't.'

Plumpton tags behind, absorbing all around her: the distant dam and huge mountain of soil; the new rear fence marking out the recently realigned boundary; and the rear vista of the inspector's home, its slate roof cutting into cumulonimbus clouds.

Street follows McMaster into the shed. Watches him remove the plywood pit cover. Peers below. Takes control. 'Okay. Stand back. We'll treat this as a crime scene.'

Two SOCO officers contain the area. One erects a portable floodlight to illuminate the deep shaft while a colleague removes the ladders for forensic analysis. Another snaps a series of photos. Camera flashes bounce from the galvanised steel walls, spotlighting the coroner. He looks to the pit: 'I'm going down. Need to see the body before you guys get to it.' He won't risk misdiagnosis by allowing the deceased's premature removal. The point of impact and body position is essential to determining cessation of life.

Strapped into a safety harness and with two torches dangling from his belt, he plummets to the earth's core. He reels off a dozen photographs, examines bruises and limb placement, and checks the deceased's pockets for ID and possessions. Nothing.

A uniformed officer hauls a stretcher from the pit, pulling on a block and tackle chain like an exhausted campanologist.

'Know him?' Street directs the question to McMaster.

'Yeah. My neighbour.'

'Any idea how he came to be in your dungeon?'

'Let's put this right first up. It's not a bloody dungeon, it's the makings of my wine cellar. And no, I've no idea how he got there.'

DS Street is not intimidated by McMaster. His status as an inspector of police means nothing in the course of an investigation. 'If you don't mind my saying, sir, it's an unusual location for a cellar.'

McMaster smiles. His ability to neutralise suggestions and accusations is unrivalled. 'Well, sergeant,' he condescends, 'it's only unusual because it doesn't make sense to you. The situation is, a covenant on the main building forbids structural changes. That prevents me removing a wall where I wanted to sink a set of stairs. The next best place, which may seem strange to you, but is practical, is to burrow under my shed where I'll be brewing strawberry wine. The 'dungeon' as you so ignorantly describe it, will serve for aging and storing my product. You may not appreciate the art of viticulture, but research shows that the deeper the cellar, the easier it is to maintain a stable temperature of 15 to 16 degrees centigrade. I could never have gone that deep under my house, so this location doubles the benefits.'

Street scratches his head, furious at allowing himself to

wander off course. 'Okay. You know the deceased, but you can't say how he came to be in your *cellar.* Could I conclude that whoever dropped him there is after you?'

McMaster pitches his voice, but maintains control: 'Conclude what you want. I'm 22-years in the job, right? There's plenty who want me out of the way. So what's the point of your question?'

'Purely procedural. I'm sure you understand.'

'I do. And I'm sure you'll understand that I'll answer nothing more unless accompanied by my solicitor. I can arrange that now or we can do it at the office.'

Street is flummoxed. He has nothing concrete to attach suspicion to his superior. 'No, that's fine inspector. We'll leave it at that for now. You can wait outside, thanks.'

'I beg your pardon?' McMaster's indignant voice enunciates outrage. 'You want me outside while you're poking your nose around in here?'

'Procedures, inspector. You know that.'

'Only if I'm a suspect. As it stands, I'm a member of the public who's phoned in a possible crime. In fact, it's more than possible, right, because the guy certainly didn't place himself in my pit, er, cellar.'

Street stands firm: 'And as I'm sure you'll understand, inspector, as a member of the public you should see that we must isolate the area. Now if you don't mind…' Street extends his arm toward the side door and continues his examination of the shed to ascertain the mode of entry for whoever had dumped Angelo's body. He concludes the roller doors' mechanism would rattle through the night; the side door lock and surrounding framework show no forced entry. He inspects the strawberry plants. Casts his eyes to empty receptacles alongside, and to moisture and soluble fertilizer lining the troughs. Errant leaf and stem fragments bear no resemblance to strawberry runners. As Street collects a sample of the greenery, the coroner approaches from behind.

'Roy, got a problem. When do say you got the call on this?'

'Couple of hours ago. Why?'

'Aside from the problem of finding a dead guy, I estimate the time of death at more than 48 hours ago. Could be up to 72. Might explain the stench down there.'

Street checks his notebook. April 29. 1217 hours. He'd logged the time on receiving the details from his duty inspector. 'Christ. Why is nothing easy in this job? What can you tell me about his condition? I mean, was he done here or was he done elsewhere and just dumped here?'

The coroner shakes his head. 'Bit early for all that. Blood lividity suggests movement post-mortem. The guy went through a horrific fall. Must be a thirty-foot drop. We've got broken bones that might have fractured from that rather than through an assault. However, there's no injury likely to have caused death, unless a rib's gone through a lung. Leave it with me and I'll call you as soon as I get a break. Sorry. Bad choice of words.'

McMaster hangs around the shed knitting together conversations and comments. He is pleased to hear the possibility of Angelo having been murdered elsewhere. Less heat on him.

He warms to the need for a serious chat with Jeff Main. There is a major disparity between encouragement and eradication. He understands it is too late for anything to be done about Angelo, despite his demise being fortuitous. His problem now lies with Main, for he has the potential to squeal under questioning and point the finger at anyone remotely associated with Angelo Caruso.

XXXVII

I ROLL INTO ASHTON HILL'S courtyard to be confronted by a pseudo used car dealership. Battenberg blues and yellows decorate the front line. An unmarked sedan I recognise as Street's, and a white van I assume to be SOCO's, sit under the portico. A scruffy Vauxhall hides behind them. McMaster's. I reverse onto the lawn, and leave my Focus next to a planter box – unlocked, should I need to make a fast exit.

I walk to the rear of the property. Blue and white tape wavers between trees and a veranda post. White-overalled officers search the shed perimeter. I approach one, with my jacket wide open below an even wider smile – which the guy doesn't even notice (the smile, that is) – and learn that Street and McMaster are inside the shed. I get the official wave to step aside. Fifteen minutes' later emerges Street and a woman who might as well have 'police' stamped on her forehead. McMaster accompanies the pair. I don't want him to spot me, but Street does. I will him to approach, but my hopes are dashed when he continues jovialities with McMaster. I pray that he will not be swept into McMaster's spell.

Street walks on, his back to me. I'm frantic to draw his attention. His offsider sees my gestures and bounds over. Introduces herself: 'DC Plumpton. And you are?'

I detest those leading questions. The little Pomeranian detective, short, squat and senseless (my initial appraisal) fronts up with her sing-song "and you are?"' I am not the archetypal bitch, except when sleep deprived: 'Waiting for DS Street. I have information.'

'And you are?'

Fuck me. 'And I *are* what?'

'Your name. What was your name?'

Bitch. 'Oh, my name. Well it *was*, and still is, Olivia Watts. I'm a private investigator and I've previously spoken with DS Street about the Caruso matter. There's a link to what you've found in the shed so I want to speak to the sergeant about it.'

'Well, as you can see, he's busy right now. You can pass anything on to me and Roy'll get it when he's finished with the inspector.'

She calls him Roy? Nice pairing that is.

I overlook the familiarity. 'Nup, it's okay. It's probably all under control. Perhaps he could phone me when he's free.' I hand Plumpton a business card and trek back to my car. I glance behind and see Street ogling me. I jiggle down my skirt.

'I'll phone you,' he yells. I wave an acknowledgement. Plumpton gawks.

I must have been mad to agree to DS Street's invitation for an 'unofficial' chat.

I sit in his kitchen, cup of tea at one side, folder of information at the other. I've offloaded detail of Angelo's relationship with his father, only to learn that I knew far more than did Street himself. And now I'm caught at crossed purposes.

Having described Gillian's association with McMaster to Thornton, I believe it equally responsible to brief Street – but I don't know how far and how deep to tread. My allegiance is to Thornton. It would border on betrayal to impart prejudicial knowledge to anyone else.

'I'll order in takeaway. What's your fancy?' Street asks.

I hadn't planned on dining with the guy. I am abusing the social call as a relationship building exercise between the constabulary and my practice. Any information I can extract about McMaster and his current predicament will be a bonus. Hunger dictates my reply: 'Chinese would be great.'

'My favourite. I'll go the Beef and Blackbean,' he smiles.

I'm forever wary of the guy who offers dinner. There's always an ulterior motive – and it's not because he thinks you're hungry. 'Sweet and Sour Pork,' I reply. 'With cashew nuts.'

He lays the table as if he is expecting royalty or the Chief Constable. One and the same, some would say. A bottle of wine shivers in an ice bucket.

Here we go. Chateau Le Gopner. He's interested in more than files.

Since my tête-à-tête with Hamilton Holt months earlier, I'd resolved to never again hook up with work colleagues. Ever. Street isn't technically a colleague, but the association, if fostered, would be too close for comfort. I'm not going to be a second-time-'round victim of locker-room banter.

We eat and drink, exchange life histories – red penned from my side – and eat and drink some more. His mercury rises to the point where he expects me to warm to his advances. There's no invite to his bed, but he suggests we 'retire' to the settee where it is 'more comfortable'. As I sink into the slippery velour, he asks my reasons for snooping around McMaster.

I explain that my role in another investigation has crossed over, and that McMaster is common to both matters. That isn't enough to satisfy him. But I hold the cards. When I let on that I witnessed, or close enough to it, McMaster's driveway incident, he shows his true colours.

'If you don't reveal your knowledge, I'll do you for withholding information.'

At this point I consider the television line: 'In that case I'll seek legal advice,' but doing so will jeopardise our connection. Thornton's paying me good money. It is in my interest to prolong proceedings so I might play a pivotal role in nailing McMaster. His involvement in this, and the threats to Rose Hernandez, could see him admonished or 'invited' to resign. The force does not need preying deadwood like McMaster.

I release tiny amounts of information like a garden enthusiast's drip-watering system trickling tiny droplets whilst the main volume remains in the pipeline. 'I already had a file on McMaster,' I lie. 'Started out as an anonymous harassment case. Surprised me when I found he was a police inspector. I have a complainant who will state that McMaster stopped her for a nit-picking motoring offence and later subjected her to various demands, the nature of which I ask you to respect my withholding for now.

'As a result of info from this complainant, I sat off the McMansion as I call it, at what turned out to be a calamitous time. I did not see who cut the trees, nor did I witness anyone depart the driveway (another lie) after the tree fell. I heard the crash and raced straight across the road from the lay by and attended the victim.

'Triple nine will have my call recorded at about 5.30 – 5.40, when I requested ambulance and police. I was there when ambos extricated the inspector from his car. Also there, was a panic stricken woman I now know to be Maria Caruso, the neighbour. She was in a bad way, so I escorted her the few hundred metres to her home where I met her son of a bitch son, Angelo Caruso. My feeling is that he had something to do with his father's death.'

Street casts me a strange look as if I am reciting the *Never Ending Story*. 'We might never know. It's Angelo Caruso who was down the hole.'

I'm not surprised that someone might want to rough up Angelo but I'm not going to give that sort of lead to Street, for fear of compromising my own case. 'I believe Angelo was working with Mac; he was assisting his mother with the sale of the family property.'

Street remains deadpan. 'So, what do you reckon of the mother? Angling for full settlement of the property?'

'You've got to be joking. You met her, have you? You're not thinking she's done the husband and the son, are you? For goodness sake, she can hardly pick up a bag of groceries, let alone chuck a 100 kilo guy down a mine shaft.'

'Just a thought. Can't close any lines until they're completely ruled out.'

'Well, I reckon you can obliterate that. Where's the motive? Maria Caruso had nothing to gain by killing her son. What's got into you? The scenario's preposterous. Now, what's for dessert?'

I shift the conversation off topic. My head is full of McMasters and Carusos and Mains.

He offers coffee and ice cream. I fall asleep before the kettle boils.

XXXVIII

I WAKE BENEATH A THICK duvet, head propped by a slab of pillow. Don't know how he did it; I usually wake at the slightest movement. I crane my head, embarrassed to have fallen asleep, but thankfully did so on the couch rather than in his bed.

I delve into my bag, grab the phone and check the time. 5.25. Double check. Morning. Reach back in and pull out a pen. Scrawl on a serviette: *Thanks for the evening and the duvet. Didn't want to wake you, had to go. I'll phone.* I slither out of his home with the same tenacity as I slither *into* homes.

I hadn't minded DS Street until he pressed me with the "I'll do you for withholding information" jibe. If ever I was short of a motivational source, Street had dangled the carrot.

I've been marinated with ambition to exceed in my chosen fields, whether they be sport, hobby or employment. I can't attribute the trait to generational DNA, because I inherited it through my step-father, a homely man who advanced through the ranks of the constabulary to inspector. "Success lies behind the face of adversity" was another of his lifelong quotes. I adopted the notion and applied it to my career in lieu of marrying at eighteen and bearing six children in a council flat before my twenty-fifth birthday, as was the custom, and, some might say, still is the custom.

It therefore makes sense to follow that ideal. I add to my responsibility of tailing Gillian and monitoring McMaster, a personal pledge to beat Street in his quest to identify Angelo

Caruso's killer. My ace is that I have an exceedingly good head start. The suspicious circumstances of Angelo's unlocked flat coupled with the files I retrieved from his under stair study complements the material I'd 'obtained' from Gillian's flat. I enjoy the ever-reliable gut feeling that I'll learn more from pursuing Gillian than I'll gain from speaking with her.

She's already flagged her involvement by revealing goings-on between McMaster and Main, and has been privy to conversations discussing Angelo's surprise appearance in McMaster's shed. That swings me to Main, so I reassemble the shredded business card. I shelve the idea of phoning, and head straight to his Worcester office. Some enjoy hanging up on me, but try to eject me from an office and you're dealing with a whole new demon.

The office complex occupies a whole floor of the prestigious Allied Finance building. After a verbal scrap with a receptionist, I am granted a ten minute concession. Jeff Main closely resembles an overweight taxi driver who's struggled into an eight-year-old charity shop suit. One should see a solicitor as a figurehead of society, sharing a pedestal with politicians. *Woops, they are both respected* and *reviled.* Perhaps I don't fit the part of a private investigator – but I do blend in with the public.

I open with an assumption: 'I believe you're acting for Gloria and Phillip McMaster in the matter of a property transaction.'

'That's privileged. What's your interest?'

'The death of two Carusos, but more particularly the suspicious death of Angelo Caruso.'

'Don't know anything about Angelo, though I am aware of his father's passing. Heart attack, wasn't it?'

Main acts extremely coy, like a Crown prosecutor yielding little while reaping heaps in return. When I first started in the constabulary, I felt so far removed from those professionals who'd spent upwards of seven years studying how to manipulate accused and witnesses into saying exactly what *they* want to hear as opposed to what the accused or witness actually wanted to say. Today, I pitch myself on par with adversaries, and accordingly articulate my words in such manner to catch my opponent napping. My head lolls: 'So how did you know Angelo was Giuseppe's son?'

Main's quick. 'I had dealings with him; he was a, er, messenger between my client and the vendor.'

Good answer from someone who, only two minutes' earlier, didn't know anything about Angelo.

Maria had mentioned Angelo handling the contracts, but I have no inkling whether those dealings meant getting together with Main. Because of his legal connexion to McMaster, professionalism should have precluded such a meeting.

'Strange,' I say, 'because Maria Caruso was, and still is, the vendor.'

Main reclines. If my vision exceeded twenty/twenty, I would see the halo glowing above his head. 'Well?' he says. 'Doesn't really concern me.'

'Mr Main. I'll be totally frank with you. I am aware of highly incriminating information supporting a meeting with Mr Phillip McMaster in which was discussed an agreement to get rid of Angelo – a "prat". You might recall the expression?'

Main jabs an intercom: 'Jade. Come and show Miss Watts out will you?'

I've dealt the big one too early. I don't move: 'Hit a nerve, did I? I'm not the only one with this information.' I turn to Jade who impersonates a trainee air hostess with extended arm ready to push me from the emergency exit.

I offer a beaming 'thank you' as Main reaches for the phone.

XXXIX

'Hello. McMaster. What is it?' Main's number glows in the display.

'You know an Olivia Watts?'

'Yeah. Ex copper. Used to work in my nick. Trouble maker. Why?'

'Just been to see me. Kicked her out after she let loose about one of our meetings and spot on quoted what we said about Angelo.'

'Fuck! Don't say another word. Meet me out front of yours in thirty.'

Main can't afford to waste the next half hour. He has tracks to cover. With haste. Phones Jill. *Come on, come on.* Voice mail. Leaves a message: 'Hi. We need to speak. Concerns a motivational session. Call me.'

Panic brews. He ends the call with a shaking hand.

In a down-market backpacker's hostel tucked away in London's East End, Jill stares at her phone. She's been expecting the call for a fortnight and is astounded it has taken Main so long to make contact.

She'd struggled with her decision to take the £1,000 and run. Since going into hiding, she's spent only forty-five of the one thousand paid. Sure, she'd tailed Angelo and devised a plan, finally settling on knocking him from his Harley as the most effective means of delivering Main's message.

For the past ten days, she's cringed to each call – before flicking it to voice mail – expecting serious consequences of not performing her part of the deal. Sooner or later a new crisis will unfold. And she'll be the victim. She swipes the screen and waits.

'Yeah,' McMaster whispers into his throwaway phone.

'Sorry to call you. It's Jill. I'm sorry about everything. You've got that Main guy on me. Can we fix this? I was going to do it; I had the time and place lined up, waited and waited and the guy never fronted. Maybe I should have called you earlier.'

'What the fuck are you on about, woman? You trying to weasel out of something 'cause you've gone too far? You got something to do with the stiff in my shed, 'cause if you have, don't come running to me for help, right? What the hell did Main tell you to do? A little hurry on was what I wanted; think the word I used was "encouragement". Fuck me, woman, you'd better make yourself scarce, and quick.'

Jill pieces together McMaster's barrage. 'Listen, will you. I haven't done anything. I don't know about your shed and I don't know what's in there. I've called you because Main's hassling me every hour. So who's the body in your shed? Whoever it is, it's got nothing to do with me!'

McMaster jumps in. 'Got news for you. It has. It's Angelo. And you were the last one to have anything to do with him. Don't try putting one over me – it'll be the last thing you do. How the hell did you think you'd get away with this? You think it's funny? A warped payback? You know my line of work. It won't take me long to sort this, so don't give me the innocence crap. I've heard it, and broken it, too many times before. Now fuck off of my phone.'

* * *

McMaster rushes to his crystal decanter. Pours a tumbler of Dewar's. No ice. Tips it down his throat like emptying a mop bucket into a drain. Sits. Scratches his head: *If Jill didn't, who did? And why dump the bastard here? Who knows about my shed? Better still, who knows about the pit? Friggin' no one because the whole show's a secret.*

He brushes his teeth and crams half a dozen mints into his mouth. Heads to Main's office. Five minutes before the hour he leans on the horn. Main whirls through a glass turnstile and leaps into Master's car. ''bout time,' says McMaster.

'What's the go?'

'More than you can imagine.' McMaster screeches away from the kerb and heads to a multi-level car park where he nudges into a corner bay on the second-top level. Turns off the engine. Removes the key. Throws his arms across Main's chest, pulls open his jacket and rifles the pockets. 'Where's your phone?'

Main leans back, hands up. 'What's that for? It's in my pocket. Here. Bloody hell.'

McMaster checks the menu. 'You're not recording this?'

'Why the fuck would I record anything we talk about? Nothing we do is above board. I'm hardly going to record it.'

'Well, you're all about arse covering. Now what's going on with that Watts bitch? Tell her nothin' you hear. What makes you think she's got word on the Angelo deal?'

Main gulps. 'Look, she just fronted my office. No appointment or anything. Conned her way in —'

'Don't think I care for your administrative obstacles.'

'All right. Said she had "highly incriminating" information.

Seems to be our conversations about fixing Angelo have been taped. That can only have come from the pub because the topic has not been anywhere else. I thought I'd better let you know, because we now have to protect ourselves.'

'You might. I don't. I've done nothing wrong. We discussed a contract which was my property deal. Anyone who might have overheard anything could construe a conversation in one of many ways. If Watts wants to make a deal of overheard snippets that *might* have sounded something like what she claims, my response would be that she's mistaken. I recommend you ponder likewise. She's got nothing. Now where's my fucking contract?'

'They've taken a back seat with all this going down. I have been assured they're being couriered to my office this afternoon, so for all intents and purposes it's a done deal.'

McMaster smiles. 'Intents and purposes, bullshit. Nothing's done 'til I've got the paperwork. For now, though, close enough is *nearly* good enough.'

Main settles back; his obligation to McMaster almost complete. But he doesn't grasp McMaster's manoeuvring him into dropping his guard.

'So tell me how Jill went with the job.'

Main grins. 'Done and dusted. Ages ago. Days, anyway. Hasn't collected the final instalment yet; I guess she's waiting for the heat to fizzle.'

'So what did she do? You verified it? You spoke to Angelo, right; to find out how receptive he is to co-operating?'

Main straightens his tie. 'I thought it best to hang back a while. Keep our association quiet. She phoned, told me the job's done, and hung up. Next thing, his mother's solicitor's telling me the documents have been executed, and they'll be in my office within 48 hours. There was a minor hiccup, but all's resolved now.'

'Would it surprise you that I've recently spoken to Jill?'

'Wouldn't surprise me at all, Phil. You're thorough with everything you do.'

A car revs around the corner, squealing its way to the uppermost deck. The sting of molten rubber wafts into McMaster's car. The distraction throws him off course. Allows thinking time before he thrusts his face into Main's: 'Now listen good, right? Jill tells me she hasn't done the job. You know what? I'm inclined to believe her. She's a good operator, but she can't lie. You're a bad operator, but you can lie. See the predicament I'm in?'

'She has done it. I got the call, and it made sense how everything fell into place after she'd seen him.'

'So tell me what she did. You did check, didn't you? Satisfied yourself how well she'd earned her money? Made sure the final instalment was genuinely deserved?'

'I took her word for it. No reason to question a professional operator.'

'Life's lesson number one. Trust no one – which is why I don't trust you. Any idea where Angelo is now? Bet you haven't. Been dumped in my place. Removed on Monday morning – to the morgue. Someone's trying to set me up. But you know what? I got the best alibi ever. I was in hospital. Hourly checks recorded on my charts; CCTV supporting my not leaving the building; and medical evidence showing I couldn't have walked twenty metres. So my best advice is to get onto this Jill broad and tell her she's gone too far. I wash my hands of it.'

'You're not going to dump me in it. All I've done is accept your instructions. I have a clear conscience. I'll not be another pawn of your bullying tactics. I'll give your file to Weston; you speak to him about the title documents. I'm out of it.' Main flicks open the door, leaps from the vehicle, and strides toward a flickering exit sign.

McMaster boils. He's not yet canvassed Main's appointment with Lowenstein and he's withheld his knowledge of Main attending his shed for measurements. So focused was he on the land contract – everything else will now have to wait.

He starts the car, draws alongside Main and yells through the window: 'I'm not done with you, Main.'

XL

FEMALE INTUITION DRIVES ME TO probe deeper into Main's role. On leaving his office, I retreat to a cold, stainless steel bench seat in a courtyard at the side of his building. I need time to gather my thoughts which are scattered like pigeon poo over Trafalgar Square. I've lost perspective amidst the multi-stranded threads of what started out as a simple tail and report. My plate is full with the death of Giuseppe Caruso – which I won't accept as natural causes – and now his son, Angelo; there is the incident against McMaster; there is the confusing association of McMaster and Rose Hernandez, and to top that, I am overdue a call from Lowenstein.

At the core was a boundary issue that triggered the offer for Blackshaw's Mill. In that respect, McMaster has a huge personal and financial interest. If my mining project theory is on the mark, it means McMaster has a vested interest in the property *and* a motive to kill. If I balance McMaster's purchase proposal with Giuseppe's refusal, I could interpret the rebuff as McMaster's motive against his neighbour. Big call, I know, but the past few days have shown McMaster's ruthlessness has no bounds.

What if *Angelo* was the stumbling block? Problem removed.

And then there is Gillian. I am unequivocally positive she has a role in this. No one can spend so much time in McMaster's company, and during so many contentious issues, without having a vivid picture of those events, or a degree of complicit involvement. If she learns of my inclination to 'leak' information to Thornton, she might become mouldable putty. I don't believe she has sufficient insight to deduce that I was the culprit who had rifled her flat. If that were the case, she would have reported her suspicion to the police. Too late now. I have my own cards to deal. And I hold the whole deck.

I boast more information about Gillian than she has about herself. The comprehensive folio provided by Thornton contains not only her personal details, but also a copy of her job application and curriculum vitae. I extract her mobile number from the résumé and log it into my phone. A car horn attracts my attention. Probably another aggrieved driver venting frustrations over a parking spot. But when Main rushes across the pavement and into the car, my awareness pricks. McMaster is the impatient driver. My attendance at Main's office must have stirred them into damage limitation. It certainly stirs me into snapping off a series of photos.

Re-enacting a low-budget American gangster movie, I flag a taxi, clamber into the back and yell: 'Follow that car,' as I thrust my arm toward the silver Vauxhall.' The driver probably thinks he's being hijacked or that I am joking, because I am laughing at my own ridiculous instruction. I reinforce it with, 'I'm serious, I'm working'. I leave it to him to determine what I am working as. To compound his confusion, two streets later I yell: 'Stop. Right here.' I pass over a tenner – which is double the fare – and rush toward a multi-storey car park. Damn. It will be like trying to find the proverbial needle in a haystack, given that by my reckoning, one in three British cars is silver.

If I were seeking a place to conduct illicit business I would not choose an empty level in a public car park. I'd use the local gym or pool where I'd mingle with women dropping gossip, calories and wayward husbands. But McMaster doesn't think like a woman. Therefore, he doesn't think with logic.

My own logic fails me as I search for the silver car. As I ascend from level to level, the vehicle density diminishes because every shopper and employee wants to park as close as possible to their favourite shop or workplace. I poke my head from the stairwell door and see that the fifth level holds only a cluster of white vans and shop fitters' gear spread across two parking bays.

I trudge up the concrete stairs, paying the price for my declining fitness. I've done nothing but run around after Gillian and McMaster for the past fortnight, and that running isn't conducive to elevating my cardiovascular capacity. My legs falter, which surprises me because many guys compliment my strong thighs, notwithstanding that some will say anything to heap praise on a woman. I puff my way to the sixth level door – or the purple floor, for the numerically challenged – and just as I open the door a car whizzes past. McMaster. And then Main springs from nowhere, smack bang into the doorway. He faces me like a boozed-up rogue about to give his wife a hiding. For once I am lost for words. But he isn't.

'Well, well. Lookee here. What's happening?' He grins an evil snigger, proud of his own joke.

I've had the line thrown at me a thousand times. Old news. Dream up something new if you want to mock my business name. He stands rigid, awaiting my reply. I blurt: 'Just doing a spot of shopping.'

Crack! He crunches me open-handed across the face, pushes me into the stairwell and pulls the door closed. 'Shopping bullshit. What is it with you? You're one piece of work, you know that? And not too good at it either. Nothing too private about the way you operate.'

I pull my hands up to caress my burning cheek. He charges his fist into my shoulder. That disables me and tells me I'm not going to get out of this lightly – if I don't defend myself. But I hold the advantage because he's leaned in to me. I execute the perfect knee-lift into his groin. He buckles over as if kowtowing to a Chinese emperor. Perfect. I clasp my hands together and crunch the back of his neck. He drops to the ground, but in doing so grabs the hem of my jacket and pulls me onto him. In a different situation, I would savour the initiative.

He rolls over, trapping me beneath him. This is nothing like Gillian straddling me. No. Main's eyes enlarge. Tears stream down his cheeks. I must have *really* hurt him. The tables are turned.

'Got a problem with me?' I ask. 'You'll suffer a bigger one after I report this.' I regret my bravado as soon as the words leave my mouth.

'You won't convince anyone a reputable solicitor attacked a woman in a car park,' he replies. 'Besides, I was with DI McMaster discussing business.'

'Yes, you were,' I agree. 'The problem you've got is that my attendance at your office will be verified by your receptionist. She knows you created a reason to leave the office shortly after I left, but she doesn't know, just as you obviously don't, that McMaster's car will be logged entering *and* exiting here. With a little luck, and you don't seem to have much going for you at the moment, there'll be CCTV of that entry and exit; one with you in the car and the other without.'

He grabs the front of my jacket, lifts me from the ground and slams me onto the concrete. I try to keep my head raised, but not high enough to prevent the back of my skull bouncing off the floor. The impact feels as if I've been whacked over the head with a brick – which I suppose is what happened, except in reverse. I am in severe trouble. Given the events of recent weeks, the guy could be capable of murder. The spark of self-preservation ignites renewed vigour. I clutch my head. Warm blood oozes onto my palm and trickles along my arm. I slide my hand to my side, glancing against his pants leg as I do so. He looks at the smear of blood. With his balance unsettled I thrust my hips upwards, toppling the oaf from me. I stagger to my feet in time to kick him to the back of the head. I thrust my foot into his back, sending him thumping down six steps to a small landing. Grey concrete dusts his designer suit, blood streaks his face, and his left arm juts out at a reverse right-angle to his elbow. I retrieve his phone from the ground.

I don't offer the conciliatory *Are you all right?* Instead, I phone DS Street, describe the attack, and ask if he can attend forthwith. I have a particular reason for asking. I know Main is merely immobilised – albeit painfully. I don't want to give him thinking time in the back of an ambulance.

With Main's phone in one hand and my own in the other I activate Bluetooth and transfer his directory to my phone. *How I love technology.* I return my phone to my pocket and recite to Main his meaningful contacts: McMaster, that doesn't surprise me; Caruso, G&M, obviously the farm; and Gill, that does surprise me – in fact it overwhelms me. *So why does he have her number?*

A door creaks from below. Footsteps. Two sets. One echoes the unmistakable click-clack of women's heels. Plumpton's rhythmic tapping precedes Street's head emerging above the stairwell railing. I choke as I imagine her clicking away with Riverdance or Celtic Thunder troupes.

Main remains mute while I speak to Street. His glazed eyes tell of a first round defeat and haze of recovery after a Floyd Mayweather championship bout. For Street's benefit, I lean over Main and whisper: 'You'll be seen to in a moment.'

'You'll go for this, bitch.' Slurred sounds and spittle spill from his swollen lower lip.

'You all right apart from your arm?'

He doesn't answer.

I don't care. No problem to me. I respect silence.

With Plumpton standing obediently behind, Street introduces himself to Main, who protests: 'She stole my phone.'

Such is the outcry of most street offenders I've apprehended since my early days of pacing beats in Worcester. They strike like a python. Their criminal philosophy manual preaches first in best dressed – as if credibility is a by-product of urgency. The offender will invariably blame someone else or offer an implausible related circumstance that renders him a suspect of theft, bashing, indecent behaviour, or one of any number of crimes they've committed since they were ten-years-old. Deflect blame. Exactly as Main has done. But I am awake to him. If we're talking streetwise, I wrote the book. Compiled the maps. I glare at Main, wink, and turn to Street. 'Sergeant, his phone's right here. I picked it up after poor Mr Main tripped down this stairwell. I was about to hand it to him when I heard you coming up the stairs. Here, please take it. Check it's not damaged. I'd hate to think Mr Main might make a claim against me. I've never had a lot of trust in lawyers.'

I offer Street a wry grin. Plumpton cringes. I'd bet she thinks I am after her partner. Not a chance. As I pass Street the phone, I activate the screen with Caruso's name and number, knowing full well the name will draw his attention.

He flicks through the menu: 'Looks okay to me,' and then turns to Plumpton and asks her to take my statement.

I think Plumpton has as much desire to interview me as I have to give her information. I recall her pretentious "And you are?", and her put-down personality. She quotes from a laminated prompt card: 'Miss Watts, I'm going to ask you some questions about an assault. You are not obliged to say anything—'

'Hang on. What the heck? Why the hell are you administering me a caution? Am I a suspect? What for?' I walk straight to Street, who's already overheard my outburst. He saves me from losing it. 'Laurel, she's a witness. Just take a statement.'

The bitch is dumb. She'd been told to take a statement. We walk a half flight down the stairwell and bail out at level five. I remind her of my on-going enquiry, and continue that I'd been walking through the car park when Main attacked me. I mention my having information important for her sergeant and that I would prefer to speak to him.

She retains her school prefect manner: 'Please wait here a moment.'

Moments later, Street approaches: 'I'll be a while. Mr Main's made serious allegations. I'm getting the ambos to look over him and then I'll take him to the station. You're coming too, so wait with DC Plumpton. She's arranging transport.'

I look at him blank-faced. 'Not so fast. What's he saying I've done?'

'We'll discuss it at the station. You can either come voluntarily or, well… let's not go there.'

'You can't be serious. I'm on the level and have already

discussed this with you. You know I'll come willingly, but you'll want a bloody good reason for threatening me with arrest.'

'As you wish.' He turns and walks to Main, now under paramedics' care.

XLI

PLUMPTON CLUTCHES THE BACK OF my pants and directs me into the station. Her actions are absurd, given my willing attendance. Brandishing a hapless suspect through the police station must be her career highlight.

Street enters the interview room with the grace of a statesman pending knighthood. *Pompous git showing off to the debutante.* 'Mr Main has indicated his preference for laying a complaint which I advise might result in your being charged with assault —'

I don't let him finish. The nerve of the guy. Sweet Laurel hasn't even taken a word from me and here is Street babbling charges before even considering my testimony. One night I'm having dinner with him and calling him 'Roy'; the next day he's preparing to charge me? Not a chance. 'Sergeant Street. I would like to speak to Mr Main privately. Mr Main is aware of my holding information that could implicate him in a crime far greater than a car park dustup. This assault crap'll go nowhere. We'll both instruct barristers who'll plea our behaviour as 'wholly out of character'; we'll be freed without conviction on our entering into a good behaviour bond for twelve months; and if we have the misfortune to stand beneath a tough magistrate, worst-case scenario would be our ending up with 100 hours' community work. Might as well save yourself the paperwork.'

Street maintains solemnity. 'You were in the job. You know

I can't do that. I can't put a complainant and a victim together in one room.'

I conjure my special occasion seductive pout: 'You can if neither of us object. Call it mediation.'

Street leaves the room defeated. He returns seconds' later to sit me opposite Main. 'No funny business. There's a camera up there,' he says, pointing to a small convex lens.

'Does it record sound?' Main beats me by milliseconds.

'No,' Street answers. 'But I wish it would.'

Neither Main nor I speak. Street accepts that as his departure hint.

I open the ledger: 'I suppose you see this as an unorthodox request.'

'What is it with you? You one of those do-gooder crusaders?'

Good start. 'You should recall that I introduced myself in your office, shortly before you had Jade evict me.' I'm proud of my ability to retain names. Think word association – Jade looked like granite. 'I was enquiring about your client Phillip McMaster. I respect your profession as a lawyer, but I ask that you respect mine as a private investigator with seven years' police experience. For the sake of this discussion I won't say anything directly against your client. However, I've been engaged in a task over the past three weeks that has exposed your association with Detective Inspector McMaster. Information includes compelling evidence of threats against a person now deceased, and knowingly attempting to facilitate a property transaction with fraudulent documents.'

'I'll not be commenting on any of that. For a start, I don't make threats against people. Secondly, I conveyed only documentation provided by the purchaser.'

'Have it your way. I'm merely trying to short-circuit what

you might later find a very trying situation. Let me throw in a name: Lowenstein. Albert Lowenstein.'

In a former romantic interlude, I viewed an autumn sunset wash over an alabaster-white rendered cottage. Main's face replicates the blushing colour change of pink to orange to red and then to a pallid grey that signals curtain fall.

'What about Lowenstein?'

'As you're not saying much, nor am I.' This is a battle of wits. I'm not a card player, but the expression 'poker face' is part of my repertoire. I don't throw in chips until I see my opponent's hand. I continue: 'You've placed a gold sample with him. Now, do you think McMaster would be interested?'

'So what's your interest? What's with the observation?'

'Privileged, as you'd say. Rest assured it's sanctioned and administered by police command. If you're up to accepting advice, mine is to distance yourself from McMaster. I also recommend you help my enquiry. Doing so will ensure your remaining in the legal profession.'

'Don't think you can bluff me. Let's say I do *co-operate*, what guarantee do I get? Do you really *know* McMaster?'

'I've seen enough and learned enough over the past fortnight to know you're in deep. Take your own advice: those who co-operate gain concessions.'

Street knocks and enters. 'Everything okay in here?'

'Fine,' we reply in unison.

I return to Main. 'I have details of your meeting with Lowenstein. He phoned me.'

'Jesus. That's some network you've got going.'

'You've not heard the half of it. I'll lay it on the table. We, and I mean myself and the police, can link you to an arrangement to fix Angelo Caruso. What can you tell me about that?'

'We discussed pressuring him to hasten a land deal. Phil desperately wants Angelo's parents' property. Started out a routine conveyance. I later heard, or was told, that gold might lie beneath both properties. After that, everything changed.'

Gold. The estate plans. The secret safe. The mining books. One objective.

'I have your business card—. Let me start again. I have a shredded version of your business card, ripped up with a threatening message on the back. I found it at the rear boundary of the Caruso and McMaster properties.'

Main looks surprised, or feigns incredibly well. 'And?'

'Just passing on info. Although it is compelling evidence when you're linked to a business card *and* to the owners of both properties *and* to a deceased later found ten metres beneath McMaster's shed.'

'I had nothing to do with that.'

'Do you know about Phil paying someone to do his dirty work?' This from Main. 'That's how he keeps his hands clean. He's in with a Russian bird – goes by the name of Jill.'

'So what did she do?'

'Don't have a clue. That's Phil's business. I steered well clear of it.'

'So what's the deal with the gold? The sample you've left with Lowenstein?'

'No need for that. Where's this going? I'm here because you assaulted me. Dislocated shoulder. And look at my suit.'

The nerve of the bastard. 'You had no reason to assault me. But that's not the issue. I'm not going for charges, although Street's offsider's CCTV footage would help my case. Think of the words 'other', 'fish' and 'fry'. You keeping your appointment tomorrow?'

'Got no reason not to. If Phil gets wind of this, he might think the worst. I intend to keep my appointment to honour my instructions of researching matters associated with mining. The sample I've left with the Guild is part of my obligation to my client.'

A complete change sweeps over Main like a restaurant transforming the casual lunch setting into the evening's starched linen tablecloths and accompanying silverware. I gauge that between the questions and answers he'd allocated time enough to assess his position, preserve his integrity and shift any burden to others – just as he's done with McMaster and Jill. His revised demeanour suits me. I have plans, and they do not include the possibility of Main tipping off McMaster with details of my involvement. I gamble: 'If we're agreed that no charges arise from this, I'll leave it at that and sign a statement of no complaint. I trust you'll do the same.'

Main looks surprised. But nowhere near surprised as he will be tomorrow afternoon.

I'm still wary of DS Street stealing my thunder. I have one chance to beat the storm. Gillian. I rip out my phone, scan the directory, and swipe 'Gill'.

It answers on the first ring: 'Hello. I'm not putting up with your shit anymore.'

I don't recognise the voice. 'Excuse me, what shit?'

'Sorry. I thought it was someone else. Who's this?'

'Olivia. Olivia Watts. Thought I was calling Gillian.'

'You are, but it's Jill. I never call myself Gillian.'

I recheck the phone. 'GILL'. *I never type in caps.* And then it clicks. Bloody Main. *This was in his phone when I did the Bluetooth transfer.* Trust a guy to not be able to spell a girl's name. 'Sorry, I got your number from Jeff Main, the solicitor.'

'That bastard? Bad news.'

She disconnects.

I won't let that go. I swipe her number over the afternoon, stopping only for blistered fingers.

At last. She's a night girl. 'Jill, please don't hang up. It's Olivia, we spoke earlier.'

'You're calling me at nearly midnight because I was a wrong number?'

'No. This is really important. You told me to watch out for Jeff Main. He's already thumped me. I need your help. Please. Tell me how you know him.'

'Personal. I don't want to talk about it. He has a police inspector on side. Do you want me to call him and tell him you're harassing me?'

I persist: 'You know *McMaster* as well?'

CLUNK.

XLII

To THE TUNE OF ELVIS's famous song, it's now or never. I scrunch my hand into a fist and rap an authoritive knock on Trotter's door.

Her viper eyes bore into me. She won't recognise me, because for the first time in months I've smothered myself in make-up, not necessarily to disguise, but to mask the yellowing bruise creeping across my jaw. Poor effort though, because I look like a ten-year-old let loose with her first make-up kit.

'Hello.' She glares, daring me to pull out a catalogue of kitchenware.

'Hi. I'm Olivia Watts. We're colleagues in a way. I'm here to help you. Can I come in?'

'Help me what?' Gillian fixes a questioning look, unsure, but confident enough to wave me inside. She leads me to a reception room where a laptop reflects a Word document. I glance at the familiar settee. A growl rumbles from behind. Considering the possibility of retribution by Benjamin, I move to my agenda. 'Gillian. I've come here to resolve a matter you're embroiled in. You're in danger. I think you know that, because of recent events concerning your work with DI McMaster. He could make you scapegoat.' I take a pausing breath. 'He'll do anything to save his own neck.'

Her eyes flicker. Assessing trust.

'I won't be anyone's scapegoat, as you so nicely put it. I'm working for the top – a Superintendent of police.'

That isn't news. Makes no impression.

'So am I, and have been for three weeks. Thornton. Want to know what my engagement is? You. I've seen it all. The pub meetings, the sit-off outside Mac's place when he was crushed, the tête–à–tête in the hospital, and the visit to the super shed where you saw Angelo Caruso's body in the bottom of a pit – information you've withheld. And the prize? I bet the Met boys will love this, some nice videos of you and McMaster going at it. Premier Motor Inn ring a bell? Think how quick *that* will circulate around the local nicks.'

She doesn't say a word. Looks to heaven for guidance – whether in desperation or quietly taking time to shape a response I cannot tell. I puncture her silence: 'Let me tell you what's happening right now. The police are mounting a case against McMaster – and you must agree they have good cause. I mean, that's why Thornton appointed you, isn't it? He'll soon be facing more than an internal enquiry.' He'll be in for a lot more than that, but I won't let slip until I have Trotter's full support.

'Okay. I'll tell you why I'm here. McMaster will take you down with him, no question. I'm giving you the chance to get in first. For that, I'll assure Thornton that you've done what you can to help me. It might save you from prosecution, but I can't make guarantees.'

Gillian raises her head. 'I'm already writing a report, so I doubt you're in a position to help me. I might have overplayed my role a fraction, making him, and a few others, think I fell for him. He's the original Mr Nice Guy, but not nice enough to fool me. Got a bloody wife at home, the hypocrite. He'll get to me somehow. You'd have no idea what he gets away with.'

'I do. Believe me. As I said, I've been onto you both for

three weeks. There's nothing I haven't seen. So why not help yourself and tell me about the deal with Angelo Caruso?'

'It was nothing. Mac found out Angelo had fiddled contracts of the next-door property he was trying to buy.'

I know that, courtesy of her memory sticks.

'Mac heavied him for part of the proceeds, but Angelo, apparently, wouldn't stand for it. He threatened Mac, or so Mac says. No one does that and gets away with it. As you know, he didn't.'

'Are you saying that McMaster killed Angelo?'

'Shit no. You think I'm stupid? I'm not saying it, but it's the most realistic conclusion. That shed was Mac's prize. He had choof growing in there. Wasn't going to broadcast *that* was he? No one knew about the pit. Could have buried a whole community down there. Haven't a clue what it was for, and I never got to ask, because 'round that time he walloped me, the bastard. Did you see that while you were snooping on us? Plain whacked me in the face he did. Was all paranoid about being followed. I haven't a clue how he twigged; guess he glued a few coincidences together. Now, I think it's bloody hilarious that we were *both* followed. How the hell d'you do it?

'Good at my job, that's how. Tell me about Giuseppe?'

'Nothing to tell. He never spoke of him.'

'Fair enough. Jeff Main?'

'The dud solicitor? So so. He's a weak bastard easily manipulated. Do anything for a quid. He was definitely up to something with Mac. They spoke of offing Angelo. But Main wouldn't swat a fly.'

'Are you for real? The guy tried to knock the crap out of me. I put it on him about his relationship with McMaster and he just lost it.'

'Well, that surprises me. I never seen him aggro, unless you count a heated discussion as aggressive.'

'So where do you stand now?'

'Thornton wants a report. He's right on to me. So's Mac. You gotta help me. Please. I'll sign anything. I'd rather be done for perverting the course of justice than be crucified by McMaster for the rest of my life. I'm an idiot for getting involved. Succumbed to seduction, you might say. It was supposed to be a straight–forward snoop and report.'

My maternal instincts kick in. I thought I'd lost them after agreeing one-night-stands suit me better than long-term relationships. I feel genuinely sorry for Gillian. However, I won't make the same mistake of pledging allegiance to the wrong side. She hasn't given me much, but she will testify against McMaster, to save her own skin rather than to uphold justice. The whys and wherefores don't interest me. It's the end result that counts.

'Don't contact anyone, not even the Knight's Arms. McMaster got your address?'

'I don't think so. But since *you* found me, I'm sure *he* can.'

'I'll speak to Thornton. Get a car out here. By the way, the name 'Hernandez' mean something to you?'

'No. Should it?

'Just asking. A little side interest.'

'Wouldn't be the slag in a bottle shop, would it? Mac scored bottles from? Got photos if you want.'

As I can't confess to already having copies, I leave with: 'All right. Cheers. I'll keep it in mind.'

* * *

Armed with McMaster's identity from the concealed camera, I prep Rose to accompany me to DS Street's office. Her history makes her indignantly reluctant to co-operate. I feel as if I've pledged my resources and compassion for nothing. I explain that Street will not be interested in her stealing the Dewar's. He will be far more interested in pursuing McMaster for bringing the constabulary into disrepute than in prosecuting a young woman for breaching probation. And whilst I don't communicate this, there is the broader picture – McMaster's involvement in the triad of disasters radiating from his property. I regret not having the power and authority to question suspects in the manner I had once enjoyed. By the same token, I do not want to pass my work to Street and cut financial recompense and the prospect of bolstering my CV.

I'd phoned ahead, so I am surprised to find that Street receives us with diffidence, as if we are there to *cause* trouble rather than to report it.

'You've got something for me,' he says as he guides us to an interview room.

I introduce Rose and detail a summary of events since her being accosted on the A44.

'So why wait a month to report this?' he directs to Rose.

'Just the way it went,' she replies. 'It was no big deal at first. I got pulled over for speeding. I admitted I was over the limit. The officer, and I didn't know his name then, didn't make anything clear about a fine or summons except to say I might hear something within a week. I thought I'd get a warning, so there was nothing to report at the time.'

I jump in. 'Sir, the officer was plain clothes, not traffic. As you're aware, it is unusual for a detective, an inspector at that, to pull over a motorist for anything other than life-threatening behaviour.'

'Yes, go on,' he motions to Rose.

She clenches her hands in her lap. 'Two days later he came into the shop where I work and invites me out for coffee. I declined. Thankfully, I was on my own and couldn't leave. But he left and returned with coffee and croissants. I felt uneasy, but even at that stage I couldn't say much because he'd done nothing wrong. I first thought he was making a move on me, that is until he told me how he'd checked up on me. He then asked for a donation to encourage him to not report my speeding. I was so scared of losing my job. I gave him two bottles of Scotch.'

Street jots neatly into his book. Dabs the ink. 'All right. You've told this woman he assaulted you?'

This woman? Thanks for nothin'. I suppose you're pissed because I didn't put out the other night.

Rose drops her head. A paler complexion would reveal flushed cheeks. 'I told her that he touched me. He wanted me to sell more weed. I refused. He grabbed my shoulders, said, "No one refuses me" and slid his hands over my breasts. I was scared and nervous because I didn't know how far he'd go. I'm lucky the shop was open and anyone could have come in. Then he said: "Sell this. Next time it won't be those lovely jugs I'm having".'

Rose passes over a wrapped foil and starts crying.

Street pulls a tissue box from an adjacent desk. Passes it to me.

I rip out a handful and press them into Rose's hand. Drape my arm across her shoulder. Again. 'It's all right.' My words probably mean nothing, although I do have an idea how she feels. It's difficult telling a guy – especially one with no empathy – about someone touching us. I press on, for Rose.

'There's camera footage,' I say to Street. 'Store security video,' I clarify, to save Hamilton's butt. I produce the SD card. 'You'll see the register on the left, and you can see McMaster's profile and full face when he turns to leave.'

Street slides the card into an adapter connected to his computer. Views the footage as described by Rose. 'Very well. You prepared to make a written statement to the effect of what we've just discussed?'

'Can we keep my work out of it?'

Street reels off a non-committal reply: 'I can't promise, but we'll do our best. There's no need for anyone else to hear about this. It's not going to court. Unless you want it to. Over the assault, I mean.'

Rose relaxes. 'Fine. I don't want it to go any further.'

'Okay,' says Street. 'Guaranteed.'

I lift my head. *And I can guarantee I've heard that sort of guarantee before.* Given this setting, I believe Street. I see the way it will play out: McMaster will claim Rose came onto *him* and offered the Scotch as encouragement. He will state that in trying to reject her advances, he admits a gross error of judgement by taking Rose by the shoulders as an attempt to curb her. The hierarchy, having considered similar defences from police across the country, would find 'no case to answer' in favour of McMaster and return him to the community. *Aah, the brotherhood.*

I wish Rose a quick recovery and tell her I'll soon visit to buy another bottle of Orange Shock. She insists on finding her own way home, a decision that pleases me. Not only does she need time to reflect, *and* to refocus; I need time to update Street about the whole McMaster debacle. I hug Rose goodbye and ask Street to spare me thirty minutes.

'All right. My office. It's more comfortable and I'll have everything at my fingertips.'

Street sits beside his desk, rather than behind, a gesture that makes me feel comfortable and not as if I am under interrogation.

He kicks off the session. 'Right. What you got for me?'

'I've been on this since March fifteenth. Superintendent Thornton engaged me to tail a private investigator by the name of Gillian Trotter. It gets messy from there. *She* was already tasked to watch over a police member who was, and now probably is, subject to an internal enquiry. Present circumstances prevent me from disclosing that officer's name.'

'You don't have to. It's all over the shop. You can't operate like he does without arousing suspicion. But remember, no one's pinned anything on him.'

'Yet,' I say with confidence. 'Anyway, turns out this officer *offered* to purchase his neighbour's 25-acre farm. The neighbour's name? Caruso. You see something developing here?'

'Only coincidence.'

'Right then. Giuseppe Caruso's death. Suspected heart attack? I'll prove otherwise: he was helped along. His wife, Maria, enlightened me with interesting facts without realising she'd dobbed someone in. She wondered if her son, Angelo, might have been involved. I don't think so. But that doesn't explain how Angelo ended up ten metres under McMaster's shed.'

Street looks uninterested. Perhaps I've spent too much time re-capping.

'Olivia. How about you tell me something I don't know? Get to the point before I drift into slumberland.'

'All right. Does the name Jeff Main mean anything to you?'

'Sure does. He's just accused you of stealing his phone.'

The guy thinks he's a comedian. Here I am trying to be serious and guide him to the identity of a killer and he's taking the piss. I shoot him a serious look. 'Ask yourself *why* he claims that. No, forget it. Cop this: *he's* facilitating the Caruso to McMaster land transaction. He's been in this for a while.'

'Now I'm interested.'

'Good. Back to the beginning, this Trotter's been having it off with McMaster – I've got juicy proof – and she was too close to the tree-felling incident.'

Street smiles. 'So you're saying that she's fucking him as well as fucking him over?'

'As a lady, I wouldn't put it that way, but it's pretty close to the mark. I don't buy everything she says. What have you done with Angelo Caruso's flat?'

'Still a crime scene. Why?'

'Because he was helping his mother with the property transaction. There'll be a paper trail.' I don't let on that I'd snaffled the manila folder. Street would jump at the chance to do me for trespass or unlawfully on premises.

'To where?'

'Main for one. Something might just spin off. Aren't you interested in why McMaster wants the adjacent property? He's not a farmer. If it's for investment, there'd be a million better opportunities. There has to be something in it for him.'

I don't disclose the contents of McMaster's secret window sill. Detailing good investigations is like working towards good sex – you have to hold back for the right moment. But I do reveal a small teaser. 'You find marijuana in that shed?'

'No. Strawberries and chilli.'

'Don't be fooled. He'd cleaned up before you guys fronted.' I flick my phone to photos of McMaster's shed: marijuana, the plastic setting, the pit and the piles of soil. *Do I tell him about the mine?*

Street isn't moved. I thought he'd be climbing over me, thanking me for handing information on a plate. Instead, he reverts to the demeanour displayed when I first met him. Emotionless. Dogmatic. He picks up a fountain pen. Plunges the end into his mouth. I hope he doesn't ask me to sign anything. And then he lets go with the force of a dam bursting its levee: 'You're barking up the wrong tree, Watts. No wonder you couldn't cut it as a detective. Still going off on bent tangents. Don't forget I've been working on this too. It's nearly done and dusted. I'll tell you what happened and then you can head off, write up an exorbitant invoice for your Thornton buddy and not bother me again.'

I nearly walk out on the spot, but stall long enough to hear him out. It could form part of the detail I endorse on Thornton's 'exorbitant' invoice.

Street pulls the pen from his jaw. 'I'll keep this brief, just to show you how it's done. First, there's no evidence to show that Giuseppe died from anything other than natural causes.'

I know about SOCO belatedly retrieving items for examination.

'We have intelligence of Angelo Caruso's association with known offenders. That's where we'll find his killer. Fact he's turned up in a copper's shed is a taunt against police. Crim mentality: set up a copper.'

All right. What about the 'fix the prat' threat?

'And this Trotter? You've got nothing. So Mac gets a bit on the side? What copper doesn't? So if there's nothing else, I've got things to do, and it's not dreaming.'

You must be blind. Trotter's implicated herself in perverting the course of justice. I can't believe he's sacrificed objectivity so clearly evident during the past fortnight. 'What's changed your view?'

'Leave it, Watts. You're out of your league. Keep your eye on the papers. You'll soon see how far off the planet you are.'

As planets are the moment's topic, I mutter: *Up Uranus.* I don't say goodbye. Just up and leave. Nothing aggrieves me more than insolence.

XLIII

THE TWO-HOUR WAIT PAYS off. McMaster lowers his head as Olivia departs Gillian's front door. He has a mind to follow her, but decides against it, knowing he can find Olivia just as he found Gill's residence.

Since his quarrel with Gillian, he has become increasingly paranoid about his relationship – or 'association' – with Gill. He's reinstated his gut feeling that something isn't quite right about her: the instant familiarity with him and the ease by which she'd floated into his arms – and bed; the implausible explanation for her sudden presence at the tree-felling incident; her soppy, patronising, "I hope you'll be all right, I'd hate to lose you" bedside mush in the hospital; and now, her entertaining Olivia Watts for more than two hours in what he is certain is an interrogation rather than a ladies' afternoon of party plan purchases and local gossip.

Determined to obtain further information, he grabs his phone:

'Afternoon. Knight's Arms.'

'Hello. McMaster, Worcester CID. Gill Trotter on at the moment?'

'Er, no, sir. Can I help you?'

'Bloody hope so. When's she on next?'

'Er, she's casual. Doesn't have a set roster, so I can't help.'

'Don't shit me, right? No one casually floats in to work when they feel like it. Who am I speaking to?'

'Paul Westacott, sir. Assistant manager. Is something wrong?'

'Bet your sweet arse something's wrong. Now put me on to the real manager.'

'Mac, how are you? What can I do for you? Brian Davies.' He speaks with the silkiness of satin pillows in an upmarket boudoir.

'I'm looking for Gill. Your bloody assistant's just fed me a line that she doesn't have a roster. Now don't feed me the same drivel, right, because I know you haven't had casual staff for Christ knows how long. You're too stingy to pay the higher rate. So cut the crap, right, and tell me what's going on.'

Davies had negotiated the deal with Thornton, a deal which had worked well in principle. Until now. Westacott hadn't a clue and nor had other staff. 'Mac, she's on a government training scheme. Mature age re-entry program with a convoluted acronym I can't remember. Works a few different sites to get a breadth of experience. That's why she's on a come and go rota. I sign her time book after she performs a block of hours.'

'You're full of it, Brian. You think I, a copper who's been around since the Bow Street Runners, can't tell when someone's winding me up? When was her last shift?'

'Can't tell you, to be honest. I'm not here all the time. Hang on a moment.'

A background shout breaks through the phone: 'Paul, when was that Gill in last?'

'Buggered if I know. About a week, I reckon. No one's missed her.'

Brian resumes the call: 'Can't tell you for sure; a week or so.'

'See, you're fuckin' full of it, right? If that were true, you could have told me up front. You sign her time book, right? So you, of all people, know to the minute when she was last in. I'll tell you what I'm thinking, right? I reckon she's slotted herself into your establishment as an informer. For who or why I'm not sure – YET! – but be assured I'll find out. And don't expect to shout me a few Dewies as a pacifier 'cause I won't be setting my arse in your God forsaken pub again – unofficially that is.'

McMaster flings the phone onto the passenger seat. *So how much do these two bitches know?*

XLIV

THE TO-ING AND FRO-ING BETWEEN Thornton and Street makes me uneasy. No one can accomplish results under these circumstances. Thornton expresses unconditional confidence in me, yet Street heads off on a power trip, ridiculing anything I put to him.

Enough is enough. I grab my laptop and small notepad. *I'll do this properly and professionally.* I yank out my phone and swipe 'Thorns': '*… I can't afford to have information flowing to anyone but me.*'

'Thornton.'

'It's Olivia. Hello. Can we get together? I've hit an obstacle. Roy Street. I'm on a merry-go-round with him. I've got plenty on Gillian; she's agreed to cooperate, and I've also got a good lead into the Caruso mishaps.'

'I'm back in London. Urgent enough for you to hop on a train?'

'It could be the best three hours I'll ever spend. I'll check the timetable and call you back.'

As luck falls in my favour, three Paddington trains run after morning peak. I have fourteen minutes to make Worcester's Foregate Street station. I don't even have to run, thanks to my living within the city precinct. But I do pass through Maccas to grab emotional company for the journey.

With spare minutes on the platform, I try to reconnect with Jill. After three failed attempts, I text Thornton my proposed arrival time. On boarding the train, I secure my laptop between my hip and the carriage wall and fall asleep. I wake to the carriage pitching across points and junctions on the Oxford approach and scoff the second Quarter with Cheese, now stone cold.

I enter his office at 3.30 p.m. What a contrast to Worcester's Government Surplus fitout. No expense spared here: velour-faced chrome chairs, plush velvet curtains, and carpet with more bounce than a Yorkshire peat bog. Climate control repels coal-black clouds gazing through floor-to-ceiling windows. I foresee a comfortable meeting. On completion, I'll submit a partial invoice, which will not be looked at for 30 days. We shake hands. A secretary jiggles in a platter of coffee and biscuits. My kind of meeting. *Here goes.*

'I've filled you in on the catastrophe of McMaster's injuries. But I'll start before that, with my initial enquiries focusing on Gillian Trotter's association with McMaster. As previously detailed, I heard fragments of conversations in the Knight's Arms, but not of sufficient weight to pass on. I hung low key for a while, upping the ante after Gillian spent an evening at McMaster's home. That whetted my curiosity. Only when I checked the shed did I understand the true gravity of the situation. I'm talking about the body. Gillian must have known. She *has* told you, hasn't she?'

Thornton sits erect, non-responsive to my assumptive leading question. A 'yes' or 'no' will do. His expressionless gaze reminds me of when my first serious boyfriend put the hard word on me. I froze. We all giggled about it at school – 'doing it' – but when the crunch came, I shook with the same fear I'd felt when facing my step-father after he'd sprung me stealing money from his wallet.

Thornton selects his words with jeweller's tweezers: 'Olivia. This is delicate. Your position was to watch Trotter —'

'Which I've done, and done thoroughly.'

He lays down the official perspective. 'I shouldn't be telling you what I've received from her. This isn't a play of one against the other.'

'Sir. I'm not here to one-up anyone. I've fulfilled your request. You can make arrests from what I'm giving you. It's to your advantage if we combine information, although I'm not suggesting you're answerable to me. No harm whether you answer or not; I'm merely trying to collate as much as possible. I understand how valuable your time is.'

I don't mind slurping my way to the top like the rest of them.

I continue: 'I know for a fact she hasn't told you. Trotter spilled her guts. Went to water. It's recorded on here.' I pull out my Samsung, place it on his desk and press 'play': *"Thornton wants a report. He's right on to me. So's Mac. You gotta help me. Please. I'll sign anything. I'd rather be done for perverting the course of justice than be crucified by McMaster for the rest of my life. I'm an idiot for getting involved. Succumbed to seduction, you might say. It was supposed to be a straight–forward snoop and report."*

I flick off the recording. 'As you can imagine, she's under pressure – McMaster pulls some heavy-duty strings. Despite her dithering, she gave me good info over forty-odd minutes.'

'Good thing too. Example of a guilty mind. She knew what she was getting into, and it sounds like she got into most of it of her own doing. But I'll keep an open mind. We appreciate how immersed one can become when we change our lifestyle for an undercover operation.'

I think about that. 'Maybe so. But the fact remains she's

seen the light and is now trying to make amends. She asked me to pass on this report. I was at first reluctant, said something to the effect of not being her messenger, but agreed to do so after telling her I'd convey to you her remorse.' I hand Thornton the report. 'She's done a good job of trying to pull the wool over your eyes, but it's full of holes. Sir.'

Report to Superintendent Thornton
Submitted by Gillian Trotter

1. On 15 April I was contracted to report on DI Phillip McMaster's movements. My instructions referred me to the Knight's Arms public house in High Street, Worcester. I adopted the trap and deceive method which requires an 'over-friendly' approach to the target to gain his confidence. Resultant from a successful connection, I monitored the target as follows:

    - Various meetings with solicitor Jeffrey Main (dates available)
    - Attendance at Westlands Council (unable to determine whether in official capacity or otherwise)
    - Attendance at Commercial Groundworks Hire (likewise as above)
    - Attendance at 63 Canning Road, Worcester, later identified as rental property of Angelo Caruso.

2. Further to the above, I attended at Worcester General Hospital where I expressed sympathy for McMaster's condition, whereupon he proposed a long-term relationship, but stopped short of engagement because of his marital status.

3. On release from hospital, he requested me to attend his house. I immediately relayed that information to your kind self.

4. That was my first attendance at McMaster's property, although at the time of the tree incident I did have the external perimeter under surveillance. During the visit, I had occasion to enter a huge shed which evidenced a hydroponic strawberry farming operation. I also noted construction works for a proposed cellar.

5. I state and declare that I have no knowledge of a deceased person inside that cellar. I do not deny an amorous association with McMaster, but I defend it as pursuing my objective of providing the most comprehensive and concise information to your office. Any inference of romantic involvement, or my giving DI McMaster operational information will constitute grounds for litigation.

Respectfully yours

Ms Gillian Trotter Lic. Investigator 22875198 April 29, 2017

Thornton glances over the two-sided page. 'If all I get from you at the end of this is a two-page précis, I'd consider my money ill-spent.'

'Not a chance, sir. I think you'll be castigating me for my verbosity.'

He shoots me a quizzical glare and flicks Trotter's report aside.

'Can I ask you to consider the pressures she might have been under?'

He responds unsympathetically: 'You've been under the same pressures, I'm sure.'

He's got me. 'Yes sir. But I am more able to deal with them. Let me go on. I'll write this up later, but for now, I'm telling you what happened. Trotter's adamant that McMaster killed Angelo Caruso to facilitate a quick settlement on the neighbour's property sale. While that's meritable, it's too easy and straightforward. It would have been more effective, and less risky, for Mac to strong-arm the young Caruso to get his point across.

'Let me backpedal a bit. McMaster's in the frame from the outset. He had something to do with old Caruso's death. Might have been totally innocent, like an out of control argument. My view is that he pulled off a well-planned, calculated hit that he believed would be attributed to another person – meaning the son or wife – or, in the best of circumstances, natural causes. Remember, that was the initial diagnosis by ambos. Remember too, if you aren't aware, that McMaster played hero at the scene by confining police interest to natural causes. By the time SOCO rolled the place, any potential weapon was well and truly disposed of.'

'Do you breathe?'

Sarcastic pig. No wonder he earned the moniker of "prick". 'Yes. Do you want me to breathe or continue my report?'

'Sorry.'

'Crucial evidence *had* disappeared, and that was the paddle thing I found in McMaster's shed. Only one person could have put it there.'

'Being analysed this very minute.'

I produce the Glad Bag of crushed cigarette I'd collected from near the Caruso fence line. Recollections of surveillance duties with tobacco-fuelled officers underscore my question: 'Sir, you remember how officers on sit-offs would drop everything, including recently lit cigarettes, as soon as a target came into view? Someone had been watching the Caruso property, and had been disturbed. It makes sense. Explains the extinguished the cigarette. I'm betting this'll shine with DI McMaster's DNA.'

Thornton rises. Ruffles his hair. Imitates a defence barrister: 'Objection, Your Honour. This is no more than conjecture and speculation. I put it to the witness that the butt could easily be the discarded product of a Caruso grandchild's first experiment with the ghastly tobacco.'

I smile. 'You'll need to be a QC to beat me because there's more. You'll not find this in DS Street's investigation. I attended McMaster's property on a number of occasions. Gloria McMaster, the estranged wife, actually *saw* her husband at the rear of the property, *and* saw him enter and leave the Caruso property only minutes before Maria Caruso ran to his home.' I flick open my notebook. 'This is what she said: *"He climbed through the fence, into the Caruso's but re-emerged only seconds later. Sprang back to the house happy as Larry. Strange. He had a cricket bat or similar under his arm. No idea why…"*.'

'Interesting.'

'"Interesting"? That's all?'

'Benefit of doubt and admissibility. You know a wife can't be compelled to testify against her spouse?'

'But sir. You don't know she won't. Anyway, there's more. Maria Caruso was absolutely certain that SOCO took three items for forensic examination. When we spoke yesterday, she asked for the items to be returned. Listen: Street confirms that SOCO removed only two kitchen items. The third item, a broken paddle from one of her son's kayaking days was definitely missing. Don't you think it more than coincidental that I found a paddle in McMaster's shed, *and* that it matches Maria Caruso's description? Can I respectfully ask you to give forensics the hurry up?'

'That's one place I can't rush. Leave it with me.'

I take another gulp: 'That thing fixes McMaster in the frame. Whether or not his wife testifies, her seeing him with something resembling a cricket bat puts him in an extremely tenuous position. You'll get his DNA for sure. The motive is clear: McMaster needs the Caruso property. Word is that it's rich in gold deposits. He's got samples with a dealer named Lowenstein—'

'Not old Alby? Thought he was out of it.'

'— one and the same. You spoken to Street about where the young Caruso was found?'

'Enough to get the gist. Go on.'

Why doesn't he see McMaster's name stamped all over this? 'All right. Mac claims it's the beginnings of a wine cellar. Cellar bullshit. It's the makings of a mineshaft. He's got books and carpentry plans, and sifting pans and shit in the shed. Now, this Lowenstein is putting a price on his sample at two o'clock tomorrow. But it's not only McMaster who'll be there because his solicitor, Main, is trying to shaft him. I've had a productive conference with Main, and as a result, I can deliver you two heads on one platter. I need to run this by you first, because it's way beyond our agreement. I sure don't want to jeopardise any prosecution.'

'We'll discuss that shortly. What else you got?'

'This might seem irrelevant, but it's not. Scattered about the rear of the Caruso farm, near the cigarette butt I spoke of, was a torn-up business card. A threatening message appeared on the back. The card is one of Jeff Main's, the puppet lawyer. Did I tell you he bashed me? The guy's crooked. He's half admitted being McMaster's right-hand-man.

'The question arises, why was a handwritten message on Main's card? More importantly, who was it given to and who threw it away in disgust or rage? It has to link to either McMaster or a Caruso, and by deduction that means Maria or Angelo. Maria doesn't strike me as one who would try anything on Mac – she adores the guy. She's in the minority, if you don't mind my saying. All this will dovetail into evidence provided.'

Thornton looks as if I've just told him I'll self-admit to psychiatric treatment. 'You've got me,' he says. 'Haven't a clue where you're heading. You're either damn good at what you do, or you've totally lost the plot.'

'I'll take the former, thank you very much. What I'm asking is, are DNA results on the glove and marijuana through yet?'

Thornton slides over a keyboard and clicks into his computer. 'The glove? Came back with a ninety-nine-nine on Caruso. The younger one. Had him on the system, as you're probably aware. Sorry. I should've let you know. Pointless exercise now. Angelo's gone. You'll not get any mileage out of it.'

I am incensed. Scarcely hold my temper. I've scratched for information, worked through the night, been bashed by a lawyer, and this Superintendent oozes a casual, meaningless apology?

'So, am I out of the loop on the Audi forensics?'

'Some things I can't pass on.'

'I'll take that as a "yes". And…?'

'Got Caruso's DNA all over it.'

'I'd expect that. It was his car.'

'True. But you wouldn't expect to find his hair – complete with follicles – trapped in the rear door jamb, and traces of saliva on the rear seat.'

I crunch my brows. 'I thought it was burnt out. I never saw it, but the radio call made it sound pretty much fu—, er, destroyed.'

'Yes, but not bad enough to have destroyed all evidence. This is one they won't get away with. It gets better. We've also got DNA of your sparring partner, Main. He might have been in the back with Angelo. Bit of close negotiation maybe?'

'Possible. This paints him right in the picture. What'd I tell you? He's Mac's puppet.'

'Not so quick. For all we know, Angelo lent him the car. Purely a devil's advocate perspective.'

I hate speculation. Futile. 'Yeah, sure. And you lent me yours. As if. So where was the DNA?'

'Smudge on the steering wheel, and a ninety-nine-point-nine-percenter from a scraping of the driver's seat. Sweating his legal arse off. Borderline conclusive that Main'd driven it; therefore follows that our Angelo was contained in the back.'

'Got enough for an arrest?'

'Can't go off half-cocked. Need to cover all bases. Problem is, we also lifted Mac's print off the driver's door.'

'Holy shit.' I let my enthusiasm settle. 'So back to Trotter. I hope she'll be as helpful to you as she was to me.'

'Hope so. She's done fuck all so far, pardon my French. So where is The Pig?'

'Getting her head together. She'll call soon, I'm sure. She's on a downer.'

'She'll be more than down once I've finished with her. Be down and out on the end of a bloody Job Seekers queue for she'll not want to set foot near a nick. Ever!'

I won't join in lambasting the wayward investigator, but I do reinforce one of her claims. 'Trotter's certain that Mac did Angelo, because he's the only one with a key to the shed.'

'Not a very reliable deduction.'

'There's another player I can't get a handle on. Woman called Jill. Main told me "Phil's got a Russian bird". Keeps his hands clean. I've spoken to her, but after I dropped Mac's name she hung up. Hasn't switched on her phone since yesterday. I'm hoping you've got resources through telecommunications investigators.'

'Leave that with me, too.'

'There's an alternative path we can take. Back streets are often easier than the direct route.' I play the video of Mac assaulting Rose Hernandez. 'I accompanied this girl to Worcester CID where she made a formal statement to DS Street. I'm not sure of the final outcome, but Street indicated he won't have a bar of writing up a fellow officer.'

'We'll see about that.'

My kind of guy.

XLV

AT 1.00 P.M. A TASK FORCE files through the Gold Guild's doors. Officers commandeer Lowenstein's security room; one observes a door monitor and two watch the shop floor. Olivia eyes three computer screens, ready to capture Main and McMaster's arrival. The playback reminds her of Hamilton's installations. 'Can this record direct onto a USB stick?' she asks.

'Not a prob,' replies Lowenstein.

Olivia pulls one from her bag. Looks at it as if she's picked up the wrong brand of nail polish in a chemist. Lowenstein plugs it in.

A menu flashes onto the screen: 'Mac' followed by a list of files. 'What the hell's this?' gruffs Thornton. He reads the file:

PM	'We had a little win yesterday.'
JM	'What do you mean "we"?'
PM	'Our old man had a heart attack. The sale should now be a breeze.'
JM	'Don't bet your bollocks on that. It could delay the whole process because of probate.'
PM	'I've got my man, Angelo, onto it. She'll be smooth sailing.'
JM	'You sure it was a heart attack? You didn't put too much pressure on the old codger, did you? Like you tried with me?'
PM	'Come now. You think I'm the kind of guy who'd do something like that?'

'Shit,' says Olivia. 'I'm not supposed to have that. I thought I put them all back.'

'Put what back? Where?'

'Memory sticks. Trotter's place, during my investigation.'

'Rip it out,' Thornton directs to Lowenstein. 'Got another one?'

Olivia sinks a shaking hand into her bag. 'Just happen to.'

'We'll discuss this later. For now, get your mind back to the intercept.' Thornton smiles and walks to the front window just as Main enters the building.

'Mr Main, welcome,' Lowenstein greets. 'Here, sit, sit. I get you coffee.' He calls his daughter: 'Danika, coffee for our customer, please.'

Thornton, posing as a customer, eyes a jewellery display cabinet, while his team monitors proceedings from the security room.

Main stands, 'I only came for a price. I'm not yet sure if I'm selling,' he directs to Lowenstein.

'Mr Main. We treat all customers important. If now you decide to not sell, maybe another day you'll remember me and return. Business flows not over one day, but over a lifetime.'

Thornton glances to a ceiling-mounted camera and tips his head.

The front door opens. McMaster. Lowenstein approaches: 'Mac, Mac. How are you? We have a good deal today, no? Come, sit with your lawyer.'

McMaster glances across the shop. 'Main? What the fuck. Alby?'

And then to Main: 'What the… what are you doing?'

Lowenstein answers for him: 'He brought in your sample,

Mac. All's well, I have the price, but you know, it's subject to daily fluctuations.'

'And where did *you* get gold from?' McMaster asks Main. 'Fuckin' my place, I bet, because I told you, didn't I? Check up on mining rights I said, and you take it as a cue to help yourself. How'd you get in? Checking a few measurements, I heard? Took time out to dump a stiff in my pit too, did you?'

'Please, no language or arguments in the shop,' Lowenstein pleads.

Thornton edges to a diamond display, nearer to the quarrelling pair.

'Don't know what you're talking about,' Main replies. 'I provide a service. You want details on mining, I have to first confirm the quality of the product. And a stiff in a pit? You're crazy.'

'Fuckin' bullshit. You knocked Angelo, broke into my shed and tried to frame me, you arsehole.'

'No need to break in. Your wife gave me a key.' Main plucks the side door key from his pocket. 'Here, have the bloody thing.'

McMaster swings his fist into Main's jaw. Main flinches, drops the key, and then, like a raging bull, charges his head into his antagonist's midriff, sending them both crashing through a display cabinet.

Lowenstein frets: 'My shop. My shop.'

Thornton, now joined by officers from the back room, rushes to separate Main and McMaster. He introduces himself and colleagues. 'Better tell me what's going on here, inspector.'

McMaster looks to Thornton. 'You know me?'

'Certainly do. Had you under obs for three weeks. Think we'll be talking for a while, don't you?'

McMaster grins. 'Not bloody likely. I'm here under

invitation of Mr Lowenstein here, right? I had a chap deliver a speck of gold for an evaluation and I've been invited back for the price. Nothing of interest to you. On the other hand, Mr Main here, my legal representative, supposedly representing my interests in a land purchase, suddenly fronts in this establishment to get a price on material stolen from – *stolen*, I stress – from my property. So, if anyone's going to be doing any talking I think it should be between you and this crook. Now what's this shit about being under observation for three weeks? You got something you want to ask me?'

'Yes, but not here. I'll invite you to my office to save embarrassment, but if you decline, I will have to act formally.'

'Act formally? You mean you'll arrest me, a long-standing detective inspector of police? Well, since you've shown your hand, I'll not give you the glory. I'm more than happy to trot along to your office and chat over coffee and croissants.'

'You'll be lucky to get a glass of water. Wait here while I tidy up.'

Main shakes plastic and glass fragments from his jacket. 'I'll be getting along then; I'll contact you later Mr Lowenstein.'

'Not so fast, Mr Main,' Thornton interjects. 'You'll be accompanying us too.'

'No, I'll be right thanks. I won't prefer charges against Mr McMaster. He seems to be under duress. I'll catch up with him later for a drink.' And then to McMaster: 'That suit you, Mac? By the way, the contracts are done. Got them in my car. Would've brought them in except I didn't expect to see you here. Perhaps Mr Lowenstein might care to explain that?'

'Mr Lowenstein will explain nothing,' chips in Thornton. 'But you'll be explaining your relationship with Angelo Caruso. Seems you've been practising a little conflict of interest.'

'Easily fixed. I'll help however I can. Mr McMaster will vouch for my ability to help in any capacity, won't you Phil?'

'Fuck off.'

Olivia jumps. She doesn't expect the reaction, thinking instead that each would cover each other. A police officer confronted with ill-doing will engage self-preservation mode, even if it means sinking everyone around him.

Thornton pulls the memory stick from the computer. 'Job well done, Watts. So far. Gotta crucify these bastards now. I've got a feeling it won't be easy. I could do with you sitting in a spare room in case I need a quick statement or memory prompt. Think I'll prop you in a see-through; give you the gist of how smart these two are at distancing themselves from trouble.'

McMaster and Main shuffle into Birmingham CID. Thornton processes Main first, predicting he will implicate McMaster in both Giuseppe and Angelo Caruso's deaths.From an adjacent window, Olivia watches Thornton and a female detective activate the recording equipment. Thornton eases into the interview: 'Jeffrey, tell me about your business relationship with Phillip McMaster.'

'I am acting for him in respect of a property purchase. I should say 'acted' as in past tense; the final documents are in my car.'

'And who is the vendor of the subject property?'

'His neighbours, Giuseppe and Maria Caruso.'

'All right. How did that transaction proceed?'

Main selects his words. 'The mechanics of a sale are generally completed prior to an offer being made. Mrs Caruso formalised the sale, supported by her son, Angelo.'

'Had you met with Angelo?'

'No. Had no need. He was not a party to the contract.'

Thornton senses a defensive edge. 'Did a situation arise where it became necessary to hasten the progress of the transaction?'

'I was not briefed of any matters that might have encumbered the sale's momentum. Parties to contracts experience differing levels of anxiety over a purchase. There might be financial obligations or deadlines to meet; there might be problems co-ordinating removalists; and there might be cumulative matters of terminating phone, electricity and gas services. In Mr McMaster's case, he, er, I'll be frank with you here, he suspected gold deposits lay beneath both his and the Caruso property. I therefore took his interest in the Caruso property as one of securing rights to those deposits.'

Thornton remains deadpan. 'So it is correct to say there *was* urgency in expediting the transaction?'

'In a fashion. I had attended meetings with Mr McMaster in which he asked me to accelerate the conveyance. I learnt the young Caruso was helping his mother. I could not establish whether a perceived delay emanated from the vendor's son or the conveyance process itself.'

Thornton ups the tempo: 'Was it during one of those meetings you were asked to "fix that Angelo prat"?

Main's face drains. 'Seems you've had words with that Watts woman. Quite obviously, I'm not privy to her reasons for snooping around. Nor will I comment on an unsupported allegation of a hearsay conversation, if such occurred at all. Having made that point, I will add that Mr McMaster's methods of communication could be construed as 'persuasive'.'

Olivia shoots a glare through the window: *Watts woman? Snooping around*?

'So, as a result of that conversation, "if such occurred", did you, in fact, *persuade* Angelo Caruso to hustle his mother or her solicitor?'

'No. I told you. I've never met Angelo. Never spoken to him.'

'I wonder then, if you could explain, Mr Main, why your DNA has been recovered from inside his black Audi?'

'Whose Audi? I think Mac may have—'

A knock on the door stops Main short. A detective enters: 'Terribly sorry, sir. There's a call. Gloucester CI. Says it's extremely urgent.'

'Can't you see I'm in the middle of a fucking interview?'

'Sorry, sir, I told him. It's a Chief Inspector Harvey. Told me to get you no matter what.'

'Okay. Thanks. I'll be right there.'

Thornton suspends the interview.

Olivia fires a surprised look through the window.

XLVI

'WAYNE. WHAT'S SO BLOODY IMPORTANT to interrupt me in the middle of a murder interrogation?'

'Sorry Jack. I wouldn't break in without good reason. We've got a situation down here. Started off as a routine response to a call over a yapping dog. "Bloody thing's been cranking off for hours" was the report. My boys attended the scene – only an hour ago – and got no answer at the door or windows. They radioed for permission to enter, and once inside, found a woman flat out on the floor. Strangled. I hesitate to say this sir, but the boys found your card on a table near a computer. Had a couple of private numbers on the back—'

'Fuck no. You got a name? Trotter? Gillian?'

'No formal ID yet, but yes, I'd say so, based on a Drivers' Licence and PI ticket.'

'Listen Wayne. This is vital. Go over the place with a fine-toothed comb. We might have a suspect. Trotter was working for me on a MET contract. She was shadowing a target for an internal investigation, so you can bet your bollocks this'll be a sensitive issue. Could be related to my current file. Put your best team on it and keep me posted. I'll get back to you later this afternoon.'

Thornton returns to the interview. Scratches his head. Feigns indecision. 'Mr Main. We were talking about Angelo Caruso, and you stated you'd never met him. Correct?'

'Yes. Correct.'

'And then I asked if you could explain why your DNA was inside his black Audi?'

Main looks as if he's fronted an ATM to find life savings flushed from his account. He stands. 'Sorry, I'm feeling ill. Haven't eaten for a while. Could you spare a glass of water?'

Olivia watches with interlocked fingers. Victory stretches across her face. This is one occasion she wishes she were still in the job and able to gloat in the glory of Main's discomfort. Three weeks of observation, pain and injury roll to fruition. *Nail him now. Block all exits.*

With a plastic cup of water centred on the table, Main continues: 'Sorry. Yes. There was a black car. All I did was open the door for McMaster.'

'And why would you do that?'

'We were going to relocate the car. As a warning.'

'A warning to who? You just told me you didn't know whose car it was.'

'I didn't. It, er, didn't matter to me. I was simply doing McMaster a favour. A gentleman's gesture of holding open a door.'

'So, did you *relocate* it?'

'Yes. No. Not personally. He did. No idea where he took it.'

'Where who took it?'

'McMaster, of course.'

'Mr Main. You've probably sat in that chair a thousand times, cautioning clients, listening to their cock and bull stories and wishing they'd just 'fess up and tell the truth. You've heard buckets of crap just as I have. What you've just told me is from the same bucket. For a start, McMaster's prints are not *inside*

Caruso's vehicle, and believe me, we've crawled over it like an Arab seeking water in the Sahara. Next, we lifted your prints from the steering wheel, not just a dainty finger here and there, but all over the damn thing. Forensic evidence shows you drove the vehicle – we'd start at thirty minutes, which, coincidentally, is about the travel time from Angelo's flat to McMaster's shed. Also, DNA from Angelo Caruso's scalp was scraped from the rear door catch. So you can see we're in a position to allege you drove Caruso to McMaster's shed and dumped him. What do you say to that?'

'No comment.'

'I put it to you that did, in fact, occur.'

'Do you know McMaster? Do you know about his "after hours" activities; his association with underworld figures who dip their fingers in more pies than Little Jack fuckin' Horner ever did? The bastard coerced and threatened me until I had nowhere to turn. I've never had problems in my life before I met him. I'm an upstanding citizen and career lawyer. The guy put me in fear of my life.'

'Did he kill Angelo?'

'I honestly don't know. I only sedated him. Ask McMaster.'

Thornton shakes his head and suspends the interview.

Thornton hands Olivia a coffee. 'What do you reckon my dear?'

'Flat white? Sorry. Going okay. I thought you struggled for a while. He knows his stuff. I half expected a no comment interview.'

'He's too wise for that. Knows where his bread's buttered.'

'You said nothing about the key. That in case he says he didn't enter the shed?'

'Well read. I've got big sleeves. Always keep a few goodies up there. I might exploit them for our friend Mac. Get ready for the climax.'

'Gladly. What's with the toilet break in the middle of the interview? You would have crucified me for that.'

'Urgent call. Official business. They track me down wherever I am.'

He withholds the information about Trotter. The recent interview with Gillian automatically slots Olivia on the suspect list. Thornton turns with an afterthought: 'By the way, I couldn't get anything on that number you gave me. Jill, wasn't it? Pay as you go? You could call yourself Santa Claus and get a dozen of those SIM cards. Unless someone tips her in, she won't be found. Right. Time for the big one. Let's crack Mac.'

McMaster, uncharacteristically gracing the *opposite* side of an interview desk, composes his defence.

'Detective Inspector Phillip McMaster, I'm going to ask questions in relation to the deaths of Giuseppe Caruso and Angelo Caruso. You do not have to say anything, but it may harm your defence if you do not mention, when questioned, something you may later rely on in court. Do you understand?'

McMaster lazes in the seat as if he were lounging in front of a television. 'Yes.'

'Did you know a person named Giuseppe Caruso?'

'Yes.'

'And by what means did you know him?'

'He was my neighbour.'

'For how long had you known him?'

'About six years.'

'And how would you describe the relationship?'

'It wasn't a relationship. He was my neighbour. We hardly spoke.'

Thornton has to open the communication. He'd expected to clash with McMaster, but not in the form of one word, restrictive answers.

McMaster also expects a clash. He is well-versed in eliciting information from suspects under the pressure of a formal interview. He knows the best way to confound an interviewer is to deliver short, snappy answers with no open ends for the interrogator to pursue.

Thornton continues: 'Tell me about your last communication with Mr Caruso.'

McMaster suddenly realises full cooperation will read better on the Record of Interview: 'A month ago. We had a boundary dispute, right? Was resolved when I produced title documentation. That led to my offer on his property.'

'And did he accept the offer?'

'We were in negotiations at the time of his unfortunate death.'

'And you subsequently engaged a solicitor to act on your behalf?'

'Much later. Yes.'

'So you were keen to gain the Caruso property?'

'More "interested" than keen. There's a distinction.'

Thornton hoists his brows. 'All right. What was your interest?'

McMaster smiles. 'A man has to plan for his retirement, doesn't he? Going to do a spot of farming. Already started. Well, I had until your lot slithered through my shed.'

Thornton won't be intimidated: 'So you had to obviate delays?'

'Part of any transaction, I suppose. Paperwork, right? Just like the burden we put up with. Never enough time.'

'Did someone help with that?'

'Told you. I had a solicitor take care of it. You've met him. Jeff Main. Not a bad guy; bit fresh around the gills, but reliable.' McMaster crosses his legs and glances at Thornton. Assumes control.

Thornton ignores the aggressive posture. 'This "paperwork" as you call it didn't happen straight away, did it? Your initial offer was refused by Giuseppe Caruso?'

'I wouldn't call that part of the negotiations. Was more an off-the-cuff teaser. I would have had no problem setting up my own land for a year and making a later offer or leasing nearby acreage. Fact of the matter is, right, I only rekindled the subject after poor Giuseppe passed away. As I said to his wife, my intention was to help eliminate a financial burden and smooth the way for her remaining years.'

Yeah, sure. What a great, big-hearted neighbour you are. 'So that's when you instructed Mr Main to oversee the contract obligations?'

'Precisely.'

'Must have made it easy with Mr Caruso gone?'

'What do you mean? I'm not familiar with the ins and outs of conveyancing. Contract's a contract, right? I'm sure Mr Main acts professionally regardless of his client's identity.'

'All right. Is it fair to say Mr Caruso's demise advantaged you?'

'Not at all, and that's a slur on my integrity. I just told you, right, I didn't care less whether I was able to buy his land or not. Had I been desperate, I might have sought other options. But I wasn't desperate. Life went on. Still does. For me, anyway.'

'Truth is, a problem did crop up, didn't it? A disparity in prices?'

'Nothing I wasn't able to solve. Bit of a mix up between solicitors, as I recall. Young Angelo, Caruso that is, had minor involvement. Was all hunky dory in the end.'

'Would you care to comment on an alleged conversation in which you're said to have told Main to fix Angelo?'

McMaster straightens. Sets his hands on the table. 'I'll comment on anything to help. Tell me the source of the allegation and I'll try to respond to the particular occasion.'

'I'll save that for later. For the moment, let's just say we have various sources.'

McMaster smiles: 'Aah, "acting on information received". Overused, but effective. Tell you something; I do recall Jeff and me talking about fixing him up for helping his mother with the paperwork. Fixing him up in a financial context – a cash reward. You're not going to do me for withholding VAT are you?'

Behind the window, Olivia cringes. She knows McMaster will walk his way out of trouble, even if it means walking *over* water.

Thornton fumes. Restrains his frustration. He won't allow McMaster the edge. 'You've investigated murders. What was your opinion of Angelo's death?'

'I was sorry for him and his mother.'

'Operationally.'

'Never got a look in, did I? Your DS Street moved me on. Went by the book: "I'm clearing the public from the scene", he said. Evicted me from my own bloody building. Thought I was on *Big Brother*: "It's time to go … Phil". All I did was go to my cellar for the first time since leaving hospital and run smack bang into a body. Didn't know who it was until Street's lot yanked him out.'

'So your friend, Gillian, never saw him?'

'I wouldn't know what she saw. She's visited my property and seen the premises and outbuildings. As to anything else she might have seen, you should speak to her.'

Olivia glares. Shuffles in her seat. *Bloody McMaster, he's good. The photos! Show him the photos.*

Thornton opens his folder. Decides against producing Olivia's photos. McMaster has not denied Gillian's presence in the shed. Shame there's no photo of Gillian looking into the pit.

'Let me revisit the boundary problem. How much time did you spend surveying the discrepancy?'

'Only as long as it took to ascertain a previous landowner had ripped me off nearly six metres.'

'Is it true you subsequently erected or realigned the rear fence?'

'Yes, it is true. I erected a new one. Great job, too.'

'And Mr Caruso was fine with that?'

'More than happy. I even offered to buy the reclaimed land, but he said take it. I paid him anyway – being the considerate neighbour I am.' McMaster smirks at his self-aggrandising compliment.

'You aware the death of Mr Caruso senior was later found to be not of natural causes?'

'Yeah. Word is SOCO stuffed up. Seized a few items for no result. When it's time, it's time. Comes to us all, right? By the way, you putting as much effort into finding out who dropped that tree on me?'

'You can be assured it's being dealt with. Your local CID, I believe. DS Street's in charge.' Thornton's turn to smile.

'Mr McMaster. It's my duty to inform you that we have a cigarette butt recovered from your property near the rear boundary.'

'Great! You could have picked up a thousand.'

'Maybe. But this is a roll-your-own. Distinctive tobacco. I'm not interested in the shit inside. It's the outside, the tip, from where your DNA was extracted.'

'So?'

'A witness has identified you as seen near your rear boundary and accessing the Caruso property through the fence.'

McMaster immediately thinks of Gill. She could have snapped photos of him twenty-four hours a day. *And* she could have written up a lengthy statement detailing his activities of the previous two weeks. The law regulating use of statements in a criminal case, which he knows clause by clause, rules they are only working documents until their originator testifies that the content of the statement is true and correct. *And that definitely won't happen.*

'Again I say, so what? The Carusos were acquaintances. I was obviously visiting.'

'Er, I forgot to mention this was April fourteen, only minutes before Maria Caruso attended your home requesting help.'

'Doesn't matter when it was. I smoke everywhere. Speaking of which, we're due for a break, aren't we?'

'Not yet. Take a look at this. Recognise it?'

'Yep. A photograph. Taken with a mobile phone, I'd say. Bit lacking in the pixels department. Too grainy for a pro.'

'Wouldn't be a wise guy if I were you. Study it. Do you agree it's a photo taken inside your shed?'

'Certainly do. And whoever took it was trespassing, right? Makes it inadmissible. No one's served a Search Warrant for access to my shed, and I've given no one permission to enter – except your lot after I found Angelo.'

'Good. Now look closer. Side wall above the bench.'

'Yep. That's my place. Pegboard, a few tools, and too much junk.'

'What can you tell me about the piece of timber wedged behind the pegboard. Looks like an oar or a paddle?'

For the first time in forty minutes, McMaster stalls. 'Er, can't tell you anything. Haven't seen it before. If someone's, er, trespassed in my property to take photos, that person, or anyone else could do whatever they wish in there. Anyway, what the hell's it got to do with me?'

'Plenty. We've received a forensics' report. It has plenty to do with you. Your palm print and DNA are on its handle. At the blade's tip, DNA comprising blood and hair follicles has been retrieved. Giuseppe Caruso's. What do you say to that?'

'Someone's planted it.' McMaster crosses his legs. Leans back in the chair. Folds his arms. 'You'll have to do much better if you're suggesting what I think you are.'

'Very well. I put it to you that you attended the Caruso property and assaulted Mr Giuseppe Caruso, the result of which caused his death.'

McMaster leans forward onto the table: 'You can put what you like. It didn't happen. Now, I'll put this to you: the interview is terminated until I arrange legal firepower – and it won't be some tin-pot clerk like that Main you've got down the hallway.'

'Very well. I'll arrange a phone. I'll remind you you're still under arrest and will be detained until such time as you are either released or bailed. It is my duty to inform you that when the Record of Interview resumes, I shall put to you questions relating to the death of Angelo Caruso.'

'You've got to be having a laugh. It was me who reported finding him! I'm hardly going to call police if I wasted him. Seriously. I'm a bloody Detective Inspector, for Christ's sake.'

'I can't comment. The interview's concluded at your request.'

Two hours' later, on arrival of Rohan Pati, a distinguished criminal lawyer recommended by the Police Association, the interview resumes.

'Mr McMaster. Before you requested Mr Pati, I put it to you that "you attended the Caruso property and assaulted Mr Giuseppe Caruso, the result of which caused his death". What do you say to that?'

McMaster looks to his lawyer. 'Yes, I attended the Caruso property. Mr Caruso was already on the floor. I attempted revival and instructed Mrs Caruso to call the ambulance.'

'Can you explain how the paddle, identified in this photo (Thornton produces the photo) came to have both your and Mr Caruso's DNA on it?'

Pati nods to endorse previously agreed responses.

'No.'

'What do you say to the proposition that you were at the dividing fence of your and Mr Caruso's property only minutes before Mrs Caruso alerted you to Mr Caruso's collapse?'

'It's entirely possible. It's a shame I didn't know what was happening—

Pati extends his hand to McMaster's leg. McMaster dips his head: 'It's okay.'

—inside the house. Most unfortunate I couldn't have helped earlier. They say time is of the essence in heart attack cases.'

Thornton shakes his head.

Olivia, still behind the window, does likewise.

'What do you say to the proposition that you were carrying a cricket bat or similar from the Caruso home?'

McMaster ponders. *Another photo? Another statement?* 'I can't recall. The shock of seeing my good neighbour dead shook me. However, it is possible I picked up a broken branch or two from down the back. Bloody windbreaks – they cop the full brunt of afternoon breeze.'

'Moving back to Angelo Caruso. You told me earlier he had "involvement" you called it, with the property contracts?'

'Correct.'

'What was the extent of that involvement?'

'He was helping his mother.'

'I have information there was a flaw in the contracts.'

How the fuck? Gill again? 'As I said, it was resolved. That's Mr Main's area.'

'And Angelo was going to be "fixed" for that?'

'Is that a question? Aren't we going round in circles? I'm on record: we spoke of a reward on his mother's behalf.'

'I formally advise that your DNA has been recovered from Angelo Caruso's vehicle.'

'Thank you.'

'Can you explain the presence of your DNA?'

'Not without checking my diary and retracing activities.'

'Is it still your position, Mr McMaster, that you gave no one permission to access your shed?'

'It is. Doesn't mean no one's been in though.'

Thornton looks to his scribbled memory prompts: 'We've been through that. You told me the paddle was planted.'

'Correct. But I just remembered my wife had a key. She'd

lent it to Main. Main told me, in Lowenstein's. Remember? Said he needed access to check measurements. Don't draw conclusions without fact. You have another two people who had access.'

Thornton drops his face into his hands. Exasperation. Four hours and he is back where he started.

He leaves the interview room. Approaches Olivia. 'Think I'll be a while on this. You can go if you want. Your role's complete. Send me your invoice and I'll hustle it through.'

'Thanks. A couple of hours' sleep won't go astray. I'll be in touch. All the best.'

XLVII

I DEPART THE MET OFFICES with Thornton's approval and gratitude. Whilst I can't claim total victory for the arrests and subsequent charges – because police exalted themselves with *my* forensic exhibits – Thornton, at least, acknowledged my contribution as the conduit to prosecution. I reflect on how the routine tail and report grew from minor thefts to harassment, deception, and ultimately, three murders.

Thornton afforded Gillian a compassionate benefit of doubt over her relationship and complicity in McMaster's dealings. Given the circumstances, he is more than kind. From my perspective, her immersion into a relationship with McMaster taints the reputation of my industry. I should harbour no grudges. However misguided she might have been, I should forgive all and let her rest in peace.

Thornton asked me to return the shed key to Gloria McMaster. I'm not sure how I'll be received, since her account of Phil McMaster's lolling about the rear boundary at the time of Giuseppe's death contributed to her husband's downfall. However, I am not one to shun responsibilities.

I drive into Ashton Hill, turn away from the gaping space in the tree-line, and soak up the sprawling mansion's view. I need no reminder of the earlier tragedy. To think I once felt sorry for DI McMaster seems disjointed. I continue down the drive to find two huge cement trucks parked near the shed entrance. The roller doors are hoisted to their maximum. Two huge plastic pipes pulse into the shed. I park, look to the house, and on seeing no activity walk into the shed. The pipes hang over the pit opening, pumping concrete into the huge void. 'Won't be long, Miss,' a contractor yells. He must think I am a resident.

'Not a problem,' I reply.

As I turn, I see an orange chainsaw hanging from a hook in a machinery cabinet. Certainly not the most unusual sight in a rural property – but it does prick my interest. *Not possible. Surely.* I struggle with the thought of Gloria McMaster wielding the chainsaw through two huge trees only fifty metres along the drive. No. No way. I walk to the rear door. Gloria greets me at the step. I guess she'd seen me drive in, or had been propped beside the rear door, wet with excitement over a shirtless contractor. 'Morning, Mrs McMaster,' I say in a voice wavering with operatic vibrato.

'Hello. You're the last person I'd expect to see around here.'

I am confused. She speaks with a smile, almost as if she is *pleased* to see me.

'I guess I'm not on your best friends list. I'm here to return this key.'

'Oh that. Won't be needing it. I got no business down there. How'd you get it?'

'Your solicitor. Main.'

'Bastard. He was supposed to hand it back the other week after he'd finished measuring.'

I play dumb – comes easy. 'So you're putting a concrete floor in the shed?'

'I'm doing nothing. Something about an O.H. & S. risk. The coppers checked with council about permits. Some guy called Stonebridge had written up a shonky permit and pocketed five hundred quid. Can you believe it? So the hole's being filled. So much for Phil's cellar.'

She still hasn't got a clue.

I bid farewell and slip next door to Maria's.

'Olivia. Come in. Here, sit, have the cup of tea with me.'

I love Italian welcomes. Gives me an insight into royalty.

Maria looks withered. She's lost a husband and son in the space of a fortnight, and has physically dried up after dealing with all attendant arrangements. She boasts about her family assisting her – both sons have returned from Italy, with Vince deciding to remain – and her daughters regularly visit to keep abreast of household chores.

The kitchen table overflows with paperwork. Visitors habitually sneak peeps to glean a little of their host's affairs. Not me. No way. I don't just 'peep' – I absorb the whole damn lot. I accidentally knock my elbow against the pile to disturb the pages, and then drag my bag across the stack to uncover further detail. That's how I derive my income: sneakily poaching others' information. From the host of legal envelopes, solicitors' letters, and Land Registry files, I leech further information: 'Looks like you're snowed under.'

'Nearly finished. My Vince helps me now. We cancel the sale to Mr Mac. He'll no be here to buy the farm and Mrs Mac's saying she's not want it. My Vince says I'm better stay here where I know everything and I'm comfortable.'

'Your Vince is very wise.'

'He's a good boy. Just like my Angelo. Why someone do that to him? Angelo's no hurt anyone.'

I keep my cool. 'Sometimes we never understand.'

'He's get involved in the things he shouldn't. I learn about the paperworks for Mr Mac and he's change the figures. Someone's make him do that. He wouldn't think like that. He's… what they call… when he's a child, the cryptomaniac. Always take things, but he's learn and gets better.'

He's certainly a cryptomaniac now. I know she means 'kleptomaniac' but correcting her seems harsh and disrespectful. I play to her hand: 'I'm sure God will look over him.'

'Yes, and his father. He leaves Angelo in the Will a cheque. What I do with this now?'

Maria shows me an executor's cheque in the sum of £88,900. In a more congenial setting I would say *just give it to me*. But here, acting with sincerity and integrity, I suggest using it to help Vince restore the farm to an income producing enterprise. I am not a religious person, but believers often say that God works in mysterious ways. I recognise the cheque as close to the figure Angelo had tried to hoodwink from his mother. Is this God's way of showing that sin can be repaid with both forgiveness *and* kindness? I guess I'll never know unless I convert – and there's fat chance of that. Never could I live up to God's expectations.

I offer Maria my best wishes and head home.

On arriving home I experience overwhelming relief and achievement. There is also apprehension – wondering what the next enquiry will bring. I can get by with routine debt collecting and summons serving, but my appetite craves the big ones. One day I'll specialise in just that. *Dream on, Liv.*

My empty fridge and foodless pantry spur me to Maccas where I purchase a tray of my usuals: Quarter with Cheese, large fries, Caramel Sundae and two Apple Pies. I pick up a tattered newspaper from the servery and slide behind a shiny fibreglass table in the dining area. I demolish the burger while I scrape silver foil off two promotional 'Scratchies' I earnt from my purchase. *What did I say to Maria about sins repaid with kindness?* I can't even fluke fifth division in Lotto, yet here, on my first card, I've scraped off a weekend for two at The Old Well Inn in Barnard Castle.

Sadly, there is no one in my life I can share a weekend with. Hamilton maybe – for a meal only – but I sure won't subject myself to his suggestive innuendo over a whole weekend. The word 'kindness' hovers. Who can I be kind to?

I am shallow. An introvert by election. Most of my friends distanced themselves after the Marchant situation, so they won't be a recipient of this windfall. Nor will I give the weekend to my step-parents who don't leave the house for longer than it takes to grab a trolley of groceries from their local Tesco.

And then I think of someone who shares similar singledom as do I. Witty, reserved, independent, and at odds with society: Rose Hernandez.

Epilogue

I lean over my bath. Platinum blonde hair colour drains from the matted mess atop my head. Since starting in this game, I flush away one identity for the sake of a new one, in line with each new contract. Whilst I am undecided about what I'll next get my teeth into – because I have the weekend in Barnard Castle to enjoy – I must be prepared.

The phone interrupts, as is its habit when I'm in the middle of doing something important. I snatch it from the toilet lid and see Superintendent Thornton's number.

'Olivia. Nice to hear you.'

Why? You want something? 'Likewise.'

'Just wanted to catch up and let you know a credit will hit your account tonight.'

'Thanks for that. I could do with steak instead of Spam.'

'I'm sure you're not pressed for a quid. Listen, you wouldn't be interested in coming back, would you? Different constabulary, new challenges.'

'No thanks. Got enough challenges of my own dispensing with the past. You can always keep me in mind for anything freelance, though.'

'Will do. Look, I didn't thank you properly for the Trotter file. The conclusion shook me, as I'm sure it did you. I could not have foreseen that Gillian might be subjected to danger, otherwise I wouldn't have assigned her, nor you for that matter. We charged McMaster with her death, had ample evidence.

He vehemently denied it. What sunk him was Trotter's technological obsession. She had a bloody camera tucked into a curtain fold. Nailed McMaster good and proper. Bastard sleazed his way into her home and wound his bloody tie around her neck. She didn't stand a chance.

'Must say I got a laugh out of your cameo comedy act… the way you flipped over that couch and appeared like a bimbo out of a birthday cake. Unbeatable.'

Shit. What a fool. I didn't even think of checking. There I was, intent on arranging a cam for Rose's shop, and I'm being recorded with my very own idea! 'Yeah, well. I've just learnt a valuable lesson.'

'So, Mac eventually coughed to doing her and Giuseppe Caruso – the forensics were too compelling. No amount of his bullshit could save him. Word is that he had enormous pressure from the brass to plea. Makes sense to me. The Chief Constable needs a clean ship. Offered Mac a cushy deal. Saves calling on you to testify.'

'That's a relief. I don't know if I could face him.'

'You won't have to worry about that for a while. Sentencing comes up in a week. I'll let you know his fate.'

'What about Main? Did Street nail him?'

'That's going down as the eighth wonder of the world. Mac absolved Main. He offered a plea to killing Angelo Caruso in an accidental rage. Definitely something going on there, because I know from the glove you produced and truck rental records, Main was up to his eyeballs. And his DNA was all over the Audi – which he couldn't even torch properly. Main had to waste Angelo to satisfy McMaster. Friggin' wimp if you ask me. He had motive and opportunity – and a key to Mac's shed for Christ's sake. I couldn't understand it.'

I do. McMaster has a massive pension lying beneath Ashton Hill. Main knows about it. I'd bet a pound to an ingot that McMaster struck a deal with him. He, McMaster, would cop the rap for Angelo Caruso's death in exchange for Main keeping mum about the gold, thereby paving the way for Mac to resume his operation after release. He'll probably be glued to a Zimmer frame and consuming life-preserving medication instead of Dewar's, but the dream of one day reclaiming his mine will help him through twenty years' prison.

Author's Note

Readers often ask: 'How did you come up with the story?'

The subconscious rewards writers with rich and fruitful material. It also produces words and scenes that, on first impression, are meaningless and incomprehensible – the very foundation of this story. *Clock face of Ills* was conceptualised of a midnight dream in which I stood before a towering clock (Big Ben, perhaps) whose Roman numerals shimmered luminous words: bill, mill, dill, sill, quill…

Through sleep-filled eyes, I scrawled a page of barely decipherable notes. After 15 minutes, the title became a work in progress.

Originally intended as 12 short stories set over 12 hours, with each story focusing on one of the 'ills' the draft swelled into the third account of Olivia Watts and her *Watts Happening? Investigations* agency. You will have recognised the 'bill' slammed on the table; Blackshaw's 'Mill'; Ashton 'Hill'; Angelo referred to as a 'dill'; the false window 'sill'; Roy Street's fountain pen resembling a 'quill' and 'Phil' McMaster.

I hope you enjoyed '*Clock face*'. Turn the page for an introduction to Olivia's next assignment in *Drain of Evidence.*

Paige offers a preview of Olivia Watts' next case in the 'Watts Happening? Investigations' series.
Drain of Evidence.
Available summer 2018.

I CURDLE TO THE PIERCING SHRIEK.

'My ring,' Rose splutters. 'I dropped it down the sink.'

No big deal. It won't be the first time a woman has lost the pledge of marriage down the drain – and it certainly won't be the last. But now is not the time for nonchalance because I am yet to fully understand Rose Hernandez. The ring obviously holds far greater significance than faded memories of a long-departed boyfriend.

'Rose,' I whisper. 'Don't worry. I'll have it for you in a second.'

'It's my grandmother's. She left it to me.'

Piece of piss, as my stepfather used to say. I drop to my knees, open the warped veneer cabinet beneath the vanity basin, and check the U-bend drainpipe. Plastic. Brilliant. I could have faced corroded steel or brass tinged with green ferrous oxide. I wrap my hand around the ribbed coupling and twist it loose. A gush of water surges over my hands and onto the cabinet's lower shelf.

I unscrew the second coupling and drop the plastic pipe into a dish Rose intuitively produces from the breakfast tray. Two clunks and a metallic tinkle drop into the bowl. The diamond encrusted gold ring glints from the silt. I scrunch my face and sink my hand into a grey clump of matted hair. I extract the ring and then repeat the exercise, hoping to souvenir the remnants of someone else's mishap.

I tease my fingers around the bowl and pull out two bullet casings and a piece of broken denture. I stall at the thought of a person leaving the motel with only half a dental plate in place. But my real attention rests with the bullet casings. Twenty-two calibre is my best guess. They are no stranger to me. We used them in the police service (ladies' loads, the macho men called them) but finding them in a drain, where they've presumably been expected to ride the waves of spent make-up, shaving cream and stubble, nose pickings and a multitude of other foreign objects destined for sewerage treatment, is not what one would ordinarily expect to find in a motel bathroom. I flick into work mode – which for me is easy – grab my camera and snap a few shots of the sink, the sink pipe, the mess in the bowl, and the casings themselves. I don't have the benefit of the tiny plastic ruler that forensic officers lay next to *their* evidence, so I lay a shiny one pound coin alongside the rounds to demonstrate perspective of size. I secure them in individual Glad Sandwich Bags, a pack of which I carry in my handbag as Watts Happening? Investigations' budget version of police evidence bags.

No one, without something to hide, would dispose of bullet casings in such a thoughtless manner.